CERIDWEN OWEN

MARTHA
MARTHA

Bringing Martha of Bethany out of the shadows

A novel

Martha, Martha

For all the Marthas out there.

Acknowledgements

I'd like to express my gratitude to: Linda Dyson who was the first ever to read part of the early manuscript – a delicate task; my sister Kirsty Wilmott, an author in her own right (you must read her books), who took up the huge task of editing, encouraging and putting me straight on the rewrite; Holly Bird for her enthusiastic input, which kept my belief in what I was doing intact; Sarah Soaring and Malcolm Down, for their part in getting the manuscript into better shape; all the friends who have listened to my endless enthusiasm and struggle in birthing this book and to the Lord, who was my inspiration and motivation throughout the long process.

Prologue

Caiaphas, high priest, head of the temple in Jerusalem, was angry. His lips pressed together in a thin white line as he swept from his dressing room, slamming the heavy door behind him. He was a busy man. It was the beginning of Shavuot, one of the three main celebrations in the Jewish calendar, and now this.

Malchus, his servant, stroked his right ear tenderly and watched him go with a grim smile. "I hope you know what you are doing, Master?" he said under his breath, shaking his head. He shuddered involuntarily, remembering the searing pain as the blunt blade, wielded so clumsily by the big fisherman, had torn at his ear. That dark night, the garden had seemed full of Roman soldiers and temple police. So many to arrest one man as he prayed. What had the temple or Rome to fear from that one man and his ragbag of followers? But Malchus knew. He had watched. He had remembered.

The priests had mocked him when he'd asked what had happened that night. So he'd kept quiet, but he knew it had happened. It was as real as the bloodstain on his cloak and the calm fearlessness in the carpenter's eyes as he had faced his captors. The authority of his voice, as he told the big fisherman to put the sword away, as he reached out to touch the wound, before Malchus had had a chance to step back. Then, as the carpenter had drawn his hand away, Malchus had heard the gasp from those around him and with dread had gingerly touched his ear. He had been astounded to find it intact, no pain, no wound at all, just clean, smooth skin.

With shaking hands Malchus began picking up his master's clothing, putting the garments away with deliberate care, as he recalled the fate of the carpenter. So now the women among his followers were also baptizing the people in the name of the one they were calling the Messiah. He chuckled. No wonder his master was so worked up. As if that wasn't enough, they were using the temple mikvehs meant for ritual purification before the festivals. Whatever next? He smiled. Gamaliel, a Pharisee and teacher of law, didn't think they had anything to worry about. If what these people were doing was inspired by man, it would fail; if it came from God, there would be no stopping it. His master had flown into a rage on hearing that. However, trouble there would be. Those men and women who had followed the carpenter had better watch out.

Contents

Chapter One

Early Morning Guests

Early spring

With a flourish of her broom, Martha flicked the last pile of debris off the veranda step and watched it settle into the damp trodden-down surface of the courtyard. Early as it was, the pale sun promised warmth, but for now there was cool, sharp air lingering after the rain. The smell of fresh bread mingled with that of the ancient olive tree that grew gnarled and twisted into the high surrounding wall of the courtyard, while chickens crooned to one another, scratching in the dirt among the roots of the tree.

Martha stretched and yawned, her umber hair swaying in long, thick cascades down her back, then rolled up the sleeves of her wool tunic and hauled rainwater from the depths of the household cistern, pouring it carefully into the waiting buckets. The donkey chewed his hay thoughtfully as he watched her over the top of the stable door. She talked to her old friend in soft, deep tones, coming over to rub between his ears and stroke the balding grey nose.

Martha listened for a moment, hearing the low murmur of voices labouring up the road outside. She couldn't help a little catch of breath as her heart quickened with excitement. The voices drew closer, more distinct; she hurried to undo the bolt on the wooden wall-high gate.

News travelled fast in the rural areas around the great city of Jerusalem. The Rabbi from Capernaum in Galilee was on his way, and until this moment, Martha had only hoped he and his followers might break their journey at her home, in Bethany. Although they had met only a handful of times, over the last year or so a strong bond had formed between Martha and the women in the group. The Rabbi Yeshua had healed their friend Simon of leprosy and had subsequently become a friend to her younger brother Lazarus. When the Rabbi and his followers were passing through they either stayed with Simon or as a guest of Lazarus, in their home.

Out in the narrow, sun-bright street, clay clad, flat-roofed houses crowded together, set like steps on the hillside below. On the other side of the gate, four women stood together, the hems of their garments dark with mud from the road. Their surprise as the gate opened turned to delight and relief when they saw the welcoming smile of Martha.

"We didn't even get a chance to knock. Were you listening out for us?" asked the older woman, Salome. Her sharp face was wrinkled even further by her broad smile. She took Martha by the hands and looked her up and down approvingly. "Where's that sister of yours? Still in bed?"

Martha was so pleased to see the women that Salome's remark didn't sting as it might have done on other occasions. Besides, she was still wondering if the Rabbi would be close behind.

"We came ahead of the men this morning, to ask if it was convenient to break our journey with you before continuing on into Jerusalem," said the tall, slender Miriam, answering her unspoken thought. Miriam's beautiful dark eyes searched Martha's face, looking for her true response to the question.

"And to lend a hand," added Salome, quickly.

Mary Alphaeus, who had stood back shyly until then, nodded vigorously, her round, eager face and rosy cheeks framed by a worn shawl.

"You'd better come in and refresh yourselves before we get started," said Martha.

"That's a yes then," said Salome.

"Who could refuse you?" replied Martha, returning the broad grin as she led the way. She bent to wash her feet in a bowl beside the stone steps to the veranda, refilling the jug for her guests.

"It will be so good to sit down and rest for a while," sighed Susanna softly, as she removed her sandals to wash her feet. Martha couldn't help noticing her expensive but practical travelling clothes and her rich dark hair flecked with gold, which matched her earrings and necklace. "It's been a long walk from the caravansary outside Jericho," she added, looking up at Martha with a grateful smile.

Martha turned to go into the kitchen, her mind already occupied with the gymnastics of preparing food for so many people. She nearly collided with the skinny nine-year-old Tabitha as she came hurrying out of the kitchen door, wiping her floury hands on her tunic.

"Oops," said Tabitha, watching guiltily as the white dust settled. She attempted to tuck a tight brown corkscrew curl behind her ear. Martha reached down and gently brushed the flour off Tabitha's cheek, shaking her head.

Tabitha was already turning excitedly to their guests, "I thought I heard voices. Is the Rabbi with you?"

"He'll be here very soon," Salome assured her.

"Along with the rest of them," laughed Susanna.

Tabitha's eyes grew even wider with excitement.

"Shall I go and wake Mary?" she asked Martha.

"Yes please. And tell her to hurry," urged Martha.

"Not before I get my hug," insisted Salome, throwing her arms around Tabitha. "Now quick, then come and help me get that dough into the oven."

"Oh, just like escaping from Egypt," called back Tabitha, as she hurried to rouse Mary. "No time to let the bread rise!"

"The bread we've baked this morning won't be nearly enough," sighed Martha, as her guests entered the warmth of the kitchen.

"Well, remind me where your flour jars are and I'll get started on another lot," said the practical Salome. "Flatbread does the job when there are hungry mouths to feed."

"And you would know," laughed Susanna. "You're a marvel, Salome."

"I'm what I ought to be, praise my maker," came the reply.

Martha's tired guests flopped down onto thick rugs scattered around the rough kitchen floor, while she handed out cups of milk and placed olives, dried figs and dates before them.

Tabitha came racing back, her hair now coiled in a tight knot. Quickly, she shaped the dough into flat hand-sized pieces while Salome began to knead the flour, salt and water she had just mixed together in a bowl on her lap.

"Take a little more time to rest," pleaded Tabitha, passing her the oil.

"I'm fine now my feet are resting," Salome reassured her, wriggling her toes, which made Tabitha giggle. "Besides, busy hands will keep me out of mischief," she added, with a twinkle in her eye.

Martha wasn't sure if her guests would be more comfortable eating indoors or out in the courtyard, until Salome pointed out that being indoors meant someone would have to sweep up afterwards, so why not be outside, where the chickens would do the job? Tabitha liked that idea, especially as she was in charge of the chickens and sweeping, usually. The furrow in Martha's brow softened.

Mary, Martha's younger sister, who was twenty, appeared just then at the kitchen door, stretching and yawning, her long, almost black hair falling in waves that were still tangled from sleep. She was short, with rosy plump cheeks and a smile that lit up the world. Her voice was still thick with sleep as she greeted their friends, giving Salome a peck on the cheek as she poured some milk. Martha opened her mouth to speak.

"Just give me a moment," Mary said to her, putting the milk down to help Miriam outside with a basket of crockery before calmly returning to her drink. "Now what would you like me to do?"

"The foot bowls, basins and towels need to be put out and the water jugs filled, please," said Martha. Mary rushed away, and Martha added more lentils and water to the previous night's stew as it began to reheat over the fire. "We'll need more water from the well," she said apologetically to Tabitha.

"I'm on my way," said Tabitha, tugging her sandals on as she left.

Mary Alphaeus helped Salome in Tabitha's absence, while Susanna began to fill jugs with wine and beer. Martha went in search of the trestles and boards crammed into the lean-to workshop that stood against the wall on the other side of the courtyard. She felt butterflies in her stomach as she hauled them out, leaning them against the wall. Miriam came to help her slide the long boards from the low rafters where they were stored.

Martha was pleased to see that Tabitha had taken time to put the chickens away in the empty stable before she'd left with the donkey. A rogue chicken perched precariously on top of the stable door, threatening to escape. "Stay there, Cluck," she commanded. The chicken jerked its head, turning away, and then dropped back down into the stable.

Miriam giggled, "Imaginative name for a chicken."

Martha sighed. "Tabitha's given them all names," she explained, "The poor donkey's called Clop, would you believe." Miriam's lips twitched with amusement as they began to set up the tables.

Martha's quick ears picked up the low, resonant rumble of a crowd coming up the road as she and Miriam worked together. The voices reached a crescendo at the open gate. Hurriedly Martha brushed the dust off her clothing, drew herself up to her full height and tried to pull her shawl over her head. Oh no, it was still hanging in the kitchen! She looked at Miriam in panic.

"He won't mind. It's the Master, Yeshua," whispered Miriam.

Martha sighed, resigning herself to the situation. Good start, she thought.

A crowd of men hung back just beyond the threshold, their muddy hemmed cloaks thrown back off their shoulders. The soft, earthy hues of their clothing intensified in the ever-brightening sunlight.

Leaving the debate, a figure turned politely from his companions and with the relaxed air of someone who belonged, walked into the tranquil courtyard. He blinked, his eyes adjusting to the deep shade under the gnarled olive tree where the two women stood. The blue tassels on his cloak contrasted with the faded brown and yellow stripes of his tunic and that morning his head was bare, showing dark streaks among the lighter, sun-scorched hair. As usual, his beard was straggly and unkempt.

Martha came forward, hands outstretched in greeting.

"Welcome, Rabbi," she said, bowing her head and lowering her eyes, then, shyly looking up to catch the familiar crooked smile with the ray of lines that led to the deep brown eyes flecked with gold.

"My dear Martha, how good it is to see you." He took her rough hands in his long-calloused carpenter's fingers and looked at her like an approving father, despite the similarity in their age. His face was lean, but there was nothing to suggest he had even noticed her uncovered head. "Is Lazarus home, and Mary and Tabitha?" His voice was deep and musical, but he spoke softly.

"Lazarus will be back soon. He's checking the flock, amongst other things, and Tabitha is fetching water. Mary will be out the moment she hears your voice." He seemed amused. "But most importantly," she finished, "breakfast won't be long."

His smile broadened. "Thank you Martha. It will be most welcome. We've been walking since before dawn, as I've no doubt you've already heard and more besides." He glanced at Miriam, who shook her head playfully.

"We've hardly had time," said Martha.

Glancing at the men still hovering at the gate, he said, "The tongues of my companions far outrun their feet."

"And I've heard there is little room to be tired when you're inspired," countered Martha.

He shook his head and reached for the water jug, hiding a wry smile. When he'd finished washing Martha handed him a towel and then he turned to those watching them, spread his arms out and welcomed them in.

Mary came rushing out of the house. The Rabbi held out his arms in greeting, not quite sure if she would kneel at his feet or hug him. He helped her up as they laughed.

With dignity Martha began to greet her guests, glad of Miriam's support, for she had travelled with the Rabbi almost from the beginning and knew everyone well. Fifteen men queued to wash in the courtyard, but one stood out: Simon son of Jonah, whom Yeshua had renamed Peter. He was the loudest and tallest by far, with broad shoulders and strong, bare arms. Long unkempt locks of black hair flopped over his face, which had been polished by wind and sun reflected off water, for he had once been a fisherman.

At Miriam's suggestion, Martha asked him and his brother Andrew if they would help to finish setting up the tables. They seemed glad to be given a task and set about the work enthusiastically. Andrew was a little shorter than his brother, but still muscular with a lighter complexion.

Philip, a tall, thin man with a short, neatly trimmed beard, approached Martha and offered his help. He and Nathanael, a young man with a broad, kind face, were given the task of straightening and loading the tables. Satisfied, Martha left the courtyard in Miriam's capable hands, hurrying to see how preparations were going in the kitchen.

Susanna and Mary Alphaeus were ready to serve drinks to Martha's guests and were closely followed out to the courtyard by young James Alphaeus carrying another basket of things for the table. He, like his mother, was short with a smooth pleasant face. The noise in the courtyard was increasing.

Mary was still chatting enthusiastically with the Rabbi. "We hear such rumours from Galilee about you. Will you be staying long in Jerusalem this time?"

"Just for Purim and then where my father sends me, as always," he said, looking down at her with kindness.

She nodded thoughtfully. "Can I ask, did some men really make a hole in the roof of your house in Capernaum, so they could lower their sick friend down to you?"

He laughed heartily. "My dear Mary, all your questions will be answered, but first your sister needs help."

"I'm sorry, Master," she said, turning reluctantly to the scene around her. "Martha will have it all in hand."

"I'm sure my friends will be more than happy to answer all your questions after breakfast," he added, as Mary went to help.

Tabitha came pushing through the throng, the water-skin-laden donkey abandoned at the gate. Thaddaeus, dark curly hair still dripping with water from his wash, greeted her and was immediately given the task of unloading the heavy skins from the patient animal. Some of his friends chuckled as he was ordered about by the nine-year-old. However, Susanna had had her eye on them and sent the lean, fit young man called Simon the Zealot to help Thaddaeus, whilst Tabitha ran in to tell Martha she was back with the water. Barsabbas was quick to stable the donkey, while his friend Matthias made farcical attempts to catch the escaped chickens, with much laughter and advice from the onlookers, especially James, Salome's oldest son, with his dark features and strong profile. Upon Tabitha's swift return, she called each chicken by name, and they strutted obediently back into the stable. The one chicken Matthias had managed to catch clucked indignantly, squirmed free of his grip and scuttled off to join the others. Tabitha closed the door decisively, to a round of applause and calls of "Well done!" With her nose theatrically in the air, she brushed the dust off her hands, turned sharply on her heels and returned to the kitchen grinning.

Miriam got Thomas, a round jovial-faced young man, and John, Salome's younger son, to manhandle benches from the large main living room onto the veranda, from where Judas Iscariot, a handsome man, and Matthew, a cousin of the Alphaeus family, carried them to the tables.

The main room of the house lay along the back wall of the courtyard, between the storeroom, on the left, and the outer stair and bedroom on the right. The storeroom led into the kitchen and washroom on that side of the house, while two smaller rooms and the lean-to workshop ran down the other side of the courtyard. The outer stair led up to a large room, on the left, for guests, and a smaller private room, on the right, with access to the roof.

The kitchen was busy as the women hurried backwards and forwards with food for the tables: dried fruit, olives, nuts, a little soft cheese and yet more bread. Martha stood in the middle giving instructions whilst stirring the lentil soup.

As Mary returned to the bustle of the kitchen, she saw the frown on Martha's face, and knew immediately her sister needed more help, so she slipped out of the gate and across the street to their neighbour. Inside the sunny courtyard, much like their own, she found Rachel with her two servants leisurely grinding corn. Mary stood for a moment trying to decide what to say.

"Good morning Mary. It sounds like that Rabbi Yeshua is back with more followers. Does Martha need some help, dear?" Rachel smiled encouragingly. Her hair was greying and her face cheerful with fine wrinkles.

"Oh, yes please Rachel. There are a lot of them and I'm not sure we have enough bread, despite all Tabitha and Salome's efforts."

Rachel had been a close friend of their mother and had helped bring all three children into the world. When their mother had become ill Rachel had cared for them along with her own boys. Eighteen years later, she was still the first person they went to in a crisis.

Quickly Rachel and her servants gathered what they needed and with Mary's help carried the loaded baskets across the street. Martha was bringing the last of the flatbread out from the oven, and wishing she had more, when Mary walked into the kitchen.

"Mary, there you are!" she exclaimed, but her irritation instantly turned to relief as she saw Rachel, arms laden, following closely behind.

"Why on earth didn't you call me earlier?" scolded Rachel. "I will handle this. You and Mary go and look after your guests."

Out in the courtyard, Martha surveyed the scene. Almost everyone was seated except the Rabbi and John. They were standing debating over the last place. Tabitha came and stood by Martha, who bent down and whispered in her ear. Tabitha quickly disappeared back into the house. Martha managed to catch the Master's eye and gestured toward the workshop and the large log they used as a chopping block. The Master was quick to catch on, carrying it with ease to the empty place at the table. Finally everyone was seated. Tabitha appeared with cushions to top off the log and was met with playful grumbles from the others.

In Lazarus' absence, the Rabbi Yeshua spoke the blessing and grace, then swiftly bowls of lentil soup were placed before the men while the women rushed to and fro. It was Mary who welcomed their brother Lazarus as he arrived. He beamed as he saw the crowded courtyard.

"As I came up through the village, our friends and neighbours have been urging me to hurry home, saying I had an esteemed guest waiting," said Lazarus cheerfully. He was tall like Martha, but his hair was fairer, with a kind, thoughtful face which was more used to smiling than frowning.

"It's certainly hard to have any secrets here," agreed Mary, handing him a drink. "We've saved you a seat, and I'm sure Martha will have put some breakfast aside."

At that moment Peter came forward, arms outstretched in greeting, a piece of bread still in one hand. The two men hugged, Peter towering over Lazarus. The Rabbi stood to greet the master of the house and Lazarus bowed to the man he called Master before they too hugged like brothers.

"Friend," said Yeshua, "come sit with us." Peter gave Lazarus his seat and took the old three-legged stool Tabitha used for milking the goats. Peter made everyone laugh as he sat down with only his head and shoulders above the table. Martha was pleased they had found seats for everyone; in the shade the ground was still damp from the rain.

Martha refilled her brother's cup and placed a full plate before him. Now she could allow herself a few moments of pleasure as she looked around at her happy guests and muttered a prayer of thanks. It was then she noticed Mary Alphaeus sitting slumped on the steps fanning herself. Immediately feeling guilty, Martha discreetly called the other women over to join Mary Alphaeus, serving them herself.

Once they were all provided for, Miriam pulled Martha down onto the step beside her. Nibbling a date cake, Tabitha joined them, leaning against Martha.

Miriam spoke softly to Martha. "Thank you for taking us in this morning. We would have been hard pressed to make it to the city, but you know the Master, he's always on a mission. It's hard to keep up sometimes."

Martha sighed. She could only imagine, and not for the first time wished she was free to follow the Rabbi, like her friend. Her responsibilities to her brother and sister and the family business tied her firmly in place.

"Will you stay in Jerusalem tonight?" she asked.

"Yes, in the lower city. Simon recommended the landlord, who is keen to meet the Master after hearing how he healed Simon from leprosy," said Miriam.

"I remember it like yesterday. It caused such a stir here in Bethany." Martha smiled at the recollection. "I think that's when the whole village began to realise this carpenter turned rabbi was different to the others, even John the baptiser. It was hard to ignore the transformation everyone saw in Simon. Mind you, that was nothing to the stir it caused in the temple when he presented himself healed and clean."

Miriam nodded. She had seen many people healed by the Rabbi since she had followed him, but still each one was a miracle untold. They sat in companionable silence for a moment watching the Master and his men.

"Will you see Joanna?" asked Martha, her mind returning as it always did to the practical.

"Chuza sent for her last week, so there must be something big going on in Herod's palace," mused Miriam.

"Or Herod wants to hear more about the Master from her," suggested Martha, hopefully.

"There could be some truth in that," replied Miriam. "Joanna was arranging accommodation with this landlord Simon suggested. Hopefully we'll get a chance to see her again. You'd like her."

Martha looked doubtful, "The wife of King Herod's steward. I'd be too intimidated."

"You, intimidated!" laughed Miriam. "That would be a first."

"The Master seems to have connections in all walks of life," said Martha, ignoring the remark.

"And it's amazing the people he collects on the way, just look at us." They both giggled.

"Ah, Lazarus is beckoning me. I'd better go and see what he wants." As Martha got up, she turned back to Miriam. "You know there is always a place for you and the others here."

"Thank you, Martha. Although we care for him as best we can while he's traveling, it's a great comfort to know we have a place to rest outside Jerusalem, away from the ever-growing crowds."

As Martha went to her brother's side, her contented guests showered her with appreciative compliments. Despite this, her heart was heavy, for they would be leaving soon, and she didn't know when they would see them again. The great city of Jerusalem, perched on the tops of its three hills and crowned with the magnificent temple, lay only three and half kilometres to the northwest, but to Martha it felt like another world.

Lazarus had been talking with the Rabbi for some time, but now he spoke privately to Martha. In her heart she had already guessed what he was about to ask, but first he spoke of farming matters. Josh and Jacob, their two young shepherds, had brought the flock off the hills and pastured them in the upper field, so they could join in the Purim celebrations the next day. He saw a little furrow appear on Martha's brow.

"There's enough grass," he added, understanding her concern. "I'll speak to Uncle Elias about our plans for the olive groves while I'm in Jerusalem." Martha nodded slowly, knowing where this was leading. "You're going into Jerusalem with them then?"

"Yes. If you don't mind. It's an opportunity not to be missed, and Uncle Elias would love to meet the Rabbi. I was going to see him next week anyway."

Martha sighed, but nodded her consent.

Their father, Reubel, had died when Lazarus was twelve, leaving him to take over running the family's extensive olive groves, a flock of sheep and goats and the barley and wheat harvest. Even with their uncle's help, most of the day-to-day management fell to Martha, who had already spent eight years supporting their widowed father, while running the home and caring for her two younger siblings. Martha had done her best to help and support the young Lazarus in his new role, but it had been hard on both of them.

Mary came over and joined them, guessing what they would be discussing, and adamant that she too would go with Lazarus and their friends into Jerusalem.

"Please Martha. It would be good to see Aunt Elizabeth and our cousins," she begged. "She's bound to have a full house for Purim, and it's so lively in Jerusalem at festival time."

"And not at all because you want to go with the Master?" said Lazarus, not fooled by his sister for one moment.

"Of course, that as well," admitted Mary, unabashed. "Please?" She looked imploringly at Martha.

"You'll need to be careful, keep your wits about you, and stay away from any clashes with overzealous factions of the population, and the Roman soldiers. Things can get very heated during festival times, especially with so many extra soldiers patrolling the streets. Our family has a good name, let's try to keep it that way." Martha spoke sternly.

"Then I can go?" gasped Mary.

Reluctantly Martha nodded, feeling it was unfair of Mary to leave her and Tabitha with all the clearing up. Besides, she worried about Mary, who could be impulsive and unconventional at times, but she consoled herself that Lazarus was steady and sensible and would do his best to look after his sister.

As Mary turned to go, Martha remembered to thank her for fetching Rachel. Mary was pleased. She knew her strengths and had helped the best way she could. Sometimes her sister didn't realise how intimidating her capabilities could be.

While Mary was gathering her things for an overnight stay in Jerusalem, Miriam and Salome also promised Martha they would keep an eye on Mary, which brought her some comfort.

Soon their guests were ready to leave, so Martha stood at the gate to say farewell with Tabitha beside her. Although Tabitha secretly wished she could go with them into Jerusalem, her loyalty to Martha kept her lips tightly sealed.

"Well done, your father would be proud," whispered Rachel, as she gave Martha a parting squeeze. "See you at sunset?"

Martha nodded. She looked down at Tabitha, who was jiggling with excitement.

"It's my favourite festival," she admitted, as Rachel shuffled across the street and slipped back into her own domain, Martha's thanks still following her.

The Rabbi was last to leave, "Why so sad, my dear Martha? Could it be all the clearing up we've left you?" Martha began to shake her head, then realised he was joking. "Or that you'll miss your brother and sister?" He raised an eyebrow questioningly. "Do you wish you could come too?" Martha knew her face was betraying her now. Yes, part of her did want to follow him, but another part wanted to stay. She felt confused.

"These are all just distractions," he said, with a warm smile on his face. "In your heart you stay for the sick and poor, for whom you care."

That was it! Astonished, Martha realised he understood her motives better than she did. The conflict melted away now she was clear about why she was staying. Purim was especially important for the poor and sick of the village, where it was traditional to give gifts, food and money. He looked pleased as he bowed his head to honour her.

"Passover's not far away," he added, with a twinkle in his eye, or was it just the sunlight? Then he blessed their home and was gone.

Martha watched them disappear down the hill, but it was Miriam who turned and waved to her in the dancing heat haze. For Martha her friendship with these women had become important, being one of the few contacts she had with people outside of Bethany and her immediate family. They had formed a connection because of the Rabbi and only now, as they left, did she realise how important it was to her. She had even begun to wonder if God has singled her brother out, for he seemed to have made an equal bond with the Rabbi and his male followers. To Mary, her sister, it was obvious and she had embraced it.

Chapter Two

Purim and Sabbath Rest

After enjoying breakfast together in the warm sunshine, Martha and Tabitha, assisted by the hungry chickens, turned to the work of clearing up. They had hardly begun when there was a gentle knock on the gate. Perhaps one of the guests had forgotten something, thought Martha, but it was Ellie, a close friend of Mary's.

"Is everything all right at home?" Martha, concerned, asked the willowy young woman.

"Oh yes, mother is doing well and since Lazarus found my brother work in Bethany, it's been a lot easier." There was an expectant pause before Ellie realised Martha didn't know why she'd come, so she explained. "Mary came and found me a little while ago. She was out of breath and in a hurry, saying if I wasn't busy this morning you would be glad of some help as she was off to Jerusalem with the Rabbi and his followers." Ellie often came to help Martha, glad of the extra income.

"You are a blessing as always, my dear," said Martha, delighted. "That's twice in one morning Mary has been thoughtful."

"And not at all because she had a guilty conscience," mumbled Tabitha, carrying a pile of things towards the kitchen.

Ellie looked round the courtyard. "It looks like you've been celebrating early. How many came for breakfast?"

"Too many to count," said Martha, with a wry smile.

"Twenty-five," Tabitha called back over her shoulder as she disappeared into the

kitchen.

* * *

It was mid-afternoon before they finished work, but for once Martha felt relaxed as the Sabbath approached. Although they would miss Mary and Lazarus, she had to admit she was feeling a little excited about joining Rachel, her husband Joseph, their sons, wives and children for Purim. It had been a while since the two families had celebrated one of the festivals together.

Ellie was dispatched home with a basket of provisions for her family and several other gifts to drop off on the way. This was usually part of Martha and Mary's Friday routine, but in Mary's absence Tabitha had begged to be allowed to go instead. Martha watched her surrogate daughter leave, giving Martha a grown-up nod as she let herself out. It had been seven years since her adoption; she was growing up so quickly.

Martha spent the remaining hours before sunset in the little garden at the back of the house. Here they also kept the household goats and sheep for milk. Martha let them into the small paddock to graze on the fresh grass while she refilled their mangers and cleaned out their bedding ready for the Sabbath. Such chores were not done on a holy day of rest. Then she began weeding and hoeing the vegetable patch. Martha had worked the plot all her life, helping her mother when she was very young. The ground had been rocky and barren then, but now, enriched by dung from their livestock, it had become a productive, green place, even in the heat of summer. Its walls were built from rocks they had removed over the years. Here, Martha felt closest to her mother and part of the land which had been in the family for as far back as anyone could remember.

Tabitha joined her, bringing weak beer to refresh them both and news of the people she had visited that afternoon. They toiled side by side until the shadows were long across the hillside, then packed their tools away and went in to prepare themselves for the fast-approaching Sabbath.

Three sharp horn blasts reverberated through Bethany, summoning the occupants to the synagogue. Tabitha's heart began to race with excitement as she and Martha joined Rachel, Joseph and their family in the street outside, and the whole neighbourhood began to flow towards the shadowed silhouette of the synagogue. Martha fell into step with Rachel as Tabitha walked ahead, holding the hands of Rachel's youngest grandchildren. Already she was eagerly recounting the story of Esther, whose central character was a brave woman from their nation's past.

The simple building was buzzing as the poor and hard-working people came together to celebrate their faith and to rest from their labours. The synagogue was the centre of the community, binding them together in its age-old traditions and beliefs, and acting as a meeting place and a school.

Martha loved the familiarity and intimacy of the place; its sounds and smells brought back memories of childhood. Each morning she had brought Lazarus here to learn from the Torah and the scrolls of the Prophets with the other boys of the village. Often, she had listened to the rhythmic chanting of scripture while she played with her little sister, before returning to her housework. Their mother had died when Mary was only two and Lazarus barely four, so running the home had become Martha's responsibility.

A nobleman, greying around the temples but with a strong, classical profile, greeted Martha courteously. It was Simon of Bethany, whose own story was a powerful one. He was a wealthy merchant who had lived in Jerusalem with his family, but leprosy had forced him into isolation. He had built a house on the edge of town where people were more tolerant of the sick, as long as they stuck to the law. A chance meeting on the road with the Rabbi Yeshua had resulted in his miraculous healing. Pronounced well by the temple priest, he was restored to his family. However, Simon was a changed man, and he remained in Bethany, becoming a good friend to the Rabbi whenever he was passing through, and building an almshouse. This drew the poor and sick from Jerusalem where they were hidden from sight on the east slopes of the Mount of Olives, which rose between the village and the city.

Martha knew that as soon as the Sabbath was over Simon too would join the Rabbi and his followers in Jerusalem for the rest of Purim. They were not permitted to travel far on a Sabbath as their God had created the world in six days and rested on the seventh, a pattern they upheld faithfully.

Martha nodded in greeting to Simon's wife Helena, but Helena barely acknowledged her, remaining aloof, more Roman in her ways than Jewish. However, her youngest daughter Anna, a close friend of Mary, gave them a cheerful wave, her fair curls bouncing around her pale cheeks. Anna looked very much like her mother, but in character she was her father's daughter.

Tabitha bounded over to speak to Anna while Martha watched anxiously. She was relieved when Tabitha remembered her manners, albeit at the last minute.

Lost in thought among the warmth and excitement, Martha recalled the first time she had met the Rabbi, as a guest of Simon;

how her hands had shaken as she had served him at dinner, how her heart had pounded when he had spoken to her and how bold she had been when she had shared the longing in her heart to see him heal the sick people of Bethany. That night she had glimpsed a hidden power in him which she could not forget, although later he'd seemed vulnerable and so human. Even now, it was difficult to grasp who he might be, and yet between the stories that had reached them between his visits, and her friends' reports, she found it increasingly difficult to doubt. Like many around her, she watched and hoped.

Martha came back to the present as Rachel squeezed in beside her. "I'll come and sit with you, otherwise I shan't hear a word with all those grandchildren clambering on me. Your Tabitha is a real gem," she whispered loudly. "It's a tight squeeze with so many visitors, but I'm so glad of it."

Joseph, a small man in comparison to the other elders and men of the village, sat opposite, but his wrinkled, shiny face beamed with pleasure as he surveyed his family.

Familiarity didn't rob the service of its magic or excitement. All faces were uplifted in the twinkling candlelight as the prayers and traditional readings were said. It was Simon who read from the Megillah that evening, bringing clarity and drama to the words. Songs were sung with great joy, and laughter filled the air as village children acted out Esther's story, herded and prompted by their own faithful, grey-haired Rabbi and Hazzan, Michael.

After the blessing the crowds dispersed in the cold night air, families and friends returning home to continue the celebration over the evening meal. Martha and Tabitha joined Joseph and Rachel, who had their whole family staying with them. The eldest son Shem, with his wife Elizabeth, lived with them for Shem was a mason and worked with his father. Their second son Noah and his wife Hadassah, lived in Jerusalem, while the youngest son, Joses, lived with his wife Adinah's parents, to the north of Jerusalem.

The meal was a lively occasion; the men were greatly outnumbered by the women who served them as they lay or sat around the low table in the centre of the main living space. Joseph sat at the head, dwarfed by his sons, but obviously enjoying himself. In one arm he held his sleeping newest grandchild, and in the other a large cup of his best wine. The lamb stew smelt wonderful and it wasn't long before Joseph invited the women with all the children to join them at the table. He told his wife it was the only sensible solution to the chaos. However Rachel wasn't fooled; she knew he loved having them all 'under his eye', as he put it.

Martha stretched out, enjoying her wine; with no responsibility, this was the most relaxed she had felt for a long while. She watched Tabitha play a board game with the children, feeling proud of the way she handled their squabbles and helped them stick to the rules. Their fathers on the other hand kept cheating, turning the whole game into a hopeless mess of mirth. A little while later, Tabitha helped to put the overtired toddlers to bed, as the men began a more serious game of checkers. Joseph was hard to beat, but after the wine his sons were hoping for a rare victory.

Noah's wife Hadassah was young, pretty and pregnant with her third child. After her marriage, Hadassah had struggled with life in rural Bethany, but Martha, out of love and loyalty to Rachel, had done her best to make the simple, caring Hadassah feel at home. It had been a relief to Martha when the couple had moved to Jerusalem, for she had been betrothed to Noah from childhood and Hadassah was largely unaware of the pain and humiliation her marriage to Noah had caused Martha.

It had taken a long time for Martha to come to terms with her feelings and realise it hadn't been Hadassah's fault, but now she was truly grateful to God for a path that was hers. She listened with interest as Hadassah talked about life in the big city and how much her mother helped with the children, and how well Noah was getting along with his father-in-law.

Rachel came and joined them, cradling her latest grandchild, who had slept in various people's arms almost the whole evening.

"Your poor mother," crooned Rachel to the sleeping bundle. "You'll wake up soon and want feeding." Adinah who sat close by, was enjoying five minutes' peace, while Tabitha and Elizabeth, who was usually called Lizzy, played a game together. Martha and Hadassah smiled sympathetically, but Adinah was looking forward to having her baby back for a while.

Hadassah stretched and yawned. "I think I'll go and join my little ones; they'll be up before the cockerel and I doubt their father will be much help," she said, loudly enough for Noah to hear. He promised he'd be along as soon as the game was won.

"That could take all night!" chorused his brothers.

Rachel sat in silence, watching Martha for a while, then reached out and touched her arm. "My dear, you know you have always been like a daughter to me, although I thank God for my daughters-in-law, our four sons and all my grandchildren. I am very blessed. But it has been a long time since we talked about what happened between our two families, between you and Noah."

Martha was a little taken aback. Her thoughts had been elsewhere.

"Oh Rachel, that was all a long time ago, you needn't worry about me. We're different people now. It really worked out for the best. Noah and I were friends, he and Hadassah have found love."

Rachel sighed deeply. "And that is why you will always be my favourite," she said, trying to smile. "You think of others before yourself."

"Moments ago you were telling the baby that she was your favourite," chuckled Martha, deflecting the compliment, which she felt she didn't deserve. "I consider myself fortunate now. I have Tabitha, and a free rein in my own home. Many of my peers have been less fortunate."

"I know dear, but you deserve love too," said Rachel softly.

"So do many others, Rachel. I believe the Lord God knows what is best for us."

"Like all those guests turning up this morning," snorted Rachel. "That was exhausting. I nearly fell asleep this afternoon."

"What do you mean, nearly fell asleep? You were snoring when I came in," chuckled Joseph, as he came over to join them. "And I know Martha enjoyed having all those guests. It was a great honour. I'm just sorry I missed the Rabbi. Did he say when he might be back?"

"Possibly Passover," Martha replied.

* * *

It was late when Martha and Tabitha returned to the dark, empty house. The night had turned chilly again, so Martha fetched their blankets and they snuggled up together beside the kitchen fire.

"Martha," said Tabitha, sleepily. "What happened between you and Noah?"

Martha sighed, "What makes you ask?

"Nothing. No one's mentioned it, if that's what you mean," said Tabitha, defensively. "But you never explained it to me and sometimes you look so sad."

"You've got a good imagination," said Martha, her wry smile concealed in the blanket.

"Please tell me. I'm old enough now."

Martha put her arms around Tabitha as she leant against her. "There really isn't much to tell. I grew up with Rachel's boys, as you know. We have always been neighbours and our parents were always good friends, so I guess it was quite natural that Noah and I were betrothed."

"Oh," said Tabitha, quietly.

"I was nearly nine by the time Lazarus came along, and up till then there had just been father, mother and myself. So we were very close, you see. After Mary was born, my mother Iscah never really recovered, so I more or less started to run the house. After Mother died, father relied on me more than ever. He was heartbroken. I don't think he ever really got over losing her."

"So you were an only child until you were my age," said Tabitha, thoughtfully. "I don't think I'd ever realised that."

"Lazarus transformed our little family, the answer to prayer, and then darling Little Mary came along, the joy of everyone's lives."

"Didn't you ever feel resentful? I'm sure I would have."

"Sometimes," said Martha. "But to begin with, having a little brother and then a baby sister was wonderful, and father was so good at making us all feel special. It's just that I was the oldest, and when my mother died, he relied on me. Besides, it was my duty. Anyhow, my marriage was postponed. Then Joseph and Father fell out, probably because Rachel was worried about me, so in the end, Father had the agreement annulled."

Tabitha felt her shrug, or had it been a shudder? It was hard to tell through the thick blanket. "Oh, Martha, that's terrible," she said softly.

"Father couldn't manage without me, there wasn't a choice. Noah was a good man and my friend, so naturally it had seemed right for us to marry. We knew nothing of love."

"Do you think he loves Hadassah?"

"What do you think?"

"Yes," whispered Tabitha, but she felt disloyal to Martha in admitting it.

"And so it shall be for you, my girl," promised Martha.

"No thank you," was the indignant reply. "I'm staying with you and Mary."

Martha laughed out loud. "Good night, Tabitha." A grunt came from under Tabitha's blanket.

Martha lay awake for a long time as painful memories paraded through her mind unbidden. She had felt trapped and condemned to a life of slavery in her own home, and further humiliation came when it was announced that Noah was to marry Hadassah. It was one of the lowest points in her life. She had felt alone and remembered those times as dark and hard, but there was little time for self-pity. Her duties running the house, looking after her two younger siblings and helping out with the harvests soon buried any feelings she had beneath a mountain of care and responsibilities. Rachel had reached out to Martha, trying to repair their damaged relationship, but Reubel and Joseph had been stubborn men and took a long time to make their peace.

Chapter Three

Tabitha

Three long horn blasts resonated through the morning air, insistently calling the inhabitants of Bethany to worship.

Martha felt groggy and stiff as she woke up; the old memories had troubled her sleep. Hastily she got dressed, the icy water feeling soothing on her hot face as she and Tabitha hurried to answer the call to the synagogue.

Josh and Jacob, their two shepherd boys, were among the crowd, and ran to greet Martha and Tabitha. With scrubbed faces, they eagerly assured her that the flock was safe and well catered for. At twelve years old, the tall, thin Josh leaned on his staff like an old man, while Jacob constantly shook aside the thick locks of black hair that partly obscured his face. She placed a tiny coin, which fortunately Tabitha had remembered, in each boy's palm and then put her finger to her lips. The boys turned the coins over with wide eyes. Josh took one of Martha's hands in both of his and squeezed it gratefully. Then he returned to his invalid mother's side and patiently helped her towards the synagogue. Jacob fell into step behind his uncle, a surly looking man. It was fortunate his uncle hadn't seen Martha give him the coin, as he would certainly have taken it. Jacob winked at Tabitha as he went by and her cheeks turned red, much to Martha's amusement. Quietly she said a prayer for the two boys; they too had been robbed of a childhood.

Once again the synagogue was full, and as an elder in the community, Joseph read and expounded the story of Esther. Simon and Lazarus were also elders in the community helping to keep the law and teach the scriptures, as well as supporting the synagogue Hazzan, Michael.

* * *

Tabitha was full of questions and comments all the way home.

"Mordecai must have been very upset when he realised that obeying God meant they might all be killed."

"Yes he was," replied Martha, as they walked along together. "But he stood by what was right, and God had known all along what was in Haman's heart, which was why Esther had been made queen. As soon as she realised that, she prayed and fasted, and so did Mordecai and his friends."

"But supposing she had been too frightened to go to the king, in case he had her killed?"

"Esther was afraid. But as Mordecai said to her, she had a choice. She could die with her people at Haman's hand, or possibly save them by risking her own life and going to the king. So she put the lives of our people before her own, and God gave her success."

"Gosh, that was real sacrificial love," sighed Tabitha.

"It certainly was," agreed Martha, as they arrived home.

In the kitchen stood a large basket decorated with herbs. Tabitha had filled it with food, clothes, beads, old toys and games and bright, neatly rolled sashes for each of Rachel's grandchildren, her own work. Together they carried the basket across the street where they were expected; everyone crowded round.

The basket was unpacked in the middle of the courtyard, and the children reached in and pulled out the gifts excitedly. Joseph just managed to grab a bottle of his favourite wine before it was dropped. Each sash had been made to measure, with a secret pocket containing a tiny shell or bead, from Tabitha's collection. Tabitha was praised for the quality of her weaving and her eye for colour.

"What dyes did you use Tabitha, especially for Joe's sash?" asked Adinah.

"Cabbage and mustard with pomegranate skins, but I'm not sure I can repeat it," admitted Tabitha. "I had a bit of an accident with the vat." Martha rolled her eyes.

The family took the noon meal in the warm sunshine of the courtyard and as soon as the men had finished eating, the children drifted across to them. Quickly all were engaged in playing with the new toys. The place rang with the sound of laughter and slowly collapsed into the chaos of family life once more.

Tabitha had another family she wanted to spend time with during the holiday. They were the only real family she had ever known before Martha, Mary and Lazarus. So she slipped away as soon as she could, hurrying down the hill carrying one of Martha's full baskets and a large bundle of clothes. Despite these, every now and again she managed to do a little skip of joy.

As she approached the single-storey house with its flaking lime plaster, tiny windows and ill-fitting doors, she was rushed upon by a gaggle of children of all ages. There were no shoes on their feet, but broad smiles danced upon their faces as they hugged Tabitha, the little ones clinging to her knees.

"Oh, Tabby, we've been looking out for you for ages. Mama

said you'd be along just as soon as you could," whined one of the little girls.

"Well, I'm here now Maemi and I can stay till prayers this evening."

"Where's Mama?" asked Tabitha, looking towards the dilapidated house.

"I'm here, my darling girl," called the widow Juthine, emerging from the house, her arms stretched out in greeting. Her hair was neatly coiled and although her clothes were worn, like her children's, they were clean and well repaired. She hugged Tabitha for a long while before they all trooped into the house. As Tabitha sat down on the raised section of the floor, Maemi immediately slid onto her lap. They chatted amiably about the children's performance of 'Esther' at the synagogue. Then Juthine, along with her older children, wanted to hear all about the Rabbi Yeshua's visit on the Friday. It was the big news in Bethany and Tabitha was delighted to tell them all about it. Although, if she gave a little more emphasis to the part she played in the proceedings, nobody minded. "Oh, and Rachel sends greetings, and she gave me this for you," finished Tabitha, handing Juthine the bundle of clothing, which turned out to be two tunics Rachel's grandchildren had grown out of.

"Oh, these are lovely," exclaimed Juthine. "Come, come," she called to two of the younger boys, "this will do very well for you Micah, with room to grow, and Joel, you will look very handsome in this one. Go into the bakery and put them on." The boys disappeared into the only other room of the house.

Juthine's only source of income to feed and clothe her eight children was the bakery. The older girls helped to grind the corn and care for the children, while the older boys found what work they could.

"Tabitha, what's in the basket? Is it for us?" asked Maemi. One of her older sisters gave her a reproachful look.

"Of course," smiled Tabitha. The two boys came back into the room to show off their new clothing. "Now the boys are back, shall we have a look?"

Tabitha picked the quietest child to go first, then each of the others took something from the basket and gave it to the one it was meant for. She and Martha had spent a lot of time putting the basket together. There were good second-hand clothes for many, a pair of sandals for one of the older boys, and an old but serviceable pair of boots for another. Tabitha had also made new bright sashes for her brothers and sisters. Mary had sent Juthine a warm blanket.

"Oh, a blanket of my own!" exclaimed the widow. "Now I won't have to share with all the little ones." There were a few wobbly lips at this remark, so Juthine said, "All right, you can all share the new blanket and I'll sleep under the old one, alone." Tabitha laughed.

Martha had made sure the basket also included dried herbs, salted fish, nuts, date cakes, raisins, olives and oil. Practical food with some treats, too. The children licked their lips in anticipation as Juthine shooed them out to play.

"Tabitha, it has blessed me so much seeing you today," said Juthine quietly, as she stood in the doorway watching her boys as they knocked wooden targets down with a sling. "I am so proud of you. Who'd have thought that poor little orphaned baby could have turned into such a beautiful, clever and gifted person."

"Martha says that too," muttered Tabitha, blushing.

"You believe us don't you?" teased Juthine, a twinkle in her eye.

Tabitha shrugged. Sometimes her own story felt like it belonged to someone else. Her mother had turned up at Juthine's door one night, pregnant and ill. Her family in Jerusalem had thrown her out and wanted nothing to do with her. The kind widow had taken her in, but it was too late, she had died in childbirth that night and she hadn't even told them her name. Juthine cared for the tiny orphaned baby like her own, and Tabitha had grown up thinking the other children were her brothers and sisters, although two of the others were orphans like herself. Martha had supported Juthine, as she supported so many others, and together they had named the baby Tabitha. Once weaned, Martha had insisted her own family adopt the toddler, with Juthine's wholehearted consent. Seven years later, Tabitha's bond was still as strong with Juthine as it was with Martha.

Tabitha had often wondered what her real mother and father had been like, but all she knew was that she had her mother's eyes and corkscrew curls. Somehow, as the years passed, not knowing her real family mattered less and less. It became hard to imagine anyone kinder than Juthine, as wonderful as Martha, funnier than Mary or as strong and wise as Lazarus. She was happy and had two families that loved her. In fact, Juthine had said she became more and more like Martha with every passing year. Mary had had a few things to say about that, but Tabitha was sure she was only joking.

* * *

During the afternoon Martha sat chatting with Rachel and her daughters-in-law, and before long the Rabbi had become the topic of conversation once again. His fame was spreading far and wide, and no one had forgotten what had happened at Passover the previous year. In anger he had driven the money changers and the livestock traders from the temple with a whip.

"It was a wonder he wasn't arrested by the temple police," pointed out Hadassah. "They still talk about it in Jerusalem."

"If he wanted to get everyone's attention that was certainly the way to do it," said Adinah.

"But what about those crooks who charge extortionate prices for the animals they sell for sacrifice?" complained Rachel. "The temple makes a fat profit out of that by insisting everything is changed into Tyrian shekels, because of the higher silver content.

That racket's been going on for years, and don't get me started on temple taxes, Roman taxes and tithes." Her daughters-in-law were a little surprised at the outburst.

"And it's all getting worse," said Lizzy, stroking the brow of her daughter, who lay dozing in her lap. "How are decent, hardworking folk supposed to be able to afford it all? Think of the men who have to come all the way to Jerusalem at least once a year, to pay the temple tax."

"But how else can they finance all the daily sacrifices?" asked Adinah.

"Out of their profits. Look how much they make from the fleeces alone. Why do you think Jerusalem is the centre of the wool trade?" retorted Lizzy. Adinah nodded, conceding.

"But surely, when you think about it, the Rabbi's action was justified, it's holy ground," said Martha, but inside she still found it hard to equate his reputed behaviour with the thoughtful teacher she knew.

"You have to admit, it resembles a market more than a temple during festival times, with everyone shouting and haggling over exchange rates and animal prices," added Rachel. The others nodded in agreement.

"Sometimes profit seems more important than holiness and serving God," whispered Lizzy.

Rachel shook her head sadly. "It does seem like that, but it won't make him popular with the priests. They don't like their God-given authority being questioned, especially the high priest, Caiaphas. There's already enough disagreement among the Pharisees, Sadducees, Essenes and the rest of them."

Martha frowned; Rachel was right. Her Uncle Elias, who usually had a fair grasp of political and religious matters in Jerusalem, had suggested that not all opinions about the Rabbi Yeshua were favourable.

"Then there was all that trouble with Herod Antipas and Herodias, Philip's wife," said Hadassah. "When John the Baptiser spoke out about their relationship, they had him imprisoned. Now is he really a prophet sent from God? How can we be sure that what he was telling us is true? Is this rabbi the Messiah prophesied about in Isaiah? Will it be him who reigns on David's throne and over the Kingdom, bringing justice and righteousness?" She took a deep breath before asking, "Martha, what do you think, is your Rabbi the Messiah?"

Taken by surprise but pleased by the question, Martha tried to gather her wits before speaking.

"Well, Andrew, Peter, the son of Jonah's brother, was a disciple of John the Baptiser before he followed Yeshua. And he told us he had witnessed John call the Master 'the Lamb of God, who takes away the sin of the world'. That's why they gave up fishing to follow Yeshua. They believed John, and I don't think Simon or Lazarus is in any doubt about John's credentials as a prophet either, or who Yeshua is."

"And my Joseph agrees too," added Rachel. "Although being a cautious man, he's biding his time, and watching." This caused some smiles among her daughters-in-law.

"So, let me see if I've got this right," said Adinah, slowly shaking her head and looking at Martha. "The Messiah was having breakfast in your courtyard on Friday morning, here in the back of beyond?"

"I know it's hard to believe," chuckled Rachel. "Only time will tell."

Noah and Shem had wandered over, overhearing some of what was being said.

"Aren't women supposed to talk about domestic things, like how many eggs the chickens are laying or the price of goods at the market?" said Shem.

"Or even more usefully, how to bring up children to respect

their fathers," said Noah, grinning. A shower of relatively harmless objects was thrown at the two men as they beat a hasty retreat pursued hotly by the children, urged on by their mothers. Noah swept his little son up over his shoulder, then caught his daughter around the waist. She squealed with delight. Shem had several children clinging to his legs as he tried to move, while his son Joe clung to his back, trying to wrestle him to the floor.

"Where shall I put them, dear?" Noah called to his wife.

"In the pen with the goats, I should think," cried Hadassah.

The children squealed and wriggled, frantically trying to escape. "Martha, Martha!" they shouted, "Save us!"

Quick as a flash, Martha grabbed an empty corn sack and with a nimble jump, popped it over Noah's head. The children squirmed free and made their escape, hiding behind their grandmother shrieking with laughter. Noah bumped blindly into Shem and the children all piled on top of them. It was a long while before they all stopped laughing.

Chapter Four

Mary and Lazarus Return

The sun had long since set, but a warm glow still lay on the land as Mary and Lazarus toiled up the hill in silence. Martha was listening impatiently for their arrival while she spun wool. Tabitha was already in bed, exhausted after the celebrations.

Tired out, Lazarus and Mary threw themselves down on the rug as Martha handed them drinks. As she joined them, she couldn't help noticing the way their faces glowed with excitement in the lamplight. They asked politely about Rachel and the family and listened patiently while Martha recounted the children's performance of the story of Esther, which had been as hilarious as ever. Martha's frustration grew. She didn't want to talk about the small goings on in Bethany; she wanted to hear the news from Jerusalem.

"What's happened?" she demanded.

Amused, Mary tilted her head.

"From the beginning," suggested Lazarus to her.

"The view of the temple, as we rounded the last bend above the Kidron valley, was truly breathtaking with the sun reflected off its vast white walls. Pilgrims were pouring in from every direction along the roads," began Mary.

Martha glared at her sister. "Yes, yes. I know all that," she said impatiently. "What did I miss?"

Mary sighed and began again.

"Salome, Susanna and Mary went off to find their lodgings, while true to her word, Miriam stayed with me in the temple courts. It was marvellous to hear the Master speak and see the crowds hang on his every word, as did we," sighed Mary. "I wish you could have been there, Martha."

"So do I," said Martha, a little more sharply than she'd intended.

"He stayed talking to the people all morning," added her brother, before briefly telling her that their uncle Elias, the head of the family, who lived in Jerusalem, had invited the Master to join them for a meal. There had been plenty of room in the large house with only their Uncles Josiah and Joachim staying. "Anyhow, the following day we met the Master out by the Sheep gate," he continued. "It was hard to make ourselves heard over the din of the animals waiting to be sacrificed."

"Why did he meet you there?" asked Martha.

"He led us to the crowded porches surrounding the pools of Bethesda. All the sick and crippled people seemed to be crammed in there."

"Many of them are helpless," said Mary, her face screwed up with indignation. Martha nodded grimly, grateful she hadn't seen them.

"Bethesda indeed. Not a lot of loving kindness and mercy around, as far as I could see," said their brother.

"And especially not if you're a sheep, goat or bullock!" Mary reminded him.

"Please, not that again," begged her brother.

"I understand very clearly that the blood of animals is used to atone for our sin so we don't have to die, but it doesn't mean I like it. Although I am grateful," Mary added more softly.

Martha rolled her eyes. She wasn't getting involved in this argument.

"Well, we certainly didn't see any angels or Greek gods in the still water," continued Lazarus. "But we followed the Master as best we could, trying not to step on anyone."

"John whispered that something might be about to happen," said Mary, the excitement back in her voice. "So I pushed my way forward. The Master was on a mission and I didn't want to miss it." Martha held her breath in anticipation. "He stood in prayer, his head bowed. I wondered if he was overwhelmed by all those sick people desperate for healing but when he looked up his eyes went searching for someone. His gaze fixed on a man lying near the back wall, propped up on an elbow. We did our best to follow, wondering what he might do."

"People were asking who we were, so I tried to explain," said Lazarus. "But I could see they hadn't heard about the Rabbi."

"Under the porch, I could hear quite clearly what the Master was saying to the man." Mary's voice shook with excitement as she spoke. "He asked the man if he truly wanted to become well. The poor man looked perplexed; he clearly didn't know who he was talking to because he started to explain why he couldn't get into the pool to be healed when the angel stirred up the water."

Lazarus raised an eyebrow, but said nothing.

"That's what they believe," said Mary defensively. "I heard someone say the fellow had been ill for thirty-eight years. Can you imagine that? How hopeless he must have felt." Tears began to glisten at the corners of her dark brown eyes. She let out a deep breath. "This time the Master was having no nonsense. In that voice which you just can't ignore, he said 'Get up. Pick up your sleeping mat and you will walk!"

Martha's mouth hung open, her pupils wide and bright. She knew what was coming, but she had to hear it. Mary continued, "The Master held his gaze unwaveringly while the man took in what had just been said to him. Then, to everyone's amazement, he began to struggle to his feet. James took a step forward to help, but the Master waved him back. At first, the man knelt shakily with both hands on the ground but then, as though gaining strength, and with one hand on the pillar to steady himself, he stood up. The crowd gasped, mouths open in astonishment. You could almost see the strength gather in his wasted body. I've never seen anything so wonderful in all my life!" Mary was almost crying with joy.

"It was like the man's faith began to stir his body, filling it with the strength of healing," whispered Lazarus, as if understanding for the first time.

Mary continued, "The man stretched up experimentally, looked around at his fellows, then slowly and deliberately he bent down to pick up the mat. I've never seen anyone enjoy rolling a smelly old mat as much as he did, before he tucked it under his arm. It was then we realised the Master had gone. We were all so focused on the miracle unrolling before us that we didn't see him leave."

"Fortunately, John had his wits about him and ushered us quickly out of the place, arguing that if the Master didn't want to draw attention to himself, then neither should we," said Lazarus. There was a pause while Martha took in what she had just been told.

"Didn't he heal anyone else?" she asked, a note of curiosity in her voice.

"No. As I said, he left abruptly," said Mary.

Now Martha was puzzled.

"Philip spotted the healed man capering between the penned flocks," laughed Mary.

"But where did the Master go? Did you find him?"

"We found him in the temple eventually, with the man he'd healed."

"But that wasn't all," said Mary, a note of irritation in her voice. "A group of witnesses hurried after the man, accusing him of breaking the law, because he was carrying his mat on the Sabbath. The poor man looked bewildered. He tried to explain what had just happened, but he didn't even know the Master's name. It made my blood boil. He'd just started walking after thirty-eight years and some overzealous law keepers were more concerned with that than the miracle!"

"Surely the Master's action was one of mercy and kindness, not work," sighed Martha. "I'm sure God never wanted it to be like that. Well, not according to some of the things the Master has said about him."

"Lazarus, have you any idea why the Master picked that man from all of the others?" asked Mary. "From what Miriam said, I got the impression he was healing almost everyone who came to him."

"Today was different," agreed her brother. "As you said, the Master picked him out. We discussed it at some length on our way back to the temple, but no one seemed to have a clear explanation."

"If those closest to him don't understand, how are we supposed to?" said Mary, exasperated.

"Miriam said he does explain a lot of things, but Susanna and Salome reckon that often his disciples are embarrassed to ask, feeling they should know and understand more than they do," said Martha.

"Well, I wouldn't be embarrassed to ask," said Mary.

"No, you wouldn't," said her brother. "We obviously need more women asking questions."

Martha laughed. "None of us know as much as the scribes and Pharisees about the scriptures. We can only do our best," she said.

"Very true," agreed her brother. "Just before we left, I asked our uncles if they had any thoughts about the incident. They suggested that as our ancestors had wandered in the desert wilderness for thirty-eight years before being led into the promised land, that might have something to do with it. But no one is quite sure at the moment what the point is."

"And no-one asked Yeshua?" reiterated Martha.

"I'd say we're all wandering around in the wilderness trying to understand this miracle," said Mary, stifling a yawn. "Perhaps all we really need to know is that he has the power to heal. I'm sorry, but I'm off to bed."

Martha lay in bed, her mind still running through the events at the pool.

"Mary, are you still awake?" she whispered. Mary grunted. "I was thinking, why did he heal that man at the pools of Bethesda? And it occurred to me, it was because everyone had put their faith in the water to heal them, through this Greek God or an angel. The other people he's healed, like Simon, had faith in the Master. That may have been the Master's point. The sick people at the pool needed to put their faith in him, not anything else. Only he has the power and authority to heal."

There was a moment of cold silence before Mary answered. "Right, as usual. Now can I go to sleep? No more questions till the morning please. Especially if you believe I'll be up early. I wouldn't put too much faith in that."

"Oh, I think Tabitha might," said Martha, brightly.

Mary groaned and turned over.

Chapter Five

Business as Usual

Tabitha had whisked through her chores and some of Martha's and was waiting for her in the kitchen. Martha felt groggy from the late night and wasn't as appreciative as she could have been. She poked the fire and put another lump of dried dung on.

"Were they very late coming home last night?" asked Tabitha, wishing she'd stayed up.

"Not especially, but they had a lot to say. I'll let Mary tell you all about it, because she'll be able to answer all your questions." Martha sounded irritated.

"Shall I go and wake Mary?" asked Tabitha, brightly.

"Give her a little longer, my love. You know she's not always at her best first thing in the morning."

Tabitha sighed heavily but perked up as Lazarus swept into the kitchen, his cheeks glowing from exercise. As he hung his cloak up, Martha looked questioningly at him.

"I thought I'd catch Josh and Jacob before they moved the flock out," he said, by way of an explanation. "I'm starving, is breakfast ready?"

"Nearly," said Tabitha, quickly pouring him a drink and laying the low table. "The bread will need a few more minutes."

"Is Mary up yet?"

"Not yet. Shall I go and wake her?" asked Tabitha quickly, avoiding Martha's disapproving look, as she tapped the bread to see if it was ready.

"Yes please!" he called back, as he went to wash.

Mary joined them just in time to pray, still rubbing the sleep from her eyes.

Over breakfast Lazarus and Martha discussed their plans for the olive groves. Harvesting would start in August. Lazarus still valued his older sister's input when it came to farming matters, so in the end, they decided to look over the groves together. They left Mary to help Tabitha with the milling, and to tell her all the news from Jerusalem.

Lazarus was poking about in the woodshed when Martha joined him, a warm cloak wrapped around her against the chill and a hastily made-up basket on her arm. They turned right out of the gate and followed the road as it climbed gently between the houses. At the far end of the village, Martha left Lazarus for a few minutes while she disappeared down an alley to deliver her basket. She returned breathless.

"Yaqim's cough has been so bad this winter," she explained. "I'm trying a new combination of herbs that Sara suggested."

"And a few other treats, if my eyes weren't mistaken," commented Lazarus.

"They're so poor, Lazarus, they can't afford to pay for medicine, and nothing really seems to help."

From there they walked briskly, following the track which led to the wheat and barley fields. They discussed the coming season, their paces evenly matched. The barley was well on its way, with strong green shoots reaching skyward, while the later wheat crop was only just showing through the furrowed earth. The fields were surrounded by olive trees which dropped away below them and marched up to meet the steeper rocky outcrops above the village.

Lazarus led the way. Old grey leaves tinged with auburn littered the ground crunching under their feet as they walked beneath the boughs. Martha caught some of the lower branches, examining the buds with expert eyes, admiring the way the grey-green leaves shone even in the overcast light.

Lazarus led her to a specific tree marked with a strip of cloth and they gazed up into its branches for a long while. Martha nodded slowly.

"It's looking very good, definitely one to take some grafts from."

"The others are nearer the road to Bethphage, so we can visit the new root stock on the way."

After a while they rounded a low outcrop and came to a smaller south-facing field which acted as a nursery. Martha smiled with pleasure as row upon row of healthy, wild olive saplings waved their stems in greeting. They were almost as tall as she was.

"They have come on," she said, gazing around. "And we've hardly lost any."

"Just one or two here and there," agreed Lazarus, tugging one up with his bare hands and carefully removing it. "A couple more weeks and we can begin grafting."

Martha nodded slowly, counting the saplings.

"You'll need enough binders, but Tabitha and I'll sort those out. I'd like to start training her so she can help too."

"As long as Mary isn't let loose on them, I don't mind," laughed her brother.

He dodged a ball of twine that flew out of Martha's hand.

"I remember a time when you never missed."

"And I remember a time when you were an easy target," she retorted.

As they left the field Martha glanced back, pleased with the healthy new trees that would, in time, continue to ensure the productivity of the family business.

They threaded their way through the olive groves, inspecting the trees and occasionally tagging one that needed dead wood cut out of it. On the way home they visited the olive presses which were in need of renovation, so it was past noon when they arrived back.

Tabitha and Mary were carrying a sack of flour across the courtyard, their arms tired after a morning spent milling. Lazarus relieved them of their burden, carrying it easily into the house. The chickens were already invading the area, searching for any escaped grains.

"I'm sorry lunch isn't ready yet," said Mary, "but Tabitha thought we should do as much as possible this morning, and honestly once we got talking the time just flew by."

Over lunch, talk quickly returned to the miracle at the pool the day before. It had had a profound effect upon Lazarus and an aura of ecstasy seemed to have settled around Mary.

However, unanswered questions still nagged Martha, as she made cheese and chopped vegetables that afternoon. Mary and Tabitha had gone to fetch water from the well where they would also meet their friends. Alone Martha prayed, but her mind kept returning to the scene at the pool. She wondered what had been going through the Master's mind, then shook her head at her own foolishness. How could she understand what he was thinking? She sighed, but couldn't let it go. It seemed important. What must it have been like to be crippled for thirty-eight years and then be healed by Yeshua? What must it have been like to wander in the wilderness for thirty-eight years before being led into the Promised Land, the land that was now occupied by the Romans? How was that significant?

What the nation of Israel should do, Martha decided, was have faith in the Master and who he was, not anything else. Then she remembered a passage from Zechariah about the Messiah building the true temple of the Lord, ruling as king and priest from his throne, bringing perfect harmony between the two roles. Could this man, a carpenter from Galilee turned rabbi, truly be the long-awaited Messiah? Martha felt pangs of doubt. It all sounded too incredible once more. Perhaps after all, he was just a man called by God, like John the Baptist. The peace she felt at this thought only lasted a moment however, as her restless thoughts turned to the religious authorities and how they thought the Messiah would come and overthrow the Romans. Martha was beginning to have serious doubts about that too. When did carrying a mat on the Sabbath become more important than a miracle that would transform someone's life? Frustrated, Martha threw the last onion into the pot as she heard the excited voices of Mary and Tabitha.

Tabitha came bursting into the kitchen. "Mary's been telling everyone about yesterday, it's caused such a stir. But now they're remembering the rumours we've been hearing from Galilee ever since the Master became known, and it's got everyone talking."

Mary walked into the kitchen, carrying a skin of water, which she hung up, grunting under the weight. Martha gave her a questioning look.

"I'd love to visit the Sea of Galilee," said Tabitha, wistfully. "I've never been further than Jericho."

Mary gave her a hug. "And so you shall, one day. Our mother's family live north of Tiberias. Martha went there many times when she was young. I should like to go again, I was only a toddler on the last trip, not long before father died."

"The trouble is everyone wants to come to Jerusalem!" laughed Martha. "But you're right, both of you, we should plan a trip. I know Aunt Jael would welcome us. It's just so hard to find enough time with all the things there are to do here," she added, breathing out deeply.

"I hope she's not like her daughter," said Tabitha.

"No, no," laughed Martha. "She's not like Rebecca at all – well, not in the way you're thinking."

"Was nosey and opinionated what you were thinking?" laughed Mary. Tabitha pursed her lips and nodded.

There was a long pause before Mary made her next comment. "We heard Noah and Hadassah returned to Jerusalem this morning," she said, watching her sister carefully for a reaction. Martha smiled woodenly, a little annoyed because she already knew that.

"Tabitha, haven't you got some milking to do?" Martha said, a slight edge in her voice. Tabitha scuttled out, glancing knowingly at Mary.

Martha added dill to her stew and tasted it. Mary watched for a while, "Did you really enjoy yourself over Purim?"

Martha looked up and frowned. "Yes, I did. What are you trying to say?"

"Well, it's just that Tabitha was concerned it had stirred up painful memories."

"It did," snapped Martha, "but as I've said before, they are old memories and they certainly have no hold on me now. I had a rough time back then, but that was ten years ago. Look how good my life is now. I regret nothing!"

Mary drew her head back and raised her eyebrows at Martha's outburst. She was silent for a while. Then she said, "Lazarus asked me to tidy the lean-to, to make room for some more wood. I've put the chopping block just inside the door. It made a very useful seat, didn't it?"

"It certainly did," agreed Martha, her face melting into a smile at the memory.

Chapter Six

Family Ties

Late spring

There was more rain, but the days grew steadily warmer as the grain harvest turned from leafy green to gold-topped feathery ears. Branches from the best olive trees had been grafted onto the wild saplings and now they watched with anticipation and prayed that God would bless their hopes for strong new trees to replace some of the ageing stock.

Martha was on a rare visit to Jerusalem's markets, and with her bags full, called on her Aunt Elizabeth. Her grandparents, Eleazar and Hannah, also lived there. Sara, her aunt's faithful servant and friend, welcomed Martha, her face lighting up with delight and surprise.

In the large, ornate courtyard, surrounded on three sides by the large Roman-styled house, her grandparents were dozing in the spring sunshine, and woke up as Martha joined them. It was peaceful there, insulated from the bustle of the city outside. Her grandmother sat tall and proud, her face framed by long white hair, as she made a point of asking after Lazarus and Mary, and as usual, Martha tactfully included Tabitha in her replies. Hannah had opposed Tabitha's adoption from the beginning and didn't disguise her disapproval whenever her name was mentioned. Martha's father, Reubel, and her grandfather, Eleazar, had opposed the adoption at first, but her grandfather had mellowed after the death of Reubel, his eldest son. Now, he called it 'women's politics' and avoided getting involved. However, he was keen to hear all about their plans to increase olive production. Martha tried to be concise, knowing full well that he would drift off to sleep soon. Eleazar had spent much of his childhood in Bethany, working with his father on the olive groves, and had fond memories of life there. It always amused Martha that when he spoke of Michael, Bethany's ageing Hazzan, it was as though he were still a young man. Although shrunken, wrinkled and frail, the old couple still held a place of high honour in the family.

Sara brought Martha a bundle of clothes to take back to Bethany, explaining that Elizabeth was taking one of her naps, but it was an ideal opportunity for the two women to catch up. They sat close together beside the fountain, listening to the gentle snores of Martha's grandparents.

Sara's skin was still tight, despite the lines and creases which multiplied every time she smiled. A widow when her oldest son had died, she was forced to become a bond servant to Elias and Elizabeth, in order to keep her family from debtor's prison. She too had grown up in the countryside, and missed the rhythm of the seasons, although, as she was always quick to point out, not the back-breaking hard work. This made Martha smile, as she knew only too well how hard Sara worked, and how lost Elizabeth would be without her.

"You'd have thought that after seven years your grandmother

would have given up her gripe about Tabitha's adoption," said Sara, who was generally accepted as a member of the family herself.

"She's not the only one," sighed Martha. "Aunt Elizabeth feels the same way."

Sara nodded, acknowledging the trial it caused Martha. "With all the wealth in this family, I could never understand why the objections were so strong. They were happy enough for Tabitha to be a servant, but when you insisted she be given the rights of a daughter, you proved you could be as stubborn as they were." Sara's eyes were smiling with approval.

"Tabitha's nearly as tall as Mary now," said Martha, changing tack.

"I hope she aims a little higher," said Sara, grinning broadly, "But under your kind hand, my love, Tabitha has turned out to be a true daughter."

"She is, isn't she," agreed Martha, but then her brow furrowed. "But sometimes I can't help feeling guilty, because I forced father to agree to her adoption. After all, he'd annulled my marriage to Noah, and then expected me to go on running his home and bringing up Mary and Lazarus. If someone had even asked me what I wanted, it wouldn't have been so bad, but they didn't. Uncle Elias only agreed because he knew it was unlikely I would ever marry and have a family of my own, and if Lazarus or Mary married, I might end up a neglected old maid. I didn't want Tabitha to be a servant, I wanted her to have the rights of a daughter, at least."

"Good grief woman, you shouldn't feel guilty. What you did was right, in my opinion. It did my heart good to see you stand up for yourself for once. They'll all come round in the end, you'll see. And despite what you might feel, you are loved so very much by them all."

There was a pause.

"I know I am, Sara. I love my life and my family now. The past is behind me. How's Aunt Elizabeth been?"

Sara sighed.

"She has her low days, usually when everyone else is busy and she's left to herself, but she hides it from Elias, Reuben and Sam. She doesn't like to worry them. Elizabeth really tries her best you know." Sara looked sideways at Martha, wondering how to broach her next question. "Although it might not have seemed like it at the time, Elizabeth tried to help you when your father died. I know she's sometimes hard to understand."

Martha was taken aback. What did Sara mean? Memories came flooding back. After their mother had died, Martha, Lazarus and Mary had been sent to stay with Elizabeth and Elias for a while, but quickly Martha had realised her aunt had little empathy for those around her. Martha mourned for her mother and pined for home. It was Sara who had stepped in to help the twelve-year-old Martha cope with her grief and contend with her two younger siblings. Out of the pain and loneliness Sara helped Martha find, buried deep inside, the resilience and resourcefulness she needed to rebuild her life.

"I used to feel such anger towards Elizabeth, but back then I was angry with everyone and everything," she said. "My world had been torn apart, and what was being asked of me felt so unfair."

"It was, my love. But the compassion you inherited from your mother began to come to the surface. I watched you shoulder those responsibilities and in the end triumph over them."

"It didn't feel like triumph. It was hard and lonely. The only two people in the whole world that were there for me were you and Rachel. I know father tried too, but he was also part of my problem."

"Like a slave in your own home," said Sara, quietly.

"That's why you understood me so well?" said Martha, through her tears.

"It was your aunt who encouraged me to reach out to you, and she never once interfered, in fact, she went out of her way to make sure I had time for you. Do you remember all that fuss over having two extra servants?"

"Oh, yes, uncle was livid. I don't think I've ever seen him so cross with her, and she can be pretty infuriating at times."

"The truth was, Elizabeth defied Elias for you when she hired those servants. She was under no illusions about herself, but she would never deliberately be unkind."

Martha blinked back more tears, taking in what she had just heard. "So are you saying she hired those extra servants so you could have more time for me?"

Sara nodded.

Martha swallowed hard, her brow crinkled. "Oh, Sara, all these years I've misjudged her, it had never occurred to me that was her reason. I just thought she was being selfish and lazy."

"I know. Perhaps I should have said something sooner."

There was a long pause until Martha, drying her face, said, "My heart feels lighter already."

"Forgiveness is like that, it sets you free," said Sara. "Unforgiveness is a heavy weight to bear."

Martha sighed. "I suppose I should be going home," she said, but she didn't move; the feeling of relief still sat with her.

"Don't worry about your aunt. I'll explain you had to get back. She'll understand."

Martha picked up her bags and slung them across her back, still reluctant to go without seeing her aunt.

"There is one thing I need to say in your aunt's absence," said Sara, looking a bit awkward. "Your Uncle Joshua sent word from Galilee to ask if the family can stay for Passover. As we're full up, and they are your mother's side of the family, Elizabeth naturally assumed you would love to have them."

"Of course, we would be glad to have them. We were only talking a few days ago about how nice it would be to visit them. Now they're coming to us," said Martha in delight, but immediately, she remembered the Master might come too. Oh dear, life could be very complicated at times, but she couldn't refuse her mother's kin, nor did she want to.

Martha walked home with her mind in a quandary, torn between seeing her family and the Master. In the end she spoke to Lazarus, who simply couldn't understand her dilemma; they could not turn family away, so if the Master came too, he and their friends would stay with Simon. That settled the matter for Martha, but a tiny bit of regret remained; being busy with relatives might mean she had no time to see her friends, whose visits tended to be infrequent and short. However, Passover lasted a whole week, so surely there would be time for everyone.

In the week leading up to Passover the crowds began to arrive, swelling the population of Jerusalem and filling the surrounding countryside. Along all the major routes into the city, camps appeared. Excitement mounted as families and friends were reunited, catching up on the news from the provinces. For many pilgrims this would be the trip of a lifetime, having waited years to visit the temple in Jerusalem to celebrate the Passover and the feast of unleavened bread.

Martha was busier than ever preparing for their arrival, and Tabitha's excitement mounted until finally, their family from Galilee arrived. It was so good to have a houseful of aunts, uncles and cousins whom they hadn't seen since their father's death. Cousin Rebecca and her daughter Calah, who also lived in Bethany, joined them, accompanied by her parents and uncle, from Galilee.

Embarrassingly, old stories from Martha's childhood were shared, but her Aunt Jael was always careful to include Mary, who had barely known her mother. Tabitha was immediately loved by everyone. Martha had no lack of help; in fact she loved the way her two aunts took over unburdening her of responsibility in her own home. Mary watched with amazed pleasure to see Martha treated like a daughter by her aunts and uncles; the years seemed to drop off her careworn face.

Martha's greatest joy had been baby Iscah, named after their mother, because she had the same sweet smile, dark curly hair and long eyelashes. Martha had taken the baby to show Rachel and her family, but it was Noah as he handed her back to Martha, who recognised how like Mary she was.

Family bonds had been retied, but there had been no word of the Master, and Martha was concerned.

Chapter Seven

Tabernacles and Harvest

Early autumn

Miriam sat down on the bench gratefully, while Martha hurriedly went to fetch her something to eat and drink. Susanna had gone straight to Simon's house to let him know the Master would be arriving later that evening, and travelling alone. He was arriving halfway through the festival and had sent the two women on ahead.

Looking up, Miriam could see the green branches of a shelter, built on the flat roof above the courtyard. Tabitha's handiwork was evident in the decoration. It was part of the celebration of tabernacles and the end of the harvest, Sukkot. She smiled, imagining Martha, Mary, Tabitha and perhaps Lazarus, at times, sleeping and eating together in the structure, as they commemorated the time their nation had lived in tents in the wilderness of Sinai.

Martha returned quickly with a laden tray, excited by Miriam's unexpected visit. It had been six months since they'd seen each other, and she was eager for news. From what Miriam told her, none of them had even been sure if the Master was coming to the festival. In the end, Miriam and Susanna had stayed in Capernaum, waiting to see what he would do. Miriam laughed as she'd told Martha that when the Master had realised they wouldn't be going with everyone else but were waiting for him, he'd sent them on ahead to tell Simon he was on his way. He would journey alone, but they hadn't known why. In the end they'd decided he was keeping a low profile and hoping not to be recognised. Martha thought about that, admitting that the approach to Simon's house was a lot less public than theirs, especially if the Master wanted to keep his arrival secret. At the same time, she was disappointed he wasn't going to stay with them, but she also had to admit to herself that they were very busy with the olive harvest. Her friends had been fortunate to find her at home. Olives were their main and most important crop, which began in the summer and usually lasted well into the autumn, when the rains began.

"Did you and Susanna come up to Jerusalem alone?" asked Martha.

"No. We joined a few of the locals who were late leaving," replied Miriam. "James John, Peter, Andrew, Philip and some of the others, all set off together joining the main caravan from Bethsaida as it came through Capernaum. Zebedee and Salome were in that party too and are now camped out on the Mount of Olives. I'm sure there'll be a big reunion at some point." She grimaced. Martha nodded in understanding; it wasn't the type of social gathering she enjoyed either.

"How did Philip come to know Nathanael? They seem such good friends. Was he from Bethsaida too?" Martha was curious.

"Oh no. Nathanael is from Cana, but he and Philip go way back. There was a sister involved, too."

Martha raised her eyebrows. "Intriguing."

Miriam rolled her eyes.

Then Martha asked the question that was really on her mind.

"Why did Yeshua come alone? Up until now you've all travelled together, haven't you?"

"Mostly, but things are changing it seems. He knows Judea isn't safe for him anymore. But he's not afraid," she added quickly, seeing Martha's concern. Martha could see Miriam was hesitating to say more, sucking her bottom lip in thought. In the end, knowing she could trust Martha, she spoke.

"Something John overheard concerns me. The Master's own brothers don't seem to care or understand about the danger he would be in if he came up to the feast. They told him he should stop hiding and show himself to the whole world if he wants to be famous."

Martha was taken aback, surprised his own family didn't seem to understand or care, but what really alarmed her was that in coming to Judea he had put himself in danger. What had happened since they had last seen their friends? Was that why the Master hadn't come for Passover?

Miriam saw the alarm on her face and tried to reassure her. "Martha, he's safe and not far behind us on the road. You'll see for yourself soon. We only hear the wisdom in his words and see the good he does, but you've heard how not everything he says and does meets with the temple's approval. And that disapproval has been growing, my friend. We can't ignore it anymore."

Martha shook her head, her eyes moist, her voice full of passion as she said, "It isn't fair. How can they be so blind?"

"They are caught up with their own rules and trying to stay in control. He might threaten that delicate balance," said Miriam, in a low voice.

Martha knew the truth, but she didn't want to face it. They would see they were wrong about him, surely.

"It must be very hard for him not to have the support of his family," she said, imagining his pain. "If they don't believe he's a prophet and the Messiah, how are the rest of us supposed to?"

Miriam spoke thoughtfully. "Sometimes, I think family are just too close, and miss the bigger picture. We must pray for them. I remember once he said a prophet was without honour in his own home. Perhaps he was thinking about them at the time. However, there was something else to give us hope. Susanna thought so too. Yeshua told his brothers he was not going up to the feast with them because 'it was not the right time'."

"The right time for what? To be revealed or arrested?" Martha challenged, but she regretted it. Miriam looked worried. "What about his mother?" she asked, more gently. "Does she believe he's the Messiah?"

"Oh yes. Salome is certain of that. They're relatives, you know. But Yeshua's mother is a widow, and her family is divided. A difficult position to be in."

"Have you met her?" asked Martha. Miriam nodded.

Martha thought about this, knowing how disagreements over faith were very different to arguments about the best way to press olives, which were far more common in her family. Nevertheless, the Master was on his way and Martha's joy was mingled with an undefined fear for him.

* * *

Wearily, Lazarus watched the donkey cart bump over the rutted ground back to the main track. It was packed with large earthenware jars of olive oil, freshly decanted from the presses that stood in a row behind him. A trail of straw, used to pack the jars, fell lightly to the ground as the cart passed from view. His attention turned back to the workers as they removed the pulp for further pressing in woven baskets. This produced a lower grade oil, used mainly for lamps, and would be sent to market or for storage along with the better-quality oil. Olives sat in baskets and piles all around them, ripening a little more in the hot sun.

A little later, Lazarus stood up to wipe the sweat from his brow and saw Simon, his friend and fellow elder, walking briskly towards him.

"You look awful, my friend," said Simon as he got closer. He was neatly dressed in fresh clothes and seemed impervious to the dust and heat. "I have good news," he said, enthusiastically, taking the water skin that was offered. "Our Lord and Master will be here soon."

Lazarus' face lit up. "When?" he asked.

"Tonight, according to Susanna. Miriam is with Martha, so she knows too, but I understand we are to keep this quiet, for he has travelled alone." Simon couldn't help glancing over to the workers nearby, but they gave no sign of having heard.

"I'd really given up," admitted Lazarus. "I thought he wasn't coming this time either."

"Well, all I know is the crowds have been looking out for him in the temple all week, so better late than never," said Simon cheerfully.

Lazarus doubted that Yeshua was ever late, but he said nothing.

"If you're free, please come to supper," added Simon. "I'm sure the Master won't object to seeing you, and you've got to eat sometime. Only do us a favour; bathe first."

Lazarus went to check the progress of the olive presses closer to home, grinning at Simon's remark. Did he really smell that bad? He had slept out in the fields last night, they had worked so late. When he arrived everything was going well. The olives from the upper slopes were already beginning to ripen, taking on a reddish tint, so he scooped some up to take home. Tonight, he promised himself, he would sleep in a proper bed. For him and his workers, sleeping in shelters in the olive groves was a reality at harvest time, not just part of the fun of the festival celebration which Tabitha enjoyed so much.

Opening the gate, he was pleased to see Martha and Mary sitting with Miriam and Susanna, deep in conversation as they pitted olives. Martha had looked so tired when she'd brought him dinner the night before, but now she looked refreshed. Tabitha ran to greet him; she had laid out clean clothes and plenty of washing water.

That night he dined with the Master and Simon, returning home to his own bed. Miriam and Susanna were staying with them. The shelter on his roof was full of women, and they were having fun, judging by the giggling he heard when he came in.

So far that week, Lazarus hadn't had time to visit the temple, so he'd decided to accompany the Master into Jerusalem the next day. He still needed to pay his temple tax and make the required sacrifices and offerings. He would also be taking the first full jar of olive oil they had made, plus some fresh olives. These Martha had carefully set aside as gifts to God from the harvest. It seemed too good an opportunity to miss, but first, he had to call Martha down from the roof to make his request. He felt guilty, knowing that she would have to take the full burden of the work in the olive groves and at the presses. To make matters worse, Mary overheard their conversation, and insisted she should go too, with Miriam and Susanna. A cloud settled over the three of them.

The next morning Martha had gone early to the olive groves, so they didn't see her before they left. Tabitha waved them goodbye. Miriam's heart felt heavy as she followed Susanna, Mary, Lazarus and the Master, over the Mount of Olives, carefully avoiding the many camps set up on its slopes. The Master seemed relaxed, talking and joking with them as they walked. If he was anxious, he didn't show it.

* * *

The light was fading as Martha bent stiffly to decant the last of the oil from the press; it was a skill she had learnt as a child helping her father. With a second jug, she ran off a little more, but still the thick golden oil poured out. However, in the third jug, the golden liquid quickly turned to the murky water produced from the pulp, and this she let run out over the ground. Straightening up and rolling her aching shoulders, she called 'Goodnight' to the last of the workers as they left. She thought longingly of the Sabbath rest in four days' time, and the celebrations that would fill the streets to conclude the festival.

She heard the thud of someone's feet on the earth close by, and spun round in alarm. Her shoulders dropped as relief spread over her tired face, it was Lazarus, but joy of joys, he was closely followed by Yeshua. Tears pricked her eyes as she swallowed the lump in her throat, for in that moment, despite the thoughts of self-pity she had battled with during the day, she knew they hadn't forgotten her, out there in the dark.

Washed and clean, she sat with her friends up on the roof listening intently to the events of the day, while Tabitha slept across her lap. Lazarus and Yeshua lay to one side, still eating and talking together.

In low voices, the women told Martha of the crowded temple, and how many of the people marvelled at how well the Master explained the scriptures as he taught. Some thought he was a good man, but others that he was leading them astray. However, the people were afraid to speak openly, because their leaders were giving them no clear indication of what they should think. In the temple courts, the Master had explained he wasn't teaching his own ideas, but God's. He only wanted God to be glorified, not himself, and those who wanted to do the will of God would know that.

Then he had challenged them, accusing them of not keeping the law of Moses, because they wanted to kill him. At this, Martha put her hands over her ears, fear welling up from inside. They had all assured him no one was trying to kill him and had dismissed his outburst as madness, but Miriam was sure some of them were trying to cover up the truth.

"Heaven forbid they should break that commandment," Mary had said in disgust.

Again, the Master accused them of breaking the law of Moses, this time because they circumcised boys eight days after their birth, even if that day fell on a Sabbath. How was it different to his healing people on the Sabbath? Many had seen his point. Martha looked over at Yeshua, remembering the lame man he'd healed at the pool of Bethesda. That had been on a Sabbath. He smiled at her reassuringly.

Martha turned her attention back to what the others were saying. Apparently, some of the people from Jerusalem had recognised Yeshua, and Mary had overheard them talking about him. They were suggesting their leaders must have come to the conclusion he *was* the Messiah, otherwise wouldn't they have arrested him by then. It had amused Mary that some of them had said 'the Messiah would just appear, like magic', so it couldn't be him, because this rabbi had come from Galilee.

"The Master doesn't miss much," remarked Susanna, "because then he called out, 'Do you really know where I come from? Do you know the one who sent me?'" She went on to say how indignant some of the leaders had become, their fingers almost twitching in their desire to stop him. Why they hadn't she and Miriam couldn't say, but for them watching and listening, it had been a nerve-racking day.

In the end, Mary told Martha that many of the people were of the opinion that he was the Messiah, because no one else could have done more miracles and signs than he had. Satisfied, Martha sat back, leaning against the wall, and closed her eyes peacefully. No one had the heart to tell her that the temple police had appeared in the crowd later that day.

After a while, it was Miriam who touched her arm gently and asked, "Are you very tired?"

"Or still cross with me for leaving you to do all the work?" added Mary, whose conscience was still troubling her.

Opening her eyes and smiling blissfully, Martha said, "Yes, I'm tired, but not cross at all. On the contrary, I'm just so happy and content right now, because you're all here and safe, and I would like this feeling to go on forever."

Hearing this, Yeshua looked over and said, "I'll stay tonight, if I may? It's getting late, and I don't want to disturb Simon's household."

Lazarus looked pleased. Then he remembered some good news.

"I nearly forgot to say, I bumped into John, Philip and Nathanael in the treasury today. Salome and Zebedee were close by, but I didn't see them. John said Salome had wanted to call in, but she knew how busy this time of year is for us, so she sends her love and hopes we'll all join them for the camp celebration at the end of the week, if not before. They were all there, and having a great time by the sound of it," Lazarus looked at Yeshua searchingly, then asked what his plans were for the following day.

"The same," he replied.

Mary sat up eagerly, ready to follow him into Jerusalem again, but a glare from Lazarus made her slump back.

"Martha, you should go tomorrow," said Lazarus. "Mary and I can take care of things here, can't we?" Mary nodded resolutely, coming to terms with the justice her brother was imposing on her.

Intently, Miriam watched Martha. She knew this would be a struggle for her. The cords of tradition, and her past, tied Martha to her home and Bethany. It would take courage to cut them.

Looking up from her lap, where Tabitha was still sleeping, Martha saw her two friends nodding encouragingly.

"I'd like that," she said. "But what about Tabitha?"

"Just you," said Miriam firmly. Then she added, more softly, "It's a long day, and with the crowds we'll see little of the celebrations." Martha nodded. Tabitha would stay safely at home. She would make it up to her somehow.

Chapter Eight

Eyes Opened

It was a bright morning as Martha stretched and yawned, standing on the roof by the shelter. Susanna and Miriam were still asleep, but Tabitha and Mary were missing. Immediately, she saw Yeshua sitting cross-legged on the roof above, a cup and some bread before him. Softly, he wished her a good morning. He looked so at home that it caused her to glow with pleasure.

Mary and Lazarus had left early for the olive grove, so for the second day running, Tabitha was in charge of the household; she handed Martha a bag of food as she was leaving with the others.

"I'm so glad you decided to go with the Master," she said. "I'll look after everyone, don't worry. Ellie will be here shortly, so I'll have company and help." Martha kissed her forehead and took the bag gratefully. She felt excited, as though she was going on an adventure. How childish, she thought.

The autumn sunshine had added to the festive atmosphere in the

65

camps, which were just coming to life as they passed by. Looking down on the city, Martha saw it wore a green cloak, the result of the shelters or tabernacles that had sprung up in courtyards, on rooftops and even in some areas of the temple. She gazed in admiration at the sheer size and magnificence of the building, crowning the hill like a great white jewel. They should bring Tabitha into Jerusalem to enjoy the parades and festivities in the streets, and soon, not that Bethany didn't celebrate in style too.

Being early, there were few people to impede their progress across the temple courts. However, a crowd gathered quickly around the Master, so he sat down and began to teach them. Eager as Martha was to hear what he said, she hung back a little, unsure of herself. Standing beside Miriam and Susanna, she became aware that their gaze was more often on the crowd than the Master. When she asked about this, they told her they were looking for Yeshua's family and the disciples, but Martha knew that wasn't the whole truth. So she pressed Miriam, and learnt they were also keeping an eye out for certain Pharisees and elders who frequently questioned the Master. They were always trying to find a way to discredit what he said Susanna had added. Miriam didn't mention that they were also watching for the temple police; she didn't want to burden Martha.

The Master, having finished what he was saying to the early crowd, began to walk away, heading for the court of women in front of the temple sanctuary. They hurried after him, anxious not to lose him in the gathering heat and noise. In the court of women surrounded by people once again, he sat down and began to teach. Listening intently, Martha was surprised when a group of Pharisees and teachers pushed through to the front of the crowd. Between them they herded a dishevelled woman, obviously determined not to contaminate themselves by touching her. Hunched and trembling, the young woman was made to stand before everyone, her eyes filled with fear. Yeshua remained calmly seated on the ground.

"Teacher," the Pharisees said, addressing him respectfully. "This woman was caught in the act of adultery. The law of Moses says she must be stoned for her sin. What do you say?"

Immediately Martha was suspicious. Why hadn't they brought the man too? That was the law.

Oddly, the Master didn't respond, but bent forward, drawing in the dust that lay over the slab-stones. Was he stalling for time, Martha wondered? Her frustration grew; she couldn't see what he was writing and the Pharisees kept pestering him for an answer. The woman raised her shaking hands to her head, as though to ward off the first blows, but still the Master didn't answer. Miriam moaned under her breath. It was too awful to watch; weren't they all bound by the law?

Martha now began to recognise what was really going on. This wasn't about the law, Miriam was right, they were trying to manipulate the Master into saying something blasphemous in front of witnesses. The poor woman had been chosen because she would draw more sympathy from the crowd when the Master condemned her, which they hoped would make him unpopular, at the very least. If he suggested otherwise, it would be breaking the law, the evidence they needed to put a stop to his teaching. Martha clenched her fists in disgust at the deviousness of the Pharisees, but also she felt angry that the woman faced this terrible punishment alone.

"Answer us!" the teachers demanded. "What do you say her fate should be?"

Slowly, Yeshua stood up and looked into the face of the crowd, his power and authority unveiled as his gaze rolled over them. Martha breathed in, and immediately felt the weight of her own sin. Weeping, Miriam reached out to steady herself, one hand clutched to her breast. Susanna's head was bowed low as she hugged herself. The whole crowd was held by the conviction of its own sin as the Master spoke.

"All right, stone her," he said. The crowd reacted to this as though they'd been condemned themselves. "But," he continued in a voice like iron, "let those who have never sinned throw the first stones." With that, he sat down and continued to write in the dust with one finger.

The silence was so loud that no one dared move. Martha found herself begging for mercy, so profound was the effect of his words. She looked up when Susanna nudged her. The eyes of the woman's accusers looked furtively one to the other, then down at the Master and what he was writing. Suddenly Martha understood; by law there should be two witnesses to the adultery, and they alone must be the ones to cast the first stones. The woman's accusers weren't credible witnesses, and somehow Yeshua had known that. He had stopped their cruel game, once more pointing them back to the law they knew so well. He had rendered them powerless to throw the stones.

The three women stood in awe watching as the crowd, with bowed heads, turned their backs on the adulteress and walked away. Defeated, the Pharisees and teachers of the law left the court with a bitter taste in their mouths.

The woman stood like a statue, afraid to look up. The Rabbi stood up and came closer.

"Has no one condemned you?" he asked, quietly.

Her mouth dropped open as she saw the empty space where the crowd had stood.

"No one, Master," she whispered back, hardly able to speak and even less to believe she was still alive.

"Then neither do I." He paused; she breathed out. "Go, but sin no more." And that was all he said.

The woman fell to her knees before him, then, overcome with shock, she fell sideways and lay still. Concerned, Martha, Miriam and Susanna began to move towards them, but suddenly, like a startled fawn, the woman jumped up and hurried from the court.

Quickly, the three women followed Yeshua towards the treasury on the northern side of the women's court, where thirteen chests stood, each like a broad inverted trumpet. Nine were for the legally required money given by worshippers and four were for voluntary gifts.

Almost immediately, the Pharisees appeared among the people, as though they had been waiting for him to begin teaching again. He seemed ready and undaunted, his opening words taking Martha's breath away.

"I am the light of the world," he said, "and if you follow me, you will no longer stumble around in the darkness but have the light that leads to life."

The Pharisees pounced on this immediately, accusing him of making false claims about himself, but he was equally quick to point out that they were judging him by human standards. He wasn't there to judge anyone. Then he said that both he and his father were witnesses to the truth that he spoke. Martha watched their hackles rise.

"Who is your father?" one of them demanded.

"Where is he?" asked another, looking to his friends for approval.

Yeshua's answer was simple in its elegance. "Since you don't know who I am, you won't know who my father is."

It was a wise answer, Martha thought, for no one ever spoke God's true name, it was too holy to be uttered by men, and if he had said God was his father, he would have been claiming to be equal to God. Blasphemy that could not be tolerated by these wise men, she thought ironically.

On the way home, Martha's thoughts still dwelt on the woman caught in adultery. She was sure the woman would never be able to adequately thank God for the restoration of her life, no matter how many sacrifices she made in the temple. Neither would Martha forget the Master's power and authority, or his compassion and mercy, when faced with all their sin. He had freed the woman from certain death. Only God could do that, but apparently, so could he.

Miriam slipped her arm through Martha's as they walked together, sorry for what her friend had had to witness that day. She knew Martha's eyes had been opened and that now they carried the same burden for their Master.

Chapter Nine

Opposition

The following day it was Mary who went with their guests, while Martha stayed to help Tabitha. Together they set off with full baskets; Martha's heart was fresh with compassion for those in need. It was almost a relief to be home after her experiences the day before, but now her eyes were open, and she had seen the danger the Master was in.

Later, Ellie came to help Tabitha, while Martha joined Lazarus in the fields, taking the weekly wages for the workers. It was nearly dark when they returned home and found Mary, Miriam and Susanna waiting impatiently for them on the roof. Martha was told Yeshua had returned to Simon's for the night. To Martha, Miriam and Susanna seemed subdued and tired, but Mary could scarcely contain her excitement. She barely waited long enough for Lazarus and Martha to begin eating the food brought by Tabitha before she began.

The crowds were already out when they'd arrived that morning and almost straight away, the Master had shouted, "Are you thirsty? Then come to me and drink living water that will flow from the heart of those who believe in me!"

Straight away Mary had known she was thirsty to hear everything he had to say; it had filled her with excitement and pleasure to hear people hailing him as a prophet, and some saying he must be the Messiah, but almost immediately others had started arguing with them because the scripture said the Messiah would come from Bethlehem, and this man came from Galilee. Mary admitted that at that point she had doubted Yeshua, until Miriam had whispered to her that he had been born in Bethlehem, of the line of King David. Martha and Lazarus' eyes opened wide when they heard this, but in their hearts they were not surprised. If it hadn't been for a timely warning from Susanna, Mary said she would have shouted this important information out to the misinformed. Susanna had learnt a long time ago that it didn't pay for women to get involved in public arguments with men, especially not over the scriptures. Silently, Martha thanked God for Susanna.

Miriam had watched the temple police with growing concern the previous day but they hadn't taken action. That morning, her stomach had twisted with anxiety as they arrived in the temple courts and among the crowds she had seen them waiting. However as the morning wore on, to her relief and amazement they'd withdrawn, and what was more, as they'd passed by she'd overheard them talking about the Master, impressed by what he'd said.

"They'll get some flak for that," commented Lazarus, sitting back and wiping his mouth, his hunger satiated for the moment.

Mary began to describe how some of the Jewish leaders had drawn the Master into a discussion, but had become puzzled when he'd said he was going away and where he was going they couldn't follow, and because they couldn't follow him, they would die in their sin. Mary laughed at the look on Martha's face, admitting it did sound complicated but explaining it all depended on your viewpoint. The leaders had probably seen the Master as the sinner, and therefore his fate would be hell. They of course assumed they were destined for heaven, so they wouldn't be able to follow him. At one point, they'd even suggested he might be planning suicide, not unheard of among some of the zealous religious factions.

Yeshua had tried again to get the point across to them, this time explaining he was from heaven and they were from the earth, and unless they believed in him, they would die sinners. Mary thought that was plain enough. Martha understood, but what really concerned her was what he'd meant when he'd said 'he was going away' as though it would happen soon. Mary admitted she didn't know, and she didn't like the implications either. Yeshua's blunt and clear reply had made the leaders more agitated, drawing the crowd with them, and demanding he told them who he was. In his reply he'd said he was who he'd always claimed to be, but Mary grinned as she repeated what came next, that there was a lot he could say about them but he wasn't going to, because he only said what he was told to say, by him who sent him. Lazarus and Martha now understood the joke.

True disciples, he'd said, would obey his teaching and know the truth, which would set them free. Miriam had noticed the effect this had had on some of the listeners, but it had also started yet another heated discussion among the leaders, and the more opinionated in the crowd. They'd insisted they weren't slaves that needed setting free, least of all from Rome. Lazarus had smiled at that. How quickly they'd forgotten their own history of slavery in Egypt. Tired, Martha struggled to understand what he'd meant, until Miriam explained that obedience to his truth, what he had taught them, would set them free from their sin. The truth of that hit home to Martha as she thought of the constant, endless, daily sacrifices that were made for people's sin in the temple. They were certainly slaves to that; and she thought of the woman who'd been caught in adultery, whom he'd forgiven and set free.

Tabitha sat up, paying closer attention to what was being said as Mary went on to tell them what Yeshua had said about slaves. "Slaves," he said, "would never be part of the family, not like a son, but if the son set the slave free, then the slave would be truly free and belong." She understood Yeshua was the son who set the slaves free from sin but it was even more poignant than that, reminding her of her adoption and how she was now a daughter in the family, with rights, when she could so easily have been a slave.

On the roof in the flickering lamplight, Tabitha often looked back on that moment as the one at which her heart finally understood who he was and just what he was capable of, and it changed her young life forever.

The arguments had continued in the temple courts that day, the teachers in the crowd saying that Abraham was their father and family lineage, but Yeshua had immediately contested that, arguing that the sons of Abraham wouldn't want to kill him. Susanna laughed wearily; the arguments were going round in circles, it seemed. Mary nodded in understanding but ploughed on, determined her brother and sister should hear it all. So, then they'd said their true father was God, but Yeshua had contested that too, much to their surprise, confessed Mary. He argued that he had come from the father and so surely they should love him too.

Miriam felt uncomfortable as she remembered the anger and frustration that was beginning to mount in the crowd. The Master had still held the upper hand at that point, but then he'd said they couldn't understand him because they were the children of the devil. At that the crowd had resorted to insults, calling him a Samaritan devil, but as Mary said cheerfully in his defence, "The devil is the father of lies."

Suddenly, a vice tightened around Martha's heart; Yeshua had gone to Simon's, hadn't he? She began to suspect that something had happened to him and the others were keeping it from her. Mary was telling them how God wanted to glorify Yeshua, and that God would be his judge and no one else. Understandably, his adversaries in the crowd had gone wild at that, shouting out that he was possessed.

When he'd repeated that anyone who obeyed his teaching would never die, the crowd had only become more incensed. They began shouting out, 'Who do you think you are? Are you greater than Abraham or the prophets?' They'd said they knew God, but again he'd called them liars. Then even more incredibly, he had added that Abraham had looked forward to his coming and had rejoiced about it.

"Can you imagine that?" asked Mary, her mouth wide open with astonishment for the second time that day.

The enraged crowd had laughed and jeered at him, saying he wasn't old enough to have met Abraham. Some had begun to reach for stones left by a mason who had been working on the temple. The Master's last words to them were, 'The truth is, I existed before Abraham was born!' Ignited, the crowd had exploded. They had gone berserk, surging towards him, so that anyone in the way would have been trampled. It had been hard to withstand such force. Miriam and Susanna had protected Mary, holding her up in the crush. In seconds the crowd had armed themselves with lumps of stone, while others had run to find more. Martha turned white as she listened, clutching Tabitha to her, her wild eyes searching Miriam's face. Oh no, they'd stoned him! Her earlier fears were true.

Miriam's soothing voice broke through her thoughts.

"It's all right Martha. He wasn't hurt, he's safe. In the seconds it took them to pick up the stones, he'd snatched his opportunity. He just melted into the crowd."

"Believers with their wits about them must have helped to cover his tracks," suggested Mary.

"God knows how he managed it. But he wasn't harmed. And I, we," said, Susanna, looking to Miriam, "Never want to witness anything like that again. I don't think I could take it."

"Some pursued him, shoving their way through the crowd, but we know they didn't find him, because we caught up with him, unharmed, on the outskirts of Bethany," finished Mary triumphantly.

Martha gave a great sigh of relief, and in the same instant realised how true Mary's words about the devil had been. However, Yeshua wouldn't be able to set foot in Jerusalem again.

There was a long silence, until Lazarus cheerfully reminded them that after the street celebrations in Jerusalem, the next day, they were all invited to the disciples' camp. Tabitha leapt up, shouting for joy.

Chapter Ten

An Invitation

Late autumn

The sloping dirt streets of Bethany were busy; it was Thursday, market day. During the morning an animated, colourful crowd had gathered near the centre of the town, where the main road widened. The rain clouds had moved off, and for the moment the streets were dry. From the marketplace, over the flat roofs of the clay-clad houses nestling in rows, you could see across the valley, which was speckled with groves of grey-green olive trees that stretched as far as the eye could see. The olive harvest was over, so, with more time to herself, Martha had been out visiting a sick friend in the lower section of the town, taking food and medicine. Wisps of umber hair escaped from under the long shawl that hung loosely about her head. She strode purposefully up the hill, intending to pick up vegetables and a few extra herbs at the market, before hurrying home to prepare the midday meal. She was surprised to find a large crowd gathered round the handful of trader's stalls. A lively conversation was going on, and there was something familiar about the Galilean accents she was hearing in amongst the more vocal and opinionated residents of Bethany. Her heart quickened; she hovered on the edge of the crowd, straining to see over the tops of heads. Could it be the Master? Surely not. There had been no news of him.

For a moment, the sun burst from behind a cloud, illuminating the earthy colours of their clothing and adding emphasis to every arm wave and movement. The source of the discussion came from one small group, partially hidden from Martha by an empty stall. Its heavy cloth flapped now and again in the warm ascending air from the valley below.

"Boo!" whispered a sudden soft voice in her ear. Martha jumped, frowning with disapproval as she realised it was Mary.

"Have you been here long? Have you heard what they are talking about?" asked Mary eagerly. "It's a passage from Isaiah, but the locals are missing the point and don't seem to understand."

Martha raised an eyebrow and gave her one of her wry sideways smiles. Sometimes Mary's grasp of scripture was remarkable.

"I've only just arrived," said Martha.

"The Rabbi Yeshua is sitting on the upturned crate," Mary informed her, in an excited whisper. "He's been talking for ages, that's why the crowd's gathered." When she saw Martha's empty basket, she added, "I don't think you'll be able to buy anything today, the stallholders packed up early." Martha grimaced. "I'm going back to listen, are you coming?" Before Martha had had a chance to reply, Mary was gone, pushing her way back into the crowd.

Martha hung back, craning her neck, hoping to spot Miriam or Salome, and feeling a little peeved that she hadn't known the Master was in the area. Instead, she saw Rachel her neighbour, Rebecca her cousin and a few other women friends, who were beckoning for her to join them. Martha was welcomed warmly, and rewarded with a better view of the crowd. She could see Mary with her two best friends, Ellie and Anna, Simon's daughter.

"Is it true that the Rabbi Yeshua is from Nazareth in Galilee, and the son of a carpenter?" asked Ellie, in a whisper. Both Mary and Anna nodded vigorously.

Quickly Mary added, "But he was born in Bethlehem." Ellie opened her mouth to ask another question, but the other two were so obviously absorbed in what the Rabbi was saying that she decided to wait.

Frustrated, Martha tried to listen, but without leaving her friends she simply couldn't hear. Also, she began to fret as Lazarus was due home soon for his midday meal, and Tabitha would be wondering where she was. In the crowd Mary and her friends had crept further forward, making it even more difficult for Martha to tell her she was leaving. She felt exasperated.

"What's wrong, Martha, dear?" asked Rachel, seeing her tense shoulders and the crease in her forehead.

"Lazarus will be back soon, and Tabitha's been alone all morning," said Martha with a sigh, torn between duty and her own desire to stay. Rachel understood, nodding sympathetically.

"Look, why don't you go on home? I'll keep an eye on Mary. My Joseph isn't back until later so I'm in no hurry, and I'd quite like to hear a bit of what the Rabbi is saying for myself."

Martha left, glancing back in the hope of spotting Miriam; she would know why the Master was in Bethany.

Lifting the latch of the gate, she entered the shady courtyard of her home. She leant back on the rough, weather-stained wood, breathing the familiar scent of the ancient olive tree that grew gnarled and twisted into the high surrounding wall. She relaxed; this was where she belonged, this was her world. A crashing noise came from the open kitchen door, making her frown. What was Tabitha doing now?

Tabitha's head appeared round the door, her wide-set eyes looking innocent. "It's all right Martha, no harm done!" she called, wiping her hands on her tunic. "How was Ellie's mama this morning?" she asked as Martha joined her in the kitchen, but before she could answer, Tabitha quickly added, "Oh, and Josh called in, asking if you or Lazarus could go up and take a look at one of the ewes. It's still limping."

"Is Lazarus back yet?" asked Martha, looking for his cloak on the peg by the door.

"Not yet," replied Tabitha from the storage room as she gathered things together for the midday meal. "Have you seen Mary on your travels?"

"Yes. She's at the marketplace, with half of Bethany. The Master is here." Martha's voice sounded bright, and Tabitha looked up expectantly.

"Is he coming to stay?" she asked. "And are we going to join everyone?"

"I don't know," said Martha, testily.

Tabitha could see something had unsettled Martha, so she busied herself with the preparations for the midday meal. Martha squeezed her shoulders gratefully.

It didn't take them long to realise that the other two weren't coming home. Martha was put out, wishing now she had stayed to listen. She and Tabitha ate together in silence. Martha soon realised it would do no good to mope around feeling sorry for herself, so by the time they'd finished, she had a plan. Hurriedly she set Tabitha to chopping more vegetables to add to the big pot of lentil stew that already sat over the kitchen fire. Next, she took charcoal and began the process of warming the clay oven. Tabitha filled a bag with bread, olives and dates, ready to take to their friends and a large water skin. Finally, together, they mixed and kneaded a large new batch of dough, which they left to prove beside the oven. Martha glanced round the kitchen to check all was in order before they hurried back to the marketplace, hoping to find everyone was still there.

They arrived out of breath. The crowd in the marketplace had grown. Immediately, Martha spotted Lazarus seated among the familiar faces of the Rabbi's followers. Mary and Anna sat close by, still listening intently, but sadly Martha noticed that Ellie had gone. She understood the burden the young woman bore having such a sick mother. Her face lit up when she spied Salome and Mary Alphaeus, but as yet, there was no sign of Miriam or Susanna.

Reluctant to approach her brother amongst the men, and unable to reach Salome, Martha waited. Tabitha, however, quickly found a way through to Lazarus, who waved when he saw her approaching. He'd been looking out for them for some time. Getting up from the floor, he dusted himself off, but was a little too close to Peter, Philip and James, who leaned theatrically out of his way. Martha felt proud, watching the good-humoured rapport Lazarus had with the Rabbi's disciples. He came over to greet her, Tabitha holding his hand.

"Oh, Martha that was thoughtful." He took the big bag of food and the heavy water skin she offered. "I'm sorry you've been waiting at home for us and have missed all of this." He gestured around. "How could we not stay and listen to what the Rabbi has to say? His teaching is so fresh, so alive," he said, wanting her to understand. "Come and sit with us." He began to tug her gently towards the others. He felt her resist, and realised how uncomfortable he was making her feel by drawing attention from the onlookers.

"Have they had anything to eat since they arrived?" asked Martha.

Lazarus shrugged. "Probably not."

"Then go and give them the food we've brought," urged Martha. "Although it won't be nearly enough."

Lazarus peeked into the bag. "I think there's enough in here to feed twice as many," he commented, before he made his way back through the largely seated crowd. To his surprise Martha came after him.

"Do you know their plans?" she asked, in a hushed voice. Lazarus shook his head. "Perhaps they would like to eat with us this evening, and stay over?" she added, trying not to sound too hopeful.

Lazarus looked pleased. "I'll see what the Master says."

"I'll help," said Mary, eagerly, as she joined them. "I could go on listening to him forever. What he's saying is amazing and you kind of know it's the truth, as well." Lazarus nodded in agreement as he backed away to return to his friends, followed by Tabitha, who carried the food bag so he could manage the water skin.

Martha watched her brother speak to Yeshua, who looked towards her, waving his hands in thanks. Out of habit and respect, she looked down, but when she glanced up he was still smiling at her gratefully. For a moment she forgot her embarrassment, standing amongst the seated crowd around her.

Mary was bursting to tell Martha about Yaqim, the child Martha had tried so hard to cure. She spoke in a low voice.

"I wish you'd stayed this morning. Yaqim was here, sitting before the Master trying to stifle that cough of his. In the end, the Master called him out and placed his hand on the child's chest and said some words. At that, Yaqim seemed to burst into life, running around excitedly telling everyone he was cured. He got very out of breath, but he didn't cough once, and his pale cheeks were glowing. He dashed back to thank the Master, shaking his hand vigorously, before racing off to tell his mother. It was so funny and quite extraordinary all at the same time." Mary spoke with joy in her voice, but she saw the tears of regret in Martha's eyes. "I'm truly sorry you missed it. I should have come home and persuaded you to come back." Mary felt guilty.

Hearing the wonderful news about Yaqim, and feeling part of what was going on once more, Martha tried to smile forgivingly at her sister.

Soon Lazarus returned to her side, bringing Salome and Mary Alphaeus with him. It had all been settled. The Master had gratefully accepted her invitation for dinner, and they would all be staying the night. Salome and Mary Alphaeus were very pleased to see Martha again, having looked for her in the crowd constantly that morning. At one point, Salome had even suggested to the Master that she should go and find Martha, but he had told her to sit still and wait. Salome then went on to tell her that Miriam had been delayed trying to find a donkey for hire, as Yeshua's mother was travelling with them. Susanna had gone ahead with Joanna, to arrange lodgings.

"We aren't going into Jerusalem," she reassured Martha. "Not after the last visit. But this is too close for comfort, if you ask me," she added, her face wrinkled with concern.

Martha and Tabitha stayed as long as they could knowing they now had guests to prepare for, but they were accompanied home by Salome, Mary Alphaeus and Rachel, for she too had meals to prepare for her own household. Mary had begged for five more minutes, which Martha had reluctantly agreed to. How she was going to be ready for all those guests in the few short hours before sunset, Martha couldn't imagine. Her steps quickened as her mind began to race with all the preparations that were needed. The others followed, out of breath.

Straight away, Tabitha and Mary Alphaeus were sent to prepare the upper rooms. Not long after, Tabitha came running down the outer stairs to take a pile of blankets from Rachel. On her way back, she called into the kitchen to get Mary Alphaeus something to eat and drink. Martha and Salome were both working hard, Martha expanding her stew and carrying piles of crockery and utensils into the main room, while Salome had set about shaping the dough that had been made earlier.

Tabitha popped back to get oil to fill the lamps and noticed Salome's flour-smeared face. She took a cloth and wiped the wrinkled shiny face before kissing it. Salome kept working, but Tabitha left a drink and some food beside her. Salome watched her go lovingly.

Martha checked the taste of the stew, adding a handful of dried dates, just to sweeten it a little and add the finishing touch. She was a good cook and housekeeper; she and her brother made a good partnership. She doubted she would have experienced the same freedoms if she had been married. The three siblings all benefited from the arrangement, especially the carefree and unconventional Mary. Despite Elias and Lazarus's best attempts to find her a husband, Mary had also managed to remain single.

The pot was bubbling gently, so Martha felt free to go and see how Tabitha and Mary Alphaeus were getting along. Martha sighed to herself as she huffed up the stairs; Mary hadn't come back as she'd promised. Didn't she realise how much her help was needed? Her brow furrowed with annoyance. Her sister could be very unreliable at times.

Tabitha was a fast worker, and with Mary Alphaeus' help they had already prepared Lazarus' room for the Master and swept the main upper room. Martha arrived just in time to help drag the thick woven rugs off the pile and spread them out on the floor. Woollen blankets topped these off, making the space look welcoming. Rising heat from the fire in the main room below would provide some extra warmth. They were all out of breath by the time the task was complete. Another job had been ticked off Martha's list.

"The stew!" she cried, running down to the veranda and into the kitchen. With relief, Martha found Salome stirring it. She smiled reassuringly at Martha.

"Everything's under control in here. The first batch of bread will be out of the oven soon. Leave it to me."

While Tabitha helped Mary Alphaeus prepare the smaller ground floor room for the women's use, Martha began to prepare the main living room for dining. Martha's anxiety grew, and with it her annoyance with Mary. Where was she? She should have been back by now. Surely Lazarus would have realised and sent her home. Besides, and not for the first time, Mary had broken her word, and that hurt.

Busy Tabitha was leading Mary Alphaeus up the ladder into the loft above the storage room. It was her own space, in the corner of the house, and she loved it. Compared to her stepbrothers and sisters she felt very fortunate. Still, Tabitha was wasting time, and this irritated Martha, who then felt guilty because the two of them had worked so hard. When Martha returned to the kitchen, she found Salome, red in the face, but with an ever-filling basket of warm flatbread. This would be torn up and used to eat the stew, instead of cutlery.

Martha returned to the main room with yet another pile of things to go on the tables, and started arranging them. At that moment Tabitha appeared.

"Shall I fill the jugs now?" she asked.

"Yes please. But use the large ones."

Tabitha pouted crossly. "I don't need to be told that!" she said.

"I'm sorry. What would I do without you," said Martha, smiling apologetically.

"I'm not going to reply to that," said Tabitha, disappearing back into the store, followed by Martha. In this room Martha kept her precious fig and date cakes, always a treat for visitors and a favourite of Lazarus, who had a sweet tooth. Clay and stone jars of every size and description, sacks, baskets and skins filled the room, all standing in well-ordered arrangements, or along sturdy shelves set into the thick stone wall. The large stone jars kept for ceremonial washing stood together and all the utensils used for food preparation were laid out neatly on a table. The house was one of the larger and better-built properties in Bethany.

Martha selected a pile of things and carried them into the main room, while Tabitha began to fill the large earthenware jugs with wine. There would be beer too. The list in Martha's head seemed endless, and they were running out of time. She stood in the middle of the room, unable to think straight. Now, what had she come in for? Why hadn't Mary come? How could she behave so thoughtlessly? Martha felt like crying.

Just then Mary Alphaeus came in, carrying a large basket of logs and kindling.

"Tabitha said you would want a fire starting in here?"

"Oh, yes please, dear Mary Alphaeus," said Martha, with such feeling and appreciation that Mary blushed.

Martha went to fetch towels for their guests. Perhaps, she should send Tabitha to fetch Mary, but that would just waste more time. Her jaw clenched tight.

Salome had found the bowls and jugs for washing and took the towels from the distracted Martha, arranging them as best she could to accommodate so many guests. She sent Martha to check on the last batch of bread. To Martha's relief they were done, so she left them to cool a little, admiring the huge pile Salome had manufactured in such a short time.

Martha shook herself and bustled into the main room where the fire had begun to glow cheerfully. It took her a while to arrange everything for the comfort of her guests and to her satisfaction.

She was just about to ask Tabitha to light the oil lamps in the yard when Mary arrived, out of breath and dishevelled, to announce that the party was on its way. Martha glared at her sister tight lipped, her anger at boiling point, but the rattle of the gate outside cut her short.

Chapter Eleven

Dinner

Red and gold spread across the fading blue horizon as Lazarus led the Rabbi and his followers into the darkening courtyard. Tabitha was stretching up to hang the last lamp back on its hook and greeted them from the welcoming yellow light that spread over the veranda steps.

The clean-shaven James came over to Tabitha, who lingered by the donkey, scratching his nose. James' youthful looks and shy manner had earned him the nickname 'Young James'. He always had time for her, although she wondered how he coped being the youngest, and having his mother, Mary Alphaeus, older brother Thaddaeus and Cousin Matthew all travelling with them.

"I guess you've had a busy afternoon," he said. She nodded vigorously. "What delights has Martha got for us tonight? It smells wonderful."

"You'll have to wait and see, but it won't be long," she assured him. At that moment, James' stomach gurgled loudly, making Tabitha giggle.

Martha appeared at the top of the steps in her shawl. She took a deep breath and went to greet her guests. Only those who knew her well would have noticed the swift rise and fall of her chest.

Mary came to join Tabitha, her face washed and her luxuriant hair combed neatly, but her tunic was still dusty from the marketplace and her run home. She plucked a wisp of hay from Tabitha's curls.

"I'm sorry about this afternoon. I just couldn't drag myself away," she whispered.

"We managed," said Tabitha.

"I broke my promise to Martha and let her down, again."

Tabitha didn't know what to say, but suddenly inspiration came. "It's a good job she loves you so much, then," she said. Mary smiled sheepishly.

The Rabbi came forward and took Martha's rough hands in his. She felt the long, strong fingers curl round hers as he held her gaze. He nodded, one side of his mouth curled up. Standing beside Martha, Tabitha curtsied, which made Mary giggle, but Yeshua courteously bowed back. Then he turned to Mary. With a wry smile he said, "You made it home before us then?"

"Only just," said Martha, sighing and shaking her head, feeling the anger rise once more.

"She's certainly fast," said Yeshua, raising an eyebrow as he looked at Mary, who hung her head, concealing a smile. "Dear friends, we are once more guests in your house, and I am very glad of it." His voice was mellow and peaceful as he looked from Mary to Martha and then Lazarus.

Martha led the way to a bench, in front of which was a row of foot bowls. Lazarus took the seat beside the Master, as she and Tabitha knelt down.

"I am honoured to serve you and have you as guests in our

house," she said quietly as she washed the dirt from his feet. When she'd finished, she stood back respectfully, almost tripping over Tabitha, who was shadowing her closely. She put an arm around Tabitha's shoulders.

Yeshua's eyes twinkled with mischief as he said to Tabitha, "Would you give Peter a hand to get his sandals off? He's so tall he has trouble reaching them."

Tabitha forgot her momentary shyness, pleased to be given a task by the Master. Approaching Peter boldly, she ushered the big man to a seat and knelt to undo his sandals.

"So is Peter your nickname?" she asked, as she began to wash off the mud.

"Yes," nodded Peter. "I'm Simon, son of Jonah, but not long after I met the Master he called me Peter, a lump of rock, and the name stuck. Although my brother Andrew would have you believe it has more to do with my brain." He grinned at her. "Miriam picked up her name in much the same way, becoming Miriam Magdalene."

Tabitha nodded enthusiastically. The Master had once told Miriam that she was a tower of strength and had sight, like looking over the sea of Galilee from the fish watchtower near her home in Magdala. Miriam had made a joke about it, but Tabitha had liked the idea, hoping that one day she might be given a nickname by the Rabbi, and see lake Tiberius.

"You could be there a while," commented John, sliding in beside Peter.

"Are you making a comment about the size of my feet?" asked Peter, one eyebrow raised.

"I don't need to," was John's quick reply. "Your feet speak for themselves."

"They certainly do. Peter is always putting his foot in it!" exclaimed his brother, Andrew, from the other end of the bench.

"Thanks, Andrew," said Peter, chucking a towel at him and

grinning. "You can always rely on family to tell you the truth."

"It's a pleasure, big brother," replied Andrew, catching the towel.

Tabitha looked from face to face as she washed their feet. She liked being with these people, especially the Rabbi Yeshua; he had a way of putting people at ease. Martha was amazed at how well he remembered people's names, accepting and valuing everyone from the strangers he met on the road to the most obstinate and outspoken villagers in Bethany. She had watched him deal with a few of them that morning.

Lazarus showed their guests into the main living room and Mary served wine and beer, while Martha moved among her guests, speaking to each encouragingly. Watching, Tabitha admired this, knowing how tired Martha was. She also knew she was still cross with Mary.

While Tabitha was putting the foot bowls away on the veranda, she heard the gate open. In the lamplight she saw the tall, slender silhouette of Miriam leading a donkey and rider into the courtyard.

"Miriam is here!" she shouted, running to greet her. Martha came out, wiping her hands on her tucked-up tunic, a look of relief on her face. Close on her heels came Salome and Mary Alphaeus, who helped the slight woman down from the donkey.

"Martha, let me introduce you to Mary Joseph, the Rabbi Yeshua's mother," said Miriam, softly. "I'm sorry we're so late. I hope you've kept us something to eat."

Martha bowed her head respectfully, as she said, "Mary Joseph, you are most welcome. It is an honour to meet you and have you stay with us." Then, turning to Miriam, she said, "We were just about to eat, you timed it perfectly."

"You've made an impression there," said Salome, winking at Mary Joseph. Then to Miriam she said, looking at the donkey, "Wherever did you find this poor undernourished specimen? Tabitha, come and take care of the poor beast, please."

Although small in stature, and leaning on Miriam's arm after the long ride, Mary Joseph spoke with the confidence of age and the grace of experience. Her sad, brown eyes searched Martha's face, and then a smile broke out, which Martha would never forget. It lit up the night and filled her with hope. "My son and his friends have all spoken well of you and your family," she said. Tabitha reappeared. "And especially young Tabitha here." Tabitha beamed with pleasure. "May God bless your family for all you do for the poor of this town, and for the kindness you show us."

Martha was touched by Mary Joseph's words as she led the way into the warmth of the kitchen, grateful that Salome and Tabitha had gone ahead to attend to the food. The house was filled with noise and bustle as they entered.

Mary hurried into the kitchen, and stopped in surprise at the sight of Mary Joseph sitting comfortably on the rug between Miriam and Mary Alphaeus. Mary Joseph returned her gaze steadily.

"Hello Mary," she said. Mary's mouth dropped open a little.

"Mary, daughter of Reubel, meet Mary Joseph, mother of our Master, Yeshua," said Miriam.

"This is going to get confusing," Salome was heard to say loudly in the background. Mary Alphaeus giggled as she took the jugs Mary was carrying and refilled them for her.

Philip's tall frame then filled the doorway. "Ah, there you are Martha. Lazarus was asking if he should say grace?" He stopped short, seeing Miriam and Mary Joseph among the women. "Oh, you're here at last," he exclaimed.

"Tell my son I'm being well looked after," said Mary Joseph, waving a goblet of wine and munching one of Martha's date cakes.

"I can see that," replied Philip. "In Martha's kitchen, I'd expect no less."

"You can tell Lazarus we're ready," laughed Martha, pleased with the compliment, as she absentmindedly checked the seasoning in the stew, yet again; she hoped there would be enough. Her guests had keen appetites.

Satisfied with the taste, she went to the door of the main room, and peered in. Men of every shape and size filled the space, some still standing, others already seated on the rugs around the low tables, and everyone was talking at once. Martha noticed with some annoyance that Mary was standing chatting to Judas, the jug held idly in her hand, her cheeks glowing with warmth and excitement. Martha tried to attract her attention, but Mary was too caught up in the conversation to notice. Automatically, Martha looked for her brother, but he was deep in conversation with Yeshua. Martha frowned and looked back at her sister, and this time Judas noticed, and sent Mary over.

Together, the sisters carried the heavy pot into the room, and placed it before Lazarus and the Master. Mary knew from Martha's restrained tone that she was still unhappy with her behaviour that afternoon.

The grace said, Martha began to ladle out the stew as quickly as she could, while the other women helped to serve. Bowls and plates were refilled, more bread produced, and the guests' beer and wine were topped up. Olives and a selection of dried fruit followed.

Her duty done in the main room, Martha turned her attention to her kitchen guests, leaving the men in Mary and Tabitha's care. The women were talking quietly, Mary Joseph at the centre. Martha felt as though she was in the presence of royalty. Mary Joseph had looked up as Martha entered, her eyes and smile animated in the candlelight. It was hard to tell her age, for in one moment she would look tired and careworn, and in the next, she seemed to be lit from within with passion and youth.

"You serve with your full heart, Martha," said Mary Joseph, beaming at her. Martha bowed her head, and if her cheeks hadn't already been glowing from exertion, they would have seen her blush. Martha was touched and longed to sink onto the mat and join her friends, but always there was something that called for her attention.

The remains of the stew were brought back to the kitchen and placed on the fire to reheat, while Martha added a little more stock. Salome produced a basket of warm bread that she had saved, and together the women ate. Martha called Tabitha and Mary to join them, but Mary's stay was brief, just long enough to comment on the fact that by some miracle, there was still stew left.

"It's just like the loaves and fishes that little boy gave to the Master," Mary Alphaeus recalled.

"But not quite on the same scale," said Salome.

"The Lord God provides what we need, and more besides," added Miriam.

Tabitha couldn't help thinking that it was Martha who had worked so hard to provide and prepare the food, with the help of others, of course. Surely she should get some of the credit. She frowned crossly.

"Tabitha, they weren't dismissing all you and Martha have done today," said Mary Joseph, seeing her face, and guessing her thoughts. "Martha's stew and Salome's bread reminded us of a great miracle we once witnessed. How God took a little boy's lunch, of fish and bread, all he had, and multiplied it over and over again, until thousands of hungry people were fed. And it was all done by the hand of his chosen one."

Tabitha had loved hearing this story from Salome, who had been there when it had happened. There had even been enough left for his disciples, she remembered.

Involuntarily, Tabitha's eyes glanced in the direction of the Master next door, and his mother gave the faintest of acknowledging smiles as she continued, "Today God provided through the skills and hard work of Martha and yourself."

"And those who helped us," said Tabitha, quietly. "I'm sorry. I understand now."

"Oh, bless you dear," said Salome. "God provides for us every day, but he does it through our skills, abilities and our work, or from the kindness of others, even miracles, like Simon being healed of leprosy. But however he does it, we always have what we need." She paused for thought, and then being Salome added, with a chuckle. "Mind you, he doesn't always give us what we want, especially if it isn't good for us." There had been plenty of events in her own life like that. "So you see Tabitha, God is always at the bottom of everything."

"Not quite how I'd have expressed it, Salome," spluttered Miriam, trying to suppress her laughter. "But the glory, honour and thanks go to God our father and maker."

"Amen," they chorused.

"There's something I've always wanted to ask," ventured Martha, still smiling at the joke. Her friends nodded encouragingly, so she said, "You must miss your homes and family, and yet you always seem so at ease travelling with the Master. How do you manage it?" Martha couldn't imagine leaving Bethany and their home, though sometimes she wondered what it would be like to cut the ties and walk into the unknown.

Miriam led the way. "You all know my story, how I built up my late husband's business by unscrupulous means. When the Master found me and released me from those terrible demons, what else could I do but follow the one who had freed me? He truly brought me out of darkness and into the light. I have very little family left in Magdala, and certainly none who care for me, so to sell all I had and follow the Rabbi was freedom and a new beginning. I couldn't stay where people were always suspicious, waiting for me to slip back into my old ways."

"A fresh start, amongst those who understood what had

happened to you," agreed Mary Alphaeus, with sympathy.

Salome spoke next after looking around at the faces of her friends, her lips pursed, her eyes filled with pain. "Without doubt, it was the hardest thing Zebedee and I ever faced. I'll never forget the day the boys announced they were leaving the family business to follow the Rabbi Yeshua. It was such a shock at the time, but looking back, I suppose we should have had some inkling of what was on their minds. We just thought he was a carpenter from Nazareth but chosen by God to be a prophet, like John the baptiser. It all happened so fast Zebedee didn't even get a chance to reason with them. Although that's probably just as well, my Zebedee's very persuasive when he's a mind to be. But God knew what he was doing, of that we are certain, because the next surprise was Peter and Andrew, Jonas' sons, dissolving their partnership with our boys. They too were off to follow the Rabbi. I thought the world had gone mad, and everyone had lost their reason. Peter has a wife and family to care for, and had a successful part in the business.

"Everything Zebedee and I had worked so hard to build up in order to provide for our families' future was about to trickle through our fingers like sea water." Salome looked down at her lap, sighing heavily at the memory, but when she lifted her face again, it was filled with a resolute smile. "But now I know differently. Talk about God providing! We were left with the biggest catch of fish on record, enough to feed all the families involved, and trade for a good while. Zebedee had no trouble hiring enough men to continue working the boats. It's funny, he's never sold the boats, just hires them out. His little wisp of hope that one day the boys will come home. And I wouldn't take that away from him, not yet." She paused for a moment, as though trying to remember.

"To begin with, it was easy to keep track of the boys. The Rabbi quickly built a reputation in and around Galilee, settling in Capernaum. But when he started to go further from home, we made a decision. By then, we'd witnessed enough to think that he could actually be the long-awaited saviour of our people. Except, he didn't always behave quite the way you might have expected." Salome glanced apologetically at Mary Joseph, who nodded, amusement tickling one corner of her mouth. She knew Salome's story well, for they were close relatives. "So we decided I would go along with them, to keep an eye on things, as it were, while Zebedee carried on running the business at home." Salome sighed. "It's been a truly amazing journey, and I wouldn't change a moment of it, but in answer to your question, Martha, yes, sometimes I really miss home, especially my cantankerous old goat of a husband and the simple predictable life I took for granted. The future changed for our family when the boys followed the Master."

"Life is never the same once my son steps into it," said Mary Joseph, shaking her head. Miriam and Mary Alphaeus nodded in agreement.

Mary reappeared to fill a jug with more beer, disturbing Martha, who rose stiffly to her feet and followed her, her irritation roused once more.

An air of contented ease filled the main room with the soft murmur of good-humoured conversation. Martha began to relax; all her efforts had been a success, only the clearing up left to do. She had fully intended to return to the kitchen and her female friends, but some internal force kept driving her on. She found herself collecting dishes from the table that surely Mary must have seen. Now exhaustion rolled in like a tide, but she couldn't stop. Automatically she continued to pick up empty bowls and cups, tidying the table as she went, smiling at her grateful guests. The tiredness threatened to engulf her. Where was Mary? Why wasn't she there to help? She of all people should understand how Martha was feeling, how far she had pushed herself on behalf of the others. Desperate, she scanned the room and saw Mary sitting at the Master's feet, like one of his disciples. Her beautiful face was upturned and animated by the words he spoke. Her anger blazed at the selfishness of her sister.

In one unforgettable moment, all her frustration, disappointment and jealousy erupted. Shaking with emotion, with bowls and cups piled up in her arms, Martha marched over to the Rabbi and stood towering over them all in her anger.

"Master, don't you care that my sister has left me to do everything?" she blurted out. "It isn't fair. She just sits here while I do all the work. Tell her to come and help me!" she pleaded, hot tears welling up in her eyes. Her feelings were gloriously on display. Already humiliation and regret were dousing the fires of her anger, but it would carry her a little further before it was quenched.

The Master sat up, looked up, and tilted his head to one side. He brushed back a greasy lock of hair as he spoke.

"Martha, Martha. My dear Martha, you are anxious and troubled about the details of many things; Mary has discovered and chosen the one thing that is really important. I won't take it away from her, would you?"

Martha stood there blinking back her tears, trying to understand what he had just said to her. Surely, he wasn't taking Mary's side, and endorsing her actions? Feeling let down and bewildered, embarrassment scalded her cheeks. Martha fled from the room, still clutching the pile of crockery, and stumbled around her guests, head down, vision blurred by tears and strands of wet hair stuck to her face.

In the silence that followed, a deeply concerned Lazarus looked from the Master's face to Mary. He could hear many in the room taking Martha's side. Hers was the cause of justice and tradition, but the Master had seemed to side with Mary, and that clearly puzzled some of the guests.

Martha hadn't heard the supportive comments as she fled to the refuge of the cool, narrow passage between the house and cistern.

Finally, she dropped her ridiculous burdens, which clattered into the stone basin. Her shoulders heaved with racking sobs as she leant over the dishes, her stomach in tight knots.

Tabitha had followed Martha but stood still at the door, her face twisted with concern, feeling Martha's humiliation as if it were her own. When Martha finally acknowledged her presence, it was with a tight smile. Tabitha saw the muscles in her jaw working for control as her eyes filled again.

"What happened?" asked Tabitha, gently, anguish shaking her voice.

Martha shook her head; she still couldn't speak. Her thoughts were jumbled, and her pulse was still racing. Tabitha waited, unsure.

Eventually, Martha splashed cold water over her face and wiped her eyes with her tunic, sniffing. "I've put my foot in it again," she said, her mouth screwed up. "I lost my temper with Mary and made a fool of myself in front of everyone."

"Oh, is that all? I thought something terrible had happened, like the wine running out," said Tabitha, risking all, not sure how Martha would react. Martha straightened up and turned towards her with a weak smile. Tabitha let out a deep sigh of relief.

"Oh, I don't mind making a fool of myself," said Martha, grimacing. "It's what the Master said, and how he said it, that upsets me. He understood. It was like he'd read my mind, knew my whole life story and knew me inside out. Now I've calmed down a bit, I understand what he meant. Mary wasn't choosing not to help, she was choosing to listen to him because what he is saying is the most important thing we'll ever hear. Mary understands that. It was me who was fussing over having the house ready, making bread and stew and then clearing up, as though that was really important. That's why I got more and more angry and frustrated with Mary for not being here to help." She swallowed hard. "I wanted to sit and listen to him too, but felt I wasn't allowed, it was my duty to serve our guests. I was jealous of Mary. And now I feel so ashamed."

"What the Rabbi has to say is very important, but I think bread and stew are quite important too, when you're hungry. I know all our guests would agree with me. Especially as you made them all feel so welcome. And if Mary had helped out this afternoon, you'd have had a chance to do some listening too, and you wouldn't have got so upset and tired."

"Oh, Tab, you're such a treasure, but the Master is right. I'm too concerned about what others might think of us, always trying to do the right thing, and fussing over unimportant details."

Mary appeared, hovering, uncertain, biting her bottom lip. She had been standing just out of view for some time.

"Oh Martha, I'm so, so sorry. Please forgive me," she begged, breaking down. Martha's brow furrowed, she was still cross with Mary for being right, and for breaking her word to come and help. She stared down at the dirty crockery, still unable to look Mary in the face. It wasn't until Mary reached out to her with a trembling hand that Martha was finally able to turn her head and give Mary a reluctant one-sided smile. Mary rushed to throw her arms around her older sister, who then wriggled her arms free and put them around Mary. They both drew Tabitha into the hug and the three of them stood locked together until the tears and apologies had finally subsided.

Eventually Martha roused them, her thoughts turning to her guests once more as they returned to the kitchen. Martha called the women to join them, but despite her brave words she followed Mary sheepishly into the crowded room. With Tabitha draped wearily across her lap, she sat as inconspicuously as she could next to her sister. Finally she was sitting at the Master's feet, where she had longed to be the whole day. The Master had watched her return to the room, and had smiled softly to himself.

Chapter Twelve

Life Goes On

Martha closed the gate quietly after the bustle of the morning's farewells; the courtyard was cool and so very, very still after the business of having so many guests. She knew she would miss them, but not just yet. Lazarus had accompanied their friends on the road, passing north of the city. He was intending to call in on Elias on his way home. Mary and Tabitha had gone with them, but only as far as the village well, reluctant to say goodbye until the last possible moment.

The events of the previous evening were still sharp in Martha's mind, but she was at peace despite everything that had happened. Martha felt good inside, like dusty-grey olive leaves washed clean after the spring rain. Although there was plenty to do, she felt in no hurry to begin; possibly for the first time in her life she made that decision free of concern about what others might think of her. She was free to decide what she would do next.

So, Martha dragged a bench into the winter sunshine and sat down. She had barely composed herself before a dull thudding bludgeoned its way through the quiet. With a wry smile on her lips, she sighed, looked up to heaven and went to see who was at the gate.

Outside, in the bright dust of the street, stood the tall, thin Joshua, leaning on his walking staff like an old man. It was only then Martha remembered Tabitha's message about the lame sheep. Apologising, she left Josh with refreshments while she went to get the things she would need.

Their two shepherd boys were reliable enough, often popping home for supplies, or to let Lazarus know where they would be grazing the flock next. Once there had been no word from them for over a week. Worried for their safety, Lazarus had set off to find them, tracking them to an area east of the Jericho road, a long way from home. After hearing rumours that bandits were operating in the area, the young shepherds had tried to find a safe route back with the flock. Relieved to find the boys, Lazarus had forbidden them to go too far without leaving word.

Martha took extra food for Jacob, and her remedy bag, which contained everything she would need for the lame ewe. From Josh's description, she was fairly certain she knew what was causing the problem.

Quickly, they left the village, following one of the many tracks that crisscrossed the tops of the hills to the south-east of Jerusalem. Josh began to lead, choosing a route that climbed steadily towards the pass from where the main road dropped down towards the city.

Soon the hazy ribbon of the road was lost in the undulations of the land as they moved south. Eventually, when Martha felt she could go no further without rest, a deep shadow appeared cutting up through the slope before them. All around were rough limestone outcrops and dried tufts of grass, rustling in the chilly wind. The main autumn rains were late, and the ground was thirsty and parched. As they reached the edge of the shadow, they were able to peer down into the cool depths of a narrow, green valley with boulder-strewn sides.

A distant figure waved enthusiastically. Jacob had been looking out for them. A few curious animals raised their heads briefly, but soon returned to their grazing. It was a steep, tortuous climb down through the larger rocks, but Martha took it in her stride. She had grown up in these hills and was as sure-footed as the goats and sheep in the flock. At the bottom of the ravine, green, velvety grass grew beside the ribbon of a stream, as it flowed down stony steps, to the valley far below.

Pleased to see the boys had tethered the sheep ready, Martha wasted no time. She tucked her tunic into her waist band, and while Jacob held its head, she examined the hoof and leg. The smell told her all she needed to know. Josh passed her the sharp knife and expertly, she pared down the rotting hoof until it began to bleed. Josh had already spread some ointment on a small clean rag and had the boot ready to fasten over the hoof. Jacob offered the sheep a small piece of bread before releasing her. Unperturbed by the ordeal, the ewe came back, searching for more. The three of them laughed.

"Make sure you change the dressing tonight and then again in the morning. She should be fine by then," instructed Martha, munching on a piece of bread herself. The ewe nibbled at her clothing, but Martha waved her away. "Go and eat the good grass Josh and Jacob have found for you." The ewe stood for a moment, as though thinking, then turned a little awkwardly in her rag boot and trotted away to join the others.

"You've done well to find such good grass hidden away like this," said Martha, waving up at the steep slopes, her mouth full.

"It's only the second time we've been here since the autumn," explained Jacob. "Lazarus warned us not to let them eat too much in one go."

"We'll move on tomorrow so the grass can recover. Overgrazing, that's what he called it," Josh added. Jacob nodded in agreement, great locks of thick, black hair flopping over his eyes obscuring his handsome face, and shy gaze.

"Any other problems while I'm here?" asked Martha. The boys shook their heads.

"I'm sorry we had to drag you all the way out here," said Josh. "We tried paring the foot like we'd been taught, but this one had got very bad and we were worried about cutting too much off."

"You were right to get help. You saw how much I had to take off. It'll come with a bit more experience," Martha assured them.

"Did Lazarus tell you about that one over there?" asked Josh, pointing to a ewe grazing close by with her grown lamb and another from the previous year. "She had one side of her udder bigger than the other when she lambed in the spring."

"It was a good birth, she did it all the right way, just like Master Lazarus said," interrupted Jacob enthusiastically.

"Well, Jacob, he catches the ewe, massages her udder, and squeezed it like you showed him. Only it squirts out suddenly and sprays me from head to foot." The boys giggled. "Then he told me to bring the lamb over and put it on the teat. It suckled like mad, dribbling milk everywhere." The boys beamed with pleasure as they told their tale.

"My tunic didn't half pong by the end of the day, so Josh made me wash it in a stream, but it didn't make much difference," Jacob said, wrinkling his nose at the memory. Martha chuckled and looked approvingly at their smiling faces.

"What are your plans for tomorrow?" she asked, stretching out in the late morning sunshine as it finally found its way into the sheltered ravine.

Jacob looked at Josh, deferring to him as usual, but Josh urged the reticent Jacob to speak up.

"Well, I haven't had time to talk with Josh about it, but I reckon we should move them down to the poorer stuff for the night, there's a small enclosure nearby that will do." Again, Jacob looked to Josh for reassurance. Josh was nodding in agreement. "Then I was thinking about taking them up on the slopes above the olive groves on the other side of the valley. We can use the walled track to get them there."

"The goats will do everyone a favour and clear the weeds out of the lane on the way through," added Josh, sagely.

"The grazing isn't so good, but after this stuff…" he pulled at the grass with one hand. "It will do fine for a couple of days," finished Jacob.

Martha was delighted to see how much his confidence was growing. They made a good team. Lazarus had chosen them well.

Shaking the crumbs from her tunic, Martha stood up; it was time to head home. After asking God's blessing over the young shepherds and the flock, she climbed slowly up and out into the cold brightness of the mountainside. She walked swiftly, aiming to stay high and enjoy the views across the surrounding hills on her long trek back to Bethany.

It was well past midday when she finally arrived home. The donkey poked his nose out with a mouth full of hay and gave her a welcoming whicker. To her surprise, Mary was sitting grinding corn in a patch of sunlight and singing softly. Judging by the pile of husks and the flour jars, she had been working for some time. A plate and cup stood on the bench.

Tabitha came rushing out, twisting her hair back with wet hands. "We guessed you'd gone to see the ewe," she said, pulling Martha down onto the bench and handing her a drink. "Do you want something to eat? I made lunch for us when you didn't come back."

"I'm fine, thank you. I ate with Josh and Jacob."

"How's the ewe?" asked Mary, getting up stiffly and coming to join them.

"Good, all sorted out. Just foot rot. A bit unusual at this time of year, but our two young shepherds are doing really well. So what's been going on here?" she asked, looking around the courtyard and spotting the mats airing, the hay in the donkey's manger, a broom leaning against the wall and Mary's full flour jars.

"Oh, Tabitha's been in charge," grinned Mary. "I've just done as I was told."

Martha laughed. "Then she'll have worked you hard."

The sisters looked up at Tabitha, who was standing in front of them with her hands on her hips.

"What do you say, Tabitha? Have I done enough flour for today?" asked Mary.

"Well," considered Tabitha, but before she could give her verdict, a large, long, grey nose gave her a shove from behind, and she found herself sprawled flat on the ground. Tabitha turned over to find Clop had wandered over to say hello.

"Someone forgot to bolt his door," said Mary, gleefully, leaning on Martha, who was laughing so hard that tears were running down her cheeks.

Chapter Thirteen

The Dedication of the Temple

Winter

By law, Jews were not required to attend the feast of Dedication, although it was still a popular eight-day celebration. So when Elias sent word to Lazarus that the Rabbi Yeshua had suddenly appeared in Jerusalem, they were taken aback, and once more Martha felt a nagging fear in the pit of her stomach.

Lazarus had just finished the last of the ploughing, so he accompanied Simon to the temple the next day. There they met Elias and his cousins, Reuben and Sam, in the hope of finding the Master. Martha, Mary and Tabitha spent a damp day sowing the remaining wheat. It was getting late, so Mary had gone ahead of them to tell Ellie, who was preparing dinner, that they were on their way home.

In the gathering dusk Tabitha unharnessed the donkey. Suddenly she heard a shout from the hillside above. Looking up, she saw Lazarus hurrying towards them, waving. He was closely followed by several other figures. Martha had heard the shout too, and had immediately recognised Miriam and Susanna picking their way down the slopes after him. The women were followed by the unmistakable figure of Peter. It wasn't until they came closer that Tabitha could make out Andrew, James and John. Martha greeted them with delight, but she kept looking back to the horizon for Yeshua. Seeing this, Miriam shook her head gently. He was with the others in Jerusalem.

It had been almost two months since they'd last seen everyone, and as they walked home in the fading light, Martha felt her tiredness disappear as they began to share all that had happened since they'd last met. Dinner was waiting when they arrived, and extra places were quickly set for their unexpected visitors. Everyone seemed relaxed and at ease as they devoured Ellie's thick, rich stew, which was almost as good as Martha's.

After dinner, the others stretched out in front of the fire while Mary said goodnight to Ellie, who was slipping off home before the rain got any worse. They could hear it drumming on the veranda roof.

Once Mary had returned, and in answer to their unspoken questions, John began to explain why they were in Jerusalem. They had arrived on the Sabbath, entering the city by the south gate. There, Yeshua had made an ointment for a blind beggar's eyes, using a mixture of road mud and his own spit. Tabitha and Mary grimaced as John described this, but were relieved when they were told that the Master had sent the beggar to wash in the nearby pool of Siloam. Swiftly, news had got around that the man, who had been blind from birth, now had perfect sight. This had caused quite a stir in his community, especially at the local synagogue. The Pharisees there couldn't agree that it was really him, so they'd called in the man's parents.

Andrew suggested that once more, the Master had deliberately chosen to heal someone on a Sabbath. The others agreed, concerned about the risk he was taking, but Miriam and Susanna knew he cared more for the people than he did for himself.

Martha's concern grew when James let it slip that the priesthood had told all synagogue leaders that anyone acknowledging the Master as the Messiah would be banned from the synagogue and excluded from their community. Immediately she thought of Michael, their ageing Hazzan. Would he comply with this mandate? Then she realised Lazarus, Simon and Joseph, as elders in Bethany's synagogue, must have known about this too. She hoped they knew what they were doing; it sounded like a dangerous game, for many people in Bethany were already convinced of the authenticity of the Master. Perhaps that was why Yeshua had stayed away?

Martha came back to the present as John was telling them how feisty the fellow had been when the Pharisees had questioned him. He had even disagreed with them. Tabitha, who like Martha tended to champion the underdog, was enjoying hearing about a beggar who dared to argue with Pharisees. John had admired the man's courage as he told them that anyone who could heal like that had to be from God. Nevertheless, he'd been thrown out of the synagogue. Mary was outraged, clenching her fists, but the best part of John's story was still to come. As soon as the Master had heard what had happened, he'd gone in search of the poor man, who had instantly recognised him as the Messiah and without hesitation, had believed in him. Mary cheered at this, until Peter pointed out that Yeshua had also said he had come into the world to separate those who would reject him from those who would believe in him, and this made her wince; it was a sharp line.

"Of course, he'd also talked about the blindness of those who thought they understood the law," Peter joked, before going on to tell them the Master had also spoken about sheep, which had made him laugh. What did he know about sheep? He was a fisherman. But he did understand why Yeshua had likened many of the leaders to thieves and robbers who climbed into the sheep fold and tried to steal the sheep.

"Look out anyone who tries to steal our sheep, or goats for that matter," interjected Tabitha. "They'll have Josh and Jacob to reckon with."

"He even went as far as saying he would give his own life for his sheep," said John.

"Like the time Josh and Jacob didn't come home, because there were bandits and they were protecting our sheep," exclaimed Tabitha. "And just like King David, when he was a shepherd boy, and protected his sheep from lions and bears." If the grown-ups hadn't fully appreciated the Master's analogy until then, they certainly did after that.

"The bit I didn't understand," said Susanna, "Was when he said he had other sheep and the two flocks would become one." The others shook their heads; they hadn't been sure what he'd meant either.

Martha got up and filled everyone's cups again, while Mary cleared some dishes. It was getting late.

"Perhaps he means people of other nationalities; gentiles, and not just Jews," ventured Martha, thinking out loud and remembering the crowds who listened to him sometimes. There were a few wrinkled brows and twisted mouths as everyone contemplated that thought. Then she asked, "Are you all going into Jerusalem tomorrow?" There were enthusiastic nods from the four men, but Miriam and Susanna looked unhappy. Martha understood their reluctance. Each day was more dangerous than the last. Mary also saw the apprehension in their eyes and this time, she wasn't sure if she wanted to go either. Lazarus looked at her questioningly, his head on one side.

"You go," she said. "Martha and I will stay."

Somehow, celebrating the rededication of the temple didn't

have quite the appeal it usually had, although the story of Judas Maccabeus, the son of a courageous priest, was one of Mary and Tabitha's favourites. The temple had been used to worship the Greek god Zeus during the Seleucid occupation. Judas had led a revolt, recapturing Jerusalem and restoring the temple back to God, and this was commemorated every year.

Martha began to drift off. There were so many differences of opinion in the way scripture was interpreted and lived out in the world around her. Only Yeshua seemed to make sense of it all, and yet he was also adding to the controversy and confusion. So why did she believe him? Even their own leaders couldn't agree. Sheep, that was it. He kept going back to the temple, putting his own life in danger, to call his sheep to him. The moment of clarity clouded over as her eyelids drooped.

When she woke up, the room was empty, but the fire still glowed and she was covered with a blanket. She soon fell asleep again.

Lazarus woke early; he always had, even as a child. Martha and Tabitha were already in the kitchen, the smell of fresh bread wafting from the hot oven. He was pleased to see that Martha looked refreshed and bright, as that made it easier for him to accompany their friends into Jerusalem.

Mary appeared with Susanna and Miriam, giggling, their damp hair combed back. They too seemed more light-hearted. Fascinated, Lazarus watched the relaxed dance the four women wove around each other as they laid everything out ready for breakfast. He felt almost as though he'd gained two more sisters.

Martha interrupted his observations. "We're ready. Go and see if the boys are up. I imagine you'll want an early start."

Did Martha just call the four men upstairs 'boys'? Amused, he climbed the steps two at a time.

John was up and washing, his blanket airing and his mat back on the pile. Funny how Martha had that effect on some people.

However, the others were still sleeping under their blanket mounds. James poked his head out and rubbed the sleep from his eyes.

"Breakfast is ready, and Tabitha has put a few more basins out in the yard for washing," Lazarus informed them.

Andrew sat up yawning, and poked his brother with a foot. "Get up, lazybones," he said.

Peter grunted but didn't move.

"Well, there's eggs, fresh bread and fruit when you're ready," said Lazarus.

"If there's any left," added John, following Lazarus downstairs.

Once again they all sat together, the rays of the sun reaching far into the room where Mary had opened the shutters along the veranda, and the fire was glowing healthily. Peter was the last to join them, dropping onto a mat beside Lazarus, while Tabitha handed him eggs fried in oil. His eyes lit up.

"What a treat! And they're crinkly round the edges, just like my wife does them," exclaimed Peter.

That caught Martha's attention. Peter seldom mentioned his family, and she was curious. Peter had once told them that his wife wasn't much of a traveller and so stayed home, looking after her mother and family. However, she'd come to the Feast of Tabernacles with Peter and had remained with him so, when Yeshua had sent out a large group of followers, in pairs, she had gone with Peter. Even now, weeks later, their friends still talked about the experience with excitement. Miriam had tried to explain to Martha that somehow the Master had transferred some of his power and authority to them. Suddenly they were telling people the Messiah was here among them, to save them, and they found they were able to heal the sick, and even the demons had obeyed them. They had felt invincible. Lazarus and his sisters had listened to this with awe and just a little envy. They would have loved to have been with them, to spread the good news that the Messiah was here, but Lazarus had encouraged his sisters that they could do that in Bethany.

After breakfast, Lazarus chopped wood while he waited for the others. Miriam and Susanna stood chatting with Martha and Mary, while Tabitha fussed with the chickens. The women all seemed to understand one another so well. Even Yeshua apparently shared this insight, but not Lazarus. At one time, he'd been fond of Anna, Simon's daughter, but she hadn't been brought up for the life he chose to lead; it wouldn't have been fair to ask to marry her. Tabitha was different to the three of them; perhaps she would marry one day, and bring children into their lives. He could hope.

His thoughts were interrupted when finally the men came hurrying down the stairs, cloaks flung over shoulders. Andrew apologised, but he didn't need to, Lazarus had heard the low murmur of prayer from upstairs. Martha was glad Lazarus was going; he would take care of their friends, no matter what happened.

They found Yeshua walking under Solomon's porch, named after King David's son, who had built the first temple in Jerusalem. The current and third temple to be built on the site had been started by Herod the Great, and was far greater than the former two. However, completing it, as his uncle always pointed out, would be a great loss to the economy of the city, as it kept many masons, carpenters and labourers in constant work.

Yeshua was pleased to see them, commenting that they were the first to arrive. Andrew was quick to point out that they would have been there sooner if Peter hadn't overslept. The others turned up not long after. Almost as soon as they'd arrived, some of the Jewish leaders had begun to appear, congregating near them, and it wasn't long before they began asking Yeshua questions. However, they came straight to the point for a change.

"How long are you going to keep us in suspense? If you are the Messiah, tell us plainly," one of them asked.

He sounded so sincere that Lazarus almost believed he was

genuine, but the Master wasn't fooled; his answer was clear. "I have told you already, but you don't believe me. The proof is in what I do in my Father's name, and by his power. My sheep recognise my voice. I know them and they follow me." The Master's reference to the day before was clear, but his next words had Lazarus and the others paying even closer attention.

"I give them eternal life and they will never perish. They are mine, because the Father has given them to me. The Father and I are one, and no one can take them from his hand." The crowd gasped, stunned by what he'd just claimed.

John and Lazarus looked at one another in alarm. The Master wasn't playing games anymore. In saying he could give eternal life, which the Sadducean priests didn't believe in, and by claiming he was equal to God, which all parties counted as blasphemy, he had just condemned himself.

Time seemed to slow down as Lazarus and John watched the men grab blocks of stone from a nearby pile. The masons began to protest, chisels in hand, but they were shoved back out of the way. The enraged attackers came forward. Instinctively, Lazarus looked for Miriam and Susanna, but they were safe behind Peter and Andrew, who stood at his back.

"He's not playing games this time," whispered Peter. "Look, he's standing his ground!"

"Under my Father's direction I have done many things to help the people." Heads nodded in the gathering crowd acknowledging this, but those who held stones only tightened their grip. At last, he was playing into their hands. What a fool, they thought.

"For which of the many merciful and good deeds are you proposing to stone me?" Yeshua asked, calmly.

"We're not going to stone you for the good things but for your blasphemy," one of them shouted back at him.

"How can it be blasphemy when the Holy One, who was sent

into the world by the Father says, I am the son of God? Even if you haven't got faith in me, at least believe in what I do, so you may know that the Father is in Me and I am in Him!"

In that moment, Lazarus felt himself tense ready to spring forward in the Master's defence. He knew that Peter, Andrew and John would follow with no thought for their own safety. He could feel the tension in the crowd as an unseen battle was fought with the armed protagonists. Panicking, some began to shout for the temple police to come, while others ran off to get them. With each slow passing moment the resolve of those who held stones seemed to waver; not all the crowd was with them. Then the police arrived and in the commotion, Yeshua recognised his moment and seized it. Lazarus was aware of his swift movement past them and turned his head, following the Master with his eyes. An urgent thump on the arm brought Lazarus' attention back to John, as it was meant to.

"We'll follow later. Stand still and look forward," he said sharply, through clenched teeth.

From the same direction that the Master had taken, the temple police came shoving and pushing through the crowd.

"Where is the Rabbi who is making blasphemous claims?" they yelled.

It went very quiet then, except for the leaders who thought they had caught Yeshua. They spun round and round, desperate to locate him.

"Where is he? Which way did he go?" they demanded, but many looked at their neighbours and shrugged.

"You!" shouted a policeman, at Peter. "Did you see which way he went?"

"No sir, I didn't," he answered, truthfully. He'd been very careful not to look.

Andrew hid a smirk. Lazarus wondered how they could behave like this, defiant, in the face of the temple authorities and an angry mob with stones. Their confidence in Yeshua, had grown.

They didn't see the Master for the rest of the day, but the crowds were certainly talking about him. Lazarus and all twelve of the disciples had left the temple towards sunset, conspicuously, through the Golden Gate. They'd found the Master waiting in a quiet corner of the the Gethsemane garden; he was eating some fruit Martha had given him that morning.

When Lazarus got home, cold and hungry, it was late and pitch dark. Martha and Mary were worried and waiting for him. After he'd said goodbye to their friends, he'd waited a long time in the shadows of the fig tree beside the main road. He had watched, but no one had pursued them, and the road had remained empty, much to his relief. The temple celebrations would continue without Yeshua, but of one thing Lazarus was sure, many more sheep had recognised his voice that day, and were following him.

Chapter Thirteen

A Sudden Death

Late winter

One evening, Lazarus arrived home later than expected. He'd felt tired all day, so he went straight to bed without eating. Martha was only mildly concerned; he would probably come looking for food once he'd rested. Mary and Tabitha were spinning wool together, and Martha was soon distracted by their chatter. As the evening wore on, they missed Lazarus' cheerful presence, so Martha went to find him, taking some food and wine. Knocking gently on his bedroom door, she waited, but when there was no reply, she tiptoed in and placed the food beside his bed. He was sleeping peacefully, but in the dim lamplight he looked a little pale. Mary had had a mild fever the previous week, caught from a patient. Perhaps he'd got the same thing, but that was most unlike her healthy brother. Mary was fully recovered and her bouncy self again, judging by the laughter coming from the kitchen.

At first light, Martha knocked on his door, but again there was no reply. For a moment she thought he might have left early for work, as he often did. Opening his door to be sure, she saw the food exactly where she had left it the night before, and his still form lying in bed. As she bent to pick up the plate she saw the sweat across his brow. Alarmed, she tried to rouse him. He was barely conscious; his bed covers felt damp. She called out to Tabitha, keeping her voice calm but urgent. Tabitha came running.

Martha bathed Lazarus' burning body while Tabitha went to wake Mary, and then, together, they changed his bed linen. She cradled his head and tried to encourage him to sip some water, while Mary bathed his feverish brow. For a short time he seemed to know they were there, smiling faintly at something Tabitha said, but then he slipped into unconsciousness again. Martha became afraid, but she hid her fear from the other two, sending Mary to find a runner to take a message to their uncle, and Tabitha to do her chores.

To their relief, Elias arrived swiftly with the family physician. Martha had nursed many sick people, and her concerns grew as she watched the physician examine Lazarus. She could see he was perplexed by her brother's condition, although his manner remained confident and reassuring. In the end, he had little to add to the care that Lazarus was already receiving from his sisters. Elias, reassured by the physician, reluctantly returned to Jerusalem. They began to pray earnestly for their brother.

As the day wore on, Lazarus continued to burn with the fever, and so did the fear in Mary's eyes as she knelt beside his bed. He didn't seem to be aware of his surroundings, and his face had become waxy and pale. Still Martha refused to give in to fear; the fever would break and release him. He was strong and healthy; he was her brother.

Finally, Mary could bear it no longer. She looked imploringly at her sister's drained face and cried, "The Master, we must send for the Master!"

Martha felt like someone had just shaken her out of a nightmare, and that spurred her into action. She didn't remember running out of the house and across the road shouting for Rachel, but she did feel Lizzy holding her tight until Rachel came. Rachel listened carefully as Martha explained all that had happened since the previous evening, and then what the physician had had to say. Rachel couldn't hide her worried frown, and the paleness of her face only added to Martha's concerns as she begged them to find someone to take a message to the Rabbi Yeshua.

Shem was working in the shed. Martha saw him walk across the courtyard towards them, taking off his apron, saying he'd go, kissing Lizzy, as he gathered his cloak and the bag of provisions Rachel stuffed into his hand.

"Please tell the Master that Lazarus whom he loves is sick, and to come quickly," pleaded Martha, biting her lip and wringing her hands.

"I will," Shem reassured her. In her gratitude Martha shook his hand. She trusted Shem. Like his father, he was a man of his word.

"Rumour says he's at the Jordan crossing, near where John used to baptise," added his mother. "But I'd check with your father before you leave, he may know more."

Shem nodded, promising he would find the Rabbi no matter what it took. Then he was gone, and Martha felt a wave of relief; the fate of her brother was no longer solely in her hands.

Returning to Mary and Tabitha with Rachel, her heart felt lighter, especially when she saw some colour return to Mary's pale, worried face. Tabitha even managed a smile, before going to fetch water from the well. Rachel now kept Martha company as they bathed Lazarus' feverish body and attempted to get him to drink.

Their cousin Reuben quietly entered the courtyard, his dark features creased with concern. He was breathing hard, his skin almost scarlet after his vigorous walk from Jerusalem. He carried medicine. Tabitha came out to him, but he didn't need to say anything, the question was written so clearly on his face.

"There's no change yet," she said gravely. "I'll take the medicine into Martha; Rachel is with her. Mary will be out in a moment."

Rachel wasted no time in releasing the sweet-smelling oils the physician had sent, in the hope they might ease the fever. Reuben waited the rest of the afternoon, hopeful for some good news to return home with. Martha was relieved when Simon called and took the anxious Reuben under his wing. Shortly after, the two men were joined by the Rabbi Michael and then others from the village. They began to pray earnestly together for Lazarus. When Reuben finally left at sunset, under dark brooding winter skies, he carried a glimmer of hope back to their uncle.

Lizzy brought food over for them, but they ate little and were very glad when Rachel stayed. Their spirits lifted when Lazarus regained consciousness in the late evening. Mary clung to his hand, tears rolling down her cheeks with joy as he attempted to speak. He smiled at Mary and squeezed her hand feebly, but then his eyes sought out Martha. She cradled his head and helped him swallow a mouthful of water, but he was too weak to do more.

"You're beginning to get better," Mary encouraged him.

Instinctively Martha looked at Rachel, who immediately went to fetch Tabitha. Tabitha came running, dropping to her knees and placing her head on his chest, and begged him through her tears to get well. Martha helped him raise a hand to Tabitha's head, where it rested for a while in blessing, slipping off as he faded back into unconsciousness. Martha sternly sent them back to the kitchen to let Lazarus sleep in peace, while her spirits sank.

Later in the night, Martha gently carried the sleeping Tabitha from the foot of Lazarus' bed to the warmth beside the kitchen fire. Rachel rested there too, gently snoring. She built the fire up before returning to Mary and Lazarus. Mary had prayed for a long while, but even she was peacefully asleep now. Her last prayer still rang in Martha's ears: 'Please keep our beloved brother alive till your son comes'. Martha continued to talk quietly to her patient while she prayed in her heart, but fear was growing and hope fading.

Martha woke with a start in the chilled room. Mary was still sleeping, and Lazarus was deathly pale. Gently she laid her hand on his forehead; it felt cold and waxy as she watched for the rise and fall of his chest. It was hard to see in the low light, so calmly she lit another candle, and went to fetch the tiny mirror from her room. The lamp was still glowing on the veranda, as it was not yet dawn. She shivered, pulling the blanket closer about her shoulders.

She knelt by his bed for a long while, alternately watching for the rise and fall of his chest and holding the mirror gently before his nose and lips. It was Mary's gentle touch on her arm that made her stop. There had been no movement and no trace of breath for a long while. Then the darkness of grief engulfed her, as she accepted that he was dead.

Martha and Mary sat together, hands clasped, heads bowed, stunned. Bursting into the room, Tabitha let out a howl. It pierced the morning and roused them. She looked at the body and then at Martha. Understanding that the worst had happened, she ran shrieking from the room, and returned, sobbing, with Rachel.

In those first few hours, Martha didn't know how she would have coped without Rachel and her family. A runner was sent to Jerusalem, and Rachel began to assemble all that they would need to prepare the body for burial. Joseph went straight to the family tomb among the rocky outcrops above the village; it would need to be opened and made ready to receive the body of Lazarus before sunset.

Mary had begged Rachel to check for signs of life once more, although she knew he had gone. A desperate hope lingered, while Martha stood impatiently by. She had already been through that, alone in the long dark watch before the dawn. Then her own despair consumed her once more, and she was grateful Rachel was there to help poor Mary.

Tabitha seemed the only one able to function, although she was wailing and crying loudly. She fed the hungry animals; the chickens stayed close to the donkey, afraid to come out, and when she collapsed onto the ground and sobbed the goats and sheep gathered around her, bleating sympathetically and nuzzling her.

Slowly, gently, Rachel began to coax Martha back into life; the body would need to be prepared for burial and word sent out that Lazarus, son of Reubel, was dead.

Simon appeared, standing in the courtyard with tears on his cheeks. Joseph had been to see him earlier, waking the household. Mary and Martha came out to him, and they wept together, although standing apart, and asked why this had happened to their brother. Simon presented Martha with a white bundle of folded linen that felt like silk between her thumb and fingers. It hurt so much Martha couldn't cry anymore.

"Your brother was like a son to me," he whispered, unable to speak clearly, his voice cracked with emotion. "My Helena had these put by, but she sends them with heartfelt regret for your brother's death. She really cared for him."

"It wasn't hard to love Lazarus," said Mary, her voice steady and clear, focused on their kindness, instead of her own racking grief.

"That's true," Simon replied, but looked away.

"Simon, would you help carry his bier?" asked Martha.

"I would have fought for a place at his side even if you had not asked me," came his reply. "Your family will be here soon, but is there anything I can do to help, in the meantime?"

Martha hugged the white linen close to her. "Simon, this means a lot to us. Now I have the courage to begin preparing his body."

Simon hesitated, but then asked, "Do you have all the help you need?"

"Rachel will help me, I don't need anyone else." Mary's face crumpled. Martha realised what she'd said. "Oh, dear Mary, I didn't mean it like that. You will have the harder task, for I will be unclean, and it is you who will have to deal with our family and friends in their grief."

Mary nodded, as she began to understand Martha's heart. It was a big sacrifice, and would isolate her from everyone but Rachel long after the burial.

"I don't suppose there's been any word from the Master?" Mary asked quietly, but Martha saw her hold her breath.

"No, not yet, but I'm sure he will come as soon as word reaches him," Simon reassured them, before letting himself out quietly and going to find Joseph.

Martha thought of her uncle and aunt and their cousins Reuben and Sam, who had been like brothers to Lazarus.

"How will the family bear such news?" Martha said out loud.

Mary's face crumpled again as she said, "Like us. One, tragic, awful, unbearable moment at a time." Martha held out her arms to her sister, then led her indoors.

They found Tabitha clinging to Rachel in her grief but she pulled away and flung herself at Martha as Rachel comforted Mary.

"Why did God take Lazarus, Martha? Why?" asked Tabitha.

Martha shook her head, as her own tears fell onto Tabitha's shoulders and into her hair. She had already asked herself that question, but her voice was calm and reasoning, as she replied, "Death happens to all, it does not discriminate, my darling girl. Do not blame God. Lazarus has simply gone ahead of us. He'll be waiting."

"The Master could have healed him. Why hasn't he come?"

"Hush, it's too soon. We don't even know if Shem has found him yet."

"We sent word to the Master too late!" said Tabitha, accusingly.

"No, we didn't," said Mary softly. "It happened so fast, it was so unexpected. Lazarus has never been ill. How could any of us have guessed this would happen?"

Tabitha looked mollified and pressed her head against Martha's shoulder.

"You won't be able to hug me once you begin to get Lazarus ready," Tabitha moaned despairingly.

"But I will," said Mary, as she held out her arms to Tabitha, and watched Martha count the first cost of her decision. With her arm round Tabitha, Mary led her into the kitchen, leaving Martha and Rachel to begin their gruelling task.

Elias, Elizabeth, Reuben, Sam and Sara arrived, with their cousin Rebecca. Mary greeted them. Elias was pale, and Elizabeth drawn as she leaned on Sara, her friend and servant. Reuben looked uncertain and Sam as though he would break into tears. Their ageing grandparents looked on bewildered. Their cousin Rebecca, from Bethany, had also joined them.

Martha hung back, keeping her distance, as her Uncle Elias approached, but Aunt Elizabeth put out a hand to gently restrain him. Then he understood, and his face filled with dismay. Why had she done this? Now she could not even receive the comfort of a hug from him, nor he from her. By law, touching a dead body made them unclean, and now she would have to wait out the long days before purification.

Elizabeth said quietly to her husband, "She never abandoned him in life, Elias. How could she in death?"

Martha looked gratefully at her aunt, comforted that she understood why she had had to do it.

Under Elizabeth's instructions and with Sam's help, Tabitha unpacked the two laden donkeys, while Sara presented Martha with the oils, aloes and myrrh they had brought. Martha felt her spirit lift as she caught the scent rising from the baskets. The courtyard was busy and full of people. Lizzy had brought refreshments and was helping her uncle and Reuben get Mary and Martha's ageing but determined grandparents, Eleazar and Hannah, up the steps and into the house. Her aunt was apologising to Mary because it had taken them so long to get there. Then she began to cry, and Martha cried too, feeling their grief as well as her own.

Her uncle had engaged professional mourners before leaving Jerusalem and they were on their way, accompanied by the musicians. Mary took their hands and thanked them for their thoughtfulness, while Martha watched but felt comforted by their presence.

Rachel put her arm around Martha and turned her to the stairs and the task ahead. "No regrets. You are right to do this, Martha," she said.

Martha nodded, but she didn't look at Rachel or speak again, although her hands trembled slightly as she wound the linen around Lazarus' limbs and added the fragrant leaves. Rachel sang softly while she worked, and Martha found it soothing, but it was Rachel who finally covered his dear face. Martha's face screwed up, and her vision blurred, as she softly shuddered with a despair that wracked her soul.

Shem had returned alone in the late afternoon cold and hungry, his message delivered, but he had been given no reply.

As everyone gathered for the funeral, Martha had never felt so alone, and any hope withered away in the winter light. She bent low over the bowl, cupping the cool soothing water to her eyes. With her face to the wall, she blinked her tears away and patted her face dry with the black shawl she wore. She wore the clothes of mourning and her movement was controlled and deliberate, as she went out to stand beside Rachel. Her family walked together with Mary and Tabitha, following the funeral bier bearing Lazarus' body, but she and Rachel walked alone, separated from the crowd that followed them.

Chapter Fifteen

Martha and the Master

It had all happened so quickly; only six days before, Lazarus had been alive. It was so hard to believe. Again and again, Martha had played the events over in her mind, from his return home, just tired, to his death. What had she missed? They had prayed almost constantly as they'd tended their beloved brother. How was it even possible that his lifeless body now lay in the family tomb with the bones of their parents? She felt empty inside, so she clung to those last few hours when he'd been alive and so full of life. She relived the helplessness and desperation she had felt in dry-eyed pain.

Shem had delivered the message to the Master five days ago, but only now had he come. Why had it taken him so long? As she thought this, Martha instantly felt a pang of guilt mixing with her anger. She didn't want to remember the attempts to stone him or that his life was in danger. Confused though her feelings were, she still longed to run and find him, hoping perhaps that even now he could do something, but not daring to imagine what that could be. Surely, by this time it was all too late. Her tearless eyes stung; overwhelmed, she felt helpless, like a child that had been abandoned once more.

Finally she threw her damp shawl around her head and shoulders and left the house to find Yeshua. The streets were busy at this time of day, despite the cold wind, so she used the steep, uneven alleyways between the houses. At one point, she crossed the main street lower down, but quickly turned off this between two low stone walls. The muddy track was narrow with vegetable patches either side, but the slope was lessening. Martha didn't hesitate; she knew Bethany like the inside of her own home.

Towards the bottom of the path, houses rose up on each side, with the odd doorway and steps. Someone called her name, and her heart sank. She had hoped to get through the cut without being spotted by Cousin Rebecca. Wearily, Martha turned back.

"Where are you off to in such a hurry, my dear?" asked Rebecca, obviously surprised to see her out and about.

"Hello, Rebecca. How's your back?" Martha asked lightly, as she continued to walk on, but backwards, unwilling to stop and chat.

"Oh, could be better, but it's kind of you to ask, especially in the circumstances. It was such a good funeral, the whole of Bethany must have been there. Such a terrible, terrible loss. He was still so young. Oh, don't mind me," she added, as Martha turned her head away to hide the pain. "What will happen to you and Mary now? Will you go and live with Elias? But you'd miss the country. You've never struck me as city girls."

"That probably won't be necessary," said Martha, stiffly. "But nothing's been discussed, as yet." Didn't Rebecca understand that she not only ran the house, but for years, while Lazarus was growing up, she had run the farm and the olive groves too? She resented the implications of Rebecca's words.

"Please excuse me, I do need to be going," she said.

"Yes, of course. You know where we are dear, if you or Mary need any guidance. You'd be a great asset to any household." There it was again, the veiled suggestion.

"Thank you," said Martha, turning away abruptly, so Rebecca wouldn't see her face.

Martha almost ran now, as the slope gently descended to the valley floor. The houses here were higgledy-piggledy, set back from the dirt road and poorly built. Tethered animals grazed between them, and ragged children hung in doorways. She strained her eyes, searching along the distant road until it disappeared into the olive trees on the other side of the valley.

Momentarily, Martha paused, standing tall, shielding her eyes with a hand, scanning the patch of common scrubland on the outskirts of the village. Her heart skipped a beat as she held her breath, for in the distance people were moving along the road, and she knew he'd come, at last.

Unsure of what to do next, Martha waited in confusion watching the approaching but distant crowd. Although she couldn't trust herself to face the Master surrounded by people, she wanted to let him know she was there. So, standing on top of a dirt mound beside the road, she let her black shawl stream out in the wind, like a flag of mourning.

The Master was talking with Barsabbas, who was not one of the twelve men chosen by him but one of those who had been with them from the beginning of his ministry. A few of the others were walking in step and listening to the conversation. It was Peter who noticed the black ribbon and the distant figure, but it was John who recognised it was Martha. John and Miriam exchanged glances, and her eyes brimmed with sorrow for her friend. The Master's reaction had been confusing when they'd heard the news that Lazarus was ill.

"Lord, Martha is coming to meet us," said John, urgently pointing to the distant figure.

The Master looked up sharply, his brown, gold-flecked eyes wide open in the bright diffused light. He motioned to the others to continue along the road, while he swiftly set off across the rough ground to intercept her.

Martha saw him coming, but being in mourning she was barefoot, so she had to concentrate hard on placing her feet on the stony ground. Picking her way around thorn bushes and prickles, she didn't look up until he was quite close. Her heart nearly stopped as he held out his arms to her. She had waited, expecting him to come every moment of every day since the message had been delivered. He felt every moment of her pain as though it was his own, and Martha saw on his face how much he had loved her brother. So why hadn't he come earlier? He was the only person who could have prevented Lazarus' death. The thought fuelled her feelings of anger towards him.

"Why didn't you come sooner? He's dead, buried. Didn't you care?" She choked back the tears.

"Oh, my dear Martha," he said, so sadly, so softly.

As she heard his words, they soothed her. Her breathing slowed as the anger melted away, and her mind felt clear and at peace.

"Even now, I know that whatever you ask God for he will give it to you, because you are his son."

A faint smile played on Yeshua's lips.

"Your brother will rise again," he assured her.

"I know that he will rise again in the resurrection on the last day," but she was puzzled. Was that what he meant? Or...

"I am the resurrection and the life. Whoever believes, trusts and relies on me, shall live, even if he dies, and whoever continues to live and have faith in me shall never die." Martha blinked, the top of her nose creasing with concentration, as she tried to work out what he'd said, but she couldn't. So her heart elbowed her mind out of the way, and then suddenly she knew the truth. truth. If they believed in him, he would give them a new spiritual life that would last forever.

"Do you believe this?" he asked, his head on one side.

"Yes," she gasped. "Beyond a shadow of doubt, you are the Messiah, the son of God, the one the world has been waiting for." A lump rose in her throat. Finally, she understood. The waiting was over, he was here and nothing else mattered anymore. She was standing before the living son of God. Awe filled her mind, joy her spirit, and from her soul came tears of relief and hope, unchecked. In that moment she trusted him completely.

He stepped forward to take her hands, but instinctively she drew back.

"I am unclean," she whispered. "You are holy."

Shaking his head, he took her hands firmly in his. "My dear Martha, you understand so much. Now trust me again. Run and tell Mary I am here. We shall be together again soon."

Together they walked back to the road, where her friends, his disciples and followers stood respectfully waiting. Martha gazed at them and they wondered at the radiance of her face. Miriam reached out and lightly squeezed her hand before Martha turned and walked quickly back into Bethany.

Once out of sight, Martha ran, making light of the steep climb back through the village. Only once did she stop to look back and check he was still there, then scolded herself for the moment of doubt.

The west wind chilled the sweat on her back as she lifted the latch quietly and let herself in. The courtyard was empty, but a low murmur of voices came from the house. Tabitha, quick-eared and missing Martha, slipped out, glancing back over her shoulder with a frown on her face. She ran to Martha, stopping short, but desperate to put her arms around her and receive the comfort she needed so much. Martha too hesitated, then remembered the Master hadn't been afraid to touch her, hadn't thought it was wrong. Filled with courage at his words, she took the thin little face in her rough, gentle hands and looked into the large, round eyes. Martha held her index finger to Tabitha's lips.

"I've spoken with the Master. It'll be all right now. You'll see."

Tabitha searched her radiant face, seeing the hope that now burned there.

"Is Aunt Elizabeth working you too hard, little one?" asked Martha.

Tabitha shook her head bravely.

"Never mind, the days of mourning will be over soon, and our guests can go home."

Tabitha sighed and tried to smile. Then Martha had an idea. "How would you like to visit mama Juthine for the rest of the day?"

Tabitha looked surprised, and then pleased. "May I go, really?" she exclaimed, relief flooding her careworn young face as she hugged Martha tightly. The Master must have brought about this change in Martha, she thought, and he was good.

"You are my beautiful gift," said Martha, softly. "Now, go quickly and don't forget to thank Juthine for the fresh bread she's sent each day. Oh, and why don't you take the donkey? He could do with stretching his legs, and you could fill up at the well on the way back."

Someone impatiently called Tabitha's name from the living room. Forcefully, she tugged the buckle up on the girth strap, causing Clop to sway under the force. The water panniers dragged on the rough gate as it closed behind them.

"Is everything all right Aunt?" Martha called, through the open door. "Tabitha has gone out. She won't be back till later."

Martha looked in at the kitchen door. Mary was still sitting on the mat. She hadn't moved, an untouched cup still in front of her.

Poor Mary had done her best with all their friends and relatives, but her own helpless grief had provided the others with something to do.

Martha called to her sister gently, longing to smooth the crumpled hair back from her face. Mary seemed startled, but relaxed when she recognised Martha's voice and turned her red, puffy eyes and ashen, salt-streaked cheeks towards her. Martha felt Mary's grief keenly, as well as her own. She longed to hold her sister and comfort her.

Then Martha whispered the words that would wake Mary from her grief. "He's here Mary. The Master's here, and asking for you. Will you go to him?"

It was like someone had breathed life into her. She was on her feet splashing water on her face and tugging her shawl over her head as she left slamming the gate behind her.

Martha welcomed the smile that spread warmly across her face as she watched Mary follow her heart without a thought of explanation to the relatives she had left behind.

"Was that Mary going out?" asked Elizabeth, wearily, as she looked out. "Has she gone to the tomb to mourn again?"

"Not directly," replied Martha. "Perhaps you'd like some refreshments before you go after her?"

"That's a nice thought. Thank you dear," said Elizabeth. "See if you can find Sara, she'll see to it." Martha went in search of Sara, pleased she had been able to buy Mary some time, at least.

Mary shot down the road, hoping and praying Martha would find a way to stop their relatives from following her, yet again. Sara had been a tremendous support, taking much of the strain off her. Especially the night she had heard Martha crying and being sick. Sara had gone to Martha, not her. At first, Mary had been filled with fear, thinking Martha too would die and leave her, but in the morning Sara had reassured her that her sister was just exhausted with grief. Mary went faster, pushing down the guilt.

Taking the same route that Martha had, Mary was watched disapprovingly by Rebecca as she passed. It was time to make another visit, she decided. Mary was so swift that she even caught up with Tabitha and the donkey.

"Hello little sister, I thought you were at home," said Mary, surprised to see her.

"Martha sent me to mama Juthine's for the rest of the day, to get away from your insufferable aunt and uncle." She looked sideways at Mary and noticed some colour had returned to her cheeks.

"That's a big word," commented Mary.

"What, insufferable? It's not big enough for them!" Mary laughed out loud, and that made Tabitha so glad.

"Elizabeth is treating me like a servant, which I don't mind, but it upsets Martha."

"I am sorry for that, but aunt is grieving too, and it's making her very grumpy. Uncle too."

Although Mary was desperate to reach the Master, seeing Tabitha's sadness, she walked along with her.

"Where are you going?"

"I'm going to meet the Master."

"Why didn't he come before?"

"I don't know, but I'm sure he had a good reason. It's very dangerous for him to even be here."

The two girls walked on in silence, until Tabitha asked, "Where will he stay? We're full up."

"There's always Simon's. Now go and have a lovely time with your brothers and sisters," said Mary, as Maemi and the other children came running towards them, shouting gleefully. Mary waved and hurried on.

Chapter Sixteen

The Family Tomb

Mary found the Master and their friends close to where Martha had left him. Word had already spread of his arrival, but Mary ignored everyone, dropping to her knees in front of him and bowing her head nearly to his feet. The Master reached down and tenderly lifted her face to look up at him. Joy and grief met his gaze, until quietly, she began to sob.

"Master, if you had been here, my brother would not have died," she said. His face was twisted with anguish at Mary's distress and words.

A crowd was rapidly gathering, and seeing Mary crying at the Master's feet, they began to call out, praising Lazarus and lamenting his loss. Normally a quiet man, Eli's brother Joe, was among the first to speak.

"Lazarus will truly be missed, Rabbi. He was kind to everyone, and always had a cheery word for you. When I lost my job, he found me work so I could go on supporting my sick mother." His voice cracked, and he fell silent.

"He was truly a godly man, always had a prayer for you, but very generous too," Yaqim's mother, called out. "Always willing to help, he was, him and his sisters. He'll leave a big hole in this community and our hearts."

"One year it was so bad, we had no oil. He brought us some himself; the first from the press, after God had had his share. So kind and considerate, no thought for his own profit," cried one of the workers from the olive groves.

Moved by the people of his village, Michael, the Hazzan, raised his voice in lament for Lazarus too. "I doubt there is a person here in Bethany who has not been blessed in some way by Lazarus son of Reubel. Many of us have known him since a boy, and seen the honourable man he grew into, serving his community and honouring our God through his word and teaching. But I will remember his humbleness best." Michael began to weep unashamedly, like many of the others. These were not the tears of duty to the dead, but of genuine loss and love, and the Master saw this.

As soon as Reuben and Sam had heard the Rabbi was there, they had hurried after Mary, joining the crowd around her and the Master. Sam cried out, "Lord comfort us, especially Martha and Mary. It is so hard to carry on without him, but we know Lazarus now awaits the final resurrection when we shall see him again. I thank you for the privilege of simply being his friend and cousin." Sam bowed his head, but Mary looked at him gratefully. Reuben stood gravely beside his younger brother, his arm round Sam's shoulders, as he wiped his nose on his sleeve. Yeshua's followers stood sorrowfully beside him. What would he do? What could he do? Death seemed so final.

Salome whispered to Miriam, "They're all waiting for the Master. Surely, he will say something to bring them comfort, especially to dear Mary."

"Just wait a moment longer, he isn't ready yet. Something's about to happen. You mark my words."

Yeshua looked from Mary's tear-stained face to the now silent grieving crowd. Mary, though heartbroken, was still at his feet, still trusting him. She was always at his feet, eager-faced, drinking in everything he offered. Then there was Martha, the first to run to him, dignity mixed with grief, but not just her own. Filled with compassion for them all, blinking back his own tears, longing for them to trust him, he sighed. It was time to glorify his father. Miriam raised Mary to her feet, as the Master spoke to the crowd, his voice firm and clear, but his cheeks shinning and wet.

"Where have you laid him?" he asked.

"Come and see," the crowd said, gesturing to the cemetery above the town.

The crowd followed Mary and the Rabbi into Bethany and as they wound their way up the hill, each collected their friends and family along the way. The pace quickened, as more and more people began to follow them.

Martha heard them coming; she had been waiting, looking out for Mary and the Master. The crowd, like the hum of bees on a sunny day, grew ever louder, and she ran out to join them, calling back for those left in the house to follow them. First Miriam, then Mary grasped her hands, and this time she did not pull away. At the highest point in the road, she glanced back. So many people were coming, more it seemed than on the day of his funeral, and Martha, with hope rising, marvelled at this. What could the Master do? What would the Master do? Anything, her heart replied.

The crowds surged out from the town, strung along the track that stretched through ploughed fields and olive groves towards the rocky outcrop that marked the town's cemetery. Sheltered from the cold westerlies by rough cliffs, door stones stood solemnly at the entrances to tombs cut into the ancient limestone.

Silently the people filed into the grassy arena, then stood reverently, waiting. Some climbed onto jumbled piles of boulders to get a better view. Mary ran forward to stand up a fallen jug of herbs and flowers, placed there that morning.

The Master stood back in the crowd, head bowed, his cheeks wet, while those around him shed silent tears. Some wondered why he had let this happen; he could surely have prevented it. Hadn't he restored a blind man's eyes? Yeshua sighed, shoulders rising and falling with each breath, as the silence grew. A crow flew cawing from the cliffs above, and many faces looked up. Tabitha came pushing through the forest of followers, dust and tears streaking her face, but determined to stand by Martha and Mary.

"Take away the stone," Yeshua said. He spoke quietly, but everyone heard the sound as it echoed off the rock face.

"But Master, he's been dead for four days, the smell will be so bad," objected Martha, anguish in her voice. Heads nodded in agreement; surely he shouldn't disturb the dead. Immediately Martha realised her mistake. Disappointed with herself for letting go of his promise so soon after it had been made, tears of shame welled up and rolled down her scarlet cheeks.

Yeshua lifted her face and held her gaze. She looked away, unable to bear his silent reproach, so she didn't see the crooked, forgiving smile as he softly and patiently said, "Did I not promise you that if you would believe and rely on me, you would see the glory of God?"

Looking into his eyes she nodded, then turned to the crowd, searching for someone to move the stone. Sam was pushing eagerly towards them, Peter in his wake. Together the two men heaved the great mill stone away from the opening. Involuntarily, the crowd stepped back, apprehensive but still fascinated. The air stirred, as if the very breath of God was with them.

The Master stepped forward, drew himself up, looked up to

heaven and said, "Father, I thank you that you always hear me, but these people need to know that too, and that you have sent me as your messenger." His voice carried through the air, elevated with authority, amplified by the cliffs. Then he focused on the tomb entrance, raising his voice in a shout. "Lazarus, come out!" The crowd jumped as his words echoed off the limestone crags.

Mary gasped, and Martha gripped Tabitha's hand as they stood frozen, eyes fixed on the darkness beyond the doorway. Tabitha rubbed her eyes vigorously. Was that movement she saw in the shadows? She looked up at Martha's face; she'd seen it too.

A figure swayed out of the grip of the tomb's black night, and leant with one hand on the lintel. The crowd gasped and backed away. The figure was still wrapped in cloth strips, which it desperately struggled to pull from its bent head. In that instant, both Mary and Martha recognised the movement of their brother and cried out his name. Unable to see in the bright light, Lazarus stood blinking, hesitant to step further from the doorway.

"Help him. Free him from his burial clothes," coaxed the Master.

Martha ran forward, her hands trembling as she reached up to remove the material from his face and head. In an instant, Mary was beside her holding his arm to steady him.

"Lazarus, oh Lazarus!" cried Martha. She and Mary took his arms and gently guided him to a boulder to sit on. The stunned crowd hung back uncertain, but fascinated while the two sisters carefully unwrapped his arms. Their confidence grew as every swathe they removed revealed more healthy, living flesh. Whispering Lazarus' name in wonder, Elias reached out shakily and touched his nephew's cheek. More relatives and friends came forward, gently touching him in wonder and disbelief.

Lazarus met their questioning eyes with his familiar and reassuring smile. Then he began to pull out the stalks caught in the cloth wound around his torso, and Tabitha knelt to help him.

"Thanks Tab. They're unbelievably itchy." Tabitha clasped his big hands, and with them wiped her joyful tears away.

Looking up, Lazarus blinked in surprise to see the sea of watching faces for the first time. Then he looked down as Tabitha touched his knee. Was this really her Lazarus alive? The last shred of doubt left her as his warm hand stroked her cheek. He felt the warmth of a cloak that Martha wrapped around him and the gentle weight of Mary's head as she rested it on his shoulder, her face shining with tears. No one seemed to notice the unpleasant odour from the cloth strips lying on the ground. The whole family cried and laughed alternately, trying to take in what had just happened.

Villagers came forward to touch the alive-dead man, speaking his name, needing to feel his warm living flesh. Lazarus called their names as he reached out to touch their extended hands. The crowd pressed in.

Lazarus shivered, and quickly a second cloak was found for him while Tabitha brought the donkey for him to ride. They led him back along the track, which was lined with people, all marvelling at the incredible sight that was Lazarus. His coming was like a rising wave in power.

Martha walked beside him as he rode on the donkey, chiding herself for all those days when her hope had died after the tomb was sealed. It had only got harder then, but a tiny flame had refused to go out. That was why she had gone to meet the Master. She cried in gratitude, twisting round to look for the Master in the crowd, but she could not see him. Somewhere, hidden quietly in the procession, he walked with them.

People ran on ahead, calling to their neighbours and family to come and see the miracle that was Lazarus son of Reubel.

"Was that Lazarus who just rode by?" cried a man from his doorway to his neighbour, "Am I seeing things?"

"Yes, and no. Isn't it incredible? Master Lazarus is clearly alive!"

shouted back the neighbour in astonishment.

"The Rabbi Yeshua did it. The one they think is the Messiah," cried a friend as he passed by. "He just called his name, and out Lazarus walked from the tomb. He looked a bit dazed, mind you," he said, coming over to join them.

"What, the Rabbi or Master Lazarus?" grinned the man.

"Lazarus, of course!" said the friend, with a chortle. "Coming back to life after being dead for four days would be enough to confuse anyone I imagine."

"My wife needs to see this. She's been moaning about what a tragedy it was leaving those poor sisters of his. I can't wait to see her face when I tell her the news," finished the man, dashing from the house.

The incredible news rapidly spread far and wide. Reaching home, the family slipped gratefully inside. Helpfully, the disciples held back the crowd from the gate, firmly telling them to go home or to the synagogue to give thanks to God for the miracle they had seen. Once they were settled back in the house, hot water was heated for Lazarus to bathe, while Tabitha, complaining of the smell, held the burial cloths at arm's length as she went to burn them in the back garden.

Simon took the disciples back to his home that night, but Yeshua stayed with them. They had been through so much, and it was a comfort to them all to have him there.

That night, their aunt and Sara took over the cooking, and even Elias helped, much to his two sons' surprise. Lazarus, dressed warmly in his best clothes, sat close to the fire, which was banked high. Elias chose the best wine, bowing to Lazarus as he handed him a cup, then broke down and wept afresh, hugging his nephew, whom he thought of as a son.

"When your father died, it was a terrible thing to bear," said Elias, addressing everyone in the room. "But your loss was unbearable, which makes our joy at your return unspeakably sweeter to my old heart. Truly, today we have seen the miracle of all miracles in our family. After this, how can anyone disbelieve that Yeshua is the Master and Lord sent by God?"

Martha watched Yeshua's face as her uncle spoke, and it seemed to her to be the face of a shepherd caring for his sheep. Today he had safely brought more strays into the fold. Martha listened while the Master talked with Elias, his elder son Reuben and their grandfather. Each question was answered skilfully, but directed to their hearts. The ageing, opinionated man who was her uncle listened, and saw the truth set before him with open eyes. Could it get any better than this, thought Martha to herself?

Mary came and sat down beside her, putting her arms round her big sister and holding her tight.

"Sitting at the master's feet," whispered Mary. Martha smiled contentedly as she stroked Mary's hair and kissed her forehead.

Lazarus turned round to them. "And what are you two whispering about?" he asked.

"Mind your own business," laughed Mary, prodding him in the ribs, before throwing her arms around him, fresh tears welling up in her shining brown eyes.

Lazarus wiped them away with his sleeve. "I suppose you'll both stop leaking, eventually," he said, seeing tears forming in Martha's eyes too.

"Not while there is so much to be joyful about," she replied.

"It's enough to make anyone dance with joy!" exclaimed Elizabeth, doing a few quick steps, and Martha felt like joining her.

Chapter Seventeen

The Tide Rises

The next morning, in the grey light before dawn, Martha stood with Peter and Andrew, who were the first to arrive from Simon's. They gladly took the food offered by Tabitha. The Master shivered in the keen west wind while they waited for the others to come, so Martha sent Tabitha into the house to fetch Lazarus' old wool cloak. Gratefully Yeshua pulled it tightly around himself. He looked tired.

"I wish you'd stay longer" she said, knowing the answer, but saying it anyway.

"It will be better if we go. You know that. Besides, you still have a houseful of guests, and you will be kept busier than you imagine." Martha wondered what he might mean. "Lazarus has caused quite a stir, and word will spread quickly," he went on. "Many people will be curious and come looking for him asking questions, and that I must leave you to deal with, for a while. But you are ready." Martha was about to ask what he meant by this last remark, but Lazarus joined them and the opportunity was gone.

The men embraced, holding one another's arms. Yeshua looked long and hard into the eyes of the man he'd called back from death.

"Where will you go?" Lazarus asked him.

"Somewhere out towards Ephraim, until it's time."

Lazarus nodded, a grim look on his fair face, as he said, "Many more will believe in you now. The demand will be great, and so will the danger."

"For you too my friend, but my father has chosen you well. Keep Martha and Mary safe, for they are chosen too and will speak to the generations of women that come after them."

Lazarus watched Martha talking rapidly to Miriam and Susanna in the short time they had before their departure. Despite everything she had been through he had never seen her so at peace, and so full of joy.

Then, with a big grin on his face, he said, "Firstly, I have the tricky problem of explaining to the temple priest that I have gone there to give thanks to God because I was dead and buried and now I'm alive. What he's going to make of that is anybody's guess. Is there a sacrifice to cover such an event?"

Yeshua was still laughing as he embraced Martha and the sleepy-eyed Mary, their uncle and cousins, who had joined them to say goodbye. Then the Master and Lord turned away silently, and left them. In the distance a dog barked as the sun bathed the land in its rose-tinted light.

By midday, the miraculous news of the resurrection in Bethany had spread to the innermost parts of Jerusalem and to the farthest outlying communities. Contagiously, it spread among the vast Jewish community and then beyond. At the heart of the story was Yeshua, the man who claimed he was God, but however people responded to the truth, the tide was rising.

Two days later, Mary marched into the courtyard, slamming the gate behind her.

"What's wrong?" called Martha from the grinding stone. She was taking advantage of the fine day to catch up with some chores.

"There were strangers up at the tomb again today. I scrubbed the whitewash off yesterday, to try and make it less obvious, but someone must be telling them where it is. Have they no respect for our family tomb?" Mary threw her hands up in exasperation, then carried on grumbling as she carelessly abandoned her boots on the steps and disappeared into the house.

Martha frowned. The number of sightseers was increasing every day. Rachel and Joseph had been plagued by friends and distant family, all eager to hear their account of the extraordinary events. Lazarus had been called upon to answer their questions, which he did willingly, sharing passionately everything he knew of the Master and his teachings. Satisfied, Joseph's visitors had finally departed to enthusiastically spread their new conviction that the Rabbi was none other than the long-awaited Messiah. More came, hopeful of finding Yeshua and being healed by the one the temple seemed so set against, but mostly they were satisfied to see and hear from Lazarus.

Hearing the gate slam and Mary's raised voice, Lazarus wandered out into the courtyard. "What's Mary riled about?" he asked.

"More sightseers disturbing the tomb. On the whole, I think most villagers are beginning to find it a bit of a nuisance. It's hard to go anywhere without being stopped and asked questions," explained Martha. "Sometimes it's hard to know what to say to them. I try to tell them about the Rabbi and who he is, so they understand he really did bring you back to life. But so often they're only interested in the petty details and they want proof."

"Some just can't seem to see it. But we mustn't give up on them. The Master would want us to keep trying."

"I know. It's just you and Mary are so good at speaking to them.

I'm more of a doer," said Martha quietly.

Lazarus shook his head vigorously. "Martha, that is simply not true. I've heard you pray for others, bringing hope and encouragement where there was none. I've seen you show extraordinary kindness and give help all your life. You speak out your faith and demonstrate it in everything you do."

"Not in everything," she muttered, but then she smiled at him and felt encouraged. "Now if our leaders behaved more like the Master and were less blind and stupid, this would all be a lot easier."

Lazarus laughed, "Now you're beginning to sound like Mary."

"Well, she's right, isn't she?"

"One thing they are not is stupid. Many are greedy and deluded, thinking things are one way when they're another, but by holding onto the little power they have left to govern our people under Roman rule, they enable us to practise the laws and customs given to us by Moses. Now, pray that I will have the right words for those I meet today," finished Lazarus, as he closed the gate behind him. Martha went to find Mary.

**

Lazarus spent every moment he could talking with those who came seeking him. The greatness of what was happening around him took his breath away. It was like a snowball gathering speed as it rolled down the slopes of Mount Hermon, and upon this Lazarus fixed his attention and hope.

It was late afternoon, and looked like rain, so Tabitha was hurriedly filling a sack with the last of the flour. She almost spilt some when someone began hammering on the gate. Then Reuben's deep voice demanded that it be opened. Hastily, she drew back the bolt and discovered that Sam was there too.

"Surprise," said Sam, cheerfully, but then added with a frown,

"Why is the gate bolted, Tab?"

"Bethany is being overrun by sightseers," she replied curtly. "Lazarus is famous, or hadn't you heard? You'd better come in before you get wet." Large drops of rain had begun to fall. Sam carried the flour sack into the house for her, but Reuben seemed agitated and kept looking around impatiently.

"Where's Lazarus? I need to speak to him urgently," he demanded.

"Father has sent us with an important message for him," Sam explained.

Tabitha told them that everyone was out, but she was wondering what message was so important that Elias had sent both his sons to deliver it.

"Typical," said Sam. "We come all this way and they're out." he winked at Tabitha. "I've always said you were the only reliable adult in the household." Tabitha giggled, appreciating Sam's sense of humour and the compliment, but Reuben ignored him, lost in his own thoughts and staring intensely into the distance.

"Now it's raining I'm sure they'll be back soon. The streets are full of strangers asking questions about Lazarus and Rabbi Yeshua, so it takes a while to get about," said Tabitha proudly. Tabitha saw the look exchanged by the two brothers; it worried her.

At that moment, the gate rattled and in came Lazarus, Martha and Mary. They were so engrossed in conversation that their cloaks were half off before they noticed Reuben and Sam seated in the gloom of the kitchen. Mary gave a gasp of delight and hurried over to greet her two big cousins. The brothers looked heartily relieved to see them.

"The Sanhedrin met yesterday. It's not sounding too good for the Rabbi Yeshua," said Reuben, ignoring the women and speaking directly to Lazarus. "Can we go somewhere private to talk?"

Lazarus looked questioningly at Sam as he led his two cousins into the main room and shut the door behind them.

Mary was cross. She wanted to know what Reuben could possibly have to say to Lazarus that he could not say to them at the same time. Martha was deeply concerned, but tried to keep her thoughts under control. Mary and Tabitha, however, felt no such constraint, and discussed all the possibilities while Martha tried to keep them busy.

A while later, Lazarus came wandering into the kitchen, leaving Reuben and Sam stretched out before the fire. Mary didn't waste a moment. "What's happened?" she demanded. "What message is so important that it required both Sam and Reuben to deliver it?"

Lazarus looked steadily at Martha when he spoke, and her calmness was reassuring.

"They came to warn us of developments in Jerusalem which may now, directly affect our family."

"What developments?" demanded Mary. "Wasn't it bad enough that they tried to stone the Master the last two times he came to Jerusalem?"

"We all know the Pharisees and Sadducees have wanted to put a stop to the Master's activities for some time, but their attempts so far have failed," said their brother. Mary glared at him. "So, my resurrection..." he paused, swallowing hard. He had no memory of his death, only waking up in the tomb and wondering at the light streaming in. He had some memories of the fever and understood what had happened to him, but only because he'd been told. The rest was a blank. He wished his friend Yeshua was still with them. "So, my resurrection has goaded them into giving an official order asking for details of the Master's whereabouts, so they can arrest him and put him out of the way."

Mary exploded with anger. "Put him out of the way? They are openly declaring their intention to kill him. Go on, say it - they fear him! But he isn't the threat." Her voice cracked with emotion. "They cling to their false beliefs rather than embracing the Messiah sent by God. Yeshua said their father was the devil, the father of lies. And he was so right."

Martha looked steadily at her brother. Despite the rapid beating of her heart, she said, "Exactly. How does this involve our family?"

Sam was standing in the doorway, having been drawn by Mary's outburst. "This house was the last place the Master was seen, and the fact that he called Laz out of the tomb in front of so many witnesses is not exactly a secret," he said. Reuben, his lips pressed together, nodded solemnly over Sam's shoulder.

Mary paused, taking in what had just been said. "So they may come looking for him here? And they'll certainly be asking for information about his whereabouts."

Again, Reuben nodded. "Specifically, they have said that anyone seeing the Rabbi must report it immediately. From what Lazarus has told us, the Master knew this would happen, that's why he's disappeared."

"That makes sense," said Martha, remembering how the Master had apologised for leaving them to deal with the aftermath of Lazarus' resurrection. She hadn't understood then, but she was beginning to now.

"But there is more," said Reuben, gravely. "Father has many good friends in the Sanhedrin and among the elders and temple staff. He is certain that Caiaphas and his father-in-law Annas will not tolerate the Master any longer. The Master's influence over the people is becoming too great and it might upset the balance of power. The last thing we need is another riot or uprising. If the high priests can't keep the peace, the Romans will step in and they'll lose what power they have. Caiaphas has prophesied that it was better that one man should die for the people than the whole nation be destroyed."

"But Caiaphas said more," interrupted Sam. "He also said that it was better that one man die for the whole nation, in order to bring the scattered children of God from far and wide and unite them into one body. Now that is a real puzzle. Many are thinking of passages written by the prophet Isaiah."

"But what does it all mean?" asked Tabitha in frustration.

"From prison and trial, they led him away to his death," said Mary. "But who among the people realised that he was dying for their sins, that he was suffering their punishment? It's in the passage about the Lord's suffering servant." Everyone turned to look at Mary, her face pale and drained. "That whole passage is about him, the Lord. But it goes far beyond anything we have yet realised. The Messiah has come for everyone, because it also says, 'I will make you a light for the gentiles that you may bring my salvation to the ends of the earth.'" Mary stared wildly at their stunned faces as the implications of her own words sunk in.

"Now it makes sense," whispered Lazarus.

"And they want to kill him, their Messiah," said Martha in disgust and tears. "This is more than blindness. Now I agree. This is the devil's work."

"Father is sure there are many sympathisers," said Reuben, with unusual passion in his voice, "but they cannot openly stand against our leaders. That would bring ruin for them and their families."

"Cowards, all of them," pronounced Mary, her voice shaking.

"Not all are as brave as you Mary," said Sam, trying to sooth his cousin. "Politics are complex, especially in Jerusalem."

"They have to think of their families and dependants, their responsibilities," sighed Reuben. "That's why Father wants Lazarus to keep a very low profile. You mustn't go on telling people about the Messiah," he begged.

Mary turned towards Lazarus. "Do you agree with this?" she demanded.

"I see that Uncle Elias loves us and wants to protect us," replied Lazarus quietly. "But I also know that our Lord and Master did not restore my life so I could remain silent. If it is his plan that I be arrested, or worse, then I am not afraid for myself, but I would not willingly put my family through that again." He winced, seeing the pain his words had caused. "Mary, you are right, God's plan for his son is far greater than we had ever realised. But do you see Mary, all choices have consequences?"

Mary frowned and held her tongue. The thought of losing Lazarus again was unbearable.

"We all have a lot to think about," said Sam, seriously. "But the smell of Martha's cooking is becoming extremely distracting. Can we please eat, dearest Martha, before I faint from hunger?"

Reuben and Sam were to stay overnight, to make the most of their time together. They sat around the fire and talked long into the night, as they had when they were younger and were still free of care. Martha felt that having time with them was a gift, and it gave her courage when the morning came.

Chapter Eighteen

The Master Returns

Late spring, seven days before Passover, Thursday

As the weeks went by and Passover approached, a green haze of new shoots began to appear in the once brown fields. Rumours reached them suggesting the Master might have returned to Galilee, and in this Martha found comfort, knowing that at least he hadn't been arrested.

The temple had sent an escort of police with Malchus, the high priest's servant, to Bethany, a few days after Sam and Reuben had brought their message. If Martha had known what was going on, she would have been terrified for her brother's safety, but by the time they heard, Malchus had already left. The good people of Bethany had been so willing to tell all they knew of Lazarus' movements and the departure of the Rabbi Yeshua that the police had been overwhelmed, and Malchus was convinced there was nothing to be gained by investigating further. He hadn't even got as far as their gate, according to Joseph, and what was more, sightseers had quickly stopped coming to their village for the time being.

When Joseph had told Lazarus all about it, he'd seemed highly amused, but Martha trembled when she realised how close they had come to being discovered. Mary, on the other hand, had been disappointed, feeling they had missed an opportunity to speak to an influential person at the temple about Yeshua. Martha was very grateful that Mary had been kept at home all day helping her clean out the storeroom and knew without a shadow of doubt that the Lord God had protected them, once more.

* * *

Mary wandered along the veranda, sleepily rubbing her eyes, and stood stretching in a pool of cold sunshine. Martha looked up, admiring the aura of calm that surrounded her sister in the mornings.

"Sorry," said Mary, "I've overslept again."

"I didn't say a word," replied Martha, as she peeled onions.

"You don't have to," said Mary. "It's all in your tone. Is Laz about?"

Martha hesitated before replying, which immediately got Mary's attention. "Where's he gone?" she asked. But she didn't need an answer; she knew from the look on Martha's face. "The Master's coming back, isn't he?" she said.

Martha nodded, unable to hide her pleasure. "He sent a message early this morning. With only seven days before the celebration of Passover, they're coming in from Jericho and they've asked to stay with us." She sounded excited. Mary did a little jig of joy.

Shouts and a loud scuffling noise came from the alleyway between their property and the next. Tabitha came running in, her cheeks flushed. For one moment Martha thought it might be the temple authorities come back, but the deep bleating of anxious sheep reminded her that Lazarus and Jacob had just brought the best of the young rams down off the hill, to be ready for the Passover.

"We're back," cried Tabitha, out of breath.

Martha sprang up and ran out to help. It took some time for the four of them to settle the animals in a separate pen at the back of the house. Jacob watched while Lazarus carefully inspected the animals before rubbing a protective layer of specially prepared oil over their legs and hooves. Lazarus explained he would make his final choice two days before the feast. The chosen lambs would need to be perfect for the sacrifice at the temple.

Martha and Lazarus returned to the house, leaving Tabitha to bring Jacob in for breakfast. The two children leant on the hurdle, deep in conversation, Tabitha was giggling.

As soon as Mary heard Lazarus was planning to go and meet the Master, she wanted to go too. Which made Martha sigh.

"Martha, are you afraid?" asked Mary.

"Of course I am. I dread his capture, I dread what they might do, but now I understand that some things are more important to God. You reminded me of some more scripture that followed on from the ones you said when Reuben and Sam came to warn us." Quietly Martha began to recite, "When he sees all that is accomplished by his anguish, he will be satisfied. And because of what he has experienced, my righteous servant will make it possible for many to be counted righteous, for he will bear all their sins. How is that even possible?"

"I don't know," said Mary, tight-lipped. "It's the beginning part of that scripture that fills me with foreboding."

"But he will be satisfied by what he accomplishes. And many will be counted righteous, just like him. Mary, he will do something wonderful we can't understand, of that I'm sure." Martha's voice was almost pleading in her need for Mary to feel the hope that she felt.

In the silence that followed Mary broke off a piece of freshly baked bread, while Martha continued to chop vegetables, adding them to the huge pot she had on the fire. Absentmindedly, Mary stirred the vegetables, listening to the comforting sizzle.

"Today, I'll need your help here," Martha ventured to say.

"I know. This time I'll stay and help you," sighed Mary, but the relief on Martha's face made it easier to bear.

Just then, Lazarus interrupted them to say he was leaving, and that he would help Tabitha load up at the well on the way.

"Did you pay the boys?" asked Martha.

He put the heel of his palm to his forehead. "No, I forgot!"

"All right, I'll see to it," said Martha, with yet another sigh. "Now go, before I change my mind."

Mary and Martha began the preparations for their guests, until Tabitha returned with the water. Mary helped her unload, while Martha went to the kitchen to check on the stew. When Mary came in alone, Martha looked up questioningly. She explained she'd sent Tabitha off to pay Josh and Jacob. After all, she was faster than either of them, and knew exactly where to find the flock.

While Mary made a second trip to the well, dropping off medicine and food to someone on the way, Martha baked and prepared for the evening meal, all the while planning for the following evening, the start of the Sabbath. She was relieved Ellie would be along soon. Her plans turned to prayer, and then her focus to the events unfolding in the world beyond her gate. The Messiah was coming back to Jerusalem. What joy for the people, what hope he brought, but her fear at what it might cost him was never far from her thoughts. Her fears for Lazarus were rekindled too. How she longed to see Miriam and the others, and to hear all that the Master had done since Ephraim.

Mary returned, saying she had seen groups of pilgrims strung out along the road coming up from Jericho. Simon had relatives staying with him already.

Later that morning, Lazarus sent word that the Master was

nearing Bethany, but intended to go straight into Jerusalem for the afternoon.

Chapter Nineteen

Going into Jerusalem

Thursday afternoon

Martha, Mary and Tabitha stepped out into the spring sunshine, and accompanied by Rachel, Lizzy and her little daughter, they joined the little pockets of villagers heading down the hill towards the main road. Ellie had run home to fetch her brother. As usual, word had travelled fast.

Bethany was set a little off the main road from Jericho to Jerusalem, near where it forked to climb steeply up to Bethphage, a town built high up on the northwest spur of the Mount of Olives. Bethphage commanded great views of the beautiful walled city across the deep Kidron gorge.

The town's people had begun to congregate near the junction with the main road, so Martha and the others joined them. They stared impatiently into the distance, hoping to see some sign of Lazarus and their friends amongst the drifts of pilgrims passing by. Two dusty men came striding hurriedly up the track, one tall and thin and the other broad and fair. Mary recognised them instantly and she waved and called out to Philip and Nathanael, who came hurrying over, relieved to see their familiar faces.

"Oh, thank goodness we've found you," gasped Philip. "Lazarus said to look out for you. The Master's sent us to find a donkey and her colt, but we haven't a clue where to start looking." He rolled his eyes.

"How hard could that be in such a small town?" joked Nathanael.

Looking knowingly at one another, Mary and Martha directed them to a nearby well-kept courtyard. It was no surprise the Master had decided to ride on into Jerusalem; the road to Bethphage was steep, and they'd already walked a good way that morning.

Pushing through the gathering crowd, Martha and Mary saw their brother waving to them. The Master and his followers were seated in the shade of some olive trees, and Lazarus left this to greet them. People pointed and stared at him as he passed by, and immediately Martha was alert and felt uneasy. Lazarus was well known to the locals. In Bethany she hadn't minded the attention, as it was a tight-knit community, but out here on the open road surrounded by strangers, the threat of arrest seemed more real.

Mary was eager to go to the Master, but Martha and Lazarus persuaded her to wait. He was already surrounded by so many people, and more were filing past all the time. Martha suddenly became aware she was stooping, anxious not to draw attention to herself. What was she doing? Trying to hide? She straightened up, feeling foolish, and got an odd look from Mary and Lazarus.

Philip and Nathanael came back, pushing through the crowds, leading an almost white donkey with a pale sandy colt trotting nervously beside her. The animals were strong and well-kept, with straight backbones, and were instantly recognisable.

"How did you get David to let these two prized animals out of his sight?" asked Tabitha, in disbelief, as she rubbed the colt's ears to soothe him.

Philip shook his head. "The yard was easy to find because the donkeys were tied up in full view, like they were waiting for us. It's true we were challenged by a few of the neighbours, but when we said that the Master had need of them and would return them later, they didn't object. Quite honestly, we were in such a hurry we simply untied them and led them here."

"I half expected an irate owner to come running after us," grinned Nathanael. "I'm amazed no one did."

"If you knew the man who owned those donkeys you'd realise just what a miracle it is," said Mary, her eyes wide in disbelief.

"But isn't that the whole point?" asked Martha, quietly. "The Master actually knows what's in people's hearts."

Martha could see the disciples with the Master, but there was no sign of Miriam and the other women. She wondered where they might be, but before she had a chance to ask Lazarus he'd introduced them to a middle-aged couple who were talking with Barsabbas and Matthias.

"Martha, Mary, how lovely to finally meet you," said the short, plump, enthusiastic Mary Cleopas. "We've heard so much about you from Miriam, Salome and the lovely Little Mary, as we call her." Her joke seemed to amuse the couple. The man was tall, greying round the temples, with a cheerful manner. Martha and Mary looked puzzled.

"My wife means dear Mary Alphaeus," her husband clarified, with a warm smile. "I'm Cleopas and this is my wife Mary." He bowed courteously.

"We're always so pleased to meet more of our beloved Rabbi's followers," said Mary Cleopas, taking Rachel and Lizzy's hands as Lazarus introduced them. "And neighbours of Martha, Mary and Lazarus too. How wonderful. Do you have family living locally?" she asked.

Rachel nodded, a little overwhelmed by the woman's breathless enthusiasm, but soon she found herself drawn into the conversation. Mary Cleopas also had grandchildren in Jerusalem. Seeing their missing women friends' approach, Martha and Mary excused themselves hurriedly and went to greet them.

Martha was particularly pleased to see Miriam; they had had so little time together with the excitement of Lazarus' return to life. Salome was pleased to see Tabitha and her siblings, who had joined Tabitha on the way passed Juthine's home. Mary Joseph was with them, riding a donkey, and Mary Alphaeus informed them that Joanna was soon to join them in Jerusalem. Everyone was talking at once, so Mary Joseph had a job to make herself heard as she urged them all to move to one side. They were partially blocking the road, causing a bottleneck for the pilgrims streaming along it.

It had taken Susanna and Salome some time to secure a donkey in Jericho, especially with all the holiday traffic heading up to Jerusalem, but they had made swifter progress with Mary Joseph riding. Despite this, they had been hard pressed to catch up with the men on the steep fifteen-mile climb, and now flung themselves down in the tiny patch of shade near the Master. Martha and Mary were even more delighted to hear that they would be staying with them for the Sabbath and at last they would have a chance to catch up on all the news. After that, the women would be moving to their lodgings in Jerusalem, courtesy of Joanna. It looked as though it was going to be a Passover to remember, with friends and family joining many of them.

The Master wandered over, exchanging a few words with his mother, obviously amused by the temporary blockage they had caused on the road. Martha wondered at his easy manner. Was she the only one who was alert to the danger around them? Looking to her friends, she saw tell-tale signs in the furrow on Miriam's brow, Salome's protectiveness towards Tabitha, Susanna's darting looks at the crowds and Mary's constant gaze on the road ahead. No, they were all alert and watchful.

The Rabbi called to his close friends that it was time to move on. The donkey and her bewildered colt were led forward. Cloaks were eagerly thrown over her bare back, causing the colt to shy. Nathanael did his best to reassure the wild-eyed and trembling beast.

"Not a good start," he remarked to Philip, who led the colt's mother.

Martha watched as some people cut palm branches from a stand of trees nearby and hurriedly came to join those who already stood waiting with theirs. She marvelled at this gesture, which was more often used to greet royalty. Now more than ever, she began to realise that many truly did understand just who the Master was.

Before Yeshua had even sat on the donkey, cloaks and prayer shawls were being strewn in their path. These the donkey stretched down to sniff before carefully stepping onto the carpet.

"Prayer shawls," Martha whispered in wonder to Miriam, who stood beside her. Wasn't this another way of acknowledging him as the Lord and King? They clasped hands, thrilled.

As the Master rode forward, people ran ahead laying palm branches in his path, while others waved them and called out. "Praised and blessed is the coming kingdom of our ancestor David," cried an old man, moved by the sight and stirred by the memory of the scripture which promised that King David's throne would be established forever. This must surely be the hoped-for descendant.

"Hosanna to the son of David, the Messiah! Blessed, praised and glorified is he who comes in the name of the Lord," cried another voice. Others joined in, and the praise became louder. "Hosanna in the highest!" they shouted, their excitement rising.

Martha, Miriam and the others hurried after the Master, their voices choked with emotion as they joined in the praise. Mary slipped her arm through Martha's and squeezed it tight. With shining cheeks, she lifted her voice to heaven and began to sing. Those nearby quickly joined in the familiar refrain. Martha felt like she was floating on air.

The white donkey stretched out her neck as she began the climb toward Bethphage carrying Yeshua, with the others following him closely. At this point, Martha and Mary reluctantly fell behind, eventually losing sight of their friends in the crowd as they turned heavy-hearted towards home. Tabitha and Ellie joined them as they made their way back through the olive groves towards Bethany. There was still plenty left to do before their guests returned that evening.

Martha had found it especially hard to tear herself away from the procession. It had brought her such joy to see Yeshua being acknowledged so openly as their Messiah, the son of God, the one who would rescue and help his people. Miriam's promise to bring back a full account that evening brought her comfort.

Mary put her arm around her as they walked together. "I'm sure he'll be safe today," she said thoughtfully.

"Having you with me is comforting too," Martha replied.

"I'm surprised she came so willingly," teased Tabitha. "But today I think we all longed to follow the Master."

"Such a wise head on such young shoulders," said Mary, tickling Tabitha from behind with a palm branch she was still carrying. Tabitha brushed it away, and then, realising what Mary was doing, she tried to grab it. Mary dodged and dashed away with Tabitha in hot pursuit. Near the back of the house, Mary climbed an olive tree and Tabitha scrambled up beside her. Here Martha and Ellie found them, still panting and looking like a pair of roosting chickens.

* * *

Lazarus walked with the Master as they began to descend into

Jerusalem. Excitement mounted as word of the Master's arrival spread ahead of them, and the greetings only got louder and more enthusiastic as the crowds grew along the route. Yeshua was surrounded closely by his disciples, but Lazarus wondered who was really protecting who. The women were further back in the crowd, but were thrilled by the response of those around them. The fear of the opposition that awaited him in Jerusalem was temporarily forgotten.

The shouts of greeting and acknowledgment reached new heights as the Master approached the bridge across the Kidron valley, drowning out the noise from the churning river below. The colt had been glued to his mother's side the whole time, but now he hesitated, afraid to cross the exposed structure with the crowd pressed so tightly against him. The man riding the mother reached back, ruffling the colt's bristly neck, and with a click of his tongue urged him to follow. The colt felt his fear subside, and stepping high he crossed over the stone bridge. Before the Golden Gate he pulled back into the crowd, his halter rope taut, his head raised over his mother's rump, eyes white-rimmed and rolling, but again the soothing voice and the steady hand of the strange man made him calm. The colt's long ears flicked back listening, and he decided to trust the man. With newfound courage, he followed his mother and her rider into the deep shadow of the imposing double arch. As he stepped out into the blinding sunlight beyond, a wall of noise and unfamiliar smells hit his senses as together, the people shouted, "Hosanna!" In his excitement the colt brayed wildly.

Chapter Twenty

An Anointing

〽

Thursday evening, the start of the sixth day before Passover

As the afternoon wore on, Martha, Mary, Tabitha and Ellie's excitement grew. Juthine had delivered bread and promised to bring more the next day, so, with what Martha had baked that day, they would have enough to feed everyone over the Sabbath.

It was almost evening when the gate rattled wildly and young James burst in, announcing that their guests were just coming up the hill.

Martha, her heart racing, dashed to get her shawl and wash her hands, while Mary and Tabitha tidied one another up. Ellie quietly showed the panting James to a seat and washed his feet. The others weren't far behind, pouring into the courtyard unceremoniously. Soon everyone was washed and seated comfortably in the main room. The women flopped down in the kitchen, heaving sighs of relief. They were exhausted, but very happy to be there. The Master and Lazarus came in last. Tabitha flung herself at the Master, hugging his waist. He lifted her high in his strong arms before embracing Mary and Martha warmly. For Martha, it felt like her family arriving home safely after a long, dangerous journey full of uncertainty, and not at all like having the Messiah, the son of God, being with them.

Simon of Bethany and Michael joined them shortly after, with Joseph close on their heels, carrying a dish sent by Rachel with the promise she'd be over to help them shortly.

In the bedlam that ensued, Martha did not miss Mary, assuming that like herself she was busy with their guests. So when Miriam asked where she was, Martha was taken aback. It was getting dark outside, and it was unlike Mary to miss a single moment of the Master's visit. Not surprisingly, Tabitha found her in the loft above the store cupboard, which they were sharing together while they had guests. However, she crept back down the ladder without disturbing Mary, and went to tell Martha.

Martha coughed as she reached the top of the ladder. "Everything all right?" she asked, seeing Mary sitting cross legged in the middle of her sleeping mat. Mary shook her head.

"I just need to be by myself, to pray and think. So much is happening, Martha. It's hard to take it all in, but I've had this feeling that this time what we fear will happen." Her voice was trembling as she spoke. "I don't know if I can bear it."

Alarmed, Martha climbed up and sat facing her, knees drawn up. There was a long pause before she spoke.

"Mary, it was prophesied long ago; he is the Messiah, the anointed one, sent by God. The scriptures say some terrible things will happen to him; his life will be an offering for sin, but they also say something wonderful will happen as a result of it. Like being made righteous before God? Only the sacrifice of animals has been able to achieve that throughout our long history. And yet he has been sent to rescue us from the consequences of our sins. What happens next is in the Almighty's hands. All we can do is pray for strength and faith not to fail him. I dread it as much as you and the others, but we will bear it together, as we did when Lazarus died – as we have born everything together since you were a child."

Martha looked down at the cloudy alabaster flask lying partly hidden in Mary's lap. "It's all I have that is truly mine," she whispered softly.

Martha paused, not sure what Mary meant.

"You will never need anything while your family surrounds you," Martha assured her. "But truly this is yours, and before heaven no one else can lay claim to it. Use it well, and trust your heart."

Mary smiled weakly, but Martha knew that whatever Mary was planning, Yeshua would be her soul concern.

"We'll be serving dinner soon," Martha called back up the ladder as she stepped off the bottom rung, wondering what the outcome of this melancholia would be. Mary could be passionate and impulsive at times, and at others, compassionate and thoughtful.

Someone called Martha's name loudly from the kitchen, so she hurried off to see what was going on. Everyone was poised, mouths watering in anticipation, as Lazarus finished praying the blessing. Mary's head was covered, and Martha's quick eyes saw a flask hanging loosely in her hand, partly concealed. Mary went forward, determinedly stepping over and around their guests seated on the floor. Immediately, all eyes were upon her. Her cheerful and unquenchable presence had been missed while they'd waited for dinner, and now they greeted her with respect, but she hardly seemed to notice them.

Yeshua sat cross-legged, close to their brother near the hearth, bathed in its warmth. He watched Mary with curiosity as he stretched out and leant on one elbow. As his eyes met hers, she dropped her gaze, unable to look him in the face, and fell to her knees. Her sudden action caused some of the guests to wonder what this extraordinary young woman was doing, kneeling with her arms outstretched, palms upwards, and her head bowed to the floor in total submission. Martha held her breath as words began to tumble from Mary's lips.

"Messiah, Son of God, Rescuer and King. Lamb of God, Redeemer and Emmanuel. Prophet, High Priest and Son of David. You are the Light of the World and the Bread of Life. You are all of these and more, Lord of all!" she said passionately, reverently worshipping him. Not a sound could be heard in the room. On the floor beside her stood the alabaster flask given to her by her father for her future, and it was all she would ever own.

Martha, drawn by her sisters' worship, found herself quietly thanking the father for sending his son to be with them and show them the way. At the kitchen door, crowded together, their faces beautified as they worshipped him too, were her women friends. Her heart swelled with gratitude to God for the love they showed her and that she felt for them. Overcome by the revelation of God's love for his creation, his people, she too fell to her knees.

Mary, her face radiant with love and understanding, held out in trembling hands the flask which was her offering. Then, in one swift movement, she broke the neck of the bottle on the hearth. There was a sharp intake of breath from the onlookers. The red oil trickled over her fingers as the heavenly aroma of the spikenard began to escape and infuse the air.

Moving closer to the Master, Mary carefully began to pour the perfumed oil over his feet and ankles. Then with a flick of her head, she released the long cascades of her luxuriant hair and stooped low so she could wipe his feet with her tresses. The room was filled with perfumed silence as Mary worshipped at his feet, honouring him with everything she had, pouring it all out onto his feet.

"His feet are already clean," whispered young James, to Matthew. "What is she doing?"

"It's extravagance beyond most of our means," his cousin whispered back. "She appears to be anointing his feet."

"What is the meaning of this?" John asked Lazarus, taken aback by Mary's action.

"Matthew is right, she is anointing his feet," whispered Lazarus.

"Her worship was beautiful," admitted James. "So fitting for our Lord."

"But all that costly spikenard poured out," said Andrew, watching it pool beneath Yeshua's feet on the flagstones.

"Surely this could have been sold and given to the poor, not wasted like this," said Judas.

"At least it's not been wasted on vanity," added Thomas, surprised at Judas' insensitive remark, but not sure whether to defend Mary's action or not.

Martha, bristling with the injustice of the remark, stepped defensively forward. Mary was devoted to the sick and poor of Bethany, as was she. Besides, this was Mary's dowry, didn't she have the right to decided how she would use it? The Lord was worth every bottle of spikenard in the world. Mary understood that, Judas clearly did not.

Martha stopped her ranting thoughts as Yeshua sat up. His gaze rested softly on Mary's bent head. "Leave her alone," he said, like an adult talking to children who don't understand. "What she has done is beautiful to me. God intended her to keep this," he pointed to the empty broken bottle, "to anoint my body, in preparation for burial." There was a gasp from the room, and Miriam caught hold of Susanna's hand and held it tight. "You will always have the poor with you, but not me. Mary's act is in recognition of my death."

His last word reverberated around the room. Mary's upturned face went pale as she fully understood the meaning of what she had done. For Martha, it was like a knife being driven through her heart. They had known this, but hearing the harsh reality from

Yeshua's own lips drove it home. Mary fell forward in a swoon. He had proclaimed his own death right here in front of them all. Lazarus stared at the Master's anointed feet and remembered the lambs whose feet he had rubbed oil over, only that morning. He closed his eyes to squeeze back the tears.

Judas hung his head, but his fists were clenched. He was right, wanton waste was not encouraged in their laws. James reached over and put a hand on his arm.

"Let it go, brother," he said, quietly. "You are our treasurer, you only thought to do your job. Sometimes we do not understand the Master's ways, or his purpose. But what he just said should be of greater concern to all of us."

"He's dangerous to be around," said Judas vehemently under his breath. James looked sideways at him, concerned. A change had come over Judas, but the Master's last words still rang loudly in his ears, drawing his attention away from Judas' dark mood.

Overcome by her actions and the Master's final words, Mary began to shake. Martha was quickly at her side, helping her to rise and leave the room. Mary's shawl lay on the flagstones, slowly soaking up the red pool of oil. The women made way for them as they passed through the kitchen and out into the dimly lit courtyard. Mary breathed deeply and became calmer. Martha watched her carefully, with pride and respect.

"Can you help me with my hair?" she asked. It hung limp and heavy, dripping with oil. A broad, loving smile crept onto Martha's face, and soon she was back with warm water, a comb and towels.

"Your hair will be as soft as silk, and the whole house will smell wonderful for quite a while," said Martha, as she combed the oil evenly through Mary's hair, then wiped the excess from it. She finished by tenderly bathing Mary's face.

The gate rattled, as though the wind was blowing it, and then they heard the low murmur of voices outside in the street. Alarmed,

Mary ran to the gate and peered through an empty knot hole, curiosity getting the better of her.

"Goodness! Come and look, Martha. There's a crowd of people out there, but I don't recognise anyone. No, wait, there are one or two villagers among them." Imploring Mary to come inside, Martha went to fetch her brother.

"It's all right Martha, I'll deal with them. They're probably just sightseers looking for the Master," said Lazarus reassuringly. He left the table and went out. Poor Martha shook her head. Invited guests were welcome, but crowds of strangers hanging about after dark made her feel uneasy. However she still followed her brother to the gate. Mary hovered nearby, her wet hair covered by a shawl. Alert, Miriam and Susanna had joined her.

As Lazarus opened the gate, there was a loud exclamation from the shadowy crowd outside. Several villages greeted him, and this caused the crowd to press forward. Unperturbed, Lazarus raised his hand, and the crowd stopped and became silent.

"What do you want, good people?" he asked.

"Are you Lazarus, the one who was dead in a tomb for four days?" asked a man standing near the front.

"I am," he replied, his voice carrying in the night air. Martha came out, enveloped in her shawl and carrying a lamp, which she hung high on a hook by the gate. A stranger tried to speak to her, but she backed politely away to the safety of the partially open gate, breathing hard.

"What was it like?" asked the man. Lazarus had been asked this many times before.

"It's hard to say really, you see, I was dead. It was only when I heard the Master's voice calling to me in the darkness to 'come out' and saw the daylight streaming in through the open door of the tomb that I really became aware of my surroundings. I staggered out and as the grave clothes were pulled off my face I felt the warmth of the sun." The crowd weren't satisfied. Many of them had come miles for a chance to see him and the Rabbi everyone was saying was the Messiah.

"But if you were dead, how could you hear anyone calling you?" asked someone else from the crowd.

"I don't know," replied Lazarus, earnestly. "But the whole of Bethany will testify to my death, yet here I am alive and well."

Joseph slipped out past Lazarus to fetch a second lamp, which he hung over his gate, on the opposite side of the street. Noah and Shem stood either side of him with their arms folded.

"Sorry about this," Lazarus called over to Joseph, who nodded and planted his feet more firmly. Lazarus regathered his thoughts, and continued, "It's Rabbi Yeshua, the Master, that you really need to speak to. He is the one who has the power and authority from God. You must all have heard of his amazing teaching, and the signs and wonders he does to accompany what he says?" Heads nodded.

"We certainly heard about him breaking the laws given by Moses," said a loud voice from the back, causing heads to turn to a large man standing in the shadows.

"But what about all the people he's healed?" pointed out Lazarus. "How do you explain that?"

"That's why some of us are here," called another.

"Then tell us where he is staying, so we can hear from him ourselves," said a woman, standing near Joseph and his sons, in the light.

"He's in this house staying with my cousin Lazarus," said the familiar voice of Rebecca.

"Good evening, Rebecca," called Lazarus, surprised to see his cousin out so late.

"Will he come out and speak to us?" she asked hopefully.

At that moment, Yeshua stepped out from the shadow of the gate and into the pool of light. He wore a smile of resignation.

"What is it you want from me?" he asked them, his arms spread wide.

"That you would speak to us and heal our sick," cried a tall man. "My wife is lame, but we believe you are the Messiah and a great prophet, and you can make her well."

"Come fully into the light," said Yeshua, beckoning the man forward.

The crowd silently let them through, his wife leaning heavily on his arm. Two sons followed, their heads bowed.

"Are you embarrassed by your father?" asked the Master, looking directly at the young men, who continued to stare at the ground.

"Our father believes you are the Messiah," mumbled one of them, like a boy who had just been found out. "But I'm not sure. For my mother's sake, I would like to believe."

"She's been lame for many years and her body is bent. Can you help her?" asked the other son, a note of pleading in his voice as he look up into the Master's face. "If you help her, we will know you are who these people claim you are."

The Master looked up into the night sky, then gently placed his hand upon the woman's head. She sighed and seemed to sag further. The whole crowd held their breath, willing her to be healed, so that they too could believe without doubt. Time seemed to hold its breath too. Then slowly she lifted her head and looked him in the face.

"Let her stand on her own," commanded the Master softly, as he stepped back to give her room. The woman waved her husband away and took a step towards the Master, and then another. At the third step she stood tall and straight, her eyes sparkling as she turned to her husband and laughed. The crowd gasped in disbelief, for her body was no longer twisted. They clasped hands and knelt before the Master. Words of gratitude tumbled from their lips, mingling with salty tears of relief and joy. Their faces were elated as she rose nimbly to her feet and flung her arms around her husband's neck.

He swung her round and round with great shouts of joy. Their sons turned to the crowd in wide-eyed wonder, laughing and shaking hands with those around them. The Master turned to go inside, but the sons called him back and sank to their knees in homage, while many in the crowd copied their action. Shem and Noah noticed that some men at the back, standing with the large man, had sour expressions on their faces and did not kneel.

Mary was still watching with Miriam, Susanna, Peter and Andrew, who had also come silently to the open gate. Peter was still eating a bowl of stew. Boldly, Ellie joined them, peering hopefully into the crowd, but she seemed disappointed.

At that moment, Salome came to Martha. "I can't find Tabitha anywhere," she whispered urgently.

"Have you tried her loft?" suggested Martha, her attention still very much on the proceedings in the street.

"Yes, yes," hissed Salome. John was standing close to them and suggested she might have been curious and slipped out of the gate to get a better view. Salome looked concerned. Martha, now fully focused, began to feel worried too.

Rachel joined them; she too had been looking for Tabitha. "There's no sign of her anywhere," she said. I had everyone left in the house looking for her."

"Where could the child have gone?" moaned Salome.

Ellie, overhearing their conversation, came guiltily to Martha's side. "Please forgive me Martha. I shouldn't have let her go. She's helping Joe bring my mother to see the Master. We didn't think other people would have the same idea."

"Oh Ellie, how thoughtless of me," cried Martha. "I'm so sorry I never thought to ask the Master about your poor mother."

It was Noah who spotted Tabitha and Joe supporting Ellie's mother between them as they came up the hill. He ran to the rescue, slipping his arm around the frail woman and helping Joe to carry her the final distance. Ellie ran forward to her mother, relieved to see them all safe. Noah caught Tabitha's eye and winked at her as she turned to face Martha and Mary.

"I know, I know. I'm in big trouble and we'll have words later," said Tabitha.

"Definitely extra chores," said Mary, relief on her face.

"I'm so proud of you," Martha whispered into Tabitha's ear, "but you're still in trouble for giving us such a fright."

Ellie's mother had crumpled into her daughter's arms, her face ashen with the effort of the walk. Noah caught her, lifting her gently in his arms.

"Please ask the Master to heal her," begged Ellie, looking from Martha to Noah. Joe put his arm around his sister, a silent plea on his face too.

"I'll ask him," volunteered Tabitha.

"What did you want to ask me, Tabitha?" said a soft, familiar voice behind her. She felt his hands resting lightly on her shoulders as she twisted round to look up into his face.

"It's Ellie's mother, Lord. She's been sick for as long as I can remember. Would you heal her, please?" Tabitha clasped her hands together. "Ellie was busy helping Martha and she didn't want to trouble you, but I said nothing troubles you. If we can't ask you, our friend, who can we ask?" Tabitha fell silent, suddenly afraid she'd said too much. Yeshua's lips twitched, compassion mixed with amusement.

"You are truly Martha's daughter," he said, turning immediately to the stricken woman in Noah's arms. Tabitha and Ellie looked at one another hopefully. Before the Master had even laid his hands on Ellie's mother, she was thanking him. Nevertheless, as he touched her, she jerked away. "Be still," came the hushed command. The woman flopped forward, bent double and then began to groan, her arms twitching and swinging. "Leave her and go," he said, firmly. For a moment her whole body was still, and then slowly she straightened up, blinking. She looked around at all the people watching her, eyes wide with astonishment. Fear flickered across her face, but instinctively she found reassurance in the Master's eyes. He nodded encouragingly. Then her mouth fell open in realisation. She was free; her sickness had gone. Leaning forward, she grasped his hand and kissed it.

"My saviour," she whispered. "My Lord, my King!" she cried aloud.

"It's done! She's healed at last!" cried Joe, grabbing his sister's hands and swinging her round and round with joy, but never taking his eyes off his mother. Ellie broke free and stared at her mother.

"Tell me it's true, please," she begged. Her mother nodded, the smile on her face crumpling under the emotion that swept through her. "It's true, my lovely daughter, I am healed. I am free at last."

The crowd cheered, as the little family clung together rejoicing. Tabitha danced around them holding Martha and Mary's hands, and Rachel and her daughters-in-law left the shelter of their gateway and joined them in the street. Tabitha continued to dance around their friends, praising the Lord Yeshua and the God of Heaven in a wonderfully undignified manner.

Yeshua healed others in the crowd that evening, but they were pleased to talk with Lazarus too, who built their faith further with his own story. It was late when the crowd were satisfied and finally dispersed.

Chapter Twenty-One

Friday

❧

The sixth day continued

"The crowds must have been up early this morning," remarked Mary, as she helped Tabitha guide the laden donkey in through the gate. The courtyard, although chilly in the morning air, was sheltered from the wind, yet several of the disciples shivered as they stood waiting for the Master and Lazarus, who was to accompany them once more.

Martha had some calls to make, so as soon as Yeshua and her brother joined them, she and Mary used this as an excuse to walk with them, at least as far as the main road. Tabitha chatted away as she walked hand in hand with Salome. The streets were already busy and there were many more sick people among the crowd near the main road. Martha's heart went out to them, but the speed with which news of the healings the night before had gone out was alarming. There were hostile faces as well. She caught her sister's eye, and Mary nodded; she had seen them too.

Philip and Nathanael, who had gone ahead of the others, came towards them leading the pale colt. Nathanael trotted the colt to Yeshua, excited to relate what had just happened.

"The owner, David, came out to greet us this morning. He had the colt already for you, and he'd spread this beautiful cloth over his back especially," he said.

"I'd half expected some rebuke after yesterday, especially after what Mary and Tabitha told us about David, but he was so generous," remarked Philip, with a wry smile.

"But you should have heard the noise the she-donkey kicked up as we led her colt away," replied Nathanael.

The Master smiled at their innocence, rubbed the colt's head, then, taking the halter rope in his hand, he mounted and sent the beast forward through the crowd. The colt was fearless this time as the sea of people parted to let him through.

Ahead of them once more, word spread through the crowds of pilgrims along the road that the great teacher who healed the sick and spoke of the kingdom of God with such authority was riding into Jerusalem. In his path fresh green palm branches were laid over the dried ones from the day before, excitement running ahead of them. People began to call out to him. "Praises and blessings to you, who comes in the name of God!" cried an old man, falling to his knees, and those around him knelt too, their arms reaching out toward the Master as he rode by.

"Bless the coming kingdom of our father David!" someone shouted, and was answered from the opposite side of the road with, "Praise God in the highest heaven!"

A woman and her family resting at the side of the road saw the Master coming, and tugging at her husband's sleeve, she ran forward, excitedly calling out, "Hosanna! Save us glorious one, King and Lord." The Master looked towards her, his hand raised in greeting, a smile of wonder on his face, as the whole family bowed reverently before him.

"Martha," asked Mary, urgently. "Do you remember that bit in Zechariah? Oh, bother. How does it go?" Momentarily Martha's brow furrowed, then her eyes and mouth opened wide with excitement as Mary chanted aloud, "Rejoice greatly O daughter of Zion! Shout aloud, O daughter of Jerusalem! Behold, your King comes to you; He is righteous and victorious, yet He is humble, riding on a donkey's colt!" People stared at her, and then back at the Master as he rode on, then they hurried after him.

Not long after this, Martha and Mary stood on a bank and watched the others until they were out of sight.

"I think I can still see Lazarus," Martha said, standing on her toes with one hand shading her eyes. "He's walking beside the donkey – Peter's not far behind."

"Good job they took the south road this morning," commented Mary, climbing down to join Tabitha, who stood on the track below.

"I think all the roads will be busy by now," replied Martha, joining them.

Mary sighed deeply. With every fibre of her being she wanted to be with the Master. If it wasn't for her sister, she would have gone. Martha always seemed to put duty and the care of others before her own desires.

"I know you want to follow him as much as I do, so how do you make yourself go home and do all the things you do?" she asked, earnestly.

"Practice," was the quick reply, but then Martha added more thoughtfully, "I suppose by focusing my whole heart into what I'm doing, knowing I'm really doing it for God, who knows and sees my heart."

"So does Yeshua. Of that I'm sure," sighed Mary, linking arms with Martha and Tabitha as they walked back through the empty streets.

"Another day's exciting chores then," said Tabitha, her mouth twitching with mischief as she looked up into Mary's face.

Rachel joined them soon after they got back, joking that she needed a break from her daughters-in-law. "This is going to be a Passover to remember," Tabitha said to her as she brushed the donkey vigorously.

"Something to tell your children about," Rachel remarked. Tabitha rolled her eyes as if such a thought was not to be countenanced, then pursed her lips disapprovingly.

"What's wrong with getting married and having babies?" said Rachel, amused but shaking her head in mock despair.

"Some of us have been set apart for other things," said Mary, winking at the indignant Tabitha.

"Well, I don't know about that," said Rachel. "Martha had good reason, she had to bring you up after your dear mother passed away. What excuses have you two got?"

"Oh, come on Rach. Could you see me running a household, obeying my husband's every wish? I'm far too spoilt," smirked Mary.

"And I'm never leaving Martha," said Tabitha, putting her arms around Martha, who was trying to sweep the veranda.

"All right, all right! You win," said Rachel, but she was grinning. There was a twinkle in Martha's eye as she put the broom away. There was a lot to do before the Sabbath began at sunset, but then her face clouded over and the knot reappeared in her stomach as she remembered the Master's words the night before.

***

As the sun dipped towards the horizon, a weary group of people, including two donkeys, slipped quietly from the city and walked back along the road to Bethany. A few pilgrims were still travelling towards the city, but most were too tired to take much notice.

Behind closed doors, in a certain part of the temple, there was turmoil and outrage. Caiaphas, the high priest, had just received a full report of the incident that had occurred in the outer court of the temple that day. The same name kept coming up. Malchus had had a hard job to calm his master down.

Chapter Twenty-Two

Turning Tables

The Sabbath begins, five days before Passover

The first star showed itself against the darkening sky, and from every dwelling in Bethany, the soft yellow glow of oil lamps welcomed them back. Strung out along the track, the Master and his disciples quickened their pace. A sharp wailing blast from the ram's horn cut through the peaceful evening. The note mellowed into rich undertones as the sound died away. There was the breath of a pause before people began to pour from their homes, making towards the synagogue, the heart of the town. The Master and his followers were quickly engulfed in the tide of people as the second call came from the horn.

"Just in time," remarked Matthew, loud enough so everyone heard.

"Where are Nathanael and Philip?" Thaddaeus asked him, looking round the hurrying crowd with concern.

"They'll be along in a minute, they had to drop off the donkey," Matthew reminded him.

"They'd better hurry if they don't want to stand. I could use a sit down," groaned Thaddaeus, to general agreement from the others.

Weary as the disciples felt, the enthusiasm of these simple people injected new vigour into their tired bodies. Salome and Susanna helped Mary from her donkey, which stood dejectedly at the tethering post outside the synagogue as they all went inside. Just then Martha and Tabitha came running down the hill. Quickly, Tabitha supplied the forlorn creature with hay and water from the Hazzan's own storehouse nearby.

The synagogue was packed, and the atmosphere expectant. All faces, young and old, were turned hopefully and attentively to one guest. Martha and Miriam exchanged knowing glances across the sea of bright cheeks between them. As the last few people squashed in, the Sabbath celebration began. The readings that evening remained etched on many memories for years to come, and the prayers and psalms had fresh vibrancy and new meaning for everyone present that evening.

The walk back was short; the gate of their home was wide open and the courtyard well-lit to welcome their guests to the Sabbath rest. Here was peace and order, and the smell of good food, that would soon fill their empty stomachs. Mary and Tabitha, having run on ahead, were there to greet everyone. Together they knelt to wash the many pairs of dirty feet.

Martha's tall figure was already bending over the stew as the other women came in, ready to do whatever they could to help, although it was clear to Martha they were exhausted. That evening, Martha called everyone through into the large living room, where wine, beer, bread and olives were laid out ready, and as the evening was cold, a fire glowed at the far end of the room. More warm air flowed in from the busy kitchen as the weary men joined them. Tabitha flitted in and out serving the drinks as Martha and Mary brought in the first pot of lamb stew, which was set down, so as many as possible could reach it. Martha paused for a moment with gladness in her heart, waiting for all her guests to come into the room.

Lazarus, taking his cue from Martha, nodded to the Master, who stood to say the blessing. Then they ate. From the middle of the room Yeshua looked towards Martha with a broad smile, holding up his bowl and waving the bread approvingly. Martha wanted that feeling to last forever.

A while later, Mary came to find Martha, and they softly spoke together. She was concerned their guests were unusually quiet and the women, who had returned to the kitchen to eat, looked worn out. Martha was especially worried about Miriam, who looked quite pale. Mary Joseph sat dozing, her empty plate tilting on her lap, so gently Miriam took it. Like a startled owl, Mary Joseph's eyes blinked open with a bright smile, but as soon as she saw what Miriam had done her eyelids began to droop again, and her chin dropped slowly to her chest as she fell asleep once more.

"She's worn out, bless her," said Salome quietly, rubbing her aching feet and stifling a yawn.

Miriam reached over to touch Martha's arm. "Joanna has found a place for us, very near the Master's lodgings," she said. "I'm sorry we're not staying any longer with you."

"It's all right, I understand. It's good that you are near the Master. If he stays with us for a few more days it will give you time to prepare for the Passover."

"We are sorry," said Salome. "You could probably do with the extra help, but many of us have family coming and relatives to see, so we must trust that God will work it out to everyone's advantage."

"Lazarus mentioned you were going to Elias and Elizabeth's for Passover, so I'm sure we'll be able to meet up," added Miriam. Martha nodded, but smiled weakly. Just then she wasn't feeling very enthusiastic about the visit.

"Would you like to hear what happened today?" asked Susanna, guessing what was really on Martha's mind. "It might help to explain why everyone's so quiet." Martha nodded gratefully, calling Mary to come and join them.

Susanna told them that the Master had been greeted like a king all the way into Jerusalem once more, and even into the temple courts. A great crowd had gone before him and others followed. The women had been moved to see him acknowledged as the Messiah, sent from God. Susanna looked lovingly at Mary Joseph, who now sat up bright but watery eyed, listening.

"He knew where he was going, and what he was about to do, of that I am certain," said Susanna, and the others nodded in agreement.

They had been a little way behind when he'd entered the temple courts, but they had heard the great roar from the crowd as he went in.

"We lost sight of them at that point," said Susanna. "But with hindsight, I'm quite glad. What happened next was disconcerting." The others clearly looked uncomfortable.

"Don't look so alarmed, Martha dear," said Miriam. "It was all right in the end."

"Although I'm sure there are many from the temple who are still beside themselves with rage," added Salome, smugly.

"They will have lost a lot of revenue because of the Master's actions today," agreed Susanna.

"Poor Martha looks even more worried," said Mary Joseph. "Susanna, please."

"Sorry. The Master was certainly very angry with what he saw going on there today. Immediately, he began driving the traders and their animals away, and with them the bewildered customers. When he got to the money exchangers, tables and chairs went flying. He was quite violent." Martha could hardly believe her ears. This wasn't a side of Yeshua she was familiar with. "After the atmosphere on the road into Jerusalem, I think we were all shocked. He was still angry when he came away. The disciples clearly didn't know what to do."

"I don't think any of us did, or expected to see it happen again," said Salome. "I remember the first time. He made a whip then, and drove out all the oxen, sheep and people, just like today. Our whole family was there. John and James didn't know what to think, but their father Zebedee told them there was a psalm with a bit in it that said we shouldn't make God's house into a marketplace, and that zeal for God's temple would eat up his chosen one, the Messiah. At the time, my Zebedee was quite clear that if this rabbi was the Messiah, then they should expect him to be angry at the way the temple was being used as a market. It's a holy place after all. Today nothing had changed," finished Salome, with a snort of anger.

"Martha, it was amazing," said Miriam, her eyes shining with enthusiasm. "After that, he slipped away for a while, but when he came back he began to heal people like never before, right there in front of the eyes of the temple."

"It was like he was in a hurry to fit in as many people as possible," commented Mary Alphaeus.

"Or as though he was running out of time," said Mary, bitterly.

This made Martha think of the lambs penned at the back of the house. Only one or two of them would be considered perfect enough to be chosen for the Passover sacrifice at the temple. The final choice would be made two days before the celebration when their woolly heads would be anointed with oil.

Mary Alphaeus broke the heavy silence. "People were being healed of some terrible things right before our eyes. But would you believe it, some of the leaders and Pharisees were asking him to stop!"

"Why?" asked Martha. "It wasn't the Sabbath."

"Because the people think he is the son of David. And when everyone, even the children, began to cry out 'hosanna, rescuer', those men got even more upset because they don't want people to say that about him, they don't believe he is. Can you believe that?" exclaimed Mary Alphaeus, exasperated by what she'd seen.

"I heard a few Pharisees asking him if he knew what was being said about him," said Miriam. The others looked at her expectantly. "I could hardly believe my ears when he nodded and said yes. Oh Martha, you should have seen their faces. They didn't know what to do to make him stop."

"Didn't they tell the temple police? They wouldn't have hesitated," said Mary.

"They couldn't," said Susanna. "It was clear the people were on his side. The temple police aren't fools. Attempting to arrest him could have started a riot. So knowing they were powerless, the Master just kept going. It was breath taking. He preached, taught and healed for hours and the people just kept coming."

"The chief priests won't let this go," said Martha, shaking her head ruefully. "Time is running out for our beloved Lord and Master, and he knows it."

Tears welled up in Miriam's eyes as she reached over and held the wrinkled hands of Mary Joseph.

"The streets were empty by the time we left," said Miriam. "All the weary way back to Bethany I kept looking behind us, half expecting to see temple police or soldiers coming after us. That was until the Master saw me. Then he looked stern and said I shouldn't be afraid, there was still time."

There was a loud roar of laughter from the other room; the atmosphere had changed. Mary went hurrying in and Martha got up stiffly to follow her. Thomas was in the middle of narrating the day's events for the benefit of the guests from Bethany. He had just got to the part where Yeshua, with the strong arms of a carpenter, had overturned a table, throwing neat piles of coins everywhere. Encouraged by the laughter, he went on to relate how the Master had been floored by the weight of the pigeon seller's table.

"It was just the excuse Peter needed to get involved," joked Thomas. "You came rushing in, lifting the whole table and its contents, sending the cages sliding to the floor, with birds escaping and flapping about all over the place."

"They flew away fast enough, though," guffawed Matthew, "releasing their bowels over our heads." He pretended to wipe guano off his shoulder.

"And if I'm not mistaken, the last two money changers to scarper were son's of Annas," said John, knowingly.

"They couldn't gather their money fast enough in that tablecloth," said Andrew, gleefully. "A very dignified escape from the rampaging rabbi."

"Oh, that's good, rampaging rabbi!" chortled Young James, lifting his wine in salute.

Yeshua, without moving his head, looked left, then right, and then went cross-eyed. That had everyone rolling with laughter.

"Some people got quite irate, defending their rights to carry merchandise through the temple area, but the Master turned them back," said Philip.

"I admit it had never occurred to me that using the temple court as a shortcut through the city was irreverent. Surely that's going too far?" queried Thaddaeus.

"No. Going too far is having to go all the way round," said Andrew, triumphantly. Peter groaned.

"Firstly, let me apologise for my brother's bad jokes," said Peter. "And secondly, I agree with the Master. The temple is supposed to be a house of prayer, not a market."

"Look at the crowds again today, despite the scenes with the traders they weren't put off. They were still flocking to hear what the Master had to say," said Nathanael.

Martha listened, fascinated, as she refilled their cups.

"The temple officials are itching to get their hands on him," Judas remarked to Simon the Zealot, who was enjoying the wine immensely. "And don't forget we have our brother Lazarus tagging along too. He is, after all, our living, breathing local miracle." Then he called across the room, "You enjoy the fame while you can brother Lazarus."

Philip's warning glare came too late. Mary was standing just behind him, her face turning scarlet with anger, a broken jug on the floor.

Lazarus seemed taken aback by the remark, but quickly regained his composure. "I'll enjoy the miracle of being alive, if you don't mind. Fame never lasts," he replied, drawing a smile from his listeners.

"Neither will staying alive, if you continue to be seen in public with the Rabbi," muttered Judas, under his breath. Thaddaeus gave him a dark look.

Mary was both outraged and upset by Judas' remarks, so understandably it took some time for Martha, Miriam and the others to calm her down. Mary Alphaeus and Susanna, with tight-lipped control, went back into the room and cleared away the broken jug.

It was Yeshua who suggested the women should come back and join them. Martha was glad the incident had passed, and now listened with renewed interest as the men went on to tell them how, on the way into Jerusalem, they had joined in with the crowd praising Yeshua. However, this had apparently upset a group of watching Pharisees who had indignantly insisted that the Master should stop his followers from behaving like that.

"You said that if they kept quiet, the gravestones on the hillside above us, and by that I took it you meant their occupants, would burst into cheers and praise!" chuckled Lazarus.

"I did," admitted Yeshua, who was sitting quietly listening with the faintest of smiles playing on his lips.

"At that point Master, nothing would have surprised me," said Young James with a grin.

The fire burned low, its warmth causing some to doze off where they sat, while others still talked quietly. Thaddaeus came over to sit with Lazarus and John, and soon it became clear he had a question to ask.

"Lazarus, you were close to the Master when he stopped and wept. What caused it?" he asked.

"It sounded like a prophecy to me," said Lazarus. "The Master said that Jerusalem would be levelled by our enemies because it had missed the visitation and salvation that was offered to it." Thaddaeus looked alarmed.

"That's right," said John. "And that peace is now hidden from the city's eyes."

"Surely God isn't going to let the Romans level his city? Or any other conquering nation, for that matter. There have certainly been quite a few in our long history. That way definitely won't bring peace to our people," said Simon the Zealot, earnestly.

"And whose visit and salvation has Jerusalem missed?" asked Thomas, who clearly hadn't been listening.

"The Lord's visit and salvation, of course," chorused Martha and Mary, together. They had been sitting nearby, listening intently.

"And because most of those who lead us in Jerusalem won't acknowledge him, despite all he's done," said Salome.

"You're quite right mother," said John. "The peace God was offering them is only to be found through his son, which is now hidden from them. They are blind."

"What an opportunity to have missed!" exclaimed Thaddaeus. "Thank you." He yawned and stretched. "Now I really must go to bed. I can't keep my eyes open a moment longer."

Those who were not already asleep climbed the outer stairs to the guest room above, and settled down in comfort. The women drifted away to their rooms on the ground floor, while Mary joined Tabitha in the cosy loft at the back of the house. Lazarus made the Master comfortable in his own room before joining his guests in the upper room. Martha sat beside the kitchen fire deep in thought before she too fell into an exhausted sleep.

Chapter Twenty-Three

The Sabbath

Five days before Passover

The house was quiet; a cool wind blew from the west, chasing across the slopes around Bethany. Lazarus' guests were slow to rise, snuggled under the warm blankets, their cloaks spread out on top. It was the wailing synagogue horn which finally roused the dozing household. Then, for a brief time, pandemonium broke out as cold water was splashed onto faces, not always by their owners, and dishevelled hair was dragged into place as they tried to make themselves presentable. They left in disorder, hurrying down the hill to the synagogue. The Master and Lazarus had left earlier. Martha and Miriam were last to leave, walking arm in arm and chatting together, enjoying the prospect of a day in each other's company.

From the women's benches, Martha watched with pleasure as Michael welcomed the Master, bowing respectfully. There was a spring in the old man's steps as he began the service that morning.

Martha nudged Miriam and whispered in her ear, "I wonder if our Hassan has heard what the Master did in the temple yesterday."

Miriam had been watching the encounter too. "If he has heard, it doesn't seem to have made any difference. He looks positively delighted the Master has agreed to read this morning," she said.

"He certainly doesn't agree with the order to arrest the Master," added Martha, who loved the old man even more for this. He had devoted his whole life to the poor rural community of Bethany, forgotten by Jerusalem, and yet here he had met the Lord.

For Martha, Mary and Tabitha it was the first time they had heard their friend read and teach from the sacred scrolls, and it was an experience none of them would ever forget. While the Master spoke, not a sound was made by the congregation. Young and old alike were held by the authority of his words and by the power of the truth of what he said.

Although their guests lingered after the service, surrounded by eager people, Martha and Tabitha raced one another home. Martha's heart felt light; for the moment, her fears had been banished. Today, she would have all her friends around her.

Quickly bread, cheese, eggs, nuts, honey and dried fruit were laid out for their guests. The house began to hum as everyone returned and ate with relish. Martha sat with Miriam and the other women among the men, enjoying the lively conversations that flowed from the scriptures read that morning.

After lunch, Martha found Ellie, Tabitha and Salome chatting in the kitchen. Ellie's eyes were wide with wonder as Salome recounted yet another story about the Master. Martha couldn't help stopping to listen.

This time, Yeshua had apparently been trying to avoid the attention of the crowds, somewhere between Tyre and Sidon, in Phoenicia, but a local Greek woman had found out where he was. James and John had tried to make her to go away, but because her little daughter was ill, possessed by a spirit, she wouldn't leave and started making a big fuss.

"In the end," laughed Salome, "my boys begged the Master to deal with her. His question to her was 'why should he heal a gentile?' and she argued that although she wasn't an Israelite, even the Master's children threw scraps to the dogs under the table. She understood how unworthy she was, but her faith in him gave her boldness to beg for her daughter. Yeshua was very impressed with her understanding and also her faith in him. So was I," admitted Salome.

"So her daughter was with her?" asked Tabitha.

"Oh no. Her daughter was at home. The Master simply healed her through his words. Miriam and Susanna went back to the house with her. They, out of all of us, appreciated what the little girl must have suffered. I think the women appreciated their support too."

"So Yeshua healed the little Greek girl without actually being present," exclaimed Martha.

"The faith of the woman was enough," said Ellie, shaking her head in wonder.

"Oh, it wasn't the first time he'd done something like that for a gentile," pointed out Salome. "He's not exclusively our Messiah, as it turns out."

"It certainly seems that way," said Martha, enjoying Salome's humour, while trying to grasp the implications of what she'd said. "However, I hope you three aren't working on the Sabbath," she added, unable to help herself, as Ellie and Tabitha began tidying up. Tabitha threw a cloth at her, while Salome pointed out that Martha, in her usual efficient way, had left them with very little to do anyway. "Well, I'll leave you to get on with 'very little then'," said Martha, but she was pleased by the compliment.

Martha joined Yeshua and Lazarus lounging in front of the fire. They were talking about the celebration Simon was planning in honour of the Master and his disciples in two days' time. Close by, Mary Joseph sat upright, but her chin rested on her chest and her eyes were closed. Martha watched her for a while as she listened to the two men talking. Yeshua's gaze then also turned to his mother.

"It was another big day for her yesterday," ventured Martha. "She must have waited a long time to see you greeted by the people as the Messiah. But then you stirred up all that trouble at the Exchange. Not that you don't have a very good point, but for her, it must have been hard to bear."

Yeshua nodded. Martha had a point.

Lazarus watched their faces, fascinated.

"Oh, my goodness," said Martha, her face turning red with embarrassment. "I didn't mean it like that."

"It's all right Martha. I understand you spoke out of concern for Mary Joseph and your fear for me. My dear friends." His smile was broad and relaxed.

Ellie, Salome and Tabitha, their ears pricked, had been going in and out of the room placing food on the low tables in preparation for the evening.

"Sometimes it's confusing," said Lazarus thoughtfully. "You're our friend, made of flesh and blood, like us, and yet on the other hand, you're the Messiah and are therefore spirit, and like God, belong to heaven." Martha nodded, it was confusing at times.

"You have spoken truly, my brother. I understand what it is to be fully human now, a creator who has become his creation, for a brief while. But I see there is something else on your mind, Martha. What is it?"

She took a deep breath before saying, "It concerns me that most of us, including your close followers, don't really understand why you do what you do, or say what you say. I know you're trying to explain God's heart and the true nature of his kingdom, but even the twelve clearly can't remember all of it. And you speak in riddles half the time." Yeshua raised an eyebrow at her candid comment, but Martha plunged on. "Riddles are hard to remember, especially if you don't understand them in the first place. Don't get me wrong, they're a great bunch of men and let's not forget Miriam and the others, but they aren't you. What you are saying is the most important thing that has ever been heard. You've come and changed us, turned our lives upside down, and you aren't content with just our nation, your aim seems to be the whole world." Martha's brow furrowed as another thought struck her. "That was always the plan, wasn't it?" He seemed pleased. "How can this happen if you aren't going to be here anymore?" she demanded, biting her lower lip, tears welling up, although her look remained challenging.

"The time is coming when I shall speak more plainly, but for now, it is better this way." For a second Martha saw the pain in his eyes, and she knew what he was going to say.

"Do you trust me Martha?" She nodded, grim faced. "Then trust the one who sent me, who chose the twelve and entrusted them to me. There has always been a plan, from the beginning, before even Adam. It will work."

"I know, I'm way out of my depth and have no right to question you, the Messiah, but you are still our friend. I cannot forget that you have spoken of your own burial, even if your men seemed to dismiss it."

"I don't think they are dismissing it, Martha. They are just afraid to confront it right now. They will have to deal with it soon enough," said Lazarus, his eyes on the Master as he spoke. The Master nodded, then looked away to hide his pain.

"It is a hard thing for us all to bear," Martha agreed.

"I am the resurrection and the life, remember. It will only seem like I have gone for a short while, but if your faith remains firm..." His voice faded away, and he seemed to be looking far into the distance. That word 'faith' again, thought Martha, but it was like cold water poured on a burn, soothing and reassuring that the pain would go.

Just then Peter and John wandered in with some of the others and threw themselves down beside them.

"You all look very serious" commented Peter. "Come on John, we'll have to cheer them up. This is our day off, to rest."

"And reflect," added John, but he knew he wasn't impressing anyone.

"Oh, I try not to do too much of that," said Peter, who was obviously in a jovial mood. "It can stop you from sleeping." This raised a smile.

"Please do some reflecting Peter, then the rest of us can get some sleep tonight," begged Matthew. "Did you all hear him snoring last night?" There was a chorus of affirmative groans.

"Perhaps Peter could swop rooms with you," suggested Thaddaeus, gleefully looking at Yeshua.

"That's fine with me, but as you know, I pray all night," he replied. The others groaned again.

"So, would some lamb's wool to stuff in your ears help?" asked Martha, merrily. The laughter woke Mary Joseph, so Martha shuffled over to sit beside her.

Martha remained beside Mary Joseph during the evening meal, curious to learn more about this extraordinary woman. She was easy to talk to, and shared freely and willingly about her life and family. She had grown up in a small village in the country and at sixteen had been betrothed to Joseph, a kind, handsome but older man. Unexpectedly, Mary had found she was pregnant, but knew without any doubt she was still a virgin. She was perplexed and didn't know who to confide in. Telling Joseph put a real strain on their relationship, until in the end he had decided to quietly divorce her. Mary was distraught, until an Angel had appeared to them, separately, explaining that the child she bore was God's child. It had all felt like a dream, but with Joseph's support she had been able to cope with the situation. Her family had sent her away to stay with her cousin Elizabeth, who was carrying John the Baptiser, the son of a priest called Zechariah. It was an incredible story to hear.

Joseph had married Mary, but they had been forced to travel to Bethlehem for Herod's census, before the baby was due. Only days after they arrived the child was born, so they'd settled in the town among Joseph's relatives. There was always work for a good carpenter like Joseph, Mary told Martha proudly. Yeshua, their little son, had barely learnt to walk when the angel showed up again, warning them to flee to Egypt to escape Herod, who wanted to kill their son. Mary Joseph shared many of the prophecies spoken over Yeshua, which she remembered clearly. Only when the angel had told them it was safe did they return to their own country. They settled in Nazareth, where Joseph's first son, James, was born. Mary had four more sons and two daughters after that, and their cup had seemed so full.

After Joseph died, Yeshua had taken over the business and he and James had worked together to support the family. As time went on Yeshua spent more and more time teaching, leaving James in charge. Resentment had crept in between the brothers, which had broken Mary's heart. At times she had felt torn in two. Things had come to a head in the family the previous autumn, resulting in Yeshua coming to the Feast of Tabernacles alone. Of course Martha knew about that, but wondered if Mary had known just how much danger he was in. Coming to the feast alone was more likely to be about protecting those around him, Martha thought.

"But James has changed his opinion, and the others too," finished Mary, her eyes shining. "Perhaps it's because they actually listened to him talking to the people at the Feast of Tabernacles. I don't really know, but my gratitude to God knows no bounds." Big watery tears filled her eyes, and Martha's too.

* * *

That evening after dinner, when everyone else had gone to bed, Martha, Miriam and Susanna sat talking quietly together. It had been such a lovely day, and Martha didn't want it to end. Besides, she was still wide awake, and Salome's story of the little Greek girl had stirred up questions she felt her two friends would be able to answer.

"How could Yeshua make a spirit leave someone without even being present?" she asked them.

Miriam blinked before she attempted an answer. "Well that's a hard one. I suppose the simple answer is, he is who he says he is, and because he only does what his father tells him to do, he has, or is given, power and authority over spirits. I suppose the spirit realm is more natural to him than this world, but to banish a spirit from someone without even being there is pretty impressive. It doesn't leave much room for doubt."

Martha nodded, then asked, "What was it like for you?"

"Oh Martha, that's even harder to explain," said Miriam, wincing at the memory. "I thought it was just me in the beginning, behaving badly and out of character. I'd make excuses, justifying my actions and blaming others for making me behave that way. I got used to being like that. Then for a while it seemed normal again. I even consulted a medium. But there was a point when it began to feel really uncomfortable. I was out of control, and my conscience began to scream inside me to stop. I wanted to so much, but I'd dug a hole so deep with my lies, deception and pride, I could see it wasn't possible anymore. Then despair took me. After that the other demons must have found it easy to torment me. By then I was a total outcast." She laughed bitterly. "I wanted the torment to stop, but they'd convinced me I was to blame; I was a terrible person, so I wanted to die." Miriam's face was twisted with pain. Martha reached out and touched her arm, sorry that her friend had been so affected by the memories.

"You're free now," she said. "They cannot touch you ever again. The Master has shown you the truth, exposed the darkness, and it has gone." And then another thought struck her. "In fact, he is the light we've all been missing in our lives. The light which drives out all the darkness, all the bad stuff that has happened to us."

Miriam looked at Martha and sighed. She straightened her shoulders and sat back.

"I am free," she repeated quietly to herself. Then, with an amused twinkle in her eye, she looked at Martha and said, "Careful, you'll be casting out demons next." Martha raised a doubtful eyebrow. "Susanna, your experience was very different from mine..."

"Yes, it was," said Susanna. "More like Ellie's mother. It just started with an illness. Nothing out of the ordinary. Everyone expected me to recover." Martha listened intently, her head on one side. "The trouble was, I didn't get better. Month by month I began to waste away. No one knew what was causing it, and no amount of money could find a cure. I became desperate as the terrible truth dawned on me; I was going to die."

"Were you in pain?" asked Martha.

"Sometimes, but mainly it was just a debilitating weakness. I could barely walk or lift a cup on the bad days. If I hadn't met the Master that day, I would certainly have died within the next few months. I could hardly eat by then, and was losing the will to live." She grimaced at the memory. "My maid heard that the Rabbi was in town. People were flocking to see him. She begged me to go to him. In the end she half-dragged me from my home, then tried to carry me through the streets. But he found us, panting and propped against a wall, too exhausted to go further. If he hadn't turned down that alley at that moment, I wouldn't be here speaking to you and sharing my story. But I needed healing, not a faith, or so I thought.

He saw the demons that were destroying my life as clearly as I see you. He spoke to them one at a time and they left. I felt each one go, like something was being pulled out of me. It was so physical." She winced as she spoke. "I understand now how it happened. My mother was from Greece, and had left me a beautiful ring, which I wore in her memory. After Yeshua sent the spirits away, he took the ring off my finger, and grasped it in his hand. When he offered it back to me, it looked so dull and ordinary sitting in the palm of his hand; my desire for it had gone. He said it was powerless to harm anyone ever again, but I buried it all the same. The memories of my mother were good and bright once more and no longer linked to the ring."

Martha thought of her own mother, and nodded in understanding.

"But that wasn't quite the end of it. At first, I was terrified the demons would come back, thinking that only the Master could keep them away from me. So I followed him. I think I only really understood that they couldn't come back after he sent the seventy of us out; the demons fled from us then. Somehow, he had given us his authority over them, and I knew then that they could never come back to me, because of my faith in who he was."

"He once told us a story about a strong man and a room being swept clean," said Miriam, knowing Martha would appreciate the analogy. "It was a while ago now, but I think his point was that he drove demons out of people by the spirit of God, making them clean, and if they believed in him, they had become part of the kingdom of God and the demons couldn't come back, because the room was full of God."

"That does make it easier to understand," admitted Susanna, looking at Martha. "I used what God has given me to help Yeshua. I left my home still in fear, but by following the Master I found peace, and purpose, and a new life."

"So was Ellie's mother sick because of a demon, or did the demon take advantage of her weakness and despair?" asked Martha.

"Most people are just sick, Martha, and want to be well," said Miriam. "But once we truly know who the Master is, there is no power that can really harm us. He is here with us, now, and if we die, then we go to his father."

"He told me, that he is the resurrection and the life, and that all those who believe in him, even if they die, they will still live in eternity with him, but I've been thinking he meant more than that," replied Martha. "He brings a new life to us, here, now, when we come to know him, and it's that new life in us that continues beyond death. He is the true life." She sighed. Looking at her friends, she hoped they understood what she was trying to say. "Thank you both for trying to explain things to me," she said, grateful for the glimmer of understanding she now had.

"So, what is your story, Martha of Bethany?" asked Susanna.

"Oh, nothing very extraordinary," replied Martha, but she did tell them of her childhood, her mother's death, the unfair demands put on her by her father, and the annulment of her marriage to Noah. Through humiliation, loneliness and disappointment she had filled her life with duty and caring for others, while part of her had died. As Miriam and Susanna listened to Martha, it was as though the story of her life belonged to someone else. The memories of her pain had gone, and when she finished, she spread her arms wide and laughing, said, "This is now my story, and you are all part of it, and I am so grateful, no matter where it leads me. I have met the one the world has been waiting for, and he has changed my life forever."

Chapter Twenty-Four

A Message

Sunday, the beginning of the week, four days before Passover

A loud hammering on the gate startled Martha. As she jumped to her feet, it flew open, revealing a sweating, panting Sam. She ran forward, calling urgently for Tabitha and Mary.

"Sam, is everything all right?" she exclaimed.

Sam threw himself down on the seat under the olive tree and poured the water he was offered over his head before gulping down a second offering. He tried to speak between gasps for breath.

"Father sent me. Warn you. Sanhedrin, Lazarus. Hoped to catch him. Before he left. Crowds slowed me down." His breath began to ease. "I came out through the Sheep Gate, but that was busy too. It took longer to come across country."

"What about the Sanhedrin and Lazarus?" demanded Martha, her heart beginning to thump.

Sam gulped down some more water. "They're going to arrest Lazarus, as well as the Rabbi Yeshua."

Martha turned white. "Where is your brother now? I must warn him."

"He left early this morning with the Master. They took the south road into the city. They said they'd be back this evening." But as she spoke, she began to doubt this.

"Father got wind of the rumours early Friday morning," Sam went on. "Apparently, Laz is being talked about almost as much as the Master. One of the rumours said Lazarus and the Master were speaking to and healing people outside this house. It was all over the city by the start of the Sabbath, so that's why the council decided to arrest Lazarus too."

At that point, Tabitha and Mary came rushing out, delighted to see Sam, but as soon as they saw Martha's face, they knew something was terribly wrong.

"Oh no," cried Mary. "They've arrested him!"

"Hush," said Martha fiercely. "Not yet, but Lazarus is to be arrested too. We must warn him as soon as possible."

"Do you have any idea what their plans were for today? Maybe I can get to Lazarus before the temple police do. Why didn't he take Father's advice and stay low?" moaned Sam.

"All we know," said Mary, biting a nail nervously, "is they were going to the temple as usual and would return this evening. It shouldn't be too difficult to find him. The Master was being greeted on the road by locals and pilgrims again this morning. That may be enough to postpone their arrest for a time," said Mary hopefully.

"Or make them easier to find," snapped Martha, beginning to feel sick.

"I'll go straight there and try and find him," said Sam, rising and resigning himself to another long run. "If you could get word to Father for me."

"Wait here! I've got an idea," commanded Mary, and dashed out. The gate slammed behind her.

Sam, Martha and Tabitha waited impatiently, but Mary was back in minutes, with Rachel.

"My boys will come with you, Sam," said Rachel firmly. "You'll stand a better chance of finding Lazarus and the Master in the crowds with their help. And you will stay here," she said, looking meaningfully at Mary. Martha could only guess at the hurried conversation Mary and Rachel had just had. "Besides," Rachel added. "You need to be here, in case there's news."

Very soon after, Sam, Shem, Noah and their younger brother Joses left, taking the shortest possible route over the Mount of Olives and down into Jerusalem. Rachel hurried back to gather her remaining family to pray, while Martha, Mary and Tabitha did the same.

"God, protect Lazarus and your son Yeshua, our friend. Please bring them safely back to us," pleaded Tabitha in prayer.

The hours passed agonisingly for the three of them. They tried to concentrate on the chores and preparations for their guests' return, but doubt nagged constantly in their minds.

"It won't stop at arrest, they want them dead," said Mary bitterly, as they finished watering the garden.

"It hasn't come to that yet," said Martha. "I trust the Master. He said they would be back this evening, and I choose to believe him."

"You're right. The Lord will keep Lazarus safe for us. Time after time we've thought they would arrest Yeshua, and it hasn't happened."

Martha thought back to the hopeful farewells of Miriam, and the others, as they'd said goodbye that morning, and the promises they'd made to meet up in the city later that week. Under what circumstances might that happen now? Would they be aware that the threat of arrest now included her brother?

In the middle of the afternoon Joses returned. They had found Lazarus and the Master, and all was well. Noah and Shem had stayed; this was greeted with mixed feelings by their families, but Martha and Mary felt only relief and gratitude. Now their faith had strengthened; their brother and Yeshua would return, as he had said.

In the quiet of dusk, Tabitha waited by the gate, her ears alert, listening for their return. Her heart quickened at every sound, although she felt a little sad that Salome and the other women wouldn't be with them.

Distant voices interrupted her thoughts. She opened the gate and looked out. There was Lazarus striding up the hill between the Master and John. She ran to him.

Brushing her tears of relief away, Martha greeted her brother. The Master hung back, staring at the ground uncomfortably. She marched over to him, took his hand and led him in amongst them.

"It's all right, I knew you would be back, because you said so. It was a sore trial, but we are through it, for today. Welcome Lord." He looked reassured. She had clung to his promise; it had kept her from being swept away with fear.

That evening seemed more precious than any so far, as Joseph, Rachel and as many of their family as could be spared from child duty joined them for the meal. Despite the fresh threat that now hung over their heads, Martha felt strangely safe.

Ellie and her mother had turned up to help. Martha suspected Rachel had asked them to come, but she was delighted to see them nevertheless. In a quiet moment together, Ellie told Martha that she was finding it hard to adjust to her mother's sudden return to health.

"I can hardly keep up with her," Ellie confessed. "It's like she's making up for lost time."

Martha couldn't help chuckling at this. "It will take time for you all to adjust to such a miraculous change," she replied. "Your role, and hers, has changed in the family. You aren't her carer any more, she wants to look after you and Joe for a change. Talk to her about it. I think you'll be surprised at how she's feeling. When a bird is set free, it sometimes perches for a while, until it figures out which direction to fly in. Your mother has been faster to fly off her perch, that's all. And you may bump into one another for a while, but that's all right, you'll work it out before too long."

Ellie laughed out loud. She appreciated Martha's wisdom and humour.

At that moment, her mother swept into the room and firmly, but politely, took the large basket of bread Ellie was still holding. "Let me take that for you, my love. You stay and talk to Martha," she said, as she hurried back to the guests.

Martha and Ellie tried their best not to laugh again, but Martha's heart was lifted for a while.

Simon of Bethany arrived after supper; he'd been into Jerusalem for purification that day and had missed them in the crowds. As soon as he'd heard about the threat to arrest Lazarus, he'd hurried over, deeply concerned. With his immediate fears put to rest, he sat at ease among them, while Thaddaeus recounted the day's events for the benefit of those who had not been with them.

He raised his glass to them and smiled at Joseph. "After Sam and your boys found us, the Master went on talking with the people as though nothing had changed," he said. "We went to pray at the usual time in the afternoon. It was so crowded it was hard to tell if we were being watched or not, but there were no outright challenges this time."

Simon of Bethany raised an eyebrow and looked at Yeshua. "Caiaphas, our high priest, and Annas, his father-in-law, ex-high priest, see you as a blasphemer, someone claiming to be the Messiah, the son of David, the rescuer of the people. And you, young man," he said, turning to Lazarus, a mischievous twinkle in his eye, "are claiming resurrection after death. There is no resurrection, as far as they're concerned. So we shouldn't be surprised they want you arrested!" He laughed, trying to make light of the situation. "I would fear greatly for us all," Simon went on, shaking his head, "if it wasn't for you." He smiled warmly at the Master.

Martha loved the way everyone was free in their conversation. Yeshua seemed to encourage that. Laws and tradition were respected too, but they were edged with kindness. Once again, she was overwhelmed by who this man was. Being Martha, she poured more wine for her guests, cleared the tables and kept busy. Almost immediately the Master caught her eye, and although she still lowered her head, blushing and wondering if he'd just read her thoughts again, she glanced up to find his warm, reassuring smile still on her.

Chapter Twenty-Five

The Fig Tree

Monday, three days before Passover

The Master and his men were up early and had left the village before its inhabitants were fully awake. Martha watched from the gate as they disappeared down the hill. She was relieved that Lazarus was on his way to meet the labourers who were going to install the new olive press and renovate the old ones. This had been arranged some time ago and the job couldn't be put off any longer. That morning she found herself wondering what might happen next. Joining the family in Jerusalem for Passover was beginning to sound very welcoming.

As her guests were to dine at Simon's house that evening, Martha did her chores at a more leisurely pace, while Mary and Tabitha had gladly gone to deliver various baskets to those in need. She was enjoying having a few quiet moments for herself, until there was a knock on the gate. It was a message from Helena, Simon of Bethany's wife, asking Martha if she would consider helping Jessica, their housekeeper, to prepare for the celebration that evening. Helena especially emphasised how important it was to her husband that the Master should be honoured before so many guests from Jerusalem.

Martha smiled to herself as she returned to her seat in the sunshine. Looking up to heaven she said out loud, "That's going to be a challenge. Jessica isn't going to appreciate my help. You know what she thinks of me." Then she sighed deeply. "But Helena hasn't given me or Jessica a choice, has she? Oh dear, I can hardly refuse."

When Mary returned, she understood Martha's predicament straight away, but knew her sister would face the difficult situation for Yeshua's sake. Mary had been looking forward to spending time with Anna, and now she had an excuse to go to their home even earlier, with Martha and Tabitha.

The house was built on the southern edge of the town, and designed somewhat like the wealthier Roman houses of Jerusalem, to please his wife. When they arrived, Helena welcomed them warmly, and with some relief. Jessica's reaction, however, was icy, to say the least.

Martha quickly appraised the situation in the kitchen, and could see that with a barrage of servants at her command, Jessica had everything well organised and under control. Helena had no cause to be so worried. Nevertheless, she retired, leaving Jessica to Martha.

Martha stood awkwardly waiting. It was hard to know what she could do to help. Anything she suggested might be seen as interference by Jessica, who obviously wasn't going to make it any easier. In the end, she simply asked Jessica what she could do to help and complimented her on her organisation. For a fleeting moment, Jessica looked surprised. Then, when Martha asked how many guests were coming, Jessica ignored her question, and began her attack.

"Is your servant any good?" she asked, glaring at Tabitha, who was standing close to Martha.

"She's not my servant, she's my sister," said Martha pleasantly, as though Jessica's question was perfectly understandable, and not the offensive barb it was intended to be. "And yes, she's a fast learner, and hardworking." Martha stared hard at Tabitha, trying to warn her not to react to Jessica's comment, but Tabitha didn't understand her meaning, and raised an eyebrow questioningly. Fortunately, Jessica was preoccupied with tasting a dish and didn't notice.

Jessica didn't seem impressed, but sent Tabitha off to help the cook. Tabitha and the cook were old friends, and soon they were folding complex pastry shapes and filling them with the Roman delicacies that Helena had insisted upon. If Jessica had intended to prove Martha's confidence in Tabitha misplaced, she was disappointed. Martha couldn't help feeling a little proud of Tabitha. The cook gave Martha a reassuring wink as she followed Jessica to the dining room to help sort out the seating arrangements for the evening.

"You must have been very busy this week. A lot of mouths to feed, with so many guests," said Jessica, as she preceded Martha briskly down the hall. "Didn't they have time for breakfast before they left yesterday morning?" she added over her shoulder, with a light-hearted sneer.

Martha was immediately on her guard. Now what was Jessica getting at?

"Yesterday they were in a hurry to get ahead of the crowds, so they left early. The Master refused breakfast, so I assumed he had other plans," replied Martha, innocently.

"Well, that is a shame. If he hadn't been hungry that lovely big fig tree down near the crossroads would still be alive, wouldn't it?" Martha was taken aback, and her brow furrowed. What an earth was Jessica talking about? Jessica saw Martha's confusion. She was enjoying having the upper hand as she continued. "The Rabbi looked for figs on it as they passed by, but when he found none, he cursed it, and now it's dead. Completely withered away." She paused dramatically, giving Martha time to take in what she'd just said. Then she added, "One of the servants witnessed the whole thing yesterday morning, and when he passed the tree on his way home in the evening, he was shocked to find it was dead. As the Rabbi is a guest in your house, I felt sure you would know all about it."

"No. I know nothing about it. It hasn't been mentioned. But I'm sure there's a perfectly reasonable explanation. Usually before a tree dies, there are signs, but they aren't always obvious to a casual passer by." Finally, Martha thought she was beginning to understand why Jessica was behaving the way she was. It was probably something Helena had said. The Rabbi Yeshua should have been staying as a guest in Simon's house, not hers. Helena would be oblivious to the danger and would only see it as a slight on her status in the community. How complicated people could be, thought Martha. Helena had little time for the people of Bethany, unlike her husband.

The dining room was impressive, but one Martha was familiar with. She had helped Simon and Helena out before. Couches and tables lay in random positions around the room, and soon Martha saw what a difficult task Jessica had been given. It was a delicate balancing act to seat everyone according to their rank and status and place the disciples as honoured guests among them. Martha knew the disciples well, and Jessica needed her to help achieve the best arrangement. It took all of Martha's diplomacy, but finally, the two women had agreed the seating plan. Jessica hurried off to attend to other pressing matters. Martha was left to direct the organisation of the furniture.

During the whole complex procedure, Helena had constantly interrupted Jessica and Martha with suggestions of her own. However, when she began to direct some of the servants away from the tasks Jessica had given them and onto ones of her own invention, Martha began to see how difficult this made things for Jessica. To make matters worse she chided Jessica in front of everyone. Helena's behaviour reminded her of her Aunt Elizabeth, who in the early days had often interfered with Sara's work because she'd felt inadequate as the lady of the house, despite the fact Sara ran things very smoothly for her.

A little later Martha returned to the kitchen, and found Helena clearly in a flap, berating poor Jessica in front of everyone and holding up the work. Tabitha looked beseechingly at Martha. The nearly eleven-year-old could plainly see Helena's behaviour was upsetting for everyone, and only served to undermine Jessica's authority with the other servants. She knew Martha was the only one who could help.

"Oh Martha dear, there you are. I'm nearly worn out, there is so much to do, and think about," complained Helena. "Please can you help Jessica sort this out?" She pointed to a salted fish lying on the table. Jessica's mouth went into a tight line.

"That looks like Galilean salted fish," said Martha, approvingly. "What a marvellous idea. I'm sure the Master and his disciples will especially appreciate it." Jessica beamed. It had been her idea. "Helena dear, don't you need to rest? Otherwise you'll be worn out before your guests arrive this evening. It's very important to Simon that you're at your best."

Helena put the back of her hand to her forehead and collapsed on a stool. "You are so right, perhaps a little rest will do me good," she sighed.

"Let me help you to your room," said Martha, nodding reassuringly at Jessica as she steered Helena to the door.

"I'll send up some of your special herb tea, to help you relax," called Jessica, realising what Martha was doing, and that she was really an ally, not an enemy.

"Oh, and some of those little biscuits you make. That would be nice," called back Helena as Martha firmly shut the door.

Jessica stood there, not quite believing what had just happened.

When Martha returned Jessica's first words to her were, "I don't know how you managed that, but thank you."

"My aunt is just the same, hasn't got a clue, but she feels she needs to look as though she's in charge. I've told Helena that if she thinks of anything else to let me know through her maid. That way she won't bother you, and you'll be free to get on with the job you do so well uninterrupted."

Jessica's relief and gratitude were plain for all to see. With Tabitha overseeing the table laying, and Martha's expert help in the kitchen, she soon had the preparations back on track. Tabitha had found a new respect for Martha as she had watched the two women work together.

Martha had seen little of Mary or Anna since they'd arrived, and supposed they were staying out of everyone's way. The two young women had spent most of their time up in Anna's room, talking as usual about the Master. Anna, like Mary, believed he was the Messiah, not just because of her father's healing two years before but because of everything he said and did. The thought that he might die because of the blindness of their leaders haunted Anna, and bound the two young women even closer together. Anna's feelings ran deep, and more than once, inspired by Mary, she too had spoken of anointing him, in preparation for the trials that they now knew lay ahead. Her own dowry of spikenard stood on the cabinet among her bracelets and necklaces, which Mary had often admired, although she had no desire or use for them. Mary's upbringing had been Spartan, and very different to Anna's.

Late in the afternoon, Martha sent Tabitha home to fetch a few extra herbs and spices for seasoning. She had snatched a brief few moments to tell her of the withered fig tree, and now, on her way home, Tabitha was curious. Despite the temptation to take a detour, she went straight there and was pleased to see Lazarus was back.

She immediately asked him about the incident, and to her surprise was told the story was true. He and the others had heard Yeshua tell the fig tree that it would no longer bear fruit, despite its green leaves.

"We hadn't realised the power behind his words or the importance of what we were seeing until we walked past the tree again this morning," Lazarus confessed. "It was Peter who pointed it out. Its leaves were dead and brown and lay on the ground beneath its black and withered branches. If it wasn't the Master's words that caused it, I do hope it doesn't affect the olive trees," he muttered to himself. "And no, I don't understand why he did it," he added, before she'd even opened her mouth to ask. "I was on my way to meet the labourers so I didn't have time to discuss it further with our friends. Now, hadn't you better get those herbs and spices back to Martha?"

Tabitha looked down at them in her hand; she'd almost forgotten. As she turned to go, Lazarus added, "Oh, and tell Martha I haven't forgotten to choose the two best ram lambs for the temple on Wednesday. The others can go back to the flock now. We'll have to let the boys know."

"The chosen ones will be very slippery customers, with their oily legs and heads," laughed Tabitha as she hurried away.

Chapter Twenty-Six

A Celebration in the Master's Honour

Monday evening, two days before Passover

Back at Simon's home, the arrangements were almost complete. Helena had been kept successfully out of Jessica's way and was now busy dressing, to be ready to receive her guests. Mary and Anna had appeared briefly during the late afternoon, and in the short conversation Martha had had with them they had seemed pensive, not at all how she'd expected. Surely these two young women should be looking forward to the evening? But then, perhaps they too couldn't forget the threat that lay over the Master's life, especially with so many guests coming from Jerusalem.

Martha had little time to consider this however, as Jessica had asked her to oversee the final details before everyone arrived. Helena had even found Martha some fine clothes to change into, to save her going home, for which Martha was grateful. Her own clothes were a bit homely for such an event.

The guests began to arrive, and were greeted graciously by Helena and Simon, who had returned home in the late afternoon. The glow of a red and gold sunset filled the sky above their colonnaded courtyard. The rooms set aside for the celebration began to fill up, but there was no sign of the Master and his disciples, nor her brother. Martha began to fret. She new Lazarus was safely at home, but what had become of Yeshua and his men? She began to wish she had gone home in case there had been news, but surely Simon would have heard if anything was amiss.

Finally, Martha heard the familiar Galilean accents of their friends as they entered the courtyard. She rushed out to greet them, almost forgetting that it wasn't her home. Lazarus was there too, bringing up the rear. While Simon and Helena greeted the others, she had a chance to speak with her brother.

"Sorry we're so late, but they've all had a wash and brush-up before coming over," he whispered to Martha, knowing she'd approve. "Did Tabitha pass on my message?"

Martha nodded. "Of course, especially about the fig tree."

"I may have a little more to tell you about that, but ask me later," he finished hurriedly, as their host Simon put his arm around his shoulder and led him away.

Martha stood quietly watching the proceedings. Besides Lazarus, all the other village elders were present, as well as many friends of Simon's from Jerusalem and relatives from both sides of the family, who were staying for Passover. The guests all seemed excited, talking and laughing loudly, while servants bustled about serving refreshments.

"A very comfortable dwelling," commented Simon the Zealot approvingly. They'd stayed with Simon in the past, so they knew the house well, but it was a little grander than they were used to.

"It looks like our host's invited everyone this evening," said Lazarus.

"Smells wonderful," remarked Thomas.

"That's not surprising," said James. "Martha's here somewhere."

"Remind me again. Why did she never get married?" queried Thaddaeus.

"If I'd had a sister like her, I'd have hung on to her," grinned Simon the Zealot.

Lazarus ignored their cheeky remarks, but was relieved that Martha wasn't around to hear them.

"We certainly couldn't have managed without her today," said Simon, their host. "Now, tell me how you got on in Jerusalem today. Was there any trouble in the end?"

"No, it was surprisingly quiet on the persecution front, but packed and noisy. Wherever the Master went he was quickly surrounded by people who wanted to hear from him and see his miracles. Only during worship and prayer did they give us any peace," sighed Thomas.

Lazarus watched Simon as he moved easily between his guests. Only the people of Bethany remembered the leper who had lived in isolation on the outskirts of their town. Anyone who had come to know him after he was healed found it hard to believe, but his zest for life was in every word he spoke, and every movement he made. Like Lazarus, his life had been restored, and now it was treasured.

Mary and Anna had appeared dutifully as the guests arrived. Anna had been whisked away by her mother to be introduced to people, leaving Mary standing alone and feeling awkward among such noble guests. Quickly, and with some relief, she joined Tabitha to watch. At one point, to their delight, the Master came over to speak with them, raising the eyebrows of a few of the more important guests.

The banquet did not disappoint. Martha stood unobtrusively at the door, directing the food to where it was needed, while Jessica kept tight control over the kitchen. Both women had been surprised at how well they had worked together. Jessica's long-held hostility towards Martha had dissolved, much to Martha's relief. Well-rested and calm, Helena sparkled like her jewels that evening, and quietly commented to Martha that it was all going very well indeed.

To begin with Anna had sat beside her mother at the table, conversing with their guests, but she seemed to have no enthusiasm for the small talk and no appetite for the wonderful food. When she excused herself and didn't return, Helena was annoyed and sent Mary to find her.

Simon's guests had finally reached a contented state of satiation, leaning back on their couches, sipping wine, or nibbling a favourite sweet fruit. It was then that Anna and Mary appeared. Anna spoke quietly to her mother, who seemed surprised that her daughter's head was now covered with a fine black shawl. However, she thought it was very becoming on Anna, if a little Jewish for her taste. Then Anna, beckoning to Mary, went and stood boldly before her father. Those sitting on the table with Simon and Yeshua looked up curiously. Anna bowed respectfully then, slowly and gracefully, she knelt before the Master, her head bowed, Mary close beside her for courage. Many in the room weren't aware of their presence, and the hubbub continued.

Anna clasped her hands together, as though in prayer, and when she looked up her face shone with a beauty that could only come from within. Those who could see her face fell silent. She reached up to heaven, her hands open in acknowledgement of the Lord, who reclined in front of them. Seeing this, others in the room bowed their heads too reverentially, acknowledging him.

Anna rose shakily, and for the first time, those watching her could see she carried an ornate alabaster flask. All eyes were now on her and a hush fell in the room. With her eyes lowered, she glided behind the Lord's couch.

"Mary anointed your feet using her hair, but it has fallen to me to finish the task that she began." Anna spoke so softly that only a few heard her.

The Lord smiled faintly and glanced down at Mary, who knelt at his feet, her head bowed. Carefully, Anna broke the seal of the flask and held it out as an offering, catching her father's eye as she did so, and taking courage from the look she saw there. Tenderly, she began to trickle the perfumed oil onto the Lord's head. Red droplets, like tears of blood, ran down his face, and rivulets formed, in his hair.

The glorious smell reached into the furthest corner of the room. The servants, summoned by Jessica, stood transfixed in the doorways, watching their mistress. Many of those from Jerusalem looked on quizzically, unsure of what they had just witnessed, but others looked troubled by her actions. This time there was unmistakable pain etched onto the faces of the Rabbi's disciples. Their host, Simon, had tears in his eyes, but he showed only approval of his daughter's actions. The silence was as thick as the perfume in the air.

"Like a lamb that is led to slaughter," thought Lazarus, remembering the lambs he had chosen for sacrifice by anointing their heads with oil, only hours before. In just two days' time they would be slaughtered. Mary looked at her brother in horror, as she too had the same thoughts. It was as though the Lord's fate had been sealed by her actions. She let out a cry of anguish. It sent ripples through the room, causing the murmurs to begin.

"Has the child any idea what she's done?" whispered one of Simon's relatives.

"Her father should have stopped her," came the harsh reply. "That perfume must be worth three hundred denarii, at least."

"What a waste," agreed someone from Jerusalem, as yet uneasy about speaking out too loudly against their host.

"That's easily a year's wages for some folk," said one of Simon's wealthier friends.

"A pitiful waste," whispered back his companion.

"It's such a beautiful smell though," sighed David, the owner of the two donkeys the Master had borrowed. "Surely the Messiah is worthy of such extravagance?" he added, in a loud voice.

A rich nobleman's eyes narrowed at the word 'Messiah'. "A vulgar display of wealth, if you ask me," he said. His friends looked down their noses at David.

Judas Iscariot began to nod in agreement with the comments. Finally, he felt he was among people who saw his point of view; after all, their laws forbade waste. His friends looked on in dismay. What was happening? This all sounded too familiar.

The nobleman piously continued, "And surely this perfume could have been sold and the money used to help the poor and needy, especially if it was not required by this woman?" He pretended he didn't know that Anna was Simon's daughter. He looked shocked when someone pointed it out to him.

Mortified by their words, Anna had fallen to her knees, supported by Mary. The Lord sighed deeply, and once again, defended the actions of a young woman.

"Leave her alone! What she has done is full of insight and good, you should be praising her. You can help the poor anytime you want, but you will not always have me here with you. This young woman has anointed my body for burial in the most fitting way she can. This will be remembered wherever the gospel is preached in the world."

"The gospel will be preached to the world," repeated Mary in an excited whisper to Anna, who did her best to smile through her tears.

Those who understood the significance of Anna's action turned their heads away in shame after the harsh comments, but others looked confused and wanted explanations. Some, like the nobleman, had made their choice, and Simon's hope of turning them had failed.

John and Peter were doubly sad. Since when had Judas started to care more about rules and money than their beloved Lord?

Martha had called Jessica to come and watch Anna, and now the two women stood in the hall talking about Anna's extravagant action, and what it meant. Judas came striding past, wearing his cloak, and Martha smiled at him, wondered where he could be going so late at night. When one or two of the other guests made their apologies and also departed, Martha felt concerned. Simon gave her a reassuring smile as he said goodnight to his hastily departing guests. Martha hoped Judas would be waiting for them back at the house; perhaps he just needed some air to cool off and clear his head.

The evening was late as Martha, a sleepy Tabitha, and Mary waited impatiently under the porch to leave, wrapped tightly in their cloaks. Lazarus was busy collecting the disciples, who seemed reluctant to leave the warm hospitality of Simon's home. Simon came over and thanked them wholeheartedly for all they had done that day. He seemed very pleased with the way things had gone, and philosophical about the few who had been offended by what had happened.

While he was saying farewell to Yeshua and his disciples, Jessica came rushing out of the kitchen calling Martha's name.

"Martha, I was so afraid I'd missed you. I wanted to especially thank you and Tabitha for all your help today. The dinner has been a great success and my mistress and master are so pleased. And that is in no small part due to you."

She swallowed hard. "The Rabbi..." she began, then started again. "The Lord has often stayed in this house, as you know, but until today I was blind. I didn't understand. But you, Mary, and my lady Anna have helped me to see who he really is. He even found time to come and speak to me – no guest has ever done that before. And what's more, he seemed to know everything about me. Things

I've never told people, from my past." Jessica struggled to hold back a sob. "But he didn't condemn me, God knows that's what I deserve. He said I was forgiven, and then I knew he accepted me, just the way I was. For the first time in my life, I felt so…"

"So loved," suggested Martha, finishing her sentence. Jessica nodded, biting her lip through her tears. "Please forgive my behaviour towards you, in the past, and today. I am truly sorry. I could not have been more wrong." She handed Martha something small, wrapped in an embroidered cloth. Martha took the gift, feeling a little guilty, as she hadn't even thought to say goodbye. Unfolding the cloth, Martha gasped with pleasure, for it contained a pot of cinnamon, a much-coveted cooking spice. Martha breathed in its fragrant aroma.

"Jessica, this is too much," she said, opening her arms to Jessica's embrace.

Finally, Simon of Bethany knelt before the Lord and kissed his hand. Yeshua raised him to his feet and embraced him.

"My friend," he said. "Peace be to your household and to your family. Now send us on our way. It is nearly time."

On their walk back home Martha and Mary found their friends still in a merry mood, especially Peter. His rugged face was flushed red, and the others teased him about the strength of Simon's wine.

"You'd think he'd be used to it by now," joked Andrew. "But as good as Simon's wine is, I don't think anything will ever match up to the wine at that wedding in Cana."

"Gosh. How long ago was that?" asked Peter. "It was the first miracle we ever saw you do."

"Glad you liked it," said Yeshua, the corner of his mouth twitching.

"And still the best," laughed Philip. Nathanael nodded his head in full agreement, as the two strode after Peter and Yeshua. They quickened their pace in the cold night air. Tabitha ran after Yeshua and caught hold of his hand, so she could keep up. In between breaths, she asked, "Is it true you are going to die soon?"

Without pausing in his stride, he looked down at her and said, "It is true."

"Aren't you afraid?" she asked, her face full of concern.

"No. Not afraid, my little one. Sad to be leaving you, but eager to return to my father and complete what I came for. There will be joy again for all who know me."

Tabitha squeezed his hand, and her eyes shone. She didn't understand the last bit of what he'd said, but it didn't matter. She knew he was the one person in the world she could truly trust, even more than Lazarus or Martha.

When they reached home, Martha was surprised that the disciples stood in a tight group by the gate, and didn't go in. Lazarus came to her side.

"They are going to pray up on the Mount of Olives tonight," he said.

Martha's stomach went into a knot and she stood shivering, trying to make out what he was saying to her. Mary came to her rescue.

"So, you are going too?" Mary asked bluntly.

"Yes," came his simple answer.

"But the night is so cold," Martha pleaded.

"We have our thick cloaks and we'll warm up in no time," Andrew reassured her, handing Peter his cloak, which Tabitha had just fetched from the house.

"And we'll be back tomorrow. Expect us late in the afternoon," said the Master. "Then we can all walk into Jerusalem together."

Martha felt numb as she watched them go, and the house felt empty and cold.

Chapter Twenty-Seven

Leaving

Tuesday

The empty feeling hadn't gone when Martha woke up, it made it hard to concentrate on everything that needed to be done before they left for Jerusalem that evening. She began by grinding corn, so there would be flour on their return. The steady rhythm of turning the handle was comforting.

Tabitha appeared, bubbling with exuberance. "I'll put the chickens in the stable just before we leave this evening. Rachel said someone will come over to let them out and feed them, until we get back. She's really pleased you've decided to go. A change is as good as a rest, she said. I've left loads of hay to top up the mangers for the sheep and goats and as soon as I've swept upstairs, I'll go and take the reject ram back to the flock," said Tabitha, almost in one breath.

Martha laughed. "Are you sure you can manage him on your own?"

"Oh yes. Josh said he'd lead on a halter all right, and they aren't far away. I should be back in no time."

Martha looked impressed. "You sound very excited," she said.

"I'm sorry, I can't help it," said Tabitha, as she helped bag up the flour. "I know Lazarus and the Master are in grave danger, and you're very worried about them – so am I. But at the same time, I'm really excited about staying in Jerusalem to celebrate and meeting all our relatives."

Poor Tabitha, Martha thought; her first real opportunity to have a holiday and spend time with the family, and all these challenging things were happening. On top of that, she still had grave concerns about the reception Tabitha would get from the family.

"Don't you dare feel guilty about being excited. You're not eleven yet." Martha smoothed back the corkscrew curls from Tabitha's frowning forehead. "It will be good to see everyone, and we'll be safe with Uncle." Rising from the ground, she asked, "Have you packed yet?"

"Nearly," said Tabitha.

"Then off you go. When you've delivered the ram I've got some things for you to take to Mama Juthine."

Tabitha raced off, nearly bumping into Mary as she came out of the house.

"Where's she going in such a hurry?" asked Mary.

"To pack," said Martha, hopefully.

"She told me she'd nearly finished, when I asked earlier. By the way, I've put all the bedding away, but our guests have left a few things behind. Hopefully they'll pick them up later."

Mary watched Martha for a few minutes, before venturing to ask, "So what happened with Jessica yesterday? What a transformation. You two seemed to be getting along really well."

"I got Helena out of her way. But the real change came when she met the Master. I don't think she'll feel the need to put others down anymore. We actually work together really well."

Mary beamed when she heard this. "I'm sure there was more to it than that, but what about the fig tree?" asked Mary, her eyes bright with curiosity. "Everyone at Simon's knew about it, as did half of Bethany."

"Only half?" said Martha, amused. "I did talk to Lazarus on the way home last night. The consensus seemed to be that it was a demonstration of the power of his words. But more importantly, it was about having constant faith, trusting and relying on the Lord, so that when we ask for things and pray, especially for others, the prayer or need is answered. It's the realisation of his power. The power of life and death, the power to move mountains, he said." She let out a long breath and shook her head. "But that gets blocked if we hold a grudge against someone, no matter how justified we feel."

Mary nodded thoughtfully. "To move mountains," she whispered, in awe. Then she remembered speaking to John. "John remembered the Master telling a story about a fig tree. In three years it hadn't produced fruit, so the owner wanted to dig it up and make room for something better. But the gardener had asked for one more year to feed it, and if then it still hadn't produced any fruit, he could cut it down."

"That's very interesting," said Martha. "Israel is often represented in scripture as a fig tree, but if it's not producing fruit, that doesn't sound so good. But I wonder who the owner and the gardener are supposed to be? What else did he say?"

"John thought God was the owner, and the Lord Yeshua was the gardener. It was like he was asking his father to give Israel more time. But the fig tree on the road to Jerusalem didn't have fruit on it, despite it being the right time. John believes the death of the tree was prophetic. Despite everything the Master has said and done, there are still so many who don't believe he is the Messiah, especially here in Jerusalem."

Mary sounded so serious that Martha went pale just thinking about what she'd just said.

Chapter Twenty-Eight

The Parting

Tuesday sunset, as the day of preparation for the Passover begins

As promised, the Master and his disciples had returned to Bethany in the late afternoon. Martha was relieved to see that Judas was with them, although he seemed quieter than usual, as they ate a light meal and warmed themselves beside the fire. The day had been bright, but the sun had been robbed of its warmth by a cold wind that swept the countryside round about.

As they sat together, Tabitha was keen to hear about their night of prayer on the Mount of Olives. It sounded like a great adventure to her, but when she asked, they all seemed reluctant to talk about it. Mary joined them, and immediately wanted to hear all about their trip into Jerusalem that day. This they were willing to talk about, but Yeshua quietly excused himself.

With one arm around Tabitha's shoulders, Lazarus told Mary how they had finally fallen asleep in a sheltered hollow on the southeast side of the hill and were woken up by the first cold rays of the sun. They had hurried down to the shelter of the temple porches, but it was still early, so some of them had gone to buy bread. The Master, by all accounts, had taken the opportunity to go into the temple while it was quiet and the priests were occupied. When they got back they had found him talking with some of the early pilgrims. He had been telling them that the Kingdom of God was now very near, and available to everyone, if only they changed their ways in the knowledge of who he was. Later, as the crowds built up, it had got a bit trickier. The Master had been approached openly by some of the chief priests, accompanied by scribes and elders of the Sanhedrin, who had questioned him in front of everyone.

"It was the usual set up," Thaddeus interjected. "They stood close together, like they were afraid, but I wasn't sure if that was of the Master or the people. They're questions were clearly designed to trap him."

"What did they ask him?" asked Tabitha.

"Where he claims his power and authority come from," said Thaddaeus.

"Can you imagine not knowing that? Are they completely stupid?" blurted out Thomas, who was helping himself to another of Martha's date cakes.

"So what did the Master say in answer to that?" asked Tabitha, curious to know why they should ask such an obvious question.

"He didn't," said Thaddeus. "He knew where their question was leading, so instead he asked them a question. 'Was the baptising that John did from heaven or from man?' Of course they didn't want to answer that, being surrounded by people who believed John was a prophet sent by God. But neither could they answer the other way."

"Why?" asked Tabitha, looking puzzled.

"Because, if they'd answered that John baptised under the authority of heaven, the people would have wanted to know why, as our leaders, they hadn't believed everything John had said and done. On the other hand, if they'd dared to say John wasn't sent by God, then there would probably have been a riot," said Matthew, a little triumphantly.

"The Master's quite smart, isn't he? Everyone knows John was a prophet, so whichever way they'd answered his question they'd have been in trouble with the people," said Tabitha, nodding her head wisely.

"And you're a smart girl. But it was good to see them get a dose of their own medicine," said Matthew.

Turning to the others, Thaddaeus said, "I quite enjoyed watching their faces as it dawned on them the Master had just backed them into a corner."

"I'm not sure the Master would have put it that way, but I take your point," laughed Lazarus.

"So, what happened after that?" asked Mary, still amused at the thought of the Master so easily outwitting such educated people.

The Master had then related a series of parables, which they had all liked, if only because they were so clearly aimed at his learned audience, but when a Herodian had asked a question about something, Thaddaeus had to confess he'd got lost part-way through the answer to that one.

"However," he remarked, "I did hear the Master say there would be no husbands or wives in heaven, and that'll please some." They all laughed.

"The Master kind of tore into them after that, almost like he was deliberately provoking them," said Philip, frowning deeply.

"I just thought the Master was losing patience with them. They'd been at him for hours," said James, passionately.

"But they still didn't arrest him!" said Simon the Zealot triumphantly, but then he added sadly, "I almost wish they'd get it over with, the suspense is hard to bear now." Some of the others nodded in sympathy.

At that moment, Yeshua came in carrying a tray laden with more wine, bread and cheese which was passed round, as he joined them.

"We rested near the treasury, later on in the day. You watched a widow drop two mites into one of the free will offerings," Lazarus said to Yeshua, wondering where he'd been. "You said she had put in more than anyone else, because she had given all she had to live on. We can learn from that, don't you think Tabitha? It's easy to give when you have plenty, but much harder when you have nothing."

Tabitha looked into his face with her big brown eyes and nodded vigorously. "I like that story," she whispered. "The things that happen with the crowds are a bit frightening. I don't like the thought of the priests trying to trap you Yeshua, so they can arrest you. It's all wrong." Lazarus squeezed her shoulder and Mary took one of her hands. "But the widow reminds me of Mama Juthine," she said, smiling, and Mary and Lazarus agreed wholeheartedly.

** *

While they'd been talking, Martha had been in the kitchen tidying away before they left. She'd been in the store cupboard for a while, and on her return was surprised to find the Master squatting before the dying warmth of the fire. He seemed deep in thought, so she carried on quietly with what she was doing.

"Would you like me to sweep up the embers?" he suddenly asked, as though he had just become aware of her presents. It was Martha's last job before they left.

"Yes, that would be really helpful. Thank you," she said, half smiling to herself with pleasure at such a rare moment.

"I used to do this for my mother when I was a child," he said, quietly.

Martha put her head on one side and watched him, realising he too might be finding comfort in simple, ordinary tasks, as she did.

She also saw how human he was at that moment, and the frailty of his body, even though it must also contain heaven. She could have wept, but instead she asked, "How is Judas?"

"Why do you ask?" he said, concentrating on sweeping up the ashes, and not looking up.

"He seems to be struggling, pulling away from us. I'm concerned about him, that's all."

Yeshua nodded and sighed deeply. "Some things have to be," he said quietly, but then another thought struck him and he looked up. A broad smile began to spread across his sad face, and she saw a twinkle of mischief in his eyes.

"My dear Martha. Sometimes, I think I should ask my father why he gave me twelve men and not twelve women. Women think with astute hearts."

She laughed, "But you have many astute women among your disciples, and they are waiting faithfully for you in Jerusalem. Now take these in for me," she said, handing him a tray laden with more wine, bread and the last of the cheese.

***

Jupiter shone out in the glow of the sunset, while voluminous purple clouds towered into the darkening sky from the north-west. Reluctantly, the disciples filed out into the courtyard ready to leave. The fire had been doused and everyone now stood waiting, wrapped tightly in their cloaks. At least they all looked less tired and strained, thought Martha as she put her bundles down and fastened the kitchen door. The branches of the old olive tree twisted and groaned in the steadily increasing wind.

"We'll all warm up once we get walking," said Matthew, putting his arm round the young James, who was shivering a little.

Martha slung one of her loads across her back and brought the other to her brother. He rolled his eyes and pushed it away playfully, so she pushed it into his chest.

"Living dangerously, I see," laughed James, as Martha let Lazarus' bundle go and stood defiantly, hands on hips. Lazarus bowed theatrically to her and picked up his bundle.

"All right, I'll carry it myself," he said to Martha, then turning to the others and shaking his head, he said, "Where did our parents go wrong?"

"I don't think they did," butted in Tabitha. "Martha was mainly responsible for bringing you up, wasn't she?"

Mary snorted with laughter. "So, Martha has no one to blame but herself."

"Are we all ready?" called the Master, wondering what was so funny.

Martha was last to leave, securing the gate against the wind. She hurried after the others, not wanting to be left behind in the fading light, even in the familiar and safe streets of Bethany.

Mary had been walking with James and John, and now she ran to catch up with her brother. They were walking fast to keep out the cold.

"Tell me what happened this afternoon," she panted, "On the Mount of Olives."

"Oh, you heard," he said.

"Yes, but nothing made sense. I didn't like to ask questions."

"Well, that must be a first," joked Lazarus. He paused to think. "After leaving the temple, we climbed back up onto the west slope, in the sunshine. Matthias was particularly struck by the view of the temple from there. Earlier he had been admiring the craftsmanship that had gone into building it, and the number of huge stone blocks it had taken." Mary nodded, unseen in the darkness. It was one of her favourite views too. "Looking out over the temple, the Master said that a time would come when not one stone would be left standing. The area would be levelled to the ground! I think we were shocked. It was something that was hard to imagine looking down on the vastness of the temple as it sparkled white in the sunshine."

"Yes, but then remember the fig tree story John told you, and the fate of that fig tree near Bethany, and don't forget he wept over Jerusalem the other day, because he knows what will happen to it."

Lazarus stood still and looked at her, his mouth slightly open in realisation.

"I hadn't connected them. Of course, you're right." He paused deep in thought, then said, 'It is no good looking to the temple and Jerusalem for help, for the real salvation of Israel comes from the Lord God'."

"The prophet Jeremiah," said Mary, recognising the quotation. "But what else did Yeshua say?"

"You will need to ask Peter, James, John or Andrew. The five of them sat talking with him for quite a while after that. The rest of us went on ahead and waited near the cairn at the top. I think it might have been a private conversation though, so tread lightly if you ask." Just then Tabitha ran up grabbing both their hands, to help keep her own warm.

The familiar road to Jerusalem seemed longer that night, as they were constantly buffeted by the restless wind. Slowly, each turned inward, to their own thoughts as they journeyed on.

Rounding the long bend, crouched like a shadow over the three hills, Jerusalem could be seen even in the gloom. Their pace quickened; everyone was keen to be inside the great walls. The silvery line of the Kidron tossed and foamed its way through the deep gorge below them. Beyond, the bridge to the Golden Gate shuddered under the force of the churning water below. Finally, numb with cold, they ascended the short stretch of road and stood before the gates.

Despite the icy wind channelled along the valley, the Master seemed in no hurry hanging at the back of the group with Mary and Martha. He stopped and looked up, his face lit from above, and seeing his expression, Martha's heart was wrenched in her chest. She had never seen such suffering before. Her eyes stung in the wind. Tabitha looked from Martha's face to the Master's, then took one of his hands in both of her own and squeezed gently. He looked down, his smile sad and far away. His free hand brushed her cheek, and then he reached out and took Martha's hands too, holding them firmly.

"Be brave, my dear friends. Hold on to what I have taught you and what my father in heaven has revealed to you. My dear Martha, you still have much to live for, your legacy is great in my Father's kingdom. Through you, others will find their healing and faith in me." Then he embraced her, Tabitha still clinging to his side, reluctant to let go. Her bottom lip trembled, and although she didn't fully understand, she knew she would never see him again. Martha shivered as she drew herself up and pulled Tabitha closer to her, trying to protect her from the inhospitable turbulence that tugged and pulled at them, but also because it brought her comfort.

Mary stepped towards him now, dry-eyed. She held herself tall and looked up at him unflinchingly, but one, white knuckled hand held tightly onto her brother. The Lord and Master, her friend Yeshua, took her hands in both of his and looked into her eyes. Tight-lipped, she tried to smile reassuringly back, her teardrops, like black pearls on her eyelashes, catching the light of night around them. Then the warmth of his peace flooded her like a kiss.

"You will be with me again," he said, softly, and she knew it was a promise.

"I know," she whispered, "but parting is so hard." Her voice dropped low as she tried to speak.

"You have work to do Mary. Teach and share all that you have learned, waste no opportunity. Reach out to all those I will send you. Do this for me and my Father in heaven."

Mary nodded mutely. She was beginning to understand the price of obedience.

Lazarus put his arm around his sister and drew her close, looking imploringly at his friend and Lord, but he mastered his voice as he spoke.

"Please, I know you called me back to fulfil the part assigned to me, but not to be allowed to follow you to the end is unbearable. Please, let me come."

Yeshua looked at the bowed heads of his sisters, and Tabitha clinging to them. "To truly follow me, you must walk the path set before you by my father in heaven. My friend, we have spoken of this. You know your way, and although as yet you do not understand how, I will be with you."

The Master embraced him, and then turned abruptly away to join the disciples, who stood huddled together in the shelter of the great arches. In another moment they were gone, passing into the shadows.

The four of them stood together, their cloaks tugging and twisting together, whipped by the wind, feeling numb. Tabitha's violent shivers finally stirred them back to life and they entered the holy city, but no one spoke.

In the vastness of night, the temple court was almost deserted, but some shelter could be found under the arches and colonnades of Solomon's porch. A few figures flitted here and there, but the little family only had eyes for their friends as they hurried to the southern steps that led down to the old town of David. Now they too began to hurry towards the west gate, which led to the upper city and their uncle's house.

Chapter Twenty-Nine

Family

🌱

They laboured uphill along broad, well-laid streets until they stood before the familiar gate in the narrow passage, beside the large house. Tabitha pulled on the bell enthusiastically until Sara let them in. She was relieved to see them, as it was getting late. Even in the lamplight, the courtyard looked grand to Tabitha, with its Roman colonnade and arched doorways. The second storey had large shuttered windows and even a tower. The sound of voices came from every direction.

Elizabeth came swooping out to greet them, scolding them light-heartedly for their late arrival. It wasn't often her nieces came to stay, and with so many relatives visiting for Passover, she was hopeful it would be one to remember. However, she couldn't help commenting on how pale they looked.

"We're just tired and cold Aunt," Martha reassured her. "Simon and Helena threw a party to honour the Rabbi last night. It was a great success, with many guests, but a lot of hard work." Martha's ploy worked well, as immediately Elizabeth's focus turned to her friend Helena. Just then Martha was feeling a little vulnerable.

Elias came hurrying out, and quickly steered them all into the warmth of the house. He immediately took Lazarus to the dining room, where all their male uncles, cousins and second cousins were waiting for him. As the two men disappeared, Martha heard Elias say, "It's been such a long time since the family were all together like this. I feel in my bones it will be a Passover to remember. Now my boy, what news of the Master, the Lord? Has he come to the city tonight? Your uncles are eager for news."

Martha, Mary and a wide-eyed Tabitha were graciously given a little time by their aunt before meeting the women and children, who, despite the size of the house, congregated in the kitchen in the traditional way. They took their bundles to the shared room which they had always used as children. Martha was surprised at how light she felt already, as though a whole weight of responsibility had been taken off her shoulders.

The room was at the top of the tower, up the main flight of stairs which gave access to the second floor. The windows looked down into the alley, the back entrance to the courtyard, and also, in daylight, to a narrow but breath-taking view of the city. As a child, Martha had spent a lot of time gazing out of these windows. Tonight, however, the shutters were tightly closed against the wind, and the room was comfortable and unchanged. Rolled up in a corner were an extra mat and blankets for Tabitha. She pulled these out and arranged them at the foot of Martha's bed, snuggling and sniffing the new creamy-white wool blanket.

"Do you think this means the old goat has finally accepted me as a member of the family?" asked Tabitha.

"Tabitha dear, you really shouldn't speak about Aunt Elizabeth like that," said Martha, as Tabitha stretched out on the deep mattress and wriggled her toes.

"Even if it's perfectly true," added Mary, as she arranged her few things on the little table. "You must be in favour, Martha and I will have to make do with our old ones."

Tiredness began to creep over Martha as she sat on the edge of her low bed. She longed to sink into it and rest, but there was a barrage of cousins, aunts and uncles to meet. Martha comforted herself that somewhere in the midst of the bedlam, Sara would be calmly and quietly overseeing everything. She splashed cold water on her face, smoothed out her clothes, combed her hair and arranged her shawl; she was ready to go. With a light tread Mary led them down the stairs, while Tabitha rushed ahead, excited.

The stairs led down to the courtyard and here an olive tree graced the centre, a symbol of their family's wealth, beside a fountain. However, any sound made by the falling water was drowned out by the hubbub of chatter that poured from the open kitchen door.

Martha took a deep breath and stepped through the wall of noise into the light. Women and children were everywhere, filling the two large rooms. She smiled with pleasure as she called greetings to cousins and aunts, bending down to hug the children and commenting on how much taller the older ones were. By the time she had waded into the centre of the room the weariness had fallen away, to be replaced by the warm glow of belonging. Mary, with her reputation for story-telling, quickly found employment among the younger children, watched by admiring aunts. Tabitha, suddenly overcome by shyness, stood beside Sara, Elizabeth's most treasured servant and friend.

At noon the next day, the temple priests would begin the ritual slaughter of thousands of lambs. At sunset, these would become the centre of the Passover meal for each family, when the week-long celebration began. The great story would be told of how the angel of death had passed over the houses of the Israelite slaves, sparing them but killing all the first-born children of Egypt. They would then go on to tell of the hurried escape from Pharaoh and his army under the guidance of Moses, a leader whose like they had never seen again.

"Ah, there you are Martha," interrupted Elizabeth. "We need you to help us decide which recipe would be best for the bitter herbs. Julia insists her mother's recipe with hyssop is best, but Sara says only horseradish will do. What do you think, dear?"

"Sara's has always been particularly pungent," remarked Martha. "But hyssop certainly lasts a while on the tongue."

"You were ever the diplomat, my dear. Can I leave it with you to sort out?" said her aunt, as she rolled away into the sea of relatives.

"A little chicory or endive gives it that extra bitterness, my mother always said," suggested the pleasant but plain Julia.

"Well, what about a bit of swine thistle, that's never hard to find, even at the last minute," suggested Martha.

"My mother used to use that too," agreed Julia, "especially during the leaner times. What do you think, Sara?"

"Best not let Elizabeth hear you say that, but I'm sure we could make it work," Sara agreed, her smile framed by frizzled grey hair and cheeks that were red from tending the fire and ovens.

"And of course, we'll use your sweet charoset," said Martha.

"Oh, I agree," said Julia. "It always brings me hope after eating all that bitterness."

"Tabitha's already grinding some of the ingredients for me, would you like to help her, Julia?" asked Sara. "Your boys seem nicely settled listening to Mary."

A while later, Martha and Sara withdrew to the cool quiet of the pantry, to do a little stocktaking but also so they could talk more freely. Martha was sad to hear of Julia's predicament. She had been married to Elizabeth's younger brother, Obadiah. After his death, their older brother Talman had dutifully taken Julia into his household along with his brother's two young sons. Over time, his wife had become resentful towards Julia, allowing their only son to bully Julia's two younger boys. Talman had refused to listen to Julia's complaints, leaving her in an almost impossible situation.

"Can't Aunt Elizabeth have them stay here?" asked Martha. "There's plenty of room and Julia would be such good company for her."

"They've talked about it, but I don't think your aunt and uncle have come to any resolution yet. It's a tricky situation, especially if Julia's older son, Silvanus, is to inherit anything."

"Poor Julia," sighed Martha.

"Oh, there's more," sighed Sara, as though they were her own family. "I don't think Josiah and Sarah are finding life easy at the moment either. From what she's told me, with Amon and Esther and the two little ones living with them and the other five children, they're a bit tight for space. And with the demands of the olive farm, Josiah has little time to think about adding another room or two."

"Couldn't Uncle Josiah employ someone else to enlarge the house?"

"Oh, you know your uncle, he likes things done properly, wants to do it himself, save money. Poor Sarah, by the sound of it she's near the end of her tether."

Martha nodded understandingly; families were complicated at the best of times.

"And how is Aunt Elizabeth doing? She seems to be revelling in her family tonight."

"Oh, she mostly puts a brave face on things, but she worries about your uncle, especially with all this business with Lazarus and the Rabbi. I don't think she's as certain as Elias is. She listens to too much gossip and is swayed by it all. And she isn't well. Having the family around takes her out of herself. What about your mother's family, aren't they coming up from Galilee for Passover?"

Martha rearranged some jars on a shelf, then said casually, "They came last year but with all the little ones and another baby on the way, I think Uncle Job thought it would be easier if just the men came this year. They'll stay with Cousin Rebecca, but I'm sure they'll call in at some point."

"So, how are you?" asked Martha.

"Nothing to grumble about," replied Sara. Martha gave her a hard look. "Well, I do get a bit tired these days, especially when the whole family comes, but it's normally only for a couple of weeks, and it makes Elizabeth so happy." There was a pause as Sara counted some sacks of flour. "That's plenty," she said to herself. "She's really been looking forward to seeing you. You remind her so much of her brother. Right, all sorted out here. Time to go back into the fray."

"Ah, there you are!" rang out Elizabeth's voice as they came into the kitchen.

Mary's stories had finished, and while some of the women were helping clear away the remains of the evening meal, the four mothers, Keturah, Julia, Sarah and her daughter-in-law Esther, were now attempting to get the younger children to bed. Slowly, almost reluctantly, the household began to quieten down.

The men stayed up a while longer, Eleazar, the head of the family, quietly snoring in a corner, while Reuben, his eldest grandson, kept a close eye on him. They were much alike in character, with piercing eyes that made lying unthinkable to anyone who met them.

Elias had been the acting head of the family for many years, overseeing the family businesses from Jerusalem. An astute businessman, he had managed to hang onto most of the family's land despite Herod the Great, and had continued to build up their olive exports, ensuring some sort of anonymity from local affairs. His brother Josiah ran the olive groves north of Jerusalem, and was married to Sarah. They had six children; Amon, their eldest, was married with two children and lived at home. Joachim, Elias' youngest brother managed the vineyards and the wool trade and was married to Keturah. They had four children and their oldest son Micah and his wife, had a baby.

Lazarus, Reuben and the affable Sam, sat together still enjoying the wine and their freedom. Martha, Mary and Tabitha had sunk into bed and fallen quickly into an exhausted sleep, Tabitha still with a smile on her face.

Chapter Thirty

A Long Night

Martha was woken by an urgent banging on the gate somewhere below their window. She kept her eyes closed, desperate to drift back to sleep, hoping that someone else would answer it. Mary was still gently snoring. The determined knocking came again, and Martha couldn't ignore it. She forced herself out of bed and down the stairs, groggily covering her tunic with a blanket.

She arrived in the courtyard just as her grumbling Uncle Joachim unlatched the gate. Even in the dim light, Martha noticed the strong resemblance he also bore to Eleazar, her grandfather. The tall, straight bearing and strong profile had been passed down to her cousin Reuben. If only he'd laugh more, she thought.

She heard Joachim's deep, gruff voice speaking urgently with the caller. As Martha watched from the shadows, he ushered two breathless men into the courtyard. They were wrapped heavily in cloaks, and refused an invitation to enter the house, standing impatiently by the gate while Joachim went to rouse Elias. Martha was intrigued and by now, wide awake, her heart was beating fast.

Elias arrived, clearly unhappy about the intrusion at such a late hour, especially with a house full of guests, but as the men spoke in hurried whispers his countenance changed. The shorter, stockier, third brother Josiah emerged from the house with Lazarus, both yawning and carrying their cloaks. Martha was surprised and stepped into the light, just as they were rejoined by Joachim. A hurried conversation took place, and then the strangers left.

Lazarus and their uncles continued to urgently debate the news they had just heard while Martha hovered awkwardly nearby, shivering a little. Finally, the four men seemed to reach a conclusion, and Elias called her over.

"My dear niece, you of all my household are awake and therefore must be the first to hear the news. It will come as no surprise, but that will not make it any easier to bear." Martha took a deep breath and braced herself. "Lazarus will explain, but you must promise me that you will not let him leave the protection of these walls." Martha nodded, her heart accelerating in fear. What could be so important to make their uncles go out at this time of night?

With grim looks on their faces, the three brothers departed into the dark streets. Lazarus closed the gate with exaggerated quietness and turned to look at his sister.

"Let's go into the kitchen," he said, shivering as he led the way. While Martha brought life back to the embers of the fire, he poured them both some wine. Martha took the goblet gratefully and sat beside the fire. Lazarus took several mouthfuls before he spoke.

"It's the Master. They've finally arrested him. He's been taken to Caiaphas' palace for trial."

"But it's the middle of the night," protested Martha.

"Nevertheless, it has begun." said Lazarus, watching her intently.

"So where did they arrest him?" Suppressed anger made her voice shake.

"The garden, Gethsemane, where he goes to pray. After they left us this evening they were going straight to the lodgings to celebrate the Passover together, a day early." Martha nodded, this she already knew. None of them had had the courage to ask why he had wanted to celebrate a day early. Peter and John had gone to see how things were going that morning. The women were all helping with the arrangements.

"So we guess they went to the garden after that," said her brother.

"He must have known he was going to be arrested tonight," said Martha, bitterly.

"It seems that way," agreed her brother. "But I don't think anyone else did. Our uncles will do their best to find out what's going on. Maybe Elias can use his influence with the elders."

"If Elias is seen openly defending the Master, the chief priests will make sure our family is ostracized from Jewish society," retorted Martha.

"I think Elias will be mindful for the safety of his family, despite his conviction about the Master." Martha nodded in agreement. Lazarus went on, "There are many good men amongst the elders and on the Great Council. Hold onto your faith. The prophecy must be fulfilled!"

Martha drained her goblet and placed it firmly on the stone floor. "I'll go and wake Mary. We need to pray."

Mary shook her head and tried to rub the sleep from her eyes. "What's the time?" she asked, sitting up.

"Somewhere past the middle of the night," whispered Martha. "Shhhh, please don't wake Tabitha." She took Mary's hand in her own.

"Your hands are freezing. What's going on?" whispered Mary, eyes wide.

"It's the Master, they've arrested him. I'm sorry to wake you, but I knew you would never forgive me if I didn't. Our uncles have gone to see what they can find out. We must gather the family to pray."

Mary drew a deep breath and exhaled slowly.

"I'm ready, Martha." Her voice was calm and steady as she looked unwaveringly into her sister's eyes.

Lazarus had been busy fetching the younger men from their beds, so Martha went to wake Sara, while Mary silently dressed. Quietly they gathered in the main room. Elizabeth joined them, bleary eyed but determined to play her part. She began by insisting Sara fetch some of the servants to get the fires going. Sara attended the fire herself.

Despite the chill air, Mary had paused in the garden, so she heard the rapid, muted knocking. Thinking it might be news from her uncle, she grabbed the lantern and ran to open it. Her mouth dropped open in surprise. Miriam, Susanna and Salome were standing huddled together in the shadows under the arch of the back gate. They were heavily veiled and cloaked, but still unmistakable. Once inside they seemed to relax.

"How on earth did you find us?" asked Mary. "But I am so glad to see you. We've only just heard the news."

"Oh, you've heard," exclaimed Miriam. "Thanks to Elias' foresight, Sara came to see us yesterday, to tell us how to find you and gather news."

"He did say we should feel free to call anytime," emphasised Salome, looking around at the darkened house. "Although he might not have meant the middle of the night," she admitted. "This must be quite a change for you all. Very grand."

"It certainly is," agreed Mary. "But poor Martha still seems to be in the kitchen." Only Salome managed a smile.

"We were just about to pray. Will you come and join us? Martha will be so pleased to see you."

"It looks as though that's why we're here," commented Susanna, as they followed Mary across the courtyard. "How did you find out?"

"Two trusted friends of my uncle's let us know. They had been summoned to an emergency meeting of the Sanhedrin because the Master had been arrested. They called in on the way there and were not pleased to have been kept waiting. My uncles left soon after the message was delivered."

The waiting family were astonished to see three heavily cloaked women enter the room with Mary. Martha cried out with disbelief and joy as she jumped up to embrace them. Elizabeth welcomed them by name, remembering them from when she had visited Helena at Lazarus' resurrection. Reuben introduced his cousins, Amon and Micah, the elder sons of Josiah and Joachim, who were also present in the room. Sara nodded to Salome and went to fetch refreshments.

"Before we pray, please tell us what you know of the Master's arrest," said Lazarus, speaking for them all.

"I should like to know a little of how you've got on this week too," added Martha.

"It was very brave of you to come," added Sam.

"Thank you, Sam," said Miriam. "What a day it's been. It began with John and Peter turning up at the guest house this morning. Our lodgings are just round the corner, and very comfortable thanks to Joanna." Elizabeth's eyes rounded with interest. She was well aware that Joanna was the wife of Chuza, Herod's steward. "It's been a while since John and Peter stayed there, so they were having trouble finding the place. Fortunately they'd bumped into the odd job man, who was carrying a pitcher of water back for the Landlord. He recognised them instantly. Yeshua had sent them to make sure everything would be ready by the evening. Magnus, the landlord, seemed to know all about it and had had the lamb prepared ready for us. We began to get worried as it got dark, but everyone finally turned up, bringing your greetings." Susanna and Salome nodded in acknowledgment, as Miriam sipped some wine.

"It was so good to see the Master, and all be together again," said Susanna.

"Was Judas with them?" Martha asked.

"No, he came along a little later," replied Salome. Her voice sounded bitter.

"They began the celebration not long after they'd arrived. We served from the kitchen below because the Master had made it quite clear the meal should be as private as possible; just the twelve," explained Miriam. "It all seemed to follow the usual traditions at first, with the Master recounting the nation's deliverance from Egypt and their setting out for the Promised Land. The first cup of wine was followed by the second and the psalms were sung with surprising enthusiasm for such a long day. But then it changed. Salome, tell us what you heard."

Salome took a deep breath before speaking. "Quite clearly I heard the Master say that one of them was going to betray him. They were all so shocked and then so busy defending themselves that I don't think they realised the significance of what he did next, but I did. Dipping some of the bitter herbs into the charoset, he handed them to Judas." Salome's face was filled with anger.

"Oh my!" blurted out Elizabeth.

"Judas left shortly after that. I opened the door for him," said Miriam, her voice cracking. "His face was cruel and hard. I hardly recognised him."

"Before they ate, I carried the water and towels upstairs for the men to wash their hands," continued Miriam. "That's when the Master stripped to the waist and began washing their feet. I had to dash back down to get more towels and water."

"We could hear Peter's protests from downstairs," said Salome, smiling. "He wasn't going to let the Master wash his feet. But Peter was missing the point, as usual. The Master was demonstrating that we should all be servants to one another, with hearts to match, no matter who we are."

"A lesson that is hard for some to grasp," said Susanna, thoughtfully.

"I know I've pushed my boys forward at times, but now I understand much better," confessed Salome.

"We can't help wanting the best for our children," said Elizabeth supportively, looking over at Sam and Reuben. Sam raised an eyebrow and got a look of reproach from his mother.

"There is more," continued Miriam. "Then the Master took a matzah, blessed and broke it and gave them all a piece as usual, but as he did so, he said, 'take and eat this, it is my body which is given for you. Remember me in this'. I had to stifle a cry. It was so difficult to hear him speak like that. I shall never forget his words, they wrenched my heart. Then towards the end of the supper, Mary Alphaeus heard him say something similar, but holding up a cup of wine. He gave thanks to God and then said, 'This cup is the new covenant, made by my blood, which is poured out for you!' Can you imagine?" Miriam's eyes were wide with horror. "He's making a new covenant before God, for us, but with his own life blood! I shudder to think how it will be accomplished."

The room was silent.

"So, what happened then? How was the Master arrested?" Lazarus asked gently.

"Patience," said Martha. "Miriam is coming to that."

"They talked for a long while. Peter raised his voice again, but we couldn't hear what was said. But just before they left, Yeshua came to us..." Miriam's voice broke for a moment. "We didn't realise at the time, but he was saying goodbye. He said they were going to Gethsemane to pray, which they often did."

"And to look out for him. That's what he said. I remember now," exclaimed Salome. "Didn't understand what he meant, still don't."

"They took swords with them, Martha." Miriam's face creased up with anguish. "Where they got those from is beyond me. They're fishermen, tax collectors, ordinary people, not soldiers, not Zealots." The others nodded. "We knew nothing of his arrest until that young friend of Peter, John Mark, turned up. There'd been a tussle with someone, he was only wearing his undergarment. He, Matthias and Barsabbas had met them after supper to pray. They prayed for a long while, and then Judas appeared out of the darkness, closely followed by some temple officials. He kissed the Master in greeting."

Salome spat, glaring defiantly at the shocked faces. Hurriedly Miriam continued. "Quickly they became surrounded by what seemed to be a battalion of armed soldiers and temple police, but they were half hidden amongst the trees. The disciples were terrified. Who would send so many to arrest one man?"

"People who were afraid of him," said Mary.

"He was betrayed by Judas," said Miriam, sadly. "My heart aches for him. It could have been any one of us. We've all struggled at times, wondering what was going on, and we all doubted him at some point. And poor John Mark, he was really angry with himself for abandoning the Master and his friends, but if he hadn't run away we might not have known the Master had been arrested until the morning."

"Has anyone else returned?" asked Lazarus, his face drawn and pale in anguish for his friends.

"Yes, Andrew came back later," answered Susanna. "Peter had taken an ill-aimed swing with his sword, managing to hack at the ear of the high priest's servant, Malchus." There was a gasp from her audience. "Andrew doesn't know how they managed to escape but to their credit, he and Peter followed the mob to the high priest's palace. He confessed he was afraid to go further, but now he's really worried about Peter, who went in. Oh, and he thinks John might have been ahead of them."

"Where are the others? Arrested too?" cried Mary.

"We don't know," said Miriam, desperately. We wondered if some might have come here or returned to Simon in Bethany. Magnus is waiting at the guest house, and Mary Alphaeus is at our lodgings. She's very worried about young James and Thaddaeus."

"As I am," added Salome. Elizabeth patted her hand sympathetically, her own eyes filling with tears. Salome shook her head, tears rolling freely down her wrinkled cheeks.

"I'll be all right when my Zebedee gets here tomorrow."

Silence fell on the room as each person pondered all that they had heard. It was a lot to take in.

It was Lazarus who brought them back to the present, speaking the words of a familiar prayer, which was taken up by Reuben and then by the others.

Chapter Thirty-One

The Brothers Return

The light of dawn crept behind the heavy, dark clouds that hung in the east as Elias and his brothers returned, pale and drawn. They would not speak until they had eaten and drunk something. Those who had been praying rubbed their eyes, stifling yawns and shivering as they waited. If Elias was surprised to see Miriam, Susanna and Salome among his family he did not show it; he greeted them courteously before he spoke.

"It's been a gruelling night. Where do I begin?" he said wearily. Then, taking a deep breath, he raised his head and looked steadily into their hopeful faces. "By the time we arrived at the high priest's palace, Caiaphas had his emergency council well under way. Annas, his father-in-law, had already interrogated the Master privately, before his son-in-law began the trial before the council.

"Those officially summoned took their seats in the inner room with Caiaphas and his henchmen, but the doors were left open, so

251

those of us who'd turned up unbidden would be allowed to hear."
Elias snorted derisively.

"I was surprised at how many of us there were," said Joachim,
with a wry smile. "This rabbi has certainly stirred up feelings
among us. Elders, scribes, Pharisees and some of the council, whose
allegiance Caiaphas obviously wasn't too sure about, were all there."

"Nevertheless, Caiaphas is still a shrewd man, and I think he
was hoping to win a few more of us over to his way of thinking, and
strengthen his case against the Master. Don't you?" said Josiah, and
Elias agreed.

"But it didn't go his way, did it!" said Joachim, with satisfaction.

"Let me explain," said Elias, to his perplexed audience. "At first,
they'd tried to incriminate the Master by asking witnesses to testify
to things he'd said, but the lack of agreement in their stories was
quite significant and so Caiaphas' plan was thwarted. You could
hear the frustration in his voice, even out in the hall. The Master
said nothing during the whole ugly process. He stood there with
his head bowed, like he was praying, and that just seemed to add to
Caiaphas' frustration."

Into Martha's head came the words her brother had spoken: 'He
was oppressed and afflicted, yet he opened not his mouth, like a
lamb that is led to slaughter, and a sheep that is silent before its
shearers, so he opened not his mouth'. Isaiah's prophecy was being
fulfilled before their eyes. The thought made her tremble as Elias'
voice rose.

"His frustration just seemed to mount. All he wanted was to
be rid of this troublemaker once and for all, and it was proving
unbelievably difficult, even with his power and authority as high
priest. In the end he lost control, screaming 'Are you the Messiah,
the Anointed One?'" Elias' audience sat up, wide awake at this, as
he continued in gentler tones, "The Master looked up, then, staring
at Caiaphas, but speaking very calmly, he said, 'I am, and you will

all see the Son of Man seated at the right hand of the Almighty and coming on the clouds of heaven.' There was an audible gasp from the whole council and it went deadly quiet," said Elias, with obvious relish.

"But old Caiaphas, Mr High and Mighty, was having none of it," said Joachim, acting the part. "He was boiling with anger. He tore his clothes and started yelling, 'We don't need any more witnesses, you heard the man's blasphemy!'"

Elias smiled for the first time, remembering the undignified behaviour of the high priest mimicked by his brother, but his face remained drawn as he said, "The council condemned the Master. No one stood up for him, not even us, and I know there were others there who believe the truth and know who he is. We were all cowards. The shame in my heart is almost unbearable. May God forgive those of us who kept silent."

Then Miriam spoke. "Don't be too hard on yourselves. We cannot foresee what God has in mind, nor how he will accomplish it. Only the Master knows that." As she tried to comfort Elias and his brothers, she remembered the Master's words at supper, that his blood would be poured out for them, and she wept.

"It wasn't very nice after that," admitted Elias. "They condemned him at first light, and he will be sent to Pontius Pilate to face a civil trial this morning, to get the Roman seal of approval on the proceedings. Let's pray the high priests don't have it all their own way." He hung his head wearily and unclenched his hands.

"Things aren't looking too good," said Reuben, shaking his head unhappily.

"Lazarus, a private word please," said Elias suddenly. The two drew aside. "You will remain here, and do not argue with me!" Lazarus' mouth pressed into a thin line, but he kept his peace as Elias continued. "I don't want anyone being reminded that you are my nephew or that our family is involved. If you will not do it for me, then think about your sisters and all the women and children asleep upstairs. Do you understand?" Lazarus nodded. It would do no good to argue with his uncle now, and although he didn't like it, his uncle was right.

Elias then returned to his guests and asked Miriam, Susanna and Salome what had become of the Master's disciples. He was able to reassure them that they had not been arrested so far.

"But I thought I saw Peter in the palace courtyard, near the fire," interrupted Joachim. "He's a big fellow and hard to miss, but in the rush to keep up with you two as we left, I didn't have time to investigate."

"So Peter did follow him," gasped Mary. "Brave man, what anguish he must be suffering."

"I may have seen John," added Josiah. "At one point in the proceedings, I'm sure I saw him standing in the opposite doorway."

"I saw him too," said Elias. "So Peter was not alone. That is good news." Miriam and the others looked relieved. "Now, so help me God, I must rest and have time to think." Leaving the room, he called back, "Sara, wake my wife and send her to bed!" Elizabeth lay slumped in a corner, gently snoring.

Mary and Martha took Miriam, Salome and Susanna to the kitchen for some breakfast before they left, not that any of them felt hungry. They were hopeful that there would be news of the other disciples when they returned.

In their bedroom, Mary found Tabitha curled in a tight ball, still sound asleep, and fell into a fitful exhausted doze herself. Unable to rest, Martha sat by the kitchen fire, as a weary Sara began the big day.

Chapter Thirty-Two

The Day of Preparation

❧

As the sun climbed a little higher behind the dense, glowering cloud it threw a momentary shadow on the upper roof of the house, although the courtyard still lay in deep shadow. Sara woke her master from a doze, and he left almost immediately, taking his sons, Reuben and Sam, with him. Martha and Lazarus returned dejectedly to the warmth of the kitchen and sat lost in their own thoughts.

The house that had felt so safe and welcoming the evening before, now felt like a prison to Martha. She longed to be free to join her friends, but she knew no amount of freedom would change the events happening around them. The shackles of duty and family seemed to encircle her heart once again. Now, more than ever, she envied the men in Jewish society. How easy it must be for them to experience the freedom the Master had promised. In a world dominated by men, women were most often treated like property, whether Jewish or Roman.

Yet again, her thoughts wandered through the night's events, and like a lump of clay being shaped by the potter, understanding slowly began to form. Through the mist of tiredness she found consolation as she realised her uncles were not free to defend or express what they believed, for fear of the consequences for their families. Nor was her brother free to follow his heart and be with his saviour and friend, because of his duty to his family. People were not free from desire, or fear, or need, or want. Only the Lord, only Yeshua, could give true freedom, but it came in the form of knowing and then finding the strength to choose the right way, and in that there was peace. Martha took a deep breath. As she let it out, she found her peace for that day, there in the kitchen.

Sophie, a young servant, bustled into the kitchen, collecting up the utensils for breakfast before she went to lay the table. "Will our Master be having breakfast this morning? I hear he and his brothers were out most of the night."

"Oh, bless you dear!" laughed Sara. "No, he's gone out already, taking Sam and Reuben. The Mistress is still sound asleep, so she won't be down either. It's just women and children for the early sitting." Sophie's eyes widened, with intrigue. "I'll explain everything once you've laid up," promised Sara. Sophie hurried off to execute her task, eager for the reward of news.

Quietly the other servants arrived and began their appointed tasks for the day. Then the children came down, filling the courtyard with their wide-awake exuberance. Today was a special day, and they were excited.

Elizabeth woke to discover her husband had gone out again, taking her sons with him, and her usually reliable niece Martha seemed distracted and restless. Sarah and Keturah were complaining because their husbands were still in bed and had been out half the night, and Sara was short-tempered. Despite Elizabeth's headache, she headed for the kitchen; it was time to take charge and get things back to normal.

Elizabeth first sought Martha, who patiently explained to her all that she had missed after she had fallen asleep while they were praying. Although Elizabeth listened attentively, it was obvious to Martha and Sara that she didn't really grasp the enormity of the events unfolding around them. Her domestic and social world just didn't encompass such things. She was annoyed by her husband's obsession with the fate of this rabbi, on one of the busiest and most important days of her domestic calendar.

Sara and Martha threw themselves as best they could into organising the aunts and cousins to prepare for the celebration that would begin that evening. Josiah and Joachim appeared a little later, followed by their sons Micah and Amon, who were besieged by their children as they attempted to eat a late breakfast. They would be going to the temple with Elias, if he got back in time, to make the all-important sacrifice. Mary and Tabitha came to the rescue of the tired fathers taking the younger children off to play, while the men shared the events of the night with their wives.

The bell jangled urgently, breaking the moody disquiet that had settled on the household. Rosh, Josiah's fourteen-year-old son, was the first to the gate, followed closely by his older sister Miriam. Reuben pushed his way in and stood panting, one hand leaning on the ivy-covered wall. Joachim motioned him to come and sit down, while refreshment was sent for. Reuben was quickly surrounded. Martha brought beer and bread, waving to the others to sit quietly while he gathered his thoughts.

In his deep grave voice, Reuben spoke. "We arrived at the Praetorium not long after the main body of the council, with the Master and his escort. We only caught a glimpse of him, but he didn't look in good shape after last night." Reuben hung his head, finding it hard to meet the anxious faces surrounding him. He wished the children weren't there. "To remain holy and clean for the day, the chief priests and elders waited outside, so Pilate had to come out to them. Not a good start from Pilate's point of view. I think he wanted the Sanhedrin to deal with the Master under Jewish law, but they were insisting Rome should authorise his death." Reuben winced. "Under our law, they can only stone someone to death, and they've tried that and failed already." His laugh sounded like a grunt. "The chief priests want to make sure he's put out of the way permanently this time, and they will do that, mark my words. The Master's popularity and influence won't stave off what is happening now." Reuben smiled sardonically. "They think crucifixion under Roman law would leave their hands free of his blood." There was a gasp from his mother, who had to be fanned by Sara.

"Surely it won't come to that!" she wailed. "What has my husband got our family mixed up in?" Reuben glared at her as Sara and Julia tried to reassure her.

Reuben continued, "They accused the Rabbi of claiming to be King, so Pilate took him inside to have a private talk. When he came out, he was shaking his head. He could find no reason to pass sentence on the Master, and he told them so. For us, that was a glimmer of hope, but it didn't last. The chief priests kept insisting he had stirred the people up, all the way from Galilee to Judea, and Pilate pounced on that like a cat on a mouse, sending the Master to see Herod Antipas, because he governs Galilee." Reuben added for the children's benefit, "He's here for Passover, staying in the Hasmonaean palace. He arrived a few days ago, luckily for Pilate."

"Pilate is shrewd," said Joachim. "It looks like just the excuse he needs to pass the problem onto someone else, and, if I know him, he hopes it will thwart the priests' and elders' plan. At the very least it will be sure to annoy them." The others nodded.

"It's difficult to decide who is worse, Pilate or our own priests!"

exclaimed Julia. Silvanus, her five-year-old, looked at his mother in shock. He'd never heard her be so outspoken before.

"So," concluded Reuben, "Sam and Father have followed the Master to Herod's palace, and I was sent back to tell you what was happening."

"I should like to know when your father intends to return," asked his mother crossly. "Is he going to follow this rabbi around the city all day? And what's to be done about the sacrifice? Did your father send no word to me?"

"Oh, yes. Sorry Mother, it has been a difficult morning. Father said to carry on as normal. Sam will be back later, to sort out the lamb, and if Father can't come then Josiah and Joachim can go to the temple in his stead. You'll have your roast dinner as usual, don't worry."

Elizabeth grumbled at this, but only Sara understood that it was out of worry for her family and not because her dinner plans were upset.

"Come on ladies, back to the kitchen," called Martha, leading the way. "We'll need a few more volunteers, there's still lots to be done."

Reuben lent back against the wall and closed his eyes. He hoped Sam wouldn't be too long. There was no point in going back and trying to find them in the crowds; he would have to wait.

As the women prepared the unleavened dough, they began to recount the tale of the Israelites leaving Egypt in such a hurry that they didn't have time to let the dough rise. Some of the younger children helped to flatten it out, making a terrible mess, but it helped lighten their hearts and bring attention back to the celebrations. Once baked, the matzah (flatbread) played an important role after the meal. One would be hidden, and the children would have the job of finding it.

Mary looked weary and pale as she left the kitchen holding

the hand of Little Mary, the seven-year-old youngest daughter of Joachim. His five-year-old and youngest son James, with Silvanus in tow, accompanied them. Tabitha and Miriam, the oldest daughter, at sixteen, of Josiah, and Noah, his four-year-old, went too. Mary was good at turning the mundane chore of laying the table into a game they all enjoyed playing, and it helped keep her mind focused.

They all heard the jangle of the bell as Sam came to get Reuben. The Master was on his way back to Pilate, but Sam was in a hurry, and didn't want to hang around.

"What was the outcome with Herod?" demanded Lazarus, who had been waiting impatiently for news.

"Herod appears to have found no cause to crucify him either," said Sam, "otherwise he wouldn't be sending him back to Pilate. I can't imagine what it must be like for the Master. They're still treating him like a common criminal. Well, actually I think they treat criminals better!" Sam swore, and then apologised to Martha as she handed him a drink. He gulped it down, wiping his mouth on the back of his hand.

"However, father did say to be sure to tell you to stay put, Lazarus. Your name has come up a few times this morning, just casually in the crowd, but it wouldn't take much to trigger your arrest. The crowd is very volatile at the moment, and there's a lot of confusion. Right now, it's best if anyone closely associated with the Master stays low."

"Surely the temple has its spies out looking, so we do need to be careful," said Joachim.

"I think Caiaphas is sure that once the ringleader is dealt with, the others will be no problem," said Josiah. "Besides, they're stretched for manpower, with the temple at full capacity with everything that's going on."

"Now we must leave," urged Sam.

Sara hurried out of the kitchen and handed him a bag of food and a bottle, to keep them going.

"Let's hope we can find Father in the crowd back at the Praetorium," Sam was heard remarking to his brother as the gate slammed shut.

Martha looked worriedly at Sara. "Have courage my love, things will work out, you'll see. My heart tells me he is the one sent from God, and he will deliver us, just like God did from Egypt and all those other times throughout our long history. God has never forsaken us, his people, and he isn't about to do so now, no matter how bad it looks."

Chapter Thirty-Three

Pilate and the Lamb

Sam returned, as his father had promised. It was nearly time to take the lambs to the temple, but first his mother insisted he tell them what was happening. Sam sat beside Elizabeth, and with the rest of the family arranged around them, he shared the next part of the trial which was unfolding in the streets of Jerusalem.

"As you all know, Father and I hung around with the crowd outside Herod's place. It seemed to take ages and we wondered if the outcome would be any different. We could only hope. Then suddenly the gate opened and there was the Master in the midst of an escort of grim, well-armed foot soldiers. They marched determinedly through the crowd, almost shoving us out of the way. The Master passed close by, and I heard father muttering, praying that we would all be forgiven." Sam shook his head, wincing at the wounds the memory left. "The Master was badly bruised, with part of his face swollen, and again his hands were bound so tightly he couldn't even straighten his clothing. Yet his eyes were bright and alert, and I wondered how that could be." He watched Mary's face as he spoke, wishing he could have spared her even the few details he'd given. The reality had been far worse.

"There was little room to move in the streets as we followed them back to Pilate. I don't think I've ever felt so angry and powerless in my life. If father hadn't been there, I don't know what I might have done. I wanted to call out, so Yeshua knew not everyone had deserted him. But our very silence must have screamed out in the face of God.

"Anyway, Father and I managed to squeeze in at the back of the courtyard in the Praetorium. Pilate wanted the elders of the Sanhedrin and the high priests up front where he could speak to them in front of the crowds. To cut a long walk short, neither Pilate, nor Herod, could find any grounds for the accusations brought against the Master, so he offered to flog him, to appease the priests and the council. Did he really think he could teach the Messiah, the son of God, a lesson, and then release him as if nothing had happened?

"The Pharisees roared with disapproval and then, driven by the priests and the council, the cry went up to release the criminal Barabbas. The crowd's cries gathered momentum. I was shocked. That man had been thrown into prison for murder and rioting!"

"Robbery and insurrection too," added Joachim. "I'm surprised the High Priests suggested a man like that. Surely Pilate wouldn't release someone who openly opposes Rome?"

"If Pilate had had any choice, he would have released the Master," Sam answered. "He has no love for our nation, but even less for troublemakers like Barabbas. Three times he tried to release the Master, but each time the crowd was stirred up by the high priests and became more and more hysterical. At one point, they told Pilate that releasing the Master would be an act of treason against Emperor Caesar."

His mother looked puzzled.

"Because the Master had claimed to be King," explained Sam.

"I bet that shook Pilate. He's on probation himself. Even Rome disapproves of his methods sometimes," added Joachim.

"So, if I've understood this correctly," said Micah. "When the priests incited the people to ask for Barabbas, a known rebel against Roman rule and a murderer, they were supporting insurrection against the Roman Empire, and yet Pilate allowed it. But then, when they insisted on the Master's sentence, because he was acclaimed to be the king, in a direct challenge to the Emperor himself, I could understand Pilate giving in. However, as the Emperor also claims to be a God, surely our priests would want him dead too, but of course there's been no mention of that." Micah stroked his chin sagely, one eyebrow raised. Joachim looked impressed by his son.

"Politics," said Sam with disgust. "But things were getting out of hand and I don't think Pilate had an option any more. He could see he wasn't going to win, and a riot could break out at any moment, so he gave the crowd what they wanted. He looked pretty fed up when he sat on the stone seat to give his judgement. The Master was brought before him, and Pilate publicly washed his hands of the whole affair, making it quite clear he was not responsible for the Master's death. As though water can wash away a man's guilt. But what was most disturbing to us, was when the Elders cried out, 'Let his blood be on us and on our children!'"

Glowering, Sam let out his breath, noisily. At the same time, there was a sharp gasp from the family.

"They have effectively cursed themselves and their families," added Sam.

Elizabeth turned pale and Sam patted her puffy hand, sorry she'd had to hear such things. Exhausted, Sam hung his head, then quietly, almost to himself, he muttered, "We were all so sure Pilate would release the Master. It was only after a servant spoke privately to him that he seemed to lose the strength of his conviction." He frowned. "There were enough soldiers around to deal with a riot, not that Pilate would willingly have gone down that road, it would have been another black mark on his career. But something changed his mind, quite definitely."

"The only person with influence over the governor, other than the Emperor, would be his wife," chuckled Eleazar, winking at Hannah, who sat with a grandchild on her lap. The tension in the courtyard relaxed a little, and the remark drew a few smiles.

"So, Barabbas is being freed, and the Master is to be flogged and then taken to Golgotha," finished Sam bitterly. He braced himself, knowing the effect his words would have on his family.

"No! Please God, no!" cried Mary. "Is there no end to their barbaric injustice?" Startled by her outburst, the children turned to their parents, fear on their faces. Little Mary took her hand and kissed it, trying to sooth her big cousin. Mary rocked and moaned as Martha held her tight, swallowing hard and blinking back her own tears.

"Quietly, my love. Don't frighten the children; it'll be all right," she whispered. She'd known this was coming, but nothing had prepared her for the agony of it.

Sam waited, not sure if he should speak again, but Micah leant over and asked quietly, "So will Uncle Elias return for the sacrifice? He is the head of the family."

"I think he intends to follow the Master," Sam answered.

Fortunately Elizabeth didn't hear that bit, as she was comforting Julia.

"Come on lad, I'll help you with the lambs. Lazarus, you come too," said Josiah as they slipped out of the courtyard. The lambs were penned in a small stable at the side of the house, where all manner of livestock were kept when needed. They would lead them out when everyone was ready to go.

Zechariah began kicking up a fuss because his ten-year-old brother, Joseph, was allowed to go to the temple and he was not. He was especially aggrieved because he would have to stay at home with his little brother Noah, whom he regarded as a baby. Even his older brothers, Rosh and Amon, couldn't reason with him. Only when his mother reminded him that Lazarus had to stay behind too was Zechariah finally pacified.

Shortly after, Josiah, with his sons Amon, Rosh and Joseph, and Joachim with his sons Micah and Joshua, followed Sam, who led the two strutting ram lambs to the temple. In the narrow alleyway, Lazarus stood like a statue watching them go, his body taut as a battle raged in his mind. He was struggling to control the urge to leave, to declare himself to the city, and hide no longer. He wasn't afraid, but he was torn between his love for the Master and his love for his family.

A creak from the gate hinges drew his attention. His grandfather stood there with piercing eyes. "Come and sit with me," he commanded. Lazarus turned and followed him.

"Those were splendid rams, my boy. Elias and I were admiring them the other day," said Eleazar, sitting down on a stone seat tucked away in a corner of the courtyard. Lazarus sat down heavily next to him. "Only the best for God. We wouldn't want to risk rejection by the priests, now would we?" replied Eleazar. "But they'll be tasty," a smile curled up on one side of the old man's face.

For a time the courtyard was silent, except for the splashing of water on stone as it overflowed the fountain. A light breeze sprang up, causing spray to drift and spatter on the surrounding herb garden. A shaft of sunlight shot through the moody sky, making the ripples in the basin look incandescent.

Mary sat quietly under the portico, Little Mary asleep in her lap.

The momentary explosion of light on the fountain lifted her heart, smoothing out the furrows on her brow. She had feared for her brother, but now the crisis was past as he sat with their grandfather.

Martha appeared and moved furtively toward the gate, winding her black shawl around her head as though she was going out. Lazarus was the first to realise what was going on and sprang after her.

Her grandfather sat up tall and straight, his voice commanding once again as he called out, "Martha, my dearest child, wait!"

Martha turned slowly, her face grim with determination. The old man sounded just like her father, his choice of words, the tone of his voice. She stood waiting, head held high, eyes locked with his.

"Martha, what difference will it make whether you are here with your family or at Golgotha watching him die?" His words stabbed at her heart.

"It'll make a difference to me!" she said, defiantly.

"This is the will of God, his father. He will be obedient to his last breath. Will you be obedient too, my child?"

Mary ran to Martha and held her hands imploringly.

"Stay with us please. He asked you to."

Martha stood rooted in angry defeat, hands clenched so her nails dug into her palms, her eyes dry with pain.

Chapter Thirty-Four

Darkness Descends

Wednesday noon

Martha had gone to her room to be alone. Mary was weary of it all, and now sat playing with her little cousin, who had been woken so suddenly when Martha had tried to leave. However, the frown had returned to Mary's brow. Keturah called to her daughter from the kitchen; Little Mary ran indoors obediently. Mary remained alone. Sometimes she muttered scripture to herself, and at other times words of prayer, as she too wrestled with her thoughts and feelings.

Later, Martha returned to the kitchen to be kept fully occupied by her aunt as the preparations began to pick up momentum. The simple routines of the kitchen helped divert her mind from the terrible events going on in the city. Dark grey clouds continued to build up from the west. It felt more like winter than spring, putting yet another damper on the atmosphere.

Elizabeth fussed over the two giant candle holders that graced the centre of the huge table, making sure everything was just right and done properly according to tradition. In the kitchen, poor Sara did her best, but it didn't matter which way she turned, there was always someone under her feet. If it hadn't been for Martha swooping in to help with all these infernal relatives she was sure she would have lost her temper many times over. Martha seemed to have recovered from her outburst earlier, but Sara knew the veneer was thin. She knew just how far this strong woman would push herself in the service of others, but she also knew how terrible the consequences could be for Martha. Sara prayed for them all as she worked.

The light in the kitchen was getting poorer by the minute; the atmosphere was so oppressive it felt like a storm was coming. Even the glow from the hearth did little to raise their spirits. Martha began to set up the great spit-roasting irons in their grooves, ready for the lamb carcasses. Only the blood, the fat and the kidneys were sacrificed for Passover, and of course the temple kept the fleece.

In that moment, in the span of a single breath, the light failed. Total darkness engulfed them. One end of the great iron bar fell to the floor with a dull clang, while the other fell among the embers, sending sparks flying. Instinctively Martha jumped clear, simultaneously pulling little James out of the way. Then, in panic, everyone began to talk at once.

Martha groped along the wall she had stepped back against, James still wrapped tightly around her, as she used her free arm to search for candles in a cupboard. Her eyes, although wide open, were useless in the dark, and her heart thumped painfully inside her chest. She fought to keep her mind clear, her hand feverishly searching. At last, she felt the long, velvety wax of the candle and took it over to the fire to light it on the embers, James still clinging to her back. At the same moment, a lamp sprang into life. Sara hadn't been idle either.

With each candle and lamp that was lit, sanity and calm was

further restored to the kitchen. Holding a lamp out, Sara looked outside. The darkness hung everywhere, but she and Martha stepped undaunted out into the shadows.

"Stay here in the kitchen, all of you, and bank up the fire. We'll be back in a minute," commanded Martha.

In the deathly quiet outside they listened, looking up at the sky. It was darker than night, and there was no reflected light from the stars or moon. Martha had to remind herself it was only midday, so how could this be? They heard faint cries from the streets. Someone not far away was hammering on a door, and then a dog began to howl.

"Martha, is that you?" came the surprisingly calm voice of Mary. "I think I'd better come in now. It's got rather chilly out here."

"Is that your attempt at a joke?" retorted Martha in relief.

"What's going on, Mary?" asked Sara.

"I don't know, but let's get some more light and get everyone together."

Lamps and candles were distributed to the adults and slowly the family began to congregate in the courtyard. There was not a breath of wind, and all the flames stretched straight and tall. Mary stood beside Martha, their hands clasped.

"He's dead," whispered Mary, though she could hardly speak.

"We don't know that," replied Martha, but her voice shook.

"It must be past midday, so the priests will have started the sacrifices," came the calm voice of Lazarus, as he stood supporting Eleazar. "The Lord, the son of the living God, is sacrificing himself for us. 'From prison and trial, they led him away to his death. But who among the people realised that he was dying for their sins, that he was suffering their punishment?' Praise him and rejoice, for he is fulfilling what was prophesied long ago by Isaiah." Lazarus began to dance round, and tears ran unashamedly down his cheeks. The others stared at him, not really taking in what he had just said. Undeniably, the words of scripture seemed to fit what was happening to the Master. But was he really dying for their sins? Being punished instead of them? Lit by pools of yellow lamplight, their faces turned up to heaven and they wept with gratitude and hope and sorrow and fear.

"May God be merciful and not judge us for his death!" cried Eleazar, still clinging to Lazarus' arm.

"The Lord is sacrificing himself!" cried Lazarus. "This is God's plan for his son. No Pharisee, no Jewish authority, no Roman civilization, nothing and no one, can prevent the will of God. Our saviour has demonstrated the mercy of the father by his death!"

"But what of this terrible darkness, what does it mean? We must find Elias, he will know what to do," cried Elizabeth, in desperation.

"He will be back soon. Reuben will take care of him, my dear," said Hannah. Then raising her voice confidently, she spoke to them all. "The temple is well lit, they will all be back safe and soon. Let us get the house back in order ready to receive them. Come, Elizabeth dear. We will celebrate."

"Mary, let's go and see if we can find out what's happened," called her brother. "We won't go far, I promise," he added, catching his grandfather's eye.

Elizabeth threw herself into activity, getting everyone back to their preparations. Whatever was causing this darkness would not last, she decided. Carry on as normal, that was what Elias had said. No need to worry. There would be a perfectly good explanation at some point, there always was.

Martha waited anxiously for Mary and Lazarus' return, but there was little to tell; a few bewildered people were wandering the streets with lamps. The immediate neighbours, like themselves, were trying to carry on, although anxious and concerned for news from the temple.

The afternoon wore on, but little changed, and the darkness held its ground. Still their uncles did not return, and anxiety grew in the household. Their aunt wouldn't hear of anyone going out to find them, for the chances of missing them in the dark was too great.

Without the sun it was hard to keep track of time, but somewhere around the ninth hour of the day, a low rumble of thunder was heard, followed seconds later by an ear-splitting crack. Jerusalem shook on its elevated bed, and the earth trembled. People lost their balance, flinging their arms out automatically in defence. Elias' family staggered and groped their way back out of the house. What new and terrifying event was this?

"Is anyone left in the house?" screamed Julia hysterically.

Lazarus spun on his heels and ran back into the building.

Time seemed to stand still as they waited, clutching one another in terror, hoping the tremors would stop. Then Lazarus reappeared, guiding Eleazar. Keturah and her daughter-in-law Naomi staggered after him, Hannah clutched between the two of them. Strapped to his mother, baby Amos was crying desperately.

"Tabitha. Where's Tabitha?" cried Martha, as another ear-splitting crack ricocheted across the city. One of the columns supporting the portico collapsed. Screams filled the air. The roof sagged, but held. Martha ran towards the kitchen door, shouting Tabitha's name. Masonry fell around her as she was flung against the wall.

"Over here!" bellowed Lazarus, grabbing Tabitha around the waist as he hauled her clear of the doorway, at the bottom of the stairs. She clung to him, terrified. Mary and Miriam managed to get Martha to her feet and help her clear of the house. Bruised and shaking, Martha lurched towards Lazarus and Tabitha, who flung herself into her arms. Tabitha was trembling uncontrollably.

The bell above the gate began to jangle in time with the tremors. Hoping beyond hope that the others might have returned, Sara fought her vertigo to reach it. Only the darkness poured in; the lamp above the gate lay smashed on the stones. They were gripped by fear, the children crying and clinging to the adults. Martha reached out to grab Mary's hand, the others supporting one another as best they could. Keturah's arms were wrapped protectively around her children. Zechariah stood stoutly beside his mother, his arms placed protectively around his little brother Noah. Sarah held her baby grandson tightly to her chest, her eyes firmly fixed on her daughter-in-law, who sat on the ground, rocking her toddler and moaning to herself.

And then light began to return to the sky, and as it did, the tremors died away. For a moment, everything was still and quiet.

"Was that the night?" asked Noah, wiping the tears away with his fist.

"Must be," replied Little Mary. "Look, here comes the dawn."

"But it's all muddled up," said Noah, frowning. "We usually have to sleep at night and it's long."

"Yeah, much longer than that," agreed Little Mary. "That night started at lunchtime and it's finishing now."

"Funny time to have dawn," commented James. "Lets go and see if Sara has something to eat. I'm starving."

The three looked up into the brightening sky, nodding sagely, and then the two boys headed to the kitchen, following Sara. Little Mary stayed, watching Mary with deep concern, as she cried aloud, "Our Lord is dead, his suffering is over!" Then, with her head in her hands, Mary broke down.

Swaying, Martha turned pale, but she managed to reach a stone bench, her arm around poor Esther, Amon's wife, who clutched her baby and sobbed.

"Martha, Martha, get up!" cried an urgent young voice beside her. Martha felt little hands tugging at her arm, trying to pull her to her feet.

"Why, whatever is the matter Little Mary?" Martha blinked

away her tears, her eyes adjusting to the light.

"Martha, get up. The seat is cracked!"

Martha jumped to her feet, pulling a dazed Esther up with her. Turning, they saw a deep crack across the solid stone bench. Instinctively Zechariah gave it a shove with his foot, and it crashed to the floor, broken in two. The children gasped and moved away. Martha scooped Little Mary up in her arms and kissed her.

"Good job, Little Mary. Martha might have squashed baby Samuel," said Zechariah nonchalantly. Their relief broke out into laughter.

"Elias will be back soon, I just know it," crooned Elizabeth, as she cuddled little Bartholomew for Esther.

Chapter Thirty-Five

The Sacrifice

Elias swayed in through the gate, his clothing dusty, his face red, beads of sweat running down his forehead. The others pushed in behind him, also looking dishevelled, but relieved to be home. Lazarus helped Elias to a seat, while mothers, sons and daughters poured from the house and threw themselves into one another's arms.

Keturah clung to Joachim, cradling their baby grandson, while Micah comforted his wife Naomi. Little Mary and James threw themselves at Joshua, clamouring to tell him what had happened to them. Sarah hugged Joseph and Rosh, her fourteen-year-old, fiercely, while Miriam clung to her father's neck, sobbing. Zechariah came running up and helped Noah into his father's lap. Josiah, full of pride, reached up and stroked the eight-year-old's face.

Amon, tears in his eyes, held Esther close, baby Samuel wedged between them, while two-year-old Bartholomew clutched his father's knees, shouting, 'Abba, Abba!' desperate to be included. Everyone was talking at once. Those few hours apart had felt like a lifetime.

Martha and Mary stood together watching their family, eyes shining with exquisite joy, despite the gulf of grief they felt. Tabitha ran up and exuberantly hugged them, then flung herself at Sara. The arms of their family enclosed them too.

"Oh, it's all been so terrible. What will become of us? Where is hope?" wailed Elizabeth, letting go of her feelings.

"The darkest day in the history of our holy city and our nation," agreed Elias, putting his arm around her and drawing her closer.

"What's happened? Why is Uncle so unhappy?" James asked Noah.

Elias saw the joy of reunion fill the anxious faces of his beloved family, and for their sakes, he rose above the despair that clutched at his heart. "We are all safe and together. For that, let us praise the most high God!" he said aloud.

"Amen!" responded everyone from their hearts.

"Was there much other damage to the house?" Josiah asked Lazarus, disentangling himself from his family and looking around at the propped porch, broken colonnade and split seat.

"We've cleared up most of it, Uncle. A few breakages inside, but nothing too serious. It was truly amazing that none of us were hurt," said Lazarus.

"We're a bit behind on the preparations. We didn't even know if there would be lamb to eat this evening," said Elizabeth, but she truly didn't seem to mind.

"You've performed miracles, as usual, my love," said Elias, the thought of food reviving his spirits a little. "And we have our lambs."

"Sara, where would you like them?" asked Lazarus, swinging a carcass up and balancing it on his shoulder. Sam hefted the other and followed them into the kitchen. Martha turned to go and help

Sara, but her uncle held her back.

"Stay my dear, and listen to the accounts that must be given. Sara will manage, she has plenty of help. Unless something has happened to the servants."

"No no. They are all safe and most of them here," his wife reassured him. Obediently Martha sat back down as the rest of the family assembled themselves around Elias and Elizabeth.

"Where do we begin?" he muttered to himself in the warm glow of the late afternoon sunshine.

"The last news we had was from Sam, when he came back to sort the lambs out," said his wife, gently. "Why don't you start from there?"

"We were at the Praetorium, weren't we?" said Elias. Reuben nodded. "Oh, how the time dragged as we waited. Eventually the Master was brought out into the courtyard by his guards. It was awful. The soldiers must have pressed a wreath of Jujube thorns on his head, like some hideous crown, so his hair was matted with blood and stuck to his forehead. Fresh blood was coming through his clothing from the lashes he'd received." Elias shuddered at the memory. "His back must have been shredded and how he managed to stand, let alone walk, was beyond me. Three of them lugged the big heavy cross beam out and dropped an end onto his shoulder."

Reuben swore, shocking some of those listening. Elias ploughed on. "The Master flinched, I thought his legs would buckle under the weight, but he bore it. I'm sorry," he choked, swallowing back the tears. "It was awful, such savagery." Elias hung his head, unable to look at the shocked faces. Even the whimpering of the youngest child was hushed, so only the fountain could be heard.

Sighing, Elias spoke again. "Oh, such suffering was on his face, yet he mastered his broken body and dragged that leaden cross beam towards the Gennath gate. It was awful to witness. At one point he staggered and fell, and the wooden weight fell across him. Then he did cry out, like a beaten dog. He tried to stand, but it was no good. In the end those heartless soldiers had to drag him to his feet, but before they could lift the beam, the Master had fallen once more.

"We could hear the angry words of the soldiers. They had two other prisoners following behind him, and they didn't appreciate the delay." Elias was overcome. Never before had the family been so close to someone sentenced to death. Crucifixion was reserved for the criminal classes, rebels and those who fell foul of politics, not respectable God-fearing families.

Reuben, at a nod from his mother, took over the narrative. "The soldiers dragged a strong-looking fellow out of the crowd and forced him to carry the cross beam."

"May God curse those soldiers for their part in the proceedings," spat Josiah, his voice shaking with anger.

"Soldiers simply follow orders. To them he was a criminal, like all the others, and deserving of such treatment. An inconvenience for Rome," finished the soft voice of Sara, who knew all about carrying out orders, even the ones you didn't agree with.

"We heard later that the man who was made to carry the beam had two children in the crowd with him. They'd come from Cyrene, in north Africa," added Reuben, with concern. "I pray someone took care of them." There was a general murmur as the parents amongst them held their children closer.

"He brought you back to us my son, only God could do that," said Elias, looking at Lazarus. "Oh, what have we done? What have we allowed to happen?" he moaned in despair.

"Elias dear, finish your story, please," begged his wife.

Elias shook himself, trying to pick up the threads. Reluctantly he began again. "Word had got around. A large crowd pressed onto the street to see the criminals, and some to watch the fate of the famous Rabbi who had performed all those miracles."

"What had the other criminals done, Uncle? Were they beaten

up like the Master?" asked Zechariah eagerly, forgetting himself. Josiah placed a firm hand on his son's shoulder to restrain him.

"I suppose some, like us, were still hoping for a miracle, but most would have been drawn by the barbaric spectacle of crucifixion."

"And stoning is better!" exclaimed Sam.

"Point taken, lad," said his father. "The other two men were simply petty criminals, thieves by all accounts."

Beads of sweat began to appear on Elias' forehead. He was obviously exhausted, and had been under considerable strain for some time. Martha watched him with concern. He clearly needed to rest.

"We tried to make our way up the crowded street, but my legs began to feel like jelly and the effort of trying to squeeze myself a few paces further became too much. I collapsed on a doorstep and thought I would be overwhelmed by the crowd, if it hadn't been for Reuben standing over me. The Master had passed out of sight by the time I was fit enough to stand."

"I watched him go; I couldn't leave father," murmured Reuben. "The two criminals weren't far behind. They had so few guards around them it was surprising, as though the Lord was the real threat."

Elias took a long deep draught of wine before continuing. "Something of interest to you," he said to Martha and Mary, who had sat motionless the whole time. "While we were waiting for the crowds to disperse, I think I saw John, Zebedee's son, on the other side of the street, there were trees shading the walkway, so it was hard to tell. He was protecting someone as they moved through the crowd. They seemed determined."

"Was it Salome?" asked Elizabeth.

"No, I'd have recognised her, this was a smaller woman," said Elias.

"It must have been Mary Joseph, the Lord's mother," exclaimed

Mary, in anguish. "Did you see anyone else, Miriam perhaps?"

"She may have been with them, but it's difficult to say for sure," replied Elias.

"Oh, his poor mother, what was he thinking of to cause her so much grief by getting into all this trouble?" wailed Elizabeth. "Just the thought of anything like that happening to my two is making me feel quite faint." She fanned herself dramatically.

"Stop your nonsense, and be grateful they are here with us," declared Elias, putting his arm around her ample shoulders. "It was clear that to try to follow the Master any further would serve no useful purpose, his fate was in God's hands." Elias lowered his eyes, afraid he would see accusation in the eyes of those listening, but if he had looked, he would have seen only compassion and sadness. "Anyway, as soon as we could, we hurried down to the temple, hoping against hope we should meet you all there," he concluded, looking up at his brothers and Sam.

"Despite being plunged into darkness on the way there, and having to negotiate panicking people and escaped animals," added Reuben, with an ironic smile.

"And by God's grace they did find us!" exclaimed Josiah.

Chapter Thirty Six

The Temple

"It was thanks to the sharp eyes of my nephew Joshua that we found Elias and Reuben in the crowds of the temple courts," began Josiah. Micah looked approvingly at his younger brother. "But we didn't get far. Even in the confusion Elias managed to bump into some of his cronies and delay us." Sam grinned at this, but Elias raised an eyebrow. "And they too were of the opinion that the creeping darkness somehow had to do with what was happening up at Golgotha. We got as far as the queue outside the Nicanor gate before the daylight failed. No one had a lamp, of course, we weren't expecting to need one. It was midday. The priests were all in confusion, no one seemed to know what was going on, and it took ages for the lamps to be lit. The only light was from the altar, which of course has been going since first light. The gate had been left open, just enough to admit the extra temple staff who ran to and fro, so we caught glimpses of what was going on in the men's court beyond. The noise from the lambs alone was deafening. It's always busy in the women's court, but mixed with the smell from the incense it was becoming oppressive in the dark.

"Eventually, enough lamps were lit for them to let us in. Our line of priests was clearly flustered and in a bit of a hurry after the delay in starting. The queues were only getting longer outside. The singers and the reed pipes sounded thin and piercing. But we were the first wave in, so the Levites probably hadn't had a chance to warm up." Amon, Rosh and Joseph all grinned, appreciating their father's little joke.

"Were any of you watching the last priest in our row?" asked Joachim, a touch of mischief in his voice. "I'd swear his hands were shaking as he threw the blood on the base of the altar. He nearly dropped the bowl. In their hurry, I bet a lot of them missed in that poor lighting."

Even Elias had to smile. You had to see the funny side in all these disturbing events.

"When it was all over, we struggled to stay together leaving," continued Josiah. "It was heaving in there, and the queue to go in was still growing. Outside, the air was less oppressive. Many were hanging about endlessly talking about what might be causing the darkness, but I'm sure plenty of them, like us, were connecting it with the crucifixion of the Rabbi from Galilee. No one spoke about their suspicions openly, mind you. Too many prying ears in the dark."

"It all looked quite beautiful by lamplight," said Amon, "and we kept bumping into people we knew, so it took ages to work our way towards the gate and home."

"Largely my fault," confessed Elias. "I met another friend near the gate, and he may have saved our lives, because while I was talking to him, a great roar suddenly exploded from the inner court of the temple. The earth shook so violently we had to hold onto each other to keep from falling over. Then with a great crack, the huge stone arch above the gate split, but at the same time, a cry went up from the temple that caused terror in our hearts."

The women and children sat frozen, mouths and eyes wide open, not knowing what to expect next. Elias continued, enjoying this part of the narrative.

"The tremors ceased, and we stood together, stunned. The silence grew, but no one dared move. Then the whispers came radiating out from the temple courts, like wind through dried leaves. Caiaphas had staggered from the inner sanctuary, white-faced, clutching his heart and unable to speak, gesticulating wildly in the direction of the Holy of Holies. The attending priests had dashed in, afraid to disobey, but terrified of what might happen to them if they did." The family drew a breath as one. "And what do you think they found?" asked Elias, raising his eyebrows.

"God," whispered James.

"No, my dear child," chuckled Elias. "Although it would have been better for us if they had. No, they found the curtain torn down the middle, from top to bottom. The two halves had fallen from the hanging. The priests came out cowering, their eyes covered. They had looked into the Holy of Holies and were probably expecting to be struck dead at any moment. Caiaphas quickly recovered his voice and had the sanctuary cleared."

"What a shame," commented Sam, but he wished he'd kept silent.

"My son, this is no joking matter," said Elias, sternly. "Only the high priest is allowed into the Holy of Holies, behind the curtain, and then only once a year and now it's exposed for all to see. What is the meaning of this?"

With authority, Lazarus answered. "The Lord, the son of the living God, has sacrificed himself for us. 'He was led as a lamb to the slaughter, from prison and trial they led him away to his death. But who among the people realised that he was dying for their sins, that he was suffering their punishment?' He has sacrificed himself for our sins, once and for all. Only his blood, the blood of the Messiah, could take away the sin of the world, the sin of those who have come to believe in him as their rescuer. Don't you see? Our sins no longer stand between us and God – the curtain, the veil, has been thrown down. The way is open to the Father, God, because of what his son has done. We don't need priests sacrificing anymore. He was the last sacrifice that will ever be needed!"

"The way is open for all who believe in him and what he has done," agreed Mary, her gaze sweeping across the faces in the courtyard. After such a blinding revelation, it was some time before anyone ventured to speak again.

"That passage even mentions he would be put in a rich man's grave," said Reuben, his eyes wide with amazement. "You must tell Joseph and Nicodemus!" he finished excitedly.

"We'll come to that part in a moment," Elias said, to assure those who had been left at home.

Josiah picked up the threads of the story once more. He could handle telling a story, but the implications of what Lazarus had just said were going to take him a long time to digest.

"Although the earth tremors had ceased, we were like drunk men for a while, disorientated and shaken to the core," he went on. "A great crowd pressed towards the courts after hearing the reports about the sanctuary. But our thoughts and concerns had turned to you, our family. So, we took our chances, commended our lives to God and rushed under the cracked arch. As you can see, it held up. We are all unscathed, except for the odd bruise. There were moments when I thought the end had come, but the light has returned and we are still alive and together. Praise God for his mercy. Now is anyone else hungry? I could eat a donkey."

"Lamb will have to do, my love," laughed his wife.

Now it was the turn of those at home to share their story, and for a while Elias listened intently. Tabitha left Martha's side and stood quietly beside him, her arms encircling his shoulders. He smiled across the sea of faces to Martha.

Then Josiah spoke quietly to Elias, his eyes drifting to Martha, Mary and Lazarus, who sat with Reuben and Sam. Elias coughed and the family came to order once more.

"Just one more thing I think you would want to hear," he said. "We ran into an old friend of mine, Joseph from Arimathea." Martha and Mary looked blank.

"He's a member of the Sanhedrin," explained Reuben. "Father and he go way back. One of the few honourable men among them."

"Many of the Sanhedrin are good men, Reuben, be careful what you say. This business has been far from straightforward. Many believe that Yeshua was who he claimed to be. They could not speak of their belief, but I know where Joseph stands. How he found peace when the Master was sentenced, is between him and God. But what I wanted to tell you is good news of a sort. Joseph watched the Lord die at Golgotha, but through that terrible experience, he had resolved to go to Pilate and ask for the body, regardless of the consequences. He has a newly cut tomb in the limestone outcrops up there; it was for his family. His hope, if it is granted, is to bury the body before sunset, according to custom. He thinks Pilate will agree, as it will save him some more trouble. Let's pray he succeeds. Our Reuben offered to help, but Joseph already had help, from Nicodemus of all people. Who'd have thought it," he chuckled to himself. "That old Pharisee is full of surprises. It makes my heart glad to think of it. Mind you, they're both running an awful risk." Elias was pleased to see he had brought a little relief to his nieces and nephew.

Immediately Mary asked, "Will Miriam, his mother and John know of this? I'm sure it would be of great comfort to them."

"I'll see if I can send word to them," promised Reuben. "But not until we know Joseph has been successful in his request." Elias nodded his approval.

"We can do no more for the moment," Martha reassured Mary. "It is in God's hands."

Pale and worn out, Elias was ushered upstairs to rest, while everyone else did their best to help Sara. Josiah, had to make do with some salted fish, while the lambs were roasting.

Chapter Thirty Seven

The Passover Meal

With the dark clouds gone, the sunset was glorious, but it did little to lift the spirits of the adults as they gathered to celebrate the Passover. However, the unquenchable excitement of the children was infectious, breathing life into the flagging adults. The colour had come back to Elias' cheeks as he sat at the head of the table, his father Eleazar at his right hand, trying hard not to nod off. The children watched him with fascinated amusement as his eyelids drooped and his head nodded.

After the blessing and with each cup of Elias' best wine, the familiar psalms and the great story of their nation's escape from Egypt, the family began to find hope and inspiration, despite everything they had been through in the past twenty-four hours.

The women took it in turns to help Sophie and Sara; every stage was well prepared, so the work was easy. Sara was pale, with her mouth set into a hard line, and Martha thought how tired she must be.

After the first blessing, James, holding little Bartholomew's hand, asked Elias the first question of the evening. "Why is this night so special and different from all others?" he asked, looking up into Elias's face innocently.

Bartholomew nodded enthusiastically, and lisped, "Storwy, please. Storwy now?"

This earned him a clap of approval, as Elias began, "We were slaves in Egypt, but God heard our cry and rescued us."

Martha felt a lump forming in her throat and swallowed hard, blinking back the tears. Oh, God. What have we done to our rescuer? She clutched Mary's hand, beside her, and felt the comforting squeeze of her sister's courage.

Miriam led the singing with her harp, her mother and aunts adding rich harmonies, while Joachim and Reuben, with their deep base voices, brought depth and rhythm to the music. Lazarus wasn't the only one to play the flute, both Micah and Joshua produced theirs and joined in heartily. Naomi surprised them all by playing Elizabeth's lyre really well, while her baby slept in his grandmother's arms.

"Mary, aren't you going to play," asked Martha.

Mary shook her head and forced a smile.

"The music is so beautiful, I wouldn't want to spoil it. Besides it's an opportunity to sing, you know I can't do both."

So together they sang, and the music was like oil soothing their grief.

The bitter herbs were met with the traditional moans and groans, some quite genuine. Sara and Julie had done an excellent job, and were commended through jaw twisting and eye squinting facial expressions from the others. Desperate, the children clamoured for the charoseth. Reuben looked concerned. "I'm afraid there'll be none left for you," teased Sam.

"I think I'd prefer slavery to Sara's mix of bitter herbs. What have you put in it this year, dear woman?" said Reuben, wincing.

Sara winked at Julia. "It's a secret," she said, raising a smile from him.

Mary remembered the Master had offered Judas the bitter herbs, and her face fell. Why had it been one of them? Why couldn't the betrayer have been an outsider? It would have lessened the Master's pain surely, and theirs, she thought bitterly.

Even now, as they washed their hands in preparation to eat, their stomachs rumbling with hunger, Martha and Mary were not alone in remembering how Yeshua had washed his disciples' feet before they had eaten their last Passover supper together. Had that really only happened the night before? To Martha, it felt as though a lifetime had passed since then. Mary rested her head on her brother's shoulder, and closed her eyes; it was all too much.

It was Elizabeth who surprised them; she seemed composed, quietly enthusiastic, as she reminded them of the things the Master had done and said at his last meal, insisting that Elias add them to the traditional format. Martha marvelled that Elizabeth had remembered and understood the importance of his actions and was now bringing them to her own table. Yeshua's influence over hearts and minds would continue long after his death, thought Martha, but it just deepened her misery.

Good humour, if a little exaggerated, prevailed throughout the meal, which was devoured with enthusiasm by most of them. Afterwards the children, supervised by the popular Tabitha and Miriam, went in search of the hidden matzah. Elias, with Joachim's help, had hidden it well, giving the adults a welcome break from the over excited children. Even Rosh was persuaded to join in.

Martha constantly found her thoughts wandering to her friends and fretting over the events of the last week. She longed for news of them and had to keep reminding herself that she had only seen them that morning. She found herself still wishing she had gone to Golgotha too. She prayed silently: 'I haven't abandoned you Lord, I'm trying to do as you asked, please give me peace.' She felt hot tears well up yet again and turned her head away.

"Martha, are you all right?" Naomi's voice cut through Martha's misery, bringing her back to the present. Martha looked round and blinked.

"I'm just very tired," she said with a sniff, grateful for Naomi's sympathetic touch on her arm.

"For you, Mary and Lazarus to lose such a dear friend in such a terrible way must be hard to bear. It was so unjust," said Naomi, with feeling, but then, almost apologetically she added, "I understand what the Master is supposed to have done in sacrificing himself, and that he was sent by God, but forgive me. After all we've been through as a family it is too much to take in right now." Martha smiled weakly. How could Naomi understand? Her world was baby Amos and Micah, her husband. To Martha, his loss felt more personal. The pain was like losing Lazarus all over again.

Tabitha came gently between Naomi and Martha, draping her long skinny arms around Martha's shoulders. Moments before she had been laughing with the children, but now her face drooped and in her large dark eyes Martha saw her distress.

"He can't be dead?" Tabitha pleaded, in a whisper. "I knew Lazarus was dead. I felt it, but I don't feel like that about the Master. It's like he's still here." Mary looked up, overhearing Tabitha's words, and nodded; she felt like that too.

"I know he's gone, but I don't feel alone," said Mary, looking closely at her brother. "Lazarus, you seem almost joyful and so full of peace. I felt it when I rested my head on your shoulder. How can you be like that, the Master meant everything to you?"

"I feel his presence too. It's a great comfort. It brings me peace, although I don't know how. I suppose what happened to him is too raw to think about."

Before Mary could comment Joachim coughed loudly, and the family were quiet, as Elias broke a matzah into pieces. The plate was passed round, and every member of the family took a bit and waited for Elias to speak.

"Take and eat this, it is his body which he gave for you. Remember him doing this."

Martha's mouth felt dry, as she tried to swallow the sharp piece of matzah. Then they drank the cup of blessing, and all who had heard Miriam and Susanna speak were reminded again of the Master's words.

"This cup is the new covenant made by his blood which he poured out for us." And then many of them wept openly, tired out as they sang of the greatness of God from Psalm one-hundred and thirty-six.

Elias raised his cup and said, "Send your wrath on the nations that despise you, Oh Lord!"

As one, the family said "Amen."

Chapter Thirty-Eight

The High Day

Thursday

The high day dawned grey and overcast, but it was a holiday. The men at least were in their places at the synagogue, dutifully following the traditions. The holy scriptures were read, the prayers said, and the psalms sung.

Surprisingly Elizabeth had insisted on going too, and was joined by Julia, whose boys were safely under the care of their cousin Miriam. Glad to see some of her friends, Elizabeth caught up with them in rapid but brief exchanges.

On the walk home, she was positively jovial, sharing with Julia her friend's experiences, which had been dull compared to her own. The collapse of the pillar, under the portico was by far the most extensive damage done to any of her friends properties. However, the men were quiet and subdued.

"They're usually so lively on the way home from the synagogue," remarked Elizabeth in confidence to Julia.

"Everyone is extremely tired, and after the things that happened and then were revealed to us yesterday – well, the implications are far reaching. It's been a lot to take in for everyone," said Julia gently.

Elizabeth frowned thoughtfully. "I suppose you're right. Yesterday there were times I thought the world might end, but it didn't. The sun came up this morning and life goes on, and for that I am grateful to God."

Through her smile, Julia said, "As am I." She was struck by Elizabeth's simple but genuine words.

A messenger arrived later that day for Elias, who immediately went in search of Martha. He found her resting with baby Samuel on her lap, but she looked so peaceful and content at that moment that he didn't have the heart to disturb her. So he went to look for Mary, instead. She was talking with some of the older boys, inside. Unobserved, Elias listened by the door as she explained some of the familiar passages from the scripture that had been read at the synagogue earlier. Mary's intensity reminded him so much, at times, of her father Reubel, his older brother.

Elias sent the boys to find their fathers and Lazarus, while he sat down beside Mary.

"My friend Joseph has sent good news," he said. "He got permission from Pilate to bury the Master's body before sunset yesterday. But even now, the chief priests cannot leave our Master in peace. They have persuaded Pilate to have the tomb sealed and guarded."

"So, they think he might resurrect himself," laughed Mary, bitterly.

"I think it's more to prevent his followers from stealing the body and claiming that he's risen. The possibility of a real resurrection is not something that our Sadducee friends could contemplate, now is it?" he chuckled.

"Has there been any other news?" asked Mary, suddenly too weary to feel angry about the suspicious mind of the priests.

"Of the disciples, no. But of the Iscariot fellow, yes. They are only rumours at the moment, and ones I don't care to repeat."

Lazarus and Sam arrived, and while Elias spoke to them, Mary went to break the latest news to Martha.

* * *

As the sun set, the family gathered to eat, and immediately realised Lazarus and Sam were missing. At first Elias was furious, but he calmed down once his brothers had reasoned with him, pointing out that the streets were quieter and for the moment the authorities were certain they had regained control of the people. Besides, it was Passover. The two young men would return safely once they had seen their friends. However, Elias remained concerned. What if Sam and Lazarus unintentionally led the temple police to the disciples, or back home?

After the meal, the children were put to bed with little argument as the adults waited uneasily for Sam and Lazarus. Reuben was angry with his younger brother for going out without consulting him, but Elias knew Reuben would have tried to stop them, and Lazarus would want to avoid that. He didn't blame his nephew; if he had been in Lazarus' position he doubted he would have been as obedient as Lazarus had, and for as long. Elizabeth alternated between despair for their safety, and the effrontery of their thoughtlessness. Martha spent her evening listening for the gate, and praying with Mary.

The household had been quiet for some time when the two men finally slipped in quietly, trying not to rattle the gate. They were surprised to find several of the family still waiting up for them. Sam looked worried, but Elias was the first to embrace them in welcome.

"At last, you are home," he said, sighing with relief. "We were beginning to think the worst. But come inside and tell us the news. Did you find his disciples?"

The two of them were flushed and out of breath from their rapid walk back in the darkness, and hungry. Gratefully they gobbled down the food Sara brought to them. Between mouthfuls, Lazarus began to share what they had learnt.

"The disciples are all safely back at the lodgings. Some didn't turn up until this afternoon, but everyone is finally accounted for. We are most concerned for Peter. He seems a broken man."

"Well, thank God for their safety," said Elias.

"Father, you weren't mistaken about seeing John on the way up to the Gennath gate," said Sam. "The Lord's mother Mary, Miriam, Susanna, Mary Alphaeus and Salome, were all there with him. They followed the Master to Golgotha. You've got to admire them, especially John. He's not exactly hidden himself since the arrest, following the Master to Caiaphas' palace and then up to Golgotha."

"Fearless, or stupid?" asked Amon.

"Faithful," came Lazarus' swift but gentle reply. "There were many others we know in the crowd at Golgotha. Cleopas and Mary were there, some of Mary Joseph's family, and Magnus' wife too, but sadly not one of us." He looked at his sisters, knowing they shared his regret too.

"The risk for you was too high," said Sam. "And what could you have done? Watched him suffer, increasing his pain and yours? He paused for a moment, before continuing. "When the crowds dispersed, no one could persuade Miriam to leave, so in the end Mary Alphaeus stayed with her, while John took the others back to their lodgings."

"Remarkable women," commented Reuben.

Mary began to cry, her heart breaking all over again. Martha felt only failure.

"But as we heard earlier today, relief did come in the form of Joseph and Nicodemus," Lazarus reminded them. "At first Miriam was very suspicious; a Pharisee and member of the Sanhedrin coming to bury the Master's body? But Joseph managed to convince her they too were believers, and then she and Mary Alphaeus wept with relief and gratitude. Where Joseph found cloth, myrrh and aloes to prepare the body we could not guess, but I'm sure Nicodemus used his influence." Elias and his brothers nodded at this.

"I've never seen a woman with such nerve and devotion," commented Sam. "Miriam has kept a vigil on the tomb since sunset yesterday, fearing some interference from the temple authorities, and dear Mary Alphaeus has stayed by her side."

"They must be exhausted, and Mary Alphaeus has Thaddaeus and Young James to think about as well," remarked Sara.

"She is an extraordinary woman, so quiet you would hardly think it of her," said Martha.

"Please let me go to them, Uncle?" implored Martha. "Surely no harm will come to you all if I go. Women are of no consequence to the authorities. The others have stood openly by him, why can't I?" Elizabeth looked concerned; surely Elias wouldn't let her go now.

"Be reasonable Martha. It's late, and none of us know exactly where the tomb is," said Elias gently.

Martha looked imploringly at her brother, but he shook his head.

"I don't care about any of that," retorted Martha, "I'll find them."

Sara slipped into the seat beside her and took her hands, holding them firmly in her own. Sara didn't speak; she waited until Martha's anger and frustration had subsided. Mary slipped her arm around her too and Tabitha crept closer.

"That big guy Peter has always had a lot to say for himself, but it was a different story after they arrested his Master," said Elizabeth, loudly. "I heard he denied knowing the Master three times, before dawn."

The whole assembly looked at Elizabeth in stunned silence. "Where did you hear all that, my good woman?" asked her husband, taken aback.

"I have my sources," Elizabeth retorted, tossing her head defiantly. Elias's brow furrowed, now who had she been talking too.

"Oh, all right. It was next door. I popped over to see Hagar and that's when I heard about Peter. Her husband was on duty at Caiaphas' palace, and had to wait for the verdict. It was only afterwards he realised Peter had been standing right there with the guards and attendants around the brasier. Perez remembers it quite distinctly, because Peter ran off as the cock crowed at dawn. Hagar was furious when Perez didn't come home until sun rise, and then he nearly nodded off in the middle of their celebrations." Elizabeth would have continued, but Elias interrupted her.

"Yes, I'm sure we can imagine how annoying that would be. Lazarus, Sam can you shed some light on this?"

"Mother is quite right," said Sam. "Peter, by his own admission, denied the Master three times. He was devastated. During the Passover super, the Master had even warned him he would do it."

"So, all that was going on in the courtyard while you were listening to the council upstairs?" queried Reuben.

"So it would seem," sighed Josiah. "A terrible night for all of us."

"No wonder Peter is so miserable, poor man," sighed Mary. "But Lazarus, you still haven't told us about the others."

"I think the initial fear and panic has subsided, but they seem confused and spend a lot of time arguing." Lazarus said. "Many share Peter's feelings of shame. But no one blames them. It grieves my heart to see them in such torment."

"Has anyone attempted to arrest them?" asked Sara.

"No," replied Sam. "It doesn't seem they are being watched either. The landlord's fairly certain of that."

"Annas will have his eye on things," said Elias thoughtfully.

"And is clearly not confident enough to leave the tomb unguarded," laughed Joachim.

"Does that mean Lazarus will be safe now?" asked Martha.

"As long as he doesn't draw attention to himself," said Reuben. Elias nodded in agreement.

"I know," said Lazarus. "We took a big risk going down there, but they're our friends, and I will not abandon them for the Master's sake. I had hoped we could bring them some encouragement and comfort but in that, I feel we failed."

"So, what about tomorrow, what happens then?" asked Josiah.

"Oh, that's easy," said Elizabeth, perking up. "We have to go shopping and make all the preparations for the weekly Sabbath. It will be a very busy day."

"A chance to get out and about for the whole family," laughed Elias, catching Josiah's eye.

"That wasn't quite what I meant, Elizabeth, but I take your point," responded Josiah.

Sam and Lazarus stretched and yawned together. As the family dispersed to bed, Martha and Mary followed their brother, still aching with questions he had not answered.

Chapter Thirty-Nine

Friday Market

Friday was usually the busiest day of the week as the Jewish community prepared for the weekly Sabbath, and with Passover celebrations and the annual holy day, the great city was busier than ever, providing another headache for the Roman governors.

Early in the morning the sun broke through the clouds, lifting everyone's spirits as they excitedly prepared to leave the confines of the house on various errands. Sara had a long list of orders and collections to make for Elizabeth, so Martha was going along to help. Elizabeth was escorting the rest of the family on a similar trip. Even Elias's parents were joining them, riding on the two donkeys kept especially for Elizabeth's shopping trips. Tabitha and Mary were to accompany the mothers with their younger children, a job Mary usually enjoyed, but today, when she most wanted freedom to roam, it felt a heavy burden.

Martha and Sara quickly left the others behind, which irritated her aunt, who had to admit she had given them a lot to do. Sara guided them swiftly through the narrow passageways between the large, ornate houses of the upper city, crossing the busy main thoroughfares. The views over the city were stunning, a far cry from that dark icy evening only two days before when Martha had said goodbye to Yeshua. Quickly they descended the streets making their way towards the market. They needed new lamps, and some blankets from the weaver's quarters. Here, Sara helped Martha pick out new tunics for two of the younger children, at Elizabeth's request.

"Why on earth couldn't Elizabeth bring them here with their mothers?" moaned Martha, as she struggled to decide on the fit.

"Ah, these days your aunt finds it too far to walk, with all the hills and steps, and to tell you the truth, I don't think she's keen on coming into the older city anymore. It's a bit too..." Sara fumbled for words.

"Squalid," suggested Martha, wrinkling her nose.

"I think that would do it," laughed Sara.

They came to a street junction, Martha looked left and right and shrugged. "You'd better lead, I am quite lost," she said.

Sara led them through several crowded streets of carpenters and blacksmiths, past a synagogue from which came the drone of boys chanting rhythmically. As they rounded a sharp corner Martha's eyes were drawn to the lively stalls crammed together in the narrow space. The fresh earthy smells reminded her of home and masked the usual odour of city life. Sara called out, but too late. Martha tripped over a pile of rubbish in the gutter and went sprawling.

People helped her up and collected the content of her basket. It took a moment for Martha to overcome her embarrassment and shock before she recognised, to her utter delight, the faces of Salome and Susanna among the helpers.

"Have you come to look for us too?" asked Salome. "It was so good to see Lazarus and his cousin last night, their visit lifted our spirits." Martha was pleased to hear this, for her brother's sake.

Blood was trickling from one of Martha's knees, so they hurried her off to their nearby lodgings, leaving Sara to join them as soon as she had finished at the market.

The house was dim inside but seemed to have a myriad of small rooms leading off the passageway, which continued on to a stair and beyond that was the back door. It was clean and well kept. Her grazed knee was tended to swiftly by Salome, while Susanna welcomed her with a drink. Martha had hardly regained her composure when Miriam and Joanna came in carrying baskets of spices and oils, followed by Mary Cleopas.

Martha was introduced to Joanna, who stood tall and erect. She had a finely chiselled profile which softened when she spoke. Martha didn't have a chance to feel awkward in front of Joanna, because Miriam engulfed her in a tight hug which left her breathless. Seeing Martha's cut knee seemed to release something in Miriam; she began to sob uncontrollably on Martha's shoulder. Martha put her arms around her friend and held her. Holding out a hand to the others, she drew them in, as they too expressed their pain and grief.

Mary Joseph came hurrying to join them, followed by Mary Alphaeus, her usually rosy cheeks drawn and grey. Martha did her best to comfort them, but inside she felt inadequate and unworthy for the task. She had not witnessed his suffering and pain as they had, and she had not stood by him or them. She felt like a fraud.

As Miriam regained her composure, she began to share the story of their ordeal at the tomb. At first, she had felt compelled to stay when Joseph and Nicodemus had left because she didn't trust the guard on the tomb. Perhaps the temple would attempt to defile his body or remove it. Exhausted, she and Mary Alphaeus had finally returned last night, and Mary Alphaeus had been reunited with her boys, and her husband who had just arrived. Miriam had engaged Joanna's help to purchase what was needed to complete the Master's burial after the Sabbath. Joseph and Nicodemus had done the best they could in the time they had had before sundown.

"Now begins the long wait," said Miriam. "We can do nothing until first light on Sunday morning. I may not bear it well." Miriam looked pale and sallow, dark rings around her dull eyes, as she unpacked the spices with shaking hands. "Pray his body is left undisturbed till then."

Salome and Mary Alphaeus were deeply concerned for the safety of their sons, but at least Salome now had the comfort and support of her husband. He was staying with the disciples at their lodgings. The other disturbing news was that Peter had talked about going back to Galilee.

"Martha, what happened? What's gone wrong? He was the Messiah!"

Martha looked at the despairing faces around her. "Don't give up your hope!" she begged, feeling helpless in the face of their grief. She cried out silently, her heart twisted by the pain she saw, and words came to her. She too found comfort as she spoke softly to her friends.

"The Lord himself shall give you a sign. Behold, the young woman who is unmarried and a virgin shall conceive and bear a son, and shall call his name Emmanuel, God with us." Hearing this, Mary Joseph straightened a little as she met the gaze of all those in the room. Scripture taught to Martha years ago by her parents came tumbling out. "Nevertheless, that time of darkness and despair will not go on forever. There will be a time in the future when Galilee of the Gentiles, which lies along the road that runs between the Jordan and the sea, will be filled with glory." Her voice grew in strength and conviction as she continued. "The people who walk in darkness have seen a great light, a light that will shine on all who live in the land where death casts its shadow. Israel will again be great, and its people will rejoice as people rejoice at harvest time.

They will shout with joy like warriors dividing the plunder, for God will break the chains that bind his people, and the rod of their oppressors is broken. For to us a child is born, to us a son is given, and the government will rest on his shoulders. These will be his royal titles: Wonderful Counsellor, Mighty God, Everlasting Father, Prince of Peace. His ever-expanding government will never end. He will rule forever with fairness and justice from the throne of his ancestor David. The passionate commitment of the Lord almighty will guarantee this!"

Silence fell. It wasn't the reaction Martha was hoping for, her heart felt light and encouraged, but her friends just stared.

"He was, no he is, the lamb of God who takes away the sin of the world. He's made the final sacrifice for all of us with his own life blood." The women looked shocked. "Please don't despair, hold on, it's not over. I just know it."

Martha was offering them hope, but the terrible scenes they had witnessed were too crushing and too overwhelming for her words to penetrate their grief.

"I have a job to finish," said Miriam, quietly into the silence. "I will go to his grave at first light on Sunday. If anyone will come with me, I shall be glad of the company, but I will go."

"Miriam," pleaded Martha. "You knew and understood before we did that he must die, we dreaded it together. Don't give up hope dear sister and friend, I couldn't bear it."

"Martha you weren't there. You didn't see him die." The cut of Miriam's words went deep into Martha, condemning her.

"But I was there in the darkness. I felt the earth tremble and saw the stones crack. My uncles were there when the sanctuary curtain was torn in two by the invisible hand of God."

"God had broken his promise to save his people," snapped Miriam.

"No, God never breaks a promise, you know that. I don't

understand either, but I still believe, I still hope."

"She can't Martha. It's too much, she is spent for the moment. We are sheep without a shepherd," whispered Susanna.

A knock on the door broke the tension. It was Sara, her shopping finished. She apologised for taking Martha away, explaining her aunt would be anxious if they didn't return soon.

"We'll come again as soon as we can," promised Sara, but Martha was silent.

Mary Joseph rose to see them out, holding Martha's hand in hers for a moment, before they parted. "Thank you," she whispered. "Your words have rekindled my hope."

The bright, boisterous bustle of the market with its surrounding streets and courtyards shook Martha from her melancholy. Sara guided her past the disciple's lodgings, the simple two storey building in which the men were barricaded, back towards the wealthier portions of the city.

Martha followed Sara, fresh guilt washing over her for failing her friends. Then anger flared up, firstly with herself and then with her friends for not listening to the words of hope she had tried to give them. As they toiled up the broad streets with their burdens, Martha became more depressed. Despair crept into her soul.

"Sara please, I want to go to Golgotha."

"But it will take too long," pleaded Sara, looking worried.

"Then I will go on my own."

"It's a terrible place, where barbaric crucifixions are done. You don't need to see the place of his humiliation. Come home."

"I'm sorry, but right now, I don't want to go back there. I can't face anyone."

Sara stopped, put the shopping down, and turned back to Martha. Placing her hands on her shoulders, she looked into her face with her piercing dark eyes.

"I've known you since you were a tiny baby and you've been

through so much. Now grab that hope of yours tight and don't let it go for anything. Everything will come right in the end, you'll see. I'm no prophet, but I know God and so do you!"

Martha felt as though she'd been slapped. Beads of perspiration broke out on her forehead, but Sara's words sank in. Then somewhere, deep down inside, like blades of tender grass in the spring, her hope began to sprout. She shook herself, and as she did her doubt was flung away and her bearing began to change.

"You're right Sara. It's only just begun. How dare we despair."

Chapter Forty

Change

"Where on earth have you been? Aunt Elizabeth is on the verge of sending out a search party!" exclaimed Mary, as Martha and Sara gratefully put their baskets and bundles down.

"Mary dear, take your sister to the kitchen and get her something to eat and drink. She's had quite a morning. Leave your aunt to me," said Sara wearily.

Mary looked inquiringly at Martha as she picked up the heavy shopping. Thankfully the kitchen was quiet, the others were resting after their trip.

"Did you get to see the women?" asked Mary, putting food on a plate.

Martha nodded. "I'm sorry you didn't get to come too. I don't think I did much good."

Mary tipped her head on one side. "What happened? Tell me everything."

"Everything?" queried Martha. "Even all the boring shopping we did?"

"No, heaven forbid. Not that stuff!" laughed Mary, glad to see her sister still had a sense of humour.

Martha poured out her story of the events of her morning, grateful for Mary's sympathetic support and understanding. In the end, Mary agreed there had been little more she could have said to help their friends. Sometimes Martha expected too much of herself.

The household servants began to appear in the kitchen, having been rooted out by Sara, who had given them tasks that were now urgent with the weekly Sabbath only hours away. At least making the matzah were quite straightforward and the children could help, but a large quantity was needed for the whole family. Sara hurriedly began the preparations to cook the meat dish, which would be accompanied by a variety of vegetables and fruit. Martha enjoyed cooking at her aunts, as they had a much wider selection to choose from. Having unburdened herself to Mary, she felt much better and threw herself into helping. Soon there was a merry party in the kitchen. The noise rose further as the men returned, carrying the goat carcass for the main dish and demanding food. They ate in the courtyard and were happy to entertain their offspring while eating. When Elizabeth woke from her nap, she was pleased to see her household in good spirits, but disgruntled to discover Elias and his brothers had gone out on business.

Tables had to be laid, and Miriam and Tabitha were instructed in the correct preparation of goat. They alone were to wait on the men that evening, a great honour and privilege. Good humour and chaos, went hand in hand during the preparations.

Seeing the preparations were well in hand, and feeling exhausted, Martha quietly retired to a corner of the courtyard, where immediately she was pounced on by some of her younger cousins who were always looking for entertainment. Mary came to her rescue, taking the little group off on some errand. To her surprise, Martha then felt alone and empty; the children had distracted her from her thoughts. Clinging to hope by her fingertips, she prayed for help.

A little while later, Tabitha came and rested her head on Martha's shoulder. With their arms around each other, they sat in silence, realising how much they had missed one another in the general melee of the last few days. Martha kissed her forehead. Tabitha seemed so grown up these days.

"Do you remember Passover last year, when the family from Galilee visited us? We certainly had a house full then," said Tabitha, looking into Martha's face searchingly. "Happy times," she said, which made Martha cry. Tabitha brushed the tears away.

Martha smoothed the tight curls, then asked, "What did you get up to this morning?"

Tabitha needed little encouragement, and her reply was full and detailed. She talked with wonder and enthusiasm of all she had seen and heard in the city, and all that had been said and done by the family.

"Elizabeth and Julia consulted me on several matters when it came to purchases," said Tabitha proudly. "And they were very complimentary at the way I handled those unruly boys." Elizabeth's acceptance of Tabitha gladdened her heart.

Just then Elizabeth came waddling over. "Martha, I'm sorry to disturb you, but could I borrow Tabitha for a while? She really is a treasure." Tabitha jumped up, smiling her best smile, and threw her arms around Martha, kissing her cheek before hurrying away with Elizabeth.

To Martha's surprise her aunt returned a few minutes later, sat down and took her hand. "How are you feeling, dear? It's been a challenging few days for all of us, but especially for you. I know how close you were to the Rabbi."

At first Martha didn't know how to respond to this uncharacteristic concern.

"I'm very tired," confessed Martha. "But I can't help thinking it's not really over. I know everyone thinks he's dead, but the hope in my heart says he's not. And scripture suggests that somehow he has saved us, not from the Romans, who I'm no longer sure are the enemy, but from our sins, which are of far greater concern to God." Martha glanced at her aunt, but her gaze remained steady and sympathetic. Encouraged, she continued, "Perhaps that's why everyone is so confused and has lost heart."

"Your friends, Miriam and the others?" Martha nodded, biting her lip. "Sara told me," her aunt confessed, softly. "I think they will come round. Be patient dear not everyone has your foresight." She sighed. "I don't pretend to understand, but I trust Elias, and if he thinks this Rabbi is the chosen one, then so do I, if for no other reason than the miracle of Lazarus. So, what I am trying to say is, I still have hope, like you, my dear niece." There was silence for a moment, before she added, "Martha, I haven't thanked you for everything you've done and in such trying circumstances. I really don't think I would have coped if I hadn't had you and my Sara to rely on. Oh, and there is something else," She hesitated, looking down at her lap. "We were all so wrong about that poor skinny child you took in."

Martha looked up sharply, but Elizabeth was smiling. "She has turned out to be a gem among the children. She shows all the hallmarks of her spiritual mother."

Martha was puzzled. "Tabitha was an orphan," she said.

"I know that, silly. You're her spiritual mother. I'm trying to pay you a compliment, dear. But seriously, she is developing into a competent and discerning young woman. Everyone in the family has come to love her. She even sounds like you at times!" She laughed.

"Thank you," was all Martha could say. She swallowed hard.

"Your uncle always said that when your father died, he couldn't have managed without you, especially as Lazarus was still so young, Elizabeth went on. "You did such a good job managing the business as well as running the home and caring for Mary. You remind me so much of your poor mother before her illness. Of course, Mary is more like your mother in looks, but heaven knows where her ways come from. She is quite an unusual young woman."

Martha tittered and squeezed her aunt's hand, appreciating this unusual side of her aunt. Elizabeth was just pleased to have brought a smile back to her niece's face.

Sara appeared, carrying two cups and her mistress's favourite dainty.

"Ah, here comes another woman I truly couldn't manage without," said Elizabeth.

Looking back over her shoulder, as if there might be someone standing behind her, Sara said, "Do you mean me, Mistress?"

"Oh, just hark at her," chortled Elizabeth. "Everyone knows she's indispensable, and I would be lost without her loyalty, understanding and friendship. She's a wise woman, like you my dear." She levered herself to her feet. "Well, I'd better get on and do something useful, Tabitha will be waiting." She waddled off across the courtyard towards the kitchen.

Martha and Sara looked at one another in astonishment. "Compliments?" they chorused.

"What a difference. What's come over her, Sara?" asked Martha.

"It'll take a bit of getting used to, if it lasts," said Sara cheerfully. She headed back to the kitchen, carrying Elizabeth's refreshments.

Chapter Forty-One

Ghosts

The Sabbath

Elias, Josiah and Joachim returned that evening with barely enough time to wash before the deep, throaty song of horns began to vibrate through the golden air of Jerusalem. In unison, each synagogue was summoning its faithful community to prayer, praise and thanksgiving. The family were gathered and ready, eager to descend the streets to the ornate synagogue that served the influential community of Jews in that part of the city.

Martha remembered trying to guess the number of synagogues in Jerusalem when she was a child. The memory gave her pleasure.

"What are you smiling at?" asked Tabitha, who walked beside her.

"Oh, a guessing game I use to play with my father. I must have been younger than you at the time."

"What sort of questions got asked? Did you guess right?"

"Oh, anything really, the number of lambs a ewe was carrying, or the weight of a grain sack, what father was thinking, or one time, the number of synagogues in Jerusalem."

"Four hundred and eighty," said Tabitha, sounding a trifle bored.

Martha was astonished, "How did you know?"

It was Tabitha's turn to look surprised, but before she could answer, Lazarus, who had been walking with them, chipped in, "Because you've told us that story many times before." Martha's jaw dropped open in protest. "Don't worry big sis, it's all part of the ageing process," he finished, with a cheeky grin. Martha just laughed.

The synagogue, although spacious and lavishly decorated when compared to Bethany, still followed the same comforting format, with set readings for each week or celebration. Mary loved the ornate gold-painted carvings on the handles of the scrolls, on which careful copies of the Torah had been made. The ark in which the precious scrolls were kept was equally beautifully decorated. Candlelight from the menorah illuminated the scrolls as they were read and was reflected in the polished stone floors.

As usual, the three texts read that morning, although written in Hebrew, were translated into Aramaic every few verses, so the congregation could understand. Blessings and traditional prayers interspersed the whole proceeding which were watched over by the Hazzan, a large self-important man.

Unlike Mary, Martha felt ill at ease amongst such finery. She found it a distraction, taking her mind off the readings and then the explanation and thoughts shared by her uncle, whose turn it was to give the commentary. Mary told her she ought to appreciate the time and devotion that had gone into the decorations, which were acts of worship in their own right, but although Martha could see that, she preferred simplicity.

On the way home, driven by pent-up energy, the youngsters ran on ahead, and had to be chased by the teenagers and brought back.

The streets were still busy. Rome did not stop for the Sabbath, nor the many other cultures that shared Jerusalem.

* * *

"Why do I feel like I've done a week's work, just like when I'm at home?" complained Micah, as they all sat for the midday meal.

"Oh, I know what you mean son," agreed Joachim. "And we're supposed to be on holiday."

"Here," called Elias. "Help yourself to wine. It'll help. We've been through testing times, and it takes it out of you."

Martha and Mary were glad to be surrounded by their family, but their thoughts turned to their friends too, many of whom were apart from their families and in deep mourning for the one person who had held them together. His followers felt as much like family to them now as their own blood relatives.

The wind increased through the night, but a bright spring day dawned as the horns rang throughout the city calling the people to prayer and worship once more. Many visitors flocked to the temple, whereas residents and visitors could attend their local synagogues. The Romans and those of other nationalities and beliefs turned over in their beds, groaned, and went back to sleep, but the Jewish God would not be denied.

Once more the family set out for the synagogue, blown like chaotic sailing ships, flapping flamboyantly while the children raced in the wind, full of excitement.

On the way home, concealed in a fine new shawl presented to her by Elizabeth, Mary listened to the male members of the family talking over the passages that had just been read. She added her own thoughts and insights to the debate, questioning and challenging her uncles and cousins. Martha listened with pride as her strong-minded sister, with quick short steps, trotted beside the men, who could not have excluded her even if they had wanted to.

This was a special time for Elias and Elizabeth, with so many members of the family gathered around them, and they worked hard together to make it a memorable Sabbath afternoon. Songs were sung and traditional dances enjoyed by young and old. Games, both boisterous and sedentary, were played by everyone, and together they found comfort in the distraction. Josiah couldn't bear to lose at board games, irrespective of who he played, and this led him to be scolded by his wife in front of his children. Elizabeth was as insensitive as ever, yet so kind. No one had changed, but because of what they had been through and the hope that would not die, each appreciated the others more.

Tabitha, with baby Amos in her arms, swept up to Martha, followed by a gaggle of the little ones. Cheerfully she unloaded the baby into Martha's empty lap.

"Everyone seems so much more lovable today," she said, before being tugged away by her followers to invent some new game for them to play.

Martha found herself watching Julia and her two boys. They always seemed a little set apart, although Julia was always smiling and pleasant, but Martha knew how much she still missed Obadiah, her husband.

The sun began to set, the last bright stabbing rays reaching into the courtyard as the wind died, and a stillness descended, almost like nature was holding her breath. Julia crept out into the stillness and sat for a moment enjoying the last warmth of the day alone.

The bell on the gate jangled gently, as if it might have been rung by the wind, or a tentative hand. Curious, Julia looked up.

Her face froze. Obadiah stood before her.

A scream pierced the silence. The living room and kitchen emptied instantly, people rushing out into the courtyard terrified.

What could have happened? Julia stood rigidly, her hand trembling as she pointed toward the gate.

"It was my Obadiah, alive!" she cried out, her chest heaving with shock.

"Julia are you all right, what's happened?" asked Sarah, who was first to reach her.

"I saw him as clear as day, right there." Julia stamped her foot and pointed to a spot. She saw the shocked, disbelieving faces around her. "I was sitting enjoying the last rays of the Sabbath sun. The bell rang faintly, so I looked up, and there he was. My Obadiah walking towards me, his arms open wide in greeting. He was smiling, but I couldn't speak and couldn't move. He came to me, lifted my hands and kissed them. I felt the warmth of his lips, saw the life in his eyes, but before I could find my voice, someone called to him. He half-turned to go, then turned back to me. Love filled his eyes as he spoke a blessing over me and his boys. He looked so happy I wanted to cry with joy myself. I'm sorry I screamed, it must have startled you all. It was trapped inside me. It was only when he'd gone and taken the joy with him that it escaped from my chest."

"You must have seen a ghost, Aunt Julia," said Joshua, sympathetically. "The Rabbi's crucifixion has upset us all."

"It was Obadiah, not a ghost. He was as solid as you or me," insisted Julia.

Elizabeth put her arm around her sister-in-law and drew her to a seat, nodding to Martha to fetch some wine.

"How was he dear? Did he look well? Did he say anything else?" she asked.

"Oh yes, he looked so well, so happy. He blessed us, Elizabeth. I heard him as clearly as the fountain. He spoke our boys' names. Then before I had a chance to take his hand or embrace him, someone called him away." Julia began to cry.

"Well, after seeing the Rabbi bring our Lazarus back to life, I'd believe anything," said Elizabeth, handing Julia the wine Martha had brought.

"How I've longed to see him again, to hear his voice and see the love in his eyes for us. I mean no disrespect towards your brother Talman, you understand. It's just so hard to be widowed after only three years of marriage, and I miss him so much."

"We all miss him my dear, but meeting you was the best thing that ever happened to him. Our parents despaired of him ever marrying, but you changed his mind. He doted on you, and the boys. Losing a husband, no matter how long you've been married, is a hard thing to bear." A tear rolled down Elizabeth's cheek as she looked up at Elias standing near.

"Well, I don't know what to believe anymore," said Elias, shaking his head. "The dead coming back to life twice in one family is quite remarkable. Life seemed so straightforward until that Rabbi turned out to be the one we had all waited for. Even the meaning of familiar scripture is being questioned now."

"Surely not, Uncle?" said Lazarus. "Our Lord was very sure that not one letter of the law should be changed, but he did say he'd come to fulfil the law according to John, and I had no trouble believing him. Only now are we beginning to understand what he might have meant by it."

"And I made the mistake of thinking things were beginning to get back to normal," grumbled Sara, as she headed back to the kitchen.

The family had barely returned to their games and entertainment when the bell started to ring wildly. Sophie ran to answer it, a little nervously. It was their neighbours Perez and Hagar. Elias and Elizabeth came puffing out to greet them.

"Welcome. What brings you both to our door this fine Sabbath evening?" asked Elias.

"Didn't your servant give you our message?" replied Perez, a little brusquely. He looked haughtily over his large hooked nose.

"Yes, of course she did. Elias has a lot on his mind at the moment. Do forgive him," said Elizabeth, charmingly.

"Come and take a seat," said Elias, politely. "Sara, a little something for our guests, please." Sara disappeared into the kitchen, returning almost immediately with refreshments. "Now, please tell us again, what's happened."

Elizabeth wasn't waiting for all that; Sophie had delivered a perfectly clear message. She dived straight in. "What a shock that must have been. It's been nearly five years, hasn't it?" she asked in a rush. The plump, usually cheerful Hagar nodded sadly. "I always remember because he and Sam were the same age. Were you frightened dear?" asked Elizabeth, patting her friend's hand.

"It certainly was a shock," replied Hagar, turning pale at the memory. "But no, we didn't feel fear, just confusion." She looked at her husband, who nodded.

"So what happened? Where is your son now?" asked Elias, finding it hard to keep up with his wife.

Perez told them what had happened. "Dan appeared while we were eating. He just wandered in and sat down with us, like he used to, and began chatting. He was always late for meals. He even picked up a matzah and nibbled it. He asked after us and the family, but as you can imagine, it wasn't much of a conversation on our part. We were speechless. Hagar recovered first, and began to ask questions, but Dan didn't seem interested in answering them. He just smiled and put his hand on hers reassuringly."

"It was warm and heavy and so real," said Hagar, looking desperately from Elizabeth to Elias, wanting them to believe her. "Anyhow, something seemed to distract him. He looked back, and that's when he suggested we should come over and see you. He said you would understand, because your nephew was raised from the dead by the Messiah. Can you explain what he meant and what has just happened? Our son appears to be alive and well!"

Elias swallowed hard and chose his words carefully before he spoke. "You are not alone in your experience. Elizabeth's sister-in-law..."

"Hagar knows Julia, dear," interrupted Elizabeth.

"Julia has had a similar experience," corrected Elias. "She saw her husband, who died three years ago. He spoke to her and kissed her. She too is adamant he was flesh and blood." Hagar and Perez looked relieved. "I must admit I doubted her, especially as we've all been under a lot of strain with recent events." Elias didn't elaborate, but Perez remembered that night at the high priest's palace too and understood. "But now I've heard your story, I'm beginning to think differently."

"It's a relief to know we're not going mad," said Perez, letting out a deep breath.

"Oh, I didn't say that," said Elias, and the two men laughed.

Elias invited them to join the family, where Julia and Hagar found comfort in discussing their experiences at great length in front of the whole family. No one could begin to explain what had happened or why, and they all wondered what might happen next.

Lazarus hung by the door, listening with Sam and Reuben. A while later the three slipped out, unnoticed. It was quite dark when they returned; Sara and Sophie were trimming the wicks and topping up the oil lamps around the courtyard.

As Sam came in he couldn't contain his excitement. "Sara, it's happening all over the city," he blurted out.

Sara finished lighting the lamp carefully, then asked, "What is happening all over the city?"

"Sightings of the resurrected dead!" he said, impatiently.

"We don't know if it's happening *all* over the city Sam," corrected Reuben. "But there are rumours and reports from many of our friends and neighbours in the Jewish quarter. At first, some were reluctant to admit to these miraculous sightings."

"They are probably afraid we'll think they were mad, or demon possessed," Sam added, grinning.

"But when we told them of Julia's experience, they seemed glad to share their own," finished Reuben.

"What can it mean?" asked the shrewd Sara, looking in Lazarus' direction.

"Why are you looking at me, Sara?" he said, laughing.

"I'm saying nothing, Master Lazarus."

Mary appeared. "What did you find out?" she asked, in hushed tones.

"These aren't isolated events. Lazarus' suspicions were correct," said Reuben. "We'd better go and report to Father. Was he cross when he discovered we'd gone?"

"You haven't been missed, yet," said Mary. "So watch out for your mother when you explain."

Chapter Forty-Two

The First Day of the Week

Sunday

Martha was awake earlier than usual, and sat in the courtyard praying. Dawn was still just a promise on the horizon. The report brought by Lazarus, Reuben and Sam had had her uncle busily searching the scriptures for anything that would shed a clearer light on what was happening. Yesterday, when the sun had set, the Master had been dead for three days and three nights, and then the dead had risen. This was the morning of the fourth day. Her brother had been in the tomb for four days.

Martha shivered with excitement; it felt like the sun was waiting to rise. She was still there when the fuller light of dawn brought a knock on the gate. She went to open it.

Miriam was leaning on the stone wall, breathing hard, her face red from running and her black shawl trailing on the ground.

"Miriam, my dearest sister, what urgent news has brought you to me so early in the morning?"

Still Miriam could not speak, but she grabbed Martha's hand and squeezed it, her face agitated but exhilarated.

"I've seen him," she finally gasped.

"Seen who?" asked Martha, carefully, her heart skipping a beat.

"The Master!" exclaimed Miriam. "He's alive! Martha, you were so right not to despair, you alone held to the hope we had shared." She took a deep breath. "I've seen the Messiah. I knelt at his feet in the garden near the tomb he was put in."

"The Master's alive," Martha repeated slowly, not quite believing what she was hearing. "Come and sit down. Tell me what has happened, for pity's sake."

Miriam sat on the edge of the seat and spoke rapidly. "The tomb is empty, only the grave clothes are left. The stone must have been rolled away by angels, or that's what I supposed them to be. The soldiers are bewildered, they saw nothing."

"Slow down. I can't take it in!" gasped Martha. "The tomb is open and empty, apart from his grave clothes? Has someone stolen the body?" Miriam shook her head vigorously. "There were angels?" Now Miriam was nodding violently. "Lazarus and Mary must hear this. Sara!" Martha shouted.

Sara had also heard the gate so she knew they had a guest, and she responded quickly, handing Miriam bread and wine before going to rouse Mary. Miriam gulped some wine, but she could not sit still and paced back and forth while they waited.

Mary stumbled down the stairs, wrapped in her blanket and rubbing the sleep from her eyes. Lazarus appeared from the opposite direction shortly after, his tunic loose and untied under his outer garment. As they joined the two impatient women, Lazarus looked from face to face bewildered, but Mary was wide awake. Martha sent Sara to wake the others, then she allowed Miriam to begin.

"We had planned to visit the tomb early this morning, to finish the anointing of the Master's body, but like you Martha, I couldn't sleep, so I left ahead of the others in the dark. I carried what I could of the prepared sweet spices, knowing the others would be close behind with the rest. I was worried about moving the stone and prayed I would be able to persuade the soldiers to do it for us. I hoped if they watched us, we would be allowed to complete the job and then the tomb could be resealed.

"When I arrived, to my utter dismay I found the stone had already been moved. It lay in its grooves to one side and there was no sign of the soldiers. I was perplexed, then deeply suspicious that Pilate had ordered the body removed, so I searched for the soldiers. They weren't far away, but they seemed afraid and as confused as I was. Nevertheless, they were adamant there had been no orders to disturb the grave. I'm afraid at that point I took to my heels in panic and ran back the way I had come in the hope of finding Mary Alphaeus, Salome and the others. I must have missed them in the dark. I was almost back at the lodgings before I realised it, so I decided to go and wake Magnus, the landlord, and see if the disciples knew what had happened.

"Peter and John were the only ones Magnus could rouse, the others were still sound asleep. We set off to Golgotha together, but I couldn't keep up. They were fresh and ran on ahead.

"I found the two Marys, Joanna, Susanna and Salome in the garden. They too had found the empty tomb, and the four terrified soldiers still on guard." Lazarus gave a wry smile at this point. "While I was fetching Peter and John, the five women had met an angel in the garden. Yes, a real angel. It spoke to them, and said Yeshua of Nazareth had risen from the dead, and was alive. Oh, and something else about him going back to Galilee." Miriam's brow furrowed. "You can imagine the state of excitement and shock they were in, even the down to earth Salome.

"Meanwhile, Peter and John had found the tomb empty. Peter

looked white and strained as Salome tried to persuade them that the Master was alive, because that's what the angel had said. But they wouldn't listen."

"Poor Peter, I doubt he could have coped with having his hopes dashed again," sighed Mary.

"But surely John would have believed his own mother?" said Sara, who had been quietly listening for some time.

"Well, you'd have thought so," agreed Miriam. "But as I share the story with you, I'm beginning to see how fantastic it must have seemed. I left Salome and the others with John and Peter, and went back to the tomb. I was in tears. I believed those women, I knew they spoke the truth.

"As I approached the tomb again, I saw something shimmer in the dark entrance and wiping my eyes I saw two figures. One sat where the Master's head had lain and the other where his feet had been. I wanted to run, but something drew me closer. Then they asked me why I was weeping. I could hardly speak and stammered that somebody had taken the body of our Master, and I didn't know where it might be. Standing in their presence, I felt terrified and began to back away. My only thought was to find the others."

"What did the angels look like?" interrupted Mary. Martha frowned at her.

"Such detail can wait. Go on with your story, Miriam," Martha urged.

"As I turned to leave, that's when I saw another figure. I assumed it must be the gardener. He asked me why I was crying, and because he seemed so concerned, I asked him if he knew what had become of the Master's body." Miriam began to shake uncontrollably. She clutched Martha's hands. "When he spoke again, he used my name. And suddenly I recognised him. Oh, Martha, can you imagine it? What exquisite joy to see him alive!"

There was a loud gasp, and Miriam realised they were not alone.

Many members of Elias' family had joined them and were standing transfixed like statues.

"Martha, Mary, dear Lazarus," she said, but she raised her eyes to include all her listeners. "The Master, my Lord, was standing right before me, that crooked smile on his lips and the golden light in his eyes. How could I have not recognised him before? It was almost unbearable. I sank to my knees, overcome with joy and fear." She paused, her face radiant and beaming. "I still don't understand what he said to me. I reached out to touch him, but he asked me not to. He said it was because he had not ascended to his father yet. Then he asked me to tell our fellowship that he was going back to his father and our father, to his God and our God."

She looked directly at Elias, "We are part of God's family. Brothers and sisters to the Lord." Elias sat down, overcome. Miriam took another sip of wine; she was calmer now.

"Salome found us, bringing the others with her. They fell down and worshipped him too, but he urged us to get up and go and find his disciples, to tell them that we had seen him. Poor Peter and John had missed him, they'd gone back to the lodgings disappointed. If only they had waited. Although between you and me, I don't think John will need much persuading, especially after seeing those neatly folded grave clothes."

"That's not exactly the act of grave robbers, Roman or otherwise," said Elias, with satisfaction.

Miriam laughed, relaxing now her story had been told. Her audience exploded, unable to contain their excitement any longer. Martha and Mary were on their feet, hugging. Lazarus and Sam were doing some sort of jig, whirling around one another. The uncles shook hands, grinning uncontrollably, but it wasn't enough to express how they felt, so they hugged and jumped for joy all at the same time. Reuben led Amon and Micah, like runaway chariots, whooping and shouting.

"He's alive!" Joachim shouted to his wife, as she appeared in the doorway, wondering what could cause such a celebration at this time of the morning.

"Who is?" Keturah asked, enjoying the spectacle of Sara and Elizabeth capering around one another in some sort of joyous dance.

"The Rabbi Yeshua, the Lord!" Joachim laughed. Keturah stared in amazement as his words sank in. Roused by the noise, the children and teenagers appeared, and very soon the whole family was celebrating in the courtyard.

"Why are we having a party before breakfast?" Noah asked Little Mary.

"Because Yeshua is alive!" shouted James, racing by waving his hands in the air.

Noah put his head on one side and frowned, so Zechariah explained.

"Like cousin Lazarus. Dead in the tomb one minute, then up and out walking and talking again. Alive!" Zechariah almost shouted. Noah blinked.

"Well that is good news," he said, nodding his little head wisely.

"Only Yeshua is much, much, much, much more important than Cousin Lazarus," added Little Mary, emphatically.

Lazarus overheard the children's conversation, but it was a while before he could explain to anyone why he was laughing so much. Another Mary in the family, full of wisdom and sharpsightedness, to keep him in his place.

Then Sara and Sophie brought out breakfast and they ate with renewed appetite.

Miriam leaned back against the wall and closed her eyes for a moment or two, listening to the joy and excitement her news had caused. For a while she rested in that good place.

"There is one other thing I suppose I should share," she said privately to Martha. "We, that is Salome, Susanna, Joanna, Mary

Alphaeus and Mary Cleopas, all hurried back to the disciple's lodgings, to tell everyone just as the Lord and the angels had asked." She took an extra breath at the thought. "But even with Peter and John's report, they didn't believe us. We explained it all carefully and calmly, but they questioned us like we were mad. Even John said nothing to help, which surprised me. It was awful. Please, we must pray for them. Perhaps the Lord will show himself to them and then they will be convinced too. Perhaps you could tell Mary, Lazarus and your uncle when I am gone."

Martha nodded, it would be better if they were told later.

Miriam stood up to leave, and Tabitha came over to say goodbye. "Salome will have a few things to say about all the money you spent on preparing for his burial," she giggled.

"Oh, she certainly will," agreed Miriam, "And a few other things besides. I must get back now, the others will be concerned. I've been away far too long as it is."

"Perhaps Mary and Martha could accompany you," suggested Elias, to their surprise. "As long as they promise to come straight back, of course." He winked at them. Miriam was both grateful and pleased to have their company.

Lazarus drew Elias aside and spoke earnestly to him. When he returned to the waiting women, he said firmly, "I'm coming with you."

Miriam thanked Elias, and the four of them left together. Elizabeth put her flabby arm around Tabitha's shoulders and gave her a sympathetic squeeze.

"Someone has to stay behind and keep an eye on this family with me, dear," she said. Tabitha was grateful.

Elias came and sat back down with his brothers, deep in thought. "He could still be in danger, and when news of this gets out, they may come looking for his disciples," murmured Elias to himself, but his brothers were listening.

"I think the Lord is powerful enough to take care of his own, don't you brother?"

Elias nodded, Joachim was right.

* * *

As they walked down the broad road together, Martha told Miriam how she had been expecting news ever since sunset the day before, because of Julia and their neighbour's experiences. It was now Miriam's turn to listen in disbelief.

"The dead have been resurrected?" she said, amazed.

Chapter Forty-Three

The Road To Emmaus

The door of the boarding house was firmly bolted when Miriam, Martha and Mary, escorted by Lazarus, arrived. Martha feared they might not be welcome because they had believed what the women had witnessed so easily. Best tread lightly, she thought to herself. They waited.

Suddenly the sound of voices and running feet were heard as the bolts were slid back, she need not have worried. They were met by the beaming faces of Salome and the other women and greeted like long, lost family. John came down and hugged Lazarus taking him upstairs to the two large rooms the men occupied. The women remained on the ground floor, using the kitchen. Here Magnus and his wife also had two small rooms for their private use; his wife came out to join them.

Relieved to see Miriam, they immediately wanted to know where she had been, although, as Salome pointed out, it was now quite obvious, especially, after the way their news had been received by the disciples early that morning. The women were all still elated, so much so that Mary Alphaeus grabbed Martha's hands and spun her round, chanting "He's alive, he's alive!" The two women rocked excitedly back and forth locked in an embrace while the others looked on with immense pleasure.

"Martha, Mary, you were so right not to despair. We should have listened to you, but the horror and injustice of what we had witnessed that day had gripped our hearts," said Susanna, shaking her head sadly, as she remembered how overwhelmed she had felt at the time.

"Thank you," said Salome. "When you left us on market day, your words took a while to sink in, but they were seeds of hope, because ours had gone."

Miriam nodded, assuring Martha it was true. Martha blushed.

The subject then turned to the disciples. "James won't talk to me, and not even my John will look me in the eye, and that hurts," said Salome.

"We have all been through so much together these last few years, and suddenly there is a gulf between us," said Susanna, sadly.

"It hurts me to see them like this, too," sighed Mary Alphaeus.

"Evil forces are the cause of this blindness," said Miriam emphatically. "We must pray for them."

"How is Mary Joseph?" asked Martha, aware she was not with them.

"Oh, you know, calm, serene, patiently waiting. A real testimony to us all. If it was one of my boys I wouldn't be acting like that," confessed Salome.

"Don't be too hard on yourself, Salome," said Mary kindly.

"Where's Joanna?" asked Miriam.

"She thought she'd better return to Herod's Palace," answered Susanna. She hasn't seen a lot of Chuza since we arrived in town. I think she wants to share the good news with him. Besides, she has connections and may be able to find out what's going on in high places. She said Herod had been wanting to meet the Master for a while."

"Well, I hope he wasn't disappointed," retorted Salome.

Just then there was a distinctive knock on the courtyard door, and everyone chorused, "It's Cleopas!"

Mary Cleopas came rushing in to join them, while her husband went to join the men upstairs. "Hello, hello," she said. "Martha, Mary, my dears. I'm delighted, but not at all surprised to see you. Are the family well? How have they taken this wondrous news of ours?"

"We are all jubilant, thank you, Mary Cleopas," replied Martha.

"As you know," said Mary Cleopas, now addressing them all, "we'd arranged to visit our daughter and family in Emmaus this afternoon. Then all of this happened, but Cleopas still thinks we should go. However, he was talking to Peter earlier and suggested he might like to come along to get out of the city for some fresh air and exercise. You know, a change of scenery might do him good. It's a bit claustrophobic upstairs. Well to his surprise, Peter liked the idea. So we've decided, I'll stay here. I'd never keep up anyway," she chuckled, seeing their surprise.

"That's a big sacrifice Mary Cleopas. I know how much you were looking forward to seeing the grandchildren," said Salome.

"We'll go again soon, but right now, we feel one of us should stay here anyway. And you never know, maybe Cleopas can talk some sense into Peter."

Miriam and Martha exchanged glances. How many other well-meaning people wanted to talk some sense into poor Peter? This could make it awkward for Lazarus to speak to him.

Upstairs, when Peter broke the news that he was planning to accompany Cleopas to Emmaus later that day, Lazarus was pleased.

"I'll go stir crazy if I don't get out of this place," Peter said, grimacing. "I need something to do."

Lazarus agreed. It might be helpful for his friend to get away. It would only be overnight, after all. However, in the next breath Peter added, "I'm still set on returning to Galilee, I haven't seen my wife and family for a long time. Anyone else fancy going home?" Then under his breath he muttered, "There's not much point hanging around here."

Lazarus caught John's eye, and John spoke up. "Peter, dear friend, I know the mention of Galilee has stirred up a longing for home, but we don't want to be parted from you."

"Then come with me. Don't you understand? I denied him, not just once, but three times even after he warned me I would. I'm not fit to be associated with the Master or you anymore."

Lazarus couldn't bear to see Peter's pain, so he said, "I believe the women. I know it's hard for you to believe them when you saw nothing but grave clothes in the empty tomb, but as yet, we have no other explanation. The soldiers saw nothing, except perhaps the angels. Your disappointment must have been unbearable, but there is more than hope, there is certainty."

Lazarus watched Peter's face, but he looked away. Lazarus tried again. "John, you told me not long ago that the Master, our Lord, had said he would go away and then in a little while, he'd return. He told us of his death, foretold by the prophets. I returned from the dead after four days. Yesterday evening, many people saw loved ones who had died, and yet were alive. I cannot help thinking that this had something to do with him. He is the Messiah! Surely, what the women have witnessed is the truth."

"Even if he has returned, he will not show himself to me," replied Peter bitterly, turning away. "He won't want anything to do with me. Your hope and truth just sting brother. I will return to Galilee,"

Lazarus turned to John, imploringly, but John shrugged with

despair. "It's hard to know what to think anymore," he said aloud, but then, as the others turned away too, he lowered his voice so only Lazarus could hear, and added, "It was the grave clothes folded so neatly. No Roman soldier does that, but the others don't see it that way, least of all Peter. Right now he can only feel his own failure and pain." Lazarus nodded, John was right.

Philip and a few of the others joined them. "What do your sisters say?" asked Philip. "And your uncles?"

"We believe," replied Lazarus, carefully. "Surely, if the angels say he has risen, who are we to question God's messengers?"

Matthias frowned. "An empty tomb, a pile of grave clothes," he said, frowning. "Hysterical women who cannot face the terrible truth. You would have us believe that, and not our own eyes?"

"Besides, if the Lord has risen, why has he not shown himself to us, his men? asked Nathanael. The others nodded in agreement.

"That I cannot answer," admitted Lazarus, "Except that the women never left his side, even in death." He turned to John, "Surely you believe the testimony of so many good and faithful women?"

John looked at Peter's back and then at the expectant faces of the others listening. "Truly my heart wants to believe, but my head can only see disappointment. This was the son of God, our Messiah and he was taken from us like a lamb to slaughter, and not one of us defended him. We all ran."

Lazarus looked from face to face, as he began to understand that each of them in their own way felt they had abandoned Yeshua, and failed in their calling as disciples. This was what blinded their eyes to the truth that he was alive. They had written themselves out of the story.

"But you heard all he said from the beginning, surely he gave you some sort of insight into what might happen," replied Lazarus. "And the women have told you what the angels and the Lord said to them himself. Can you remember nothing that he said beforehand that might dispel this doubt you are all feeling?" Even he could not keep a rising note of exasperation from his gentle voice.

"Miriam and the others have spoken a lot this morning, but we cannot see it. What was said or hinted at back then, has no bearing on what has happened now," said Peter firmly as he turned back to Lazarus, and many of the others nodded in agreement.

"They are women, and these weighty matters are for men," said Simon, decisively.

At that moment Miriam came boldly up the stairs, followed by Susanna and Salome. "Brothers!" she said loudly. "Open your hearts. This is how men talked before the Master came to shine his light. Come, my dear friends, let us throw open the shutters and let the light in while we eat together." To that, no one objected. It was at that point too, that Lazarus and his sisters left, promising Miriam and the other women they would send word if they heard anything more.

On the way back, as the three siblings began to climb the broad roads of the upper city, they saw a familiar figure ahead of them. It didn't take long to catch up with the puffing, wheezing Elias. Mary and Martha linked arms with him, one on each side. Elias had been to visit his friend Joseph. How the body could have been taken or the tomb opened without the guards' knowledge, they could not discern. So, with great joy, Elias had shared the news of angels and the Lord's resurrection with Joseph. Nicodemus had turned up, part way through his account, and was overwhelmed by the news, weeping and laughing at the same time. Nicodemus had news too. The Roman sentries had had an audience with Caiaphas, at their request. Nicodemus had been sure something fishy was going on and assured them that Caiaphas would probably bribe the guards to keep quiet.

Chapter Forty-Four

Wait!

They returned home to find everyone in high spirits. Elizabeth was planning a big celebration for the evening and had got the whole family involved, with music, singing, sumptuous food and games.

Martha, Mary and Lazarus felt awkward. On the way back from visiting their friends they had decided it was time to return home. They had been in Jerusalem for five days and were concerned about the vital barley crop and the spring lambs and kids, which had been left under Josh and Jacob's care. Mary struggled with the decision, but she could see that for Lazarus and Martha, who carried the responsibility, there was little option. So when they got back, Lazarus broke the news to their aunt. Elizabeth began her lament straight away, and Martha found it quite touching.

Mary spent a lot of time with the children that afternoon, telling them the story of the Lord's life to ensure that they too understood what had happened. They too were witnesses and as important to

God, and Yeshua as the grown ups.

As the sun set gloriously over the hills towards the west, the family celebrated the Lord's resurrection, which also became a farewell to Martha, Mary, Lazarus and Tabitha. Joshua and his older brother Micah began to play their flutes merrily, then Miriam and her older brother Amon joined them with a harp and lyre. Miriam's beautiful voice led them in a traditional folk song, while baby Amos was bounced boisterously on his grandfather Joachim's knees. Soon the whole family were joining in, cavorting around the room dancing. Sam linked arms with Sara and spun her round, Eleazar and Hannah managed a turn about the floor before collapsing into their seats. Silvanus and Zadok danced with their mother, and Julia and Reuben joined them. Rosh twirled baby Samuel under the watchful eye of Esther, while Joseph swung Bartholomew, who shrieked with laughter. Sarah danced gracefully with her husband Josiah, followed closely by Little Mary and Zechariah. Lazarus took Naomi's hand as Micah was busy playing his flute, while Mary danced with little James, and Martha with Noah. Keturah grabbed Tabitha and finally Elias and Elizabeth rose and danced with them all.

Before they ate, Elias broke a matzah and gave everyone a piece. Then they drank wine and remembered what the Lord had done. The family had become even closer, and Martha knew it would be hard to leave in the morning.

Martha and Sara were enjoying a few quiet moments in the kitchen, on the pretence of clearing up, when they heard the gate. "What now?" remarked Sara, rolling her eyes heavenward.

A few moments later, Sam popped in through the kitchen door. "I think you might want to come and join us ladies, Susanna and sweet Mary Alphaeus have just arrived," he said. Martha and Sara exchanged glances as they hurried out.

The children were being put to bed, so it didn't take long for the rest of the household to congregate.

"Miriam knew you would want to hear this as soon as possible," Susanna confided in Martha. "And I'm glad we came, now we know you're going home tomorrow."

"So what news do you bring?" asked Mary, impatiently.

Susanna gave a big grin and plunged in. "As you know, Peter accompanied Cleopas to Emmaus. Unexpectedly, they returned early this evening, very excited. The roads are still very busy, and they began talking with a stranger, who hadn't heard about the tragedy of our Lord's death in Jerusalem. Naturally when they arrived at Cleopas' daughter's, they invited him in for the evening meal. It wasn't until he broke bread that they realised who he was! It was remarkable, considering they had walked nearly the whole seven miles with him. Cleopas fell over backwards when he realised who it was! And Peter was speechless." She paused, looking around excitedly.

Mary was jiggling about with impatience. "Who was the stranger? Why all this mystery?"

"It was the Lord!" exclaimed Mary Alphaeus, almost jumping off her seat.

Susanna laughed with joy, then said, "He was as large as life, eating and drinking and talking like nothing had happened in between."

"The miracle we'd hoped for," exclaimed Martha.

"He's appeared a second time," cried Elias. "How marvellous. And this time to Peter, the one who most needed to see him."

"Oh, this is so good," whooped Josiah, stamping his feet with excitement.

"How could they have not recognised him?" Mary demanded.

"I know, it's hard to believe, but remember Miriam didn't recognise him at first, she thought he was the gardener," Susanna reminded them.

Mary was still frowning. "Miriam had just seen angels, she may have been a bit dazzled, but Peter had been walking and talking with him for a good part of the afternoon."

Susanna shrugged, "I have no answer, Mary."

"What did he say to them, and did he walk back with them to Jerusalem? Is he here now?" asked Sam, eagerly.

"He said a great deal on the road, apparently," said Susanna. "He went over all the scripture concerning himself, from Moses to the prophets, but as soon as they recognised him, he disappeared." Sam's face dropped.

"Typical," whispered Sara, rather too loudly. Then realising everyone had heard, she turned scarlet with embarrassment.

Mary Alphaeus, grinning widely, caught Susanna's eye.

"Out with it!" cried Joachim. "It's plain there is more to tell!"

"More?" exclaimed Sara. "That I should live to see and hear of such miracles."

Once again Susanna took up the narrative in her calm, clear voice. "Poor Cleopas was exhausted when they got back. Peter had made him walk back in record time in the dark, no less, but I'm so glad they did. They were in the middle of telling the others what had happened, when, you'll never guess what..." She took a deep breath and almost shouted, "The Master, our Lord appeared in the room, right there in front of them all."

There were gasps from her audience, and the general hubbub of excitement rose again and filled the room.

Mary Alphaeus leant over to Martha and Sara and said quietly, "Not everyone was there. Thomas had gone to visit relatives, he'd been putting it off for days. Poor lad was devastated when he got back and discovered he'd missed seeing the Lord. He quite refused to believe the rest of us, saying we were all playing a nasty joke on him. He was so disappointed." She looked sad for Thomas.

"So how did he reappear? What did he look like?" asked Mary, as curious as ever.

"Miriam was upstairs helping Magnus' wife clear away after the evening meal," said Susanna. "So Miriam let Peter and Cleopas in, and sent word to Mary Cleopas that her husband had returned unexpectedly. Mary Alphaeus and I were at our lodgings, so we walked over with her. We were still clearing up downstairs when we realised it had gone very quiet upstairs. It was then we heard the unmistakable voice of the Master coming from the upper room. As one we started for the stairs, but it was you, dear Mary Alphaeus, who held us back. You said it was their time, they needed to see him for themselves. They were the ones who needed convincing, not us. You were so right my friend, but it was so hard not to creep up the stairs. We needed every shekel of willpower. Later, Salome was sure she'd heard the Lord admonish the disciples for not believing us."

"Quite right too," chipped in Sara. "Would have saved all this fuss and bother, not to mention the heartache." The women nodded in agreement, and some of the men too.

"He showed them his wrists, his feet too, and he even ate something to prove he was real," continued Susanna. "It's quite hard to remember everything we overheard. I do hope it doesn't make us sound like eavesdroppers, but he did explain that the Messiah had to suffer, and on the third day rise from among the dead. I remember that, because it helped to explain what had happened."

"Our brothers must feel so different now they believe, now they've seen him. I almost feel jealous," confessed Lazarus.

There was a general murmur of agreement.

"Is he still there now?" asked Mary, beginning to rise to her feet at the sudden thought.

"No, sorry Mary. I should have said. He was with them for quite a while and then he wasn't. But it felt like he'd just popped out and he'd be back in a minute." Susanna shrugged, it was hard to find the right words.

"He didn't walk through any walls, but neither did he use the door. It really is hard to explain," agreed Mary Alphaeus.

"There is one other thing I must tell you, though; Miriam was very insistent. It was the last thing he said, before he left." Susanna looked steadily into each of their faces, as she spoke. "We are to wait here in Jerusalem, until power comes from on high!" Then she sighed, "We don't understand what he meant and wondered if you had any idea."

Elias looked thoughtfully at his brothers, before he spoke.

"The prophet Jeremiah mentions something and Ezekiel speaks of God saying he will give us a new heart and a new mind, and put his spirit in us and cause us to walk in his statutes and obey his rules. Some think that is for another time, but now I'm not so sure. Truly though, if the spirit of God were in us, we would be very different people." His brothers nodded vigorously.

"We would be more like Yeshua was," said Lazarus sadly.

Mary looked anxiously at her brother. "Should we stay in Jerusalem?" she asked.

"I think Bethany is close enough," he reassured her.

"A little rest from all this emotional excitement suddenly sounds very attractive," laughed Martha. "Yeshua, I mean the Lord, might even pop in for breakfast, like he used to, although I think he may have gone beyond that now."

"Do you really think we might see him again?" asked Mary, her eyes bright with the thought. Then she laughed at her own folly. "Of one thing I am sure, there'll be no rest with the harvest, the flocks and the sick."

Elias stood up stiffly and turned to Susanna and Mary Alphaeus. "I will, if I may, visit you all tomorrow," he said, "when we have had time to think about this message. And we are forever indebted to you both for bringing us such important and joyous news and so late in the evening. It has gone a long way to settling any remaining doubts. Now we can all be certain that the Lord is truly risen, as was prophesied. We must wait, as he has asked, for this power from on high."

"I don't know how we are supposed to go back to our everyday lives," remarked Josiah. "Some of us have family and business elsewhere in the country, and they will not run themselves. It will certainly be a challenge."

"These are matters we must pray about," said Joachim firmly.

Mary Alphaeus and Susanna departed, and the household finally prepared for bed. As Mary blew out the lamp, Tabitha's sleepy voice was heard from under her blanket. "I shall miss the city and all our family, but I am so looking forward to going home. Things always make more sense when we are there." Martha and Mary agreed silently, but Tabitha hadn't finished her little pearls of wisdom. "The Lord, my Rabbi Yeshua, is so thoughtful to come back and explain to his followers what the scripture said about him, and to remind them of the things he had said that they had forgotten. Now they will be happy again." There was a pause, then in a dreamy voice she added, "Martha you didn't need to see him alive after he was killed, did you? You and Mary both knew he had something up his sleeve all along." Then there was another pause. "And I don't mind waiting, but it would be easier if we knew what power we were waiting for, wouldn't it?"

"Good night Tabitha," whispered Martha and Mary together, but they were nodding their heads in agreement.

Chapter Forty-Five

Going Home

With mixed feelings the four of them picked up their bundles early the next morning. Elias had suggested they would accompany Lazarus, Martha, Mary and Tabitha as far as the temple, as he and his brothers were off to make a peace offering amongst others. Elias was also reluctant to let them go.

It had been hard leaving the younger children, who clung to Martha, Mary and Tabitha. Little Mary cried until the resourceful Miriam, with help from Sam and Josh, distracted them with a game of piggyback. As they walked down the broad road towards the temple enclosure, Sam, Josh and Miriam caught up with them, puffing and laughing, having made their escape from the children.

Martha now began to feel eager for home, no longer concerned for her friends and secure that they would see everyone again soon. Tabitha had been right; she knew the Lord was alive and didn't need to see him, her faith was enough. Besides, she was no one of consequence or significance amongst so many who now believed in him. Deep down, nevertheless, her heart longed to see her friend once more. Had he changed? Would she recognise him?

Martha and Mary remained in the court of women with Miriam, where they prayed and worshipped with those who had gathered early for that purpose. Tabitha and Mary knelt on one side of Martha and Cousin Miriam on the other, their heads bowed and covered. The ornate grandeur of the building that towered around them only emphasised to Martha her smallness and how mighty God was. This was for his glory, and through his son, God was restoring his people. As they waited, they could hear the sound of music and singing in the inner court, where the sacrifices were taking place.

Finally, as the gate opened, she heard the voices of her uncles, and they came down the steps towards them. Martha was definitely becoming impatient for home. They walked together to the Golden Gate, then said their farewells, Elias promising to let them know immediately if anything else happened. He also cautioned Lazarus to be careful still, which made them both laugh; Bethany wasn't exactly a public or well-known place. Tabitha held onto his great big hand with both of hers and kissed it.

"We expect to see you again very soon, young lady. And mind you keep your promise to Elizabeth, as soon as Martha can spare you." Tabitha nodded vigorously, which brought such joy to Martha's heart. She turned to go with a spring in her step.

"Oh dear, I shall have to pull my weight in the kitchen if you go on holiday Tab, which I'm not sure is fair on Martha," said Mary, trying to keep a straight face, as they headed for home. Tabitha looked uncertain for a moment, until everyone burst into laughter.

As it was still early and there was a good breeze, the four of them chose the familiar track that led close to the top of the Mount of Olives and down the eastern slopes to Bethany. It was lovely to look down on their home and approach the house through the rough pasture behind the village.

The donkey spotted them coming, and trotted up and down his paddock, braying his welcome for the whole village to hear. Tabitha threw her arms around his neck, ruffled his poll, then kissed his nose. The goats and sheep crowded round too, wanting their ears rubbed or their backs scratched. Mary and Lazarus carried on, leaving Martha and Tabitha to admire and lament the changes in the vegetable plot.

Once back in the courtyard, Mary fetched grain for the chickens, scattering it about.

"It's good to be home," sighed Lazarus.

"Really?" queried Mary. "My heart is still in Jerusalem."

"Is that a new shawl you're wearing?" asked Lazarus, noticing it for the first time.

"As observant as ever," remarked Mary, throwing a handful of grain at him. "It was a present from Aunt Elizabeth, if you must know."

"Ouch! Careful you stupid birds, mind my toes," he exclaimed, hopping from one foot to the other, as the eager birds pecked at his feet trying to get the grain.

"Stop standing on their food then," retorted Mary, beginning to laugh.

At that moment, the gate rattled, admitting Tabitha and Clop.

"I'm off to get fresh water, and to check on things," said Tabitha, as she fetched the water skins and harnessed the donkey. "Do you want to come, Mary? We could make some calls on the way back and catch up with a few friends."

"No. I think I'll stay and help Martha, if it's all the same to you Tab."

If Tabitha was surprised by Mary's response, she hid it well. Martha appeared.

"Oh, you're still here," she said to Mary.

"I thought I'd stay and give you a hand."

"Thank you," said Martha, and began listing the things that ought to be done. Mary listened patiently.

"I'll start the new leaven," she offered. "Only one more day of matzah."

"Yes please. Oh, and could you get the fire going and organise some more wood? The store is low."

Mary slipped away quietly to the kitchen, revelling in the simplicity of her tasks. Now she would have time to herself.

Rachel knocked on the gate and came straight in. She was so pleased they were back, and full of the events in Bethany. She told them how Joseph and their sons had gone bravely to the temple to make their sacrifices, despite the darkness, and had experienced the terrible earth tremors. In the long hours of darkness, Rachel and her daughters-in-law had waited for the men to return in fear and foreboding. When they did return, they brought horrendous stories of the Master's arrest and death, and chaos in the temple when the curtain was torn down. One thing she did mention, which caught Martha and Mary's attention, was that the quakes seemed far worse in the city, which Martha and Mary now knew was true. Wisely, Rachel invited them all to dinner that evening, so that they could fully share what they knew of the events surrounding the death and resurrection of the Messiah, Yeshua. As soon as she left them, Rachel hurried off to invite a few others to supper, including Simon and Michael.

Martha relaxed a little, finding herself looking forward to seeing everyone. She would gladly wait another day before rolling up her sleeves and beginning her usual hard work.

Lazarus interrupted her thoughts. "I'm off to track down Josh and Jacob. Joseph says they're over on the other side of the valley, near Malachi ravine. Hopefully not in it. Do you want to come? It might take some time to find them."

Martha thought for a moment; she would enjoy seeing the new lambs and kids, but she was more anxious about the barley harvest, so they decided to split up and meet later. On her way to collect her shawl from the kitchen, Martha checked the cistern. It had filled again nicely and would last a while longer. Mary was on her knees, working on the fire, and the leaven lay in its bowl.

"I'm going to check the crops, do you want to come?" asked Martha.

"I'll stay and wait for Tabitha, then I can help her in the garden, and the veranda is covered in leaves from the high winds we've had" said Mary. She shook her head. "Has it really only been six days? It feels like a lifetime."

Once clear of the town, the cooling breeze, shimmering views of the valley and surrounding hills brought purpose and strength to Martha's steps. Her hair flew free, the shawl draped over one shoulder. She began to run, her shawl flying behind her. She didn't stop until her breath came in ragged gasps, and by then she was far beyond the barley fields. She gazed out to the horizon, smelling the earth, hearing the breeze in the dried grass, feeling the sun and space around her. Her breathing slowed. It felt so good after the confined claustrophobia of Jerusalem.

When they had arrived home that morning, she had felt the peace and contentment of knowing who she was and her place in the world. She had looked forward to getting back to a simple life that revolved around the seasons and the harvests. Now she realised that none of it could satisfy the longing in her heart; the Lord had changed all that.

Still unsettled, she turned back to the barley. Close inspection revealed that the ears were full, standing erect and golden. The wind of a few nights ago had seemed to pass these fields by, and the rain had only done them good. The graceful heads waved like ripples on the sea as Martha walked around the fields. She picked some ears and put them safely in her sash to show to Lazarus later. Just a few more days if the weather continued fine, then they could begin to harvest.

Harvesting involved most of the village. There would be a lot to do over the next few days; food would need to be prepared to feed everyone, the threshing floor would need inspecting and the surface repaired after the winter, and the poorer folk must be alerted, so they would be ready to glean any fallen grain. Each field was cut and threshed in turn, and Martha noticed that some of the neighbouring fields were almost ready too. Harvesting such a good crop would be hard work, but socialising and having fun was an important part of it, as neighbour worked alongside neighbour.

With a light step she descended the track to the lower slopes and cast her eyes over the wheat crop. It too was doing well, but there would be another full month before it would be ready. Martha reminded herself to check the grain storage pots at home; they might need some new ones.

It was much hotter lower down the slopes, so she was glad to reach the shade of the narrow streets of Bethany on her way home. Her thoughts drifted back to Jerusalem, wondering if the Lord might appear to other people, perhaps to his followers in Bethany, though why should he? She could see now that the real spiritual battle had been in Jerusalem.

She thought back to the day she had met him on the road after Lazarus had died, which had led to the four longest days of her life, and what he had said to her then. At first, when he'd told her that her brother would rise again, she hadn't understood what he was getting at, assuming he meant the last days when all people, living or dead, would be raised up for judgment. It was only when he had said, 'I *am* the resurrection and the *life*, whoever believes in me, although he may die, yet he shall live,' that she knew he was going to bring her brother back.

Now his words suggested more to her than she had understood back then. It was their belief in him, and who he was, which was the key. If you believed in him, he would raise you to a new life with him while you still lived, and then when you died, you would still live, but in heaven. That was what he must have meant by 'whoever continues to live and have faith in me shall never actually die'.

Martha's pulse quickened. Her thoughts turned to the darkness that had come when Mary had thought Yeshua was dead, but Lazarus had danced with joy. He had known that Isaiah's prophecy was being fulfilled. The Messiah had been punished, suffering instead of them, dying for their sins, the lamb slaughtered, as the law demanded. But the grave could not hold him; he had come back to life, conquering both physical and spiritual death for them. The veil had been torn down between them and God. It seemed so clear now. He had made a new way for them, a new covenant, instead of the laws and sacrifices. He had given his life for theirs, the final sacrifice, so they were no longer separated from God by their sin, but if they were no longer separate, how were they connected? She put her hands to head in frustration.

Then her thoughts turned to the dead people who had reappeared alive, in Jerusalem that evening. Surely the dead must have been resurrected too, it had to have been at the same time he'd left the tomb. Three days and three nights, that was it. His power was so great that as he came back from the dead he had caused many of those in the graves to rise too.

Stopping in her tracks, Martha suddenly became aware of her surroundings. She ran the last bit home. As she came breathlessly in, Tabitha looked up from grinding corn.

"Where's Mary?" asked Martha.

"Out the back watering. Why? What's up?"

"I have something I want to tell her," Martha called back, as she disappeared.

Martha found Mary bent double, carefully scooping water out of a bucket and pouring it around each plant. She stood up stiffly.

Martha flung herself down in the shade and tried to explain the thoughts she had just had. Mary listened carefully.

"You are right," she exclaimed, when Martha had finished. "You have put it all together, and my heart is hearing the whole truth for the first time."

"What should we do?" asked Martha, eagerly.

"We'll share it with Lazarus and Simon this evening, and Uncle as soon as there is an opportunity."

Martha saw the wisdom in that; she only hoped she would be able to explain it as clearly as she had understood it.

"And we still have the power from on high to come. Whatever that is," she said happily as she went to help Tabitha. It was hard to concentrate on the chores after that, so she and Tabitha sang psalms together while they worked.

At the midday meal, Martha and Lazarus discussed how they would divide the flock, as it was becoming too large. The other two listened with boredom. As Tabitha and Mary began to clear away, Lazarus looked up and said, "Oh, Tabitha, I've brought you back a gift from Josh and Jacob, it's in the pen." Tabitha was gone like an arrow from a bow. She returned quickly with a scrawny kid tucked under one arm and fresh milk to feed him.

"I shall call him Jacob," she announced. "On account of his big floppy black ears."

"They do remind me of Jacob's hair," agreed Martha.

"Perhaps we could give the boys a lamb or kid of their own this year, so they can start their own flocks, as ours are doing so well," suggested Mary.

"That's a very good idea," said Lazarus.

"But this one's mine," said Tabitha firmly, cuddling the cream and black bundle.

"He looks better already," said Mary.

Martha looked inquiringly at her brother, and asked, "Twins?"

Lazarus nodded. "It wasn't getting enough milk, but the other one is doing well."

The rest of the afternoon passed swiftly: Lazarus chopped wood, the house was aired, and Tabitha, in between fussing over her new pet, helped Martha to set up the loom. When the sun was low in the sky, they drifted next door to be welcomed home by their friends.

Chapter Forty-Six

The Early Harvest

Mary was surprised at how quickly they all settled back into life in Bethany. The sheep and goat flocks had been split in the first week, and the barley harvest begun in the second. Tabitha was rushed off her feet looking after the livestock and the garden, baking and cooking. Once the harvesting began in earnest, Martha and Mary were busy in the fields from sunrise to sunset, but between them, they still managed to give care and food to those who needed it. Always cheerful and encouraging, Lazarus helped co-ordinate the villagers in the fields. Once the winnowing began, with the ever-lengthening daylight hours, he often worked till dark if they had enough breeze.

Despite the harvest, Lazarus had still managed to slip off one evening to see their friends in Jerusalem, returning in the early hours of the morning. Martha wondered how he managed with so little sleep, but he seemed invigorated by the discussions they had had recalling all they could of what the Lord had said and done in the time they had known him. He had felt so privileged to be among them. His only concern had been for Peter, whose initial joy at the Lord's reappearance had turned once more to deep despair.

In the second week, as the harvest became more demanding, Lazarus' longing for news of his friend grew deeper. Everyone was working hard in the fields, so it was out of the question for him to leave, even for a few hours.

The next day, out in the fields, Martha straightened up from the row of sheaves she had just tied. Arching backwards and flexing her aching shoulders, she wiped the beads of sweat from her neck and brow as she gazed across the hot, shimmering hillside, her hand shading her eyes. Hazy figures were coming along the track towards them; she could just make out Tabitha's quick step and slender shape ahead of the group, but the rest she didn't recognise. Calling out to Mary, she pointed in their direction. Mary dumped her sheaves onto the hand cart and stared. Suddenly, with a cry of delight, she began to run, half turning and nearly tripping, as she called back,

"It's Peter, John, and Miriam! Come on!"

Joseph, who was working in the same field, looked up and said to his neighbour, "Where are those two off to in such a hurry?"

"Seen some people coming, so gone to meet them," the neighbour replied, holding the sheaf while Joseph tied it off.

"On a Wednesday?" remarked Joseph, tying the next sheaf.

"What, is it Wednesday already? Where does the time go?"

"Oh, and there goes Lazarus too," said Joseph, watching him run after Mary and Martha.

Lazarus and Martha were the first to reach them, and they greeted their friends with surprise and delight. Susanna, James and Andrew were in the party too.

"We thought you might like a hand," said Peter, slapping Lazarus on the back. "I could use some exercise and the feel of sun on my back. We're still simple hard-working fishermen at heart." Lazarus looked hard at Peter, but he seemed cheerful enough.

"That was until we met the Lord, of course," grinned Andrew.

"I don't think any of us know who we are now," said James thoughtfully.

"We're all works in progress," said Lazarus, as Mary joined them out of breath.

"Surprise!" said Susanna.

"A wonderful one," gasped Mary. "And well timed for lunch, I see."

Miriam put down the large basket and began to help Tabitha unload the donkey and lay out the food under the tree.

"Salome sends her love, and hopes you'll forgive her for not coming," said Susanna.

"I think it's a bit too much for her these days," said James.

"Don't let her hear you say that," said John, rolling his eyes in mock horror. "The others all send greetings and love. More would have come to help, but we decided too many of us might have been in the way." They laughed.

"Definitely lunchtime," grinned Lazarus, patting his gurgling stomach. "I'll go and let the others know."

As they settled themselves in the shade, Susanna went to help Martha fetch a water skin from the donkey.

"Martha," she said, hesitatingly. "I came to help, but I've never done anything like this before, and I don't know what to do."

Quickly Martha reassured her friend. "You can help put the sheaves in the cart or tie them up. It's just like braiding hair, and you're a genius at that, even on Tabitha's unruly head." Susanna looked relieved.

They joined the others just as John announced he had something to tell them. Over the midday meal, they learnt that the Lord had appeared yet again to his disciples. It had been on the Monday eight days after his resurrection, and this time Thomas had been with them.

"Oh, what a relief for poor Thomas," exclaimed Martha.

"It was almost like the Lord had heard Thomas' sceptical remarks after he'd missed him the first time," said John. Martha saw a dark cloud pass over Peter's face, and thought perhaps Thomas' doubt had seemed small and forgivable in Peter's eyes, whereas his own denial was unforgivable.

"This time the Lord was standing in front of Thomas and asked him to touch the nail scars in his wrists and the hole left by the spear in his side," said John, making Miriam shiver at the thought. "Thomas was overwhelmed," he finished.

"Afterwards, he'd admitted feeling a bit foolish," added Andrew, chuckling. "Until young James suggested the Messiah had put in a special appearance just for him. I think he liked that idea."

"That's just typical of the Lord's kindness," said Tabitha, and the others agreed.

"However, in some things he hasn't changed," said Miriam, suppressing a smile. "He was also making the point that those who believe in him but have not seen him are blessed and to be envied. That is true faith."

She looked at Martha, remembering how her friend had held onto her faith, despite everything that had happened to Yeshua, and even now, though she had not seen him resurrected, Martha and Mary were unwavering in their belief. Martha also remembered Tabitha's wise words on their last night in Jerusalem, and felt encouraged.

Through the early afternoon, Suzanna tied sheaves and loaded the cart with Tabitha, concealing how badly blistered her hands were becoming. It was only when she dropped a cup of water that they realised how bad her fingers were. Ashamed, she tucked them behind her back, but it was clear she couldn't continue. It was

Tabitha who suggested she could help with preparations for the evening meal.

"It'll be nice to have your company," said Tabitha as they led the donkey away, accompanied by Rachel, who was also to help Tabitha. "Although I am sorry to see your poor hands like that." Tabitha looked at her own long brown fingers, which were well used to manual labour.

"How old are you now, Tabitha?" asked Susanna.

"Ten, soon to be eleven," came the reply.

"My goodness nearly eleven, already," said Susanna. "Where did that shy little nine-year-old go? And look at you now, practically running the household while Martha's busy." She was pleased to see the effect her words had had on Tabitha as they walked back along the track together.

Peter, Andrew, John and James worked hard that afternoon, glad of a change from the city. The remainder of the barley was cut and sheaved in record time. The villagers took the opportunity to ask questions about recent events in Jerusalem and were especially pleased to hear first-hand of the Lord's further appearances. Lazarus was pleased to see his friends so at ease joking and talking with the villagers. In fact, both he and Miriam remarked at the change that had come over Peter during the afternoon.

"Let's hope the dark mood has left him," she said to Lazarus, as they watched the four men swinging scythes with such strength and purpose.

"Amen," agreed Lazarus.

"They have no idea how much the villagers are in awe of them," chuckled Lazarus, as Peter waited patiently for Joe, Ellie's brother, to sharpen his scythe. "Look at them, bathed in sweat and scorched by the sun, working alongside these farmers."

"We are all God's people, rich, poor, young or old, and hopefully bonded by one common belief in the Lord, our Master," said Miriam.

"Wise words, my friend," said Lazarus, smiling into her beautiful face. "Shall we go and lend a hand?"

"No, I don't think so," she said, with a straight face. "They seem to be doing very nicely without us." For a moment Lazarus was taken aback, until he realised she was joking. Laughing, Miriam almost skipped off to join the other women, calling back over her shoulder, "Never underestimate a woman."

Lazarus shook his head. "How could I? I live with Martha and Mary!"

"And Tabitha," was Miriam's parting comment. Grinning to himself, he went to join the men.

It was dark when they finally left the threshing floor. Peter held the lamp aloft so all could see the way.

Martha's home was crammed that evening, but with Tabitha and Susanna's great pot of stew, Rachel, her household and Jessica, with others of Simon's household, bringing many more welcome additions to the table, all were well fed and their thirst quenched. Michael said the blessings and was given the seat of honour, but it was John, Peter, Andrew and James who commanded attention. Lazarus slipped into a quiet corner to sit between Simon and Joseph to watch.

As the villagers asked questions about the recent events connected with the Lord's death, resurrection and reappearances, the four men had to search their hearts and minds deeply for the answers. A process that had begun earlier that day in the fields grew, keeping them busy. The good people of Bethany were hungry for more, and although the brothers felt unsure, they did their best to satisfy their audience.

After the hard work of the day, Peter's confidence and spirit seemed to have grown even more, gladdening the hearts of Miriam,

Martha and Susanna, who watched quietly from the sidelines, Jessica standing with them. She and Martha had not seen one other since Simon's party, so she was glad to be able to help out.

Very late in the evening, the villagers drifted away, exhausted but satisfied. Simon said good night and escorted Michael home. Jessica and the others followed shortly after. Under Tabitha's guidance, the kitchen had been left in good order, which had earned Rachel and Jessica an extra grateful hug from Martha. The house was soon quiet except for the gentle snores from the tired disciples upstairs.

Chapter Forty-Seven

More Visitors

It was with heavy hearts that Martha and Mary walked along the dusty track to the threshing field in the chill air of the dawn light. Lazarus had gone on ahead. It had been hard to leave home and their guests, who would be returning to the city that morning. Neither of the women spoke; they were lost in their own thoughts, but still glad of each other's company.

They arrived shivering, but the breeze was welcomed as it meant threshing would be quicker. Children squabbled over whose turn it was to ride on the boards as these were harnessed to the oxen, and the work began, rolling over the barley on the hard-baked earth. The extra weight of the children helped to press the jagged iron strips in to separate the ears from the stalks. Once winnowed, the stalks were quickly gathered into bundles for bedding and building, then distributed to everyone under Lazarus' fair hand.

The golden grain was carefully swept into sacks to be transported home. A constant stream of people could be seen slowly wending their way up and down the track from the village in the rising dust and heat.

Shem and Joseph helped out at harvest, when they hadn't any pressing masonry work to do, and were always amazed that the chaos that still seemed to result in everyone getting their crops gathered in and stored. Even now, two or three of the poorer members of the community came by to chat, their gleaning sacks bulging with fallen grain.

Martha was concerned that one of the poorer women of the village, being unwell, had not been able to come and glean as usual. The fields were all finished, and what fallen grain was left would soon be finished off by the birds. Quickly Martha bent to the threshing floor scooping grain into a sack, which she then handed to one of the women, asking her to give it to the sick woman. Lazarus gave her a nod; he would make sure that the family whose grain was being threshed just then would not go short.

A few days later Elias sent word to say he and Reuben would be calling in on the way to the vineyard. Tabitha was waiting to greet them, flinging her arms around Elias' considerable girth. The old man looked pleased.

"Hello, Tabitha dear, are the others up yet?"

"They've just come back," said Tabitha, taking the hired donkey from Reuben as Elias took a seat under the olive tree, where she had refreshments all ready. Martha, Mary and Lazarus, came hurrying from the house, sun-tanned and dripping water after their hasty washes. Despite the donkey he rode, Elias was sweating profusely, and mopped his brow as he sat down. Clop brayed his customary greeting to her uncle's donkey, which Tabitha fed and watered with her usual kindheartedness, convinced that even Elias didn't care for his donkey as he should.

Elias was glad to hear about the flocks and the grain harvest and in their turn, they were glad to hear news of the family, who had all finally returned to their own homes. However, Julia was to stay on an extended visit with Elizabeth. "It'll keep Elizabeth occupied," explained Elias, but Martha knew it was also a kindness to Julia and her sons.

"You don't sound too sad about having your house back," said Lazarus, but before Elias could reply, Reuben jumped in. "Father is delighted to have the peace and quiet back," he said.

"I can't deny it," confessed Elias.

"I expect Sara is glad too," said Martha. "I don't think she would welcome another Passover like the last."

On a more serious note, Lazarus asked if anything had changed in the temple.

"Oh, same old stuff," said Elias, wearily.

"Except they have put a new curtain up and have spread a rumour that the old one fell apart because of an infestation of moths," said Reuben incredulously.

"Oh, I was told it was dry rot in the poles," Elias chuckled, shaking his head. "On the surface nothing has changed, sadly, it's been business as usual." A glint appeared in his eye as he continued, "but since there is now an empty tomb and reported sightings of the Messiah, people are asking questions and wondering about the story that has spread like wildfire through the city."

"The more the temple seems to quash the rumours, the more it seems to fuel the fire," Reuben added with satisfaction.

"Surely your friends mentioned this when they visited?" asked Elias.

"Nothing gets past you, Uncle," said Mary.

"Well, I thought you might be feeling a bit out of things here in Bethany, and in need of some extra hands," said Elias, narrowing his eyes, just for a moment.

"Thank you, Uncle," said Mary, kissing his cheek. "They did

tell us that behind closed doors a growing number of people were talking frankly about events, questioning what had happened, and remembering the miracles he did and the things he said."

"I think your friends are underestimating what's happening around Jerusalem. There is a confused hope emerging and growing," said Elias emphatically.

"And you can bet your last shekel that Father is at the bottom of it," laughed Reuben. Elias put a finger to his lips.

"Your friends are in great demand, people are looking for them," said Reuben. "Although Mother is insisting that it's been the women who have led the way, from the start."

"Is that so?" said Elias, the corner of his mouth twitching.

Mary looked challengingly at them both. "Do you have a problem with that?" she asked, a little fiercely.

"No, I don't. It's quite clear to me that Miriam and the others have a network that extends far and wide, and their boldness and confidence is growing all the time," said Elias, and Reuben quickly agreed.

"It's true," said Lazarus. "Those in authority over us think little of women, but it leaves you free to come and go as you please." Martha wanted to disagree, but now wasn't the time.

"A grave oversight," said Mary, "And a truth we will exploit."

"Mary, you sound like a Zealot," said Martha accusingly.

"But very apt," laughed Lazarus. "The Romans and the priests certainly overlooked the women at the tomb, as God knew they would." Elias agreed. "And neither is Mary afraid to speak the truth to those who need to hear it."

"We all have our parts to play in what's to come next. Let's hope we may be alert to what God asks of us," said Elias thoughtfully.

"Are his eleven chosen men still reticent?" asked Reuben, frowning.

"Yes, but now it's only because they don't know what to do.

We all need patience," said Lazarus. "We are fortunate to have our livelihoods and families; many of them have given up everything to follow the Lord. They long for occupation, we long for freedom to follow him. I am grateful to God that we have our farm, and a community in which to practise what the Lord has taught us. We can share what we know of him, but his disciples don't have that yet. I think this time of waiting is a time of preparation, after which they will know with certainty, what it is they are called to do. We all will."

Tabitha had been listening intently while quietly spinning, and now she ventured to speak. "Is part of Peter's problem that he still can't forgive himself and so doesn't think Yeshua can forgive him either? I mean it was no surprise to the Lord that Peter denied him, after all he tried to warn him that would happen. And then when Peter had a chance to believe he was alive, at the tomb, he passed that by too, and once he realised it, he felt worse than ever. He just can't see that out of all the disciples the Lord chose to reveal himself to Peter first. Now that's the action of a forgiving Messiah, not one who holds a grudge. And as for the rest of them, well, I think they struggled because they couldn't see past his humanness." She giggled. "They'd spent so long eating, sleeping, smelling and living alongside Yeshua the man that when he died so cruelly, they were so very disappointed and so very focused on what was happening in this world that it blocked out their ability to see the heavenlies, to have faith. As far as I can make out, from what the Master said to Miriam that morning at the tomb, he exists in heaven as well as on earth now, and because of that, she, and Peter and Cleopas, had trouble recognising him. Things like harvest and chores and daily life take over, they seem more real to us than the spiritual realm, which is real too, and really matters." She shrugged and carried on spinning. The others looked on wide eyed with astonishment.

"Where did that come from, young lady?" said Elias. "I do believe you have spoken with great wisdom and insight. You're right, it is easier for us to believe than those who were closest to him."

"You've lost me," groaned Reuben.

"Don't worry lad, I'll explain on the way out to the vineyards," said Elias. "We must be going soon, but I have one more important piece of news." He paused and took a very deep breath. "Seven of the eleven departed for Galilee the day they left here. I had a good chat with Andrew after they'd gone. I really like the fellow. Apparently, Peter remembered something the Lord had said to them all the night before his arrest." He paused, trying to remember. "Oh yes, that was it. After the Lord had risen, he would go ahead of them to Galilee. Apparently, their memories are beginning to work again. There was more besides, but you will have to get them to tell you."

"So Peter is finally going to Galilee, no longer to run away but to meet his Master once again," exclaimed Mary.

"Just like the angels told Miriam and the others," added Tabitha.

"Who has gone with Peter?" asked Martha.

"John, James, Thomas, Nathanael and Philip, and Simon the Zealot," said Reuben.

"Seven of the eleven, the perfect number," said Lazarus, triumphantly.

"But we still have to wait for the power, don't we, here in Jerusalem?" asked Tabitha, a little concerned.

"Oh yes," said Mary confidently.

Reuben slipped something into Tabitha's hand as Elias mounted his donkey. "Your aunt says that as the barley harvest is over, if Martha could spare you, perhaps you would consider coming to see us for the Sabbath? She quite misses your lively company."

Tabitha opened the beautifully embroidered pouch Reuben had just given her. Inside was an exquisite bracelet. She slipped it on, turning her wrist to admire it. "A present from Elizabeth to me!" she said, a little overawed. "She must have seen me admiring it in the market. It's the most beautiful thing I ever saw."

On the way back to the fields, Mary and Lazarus looked wistfully to the horizon beyond Bethany, and thought longingly of the sparkling waters of the Sea of Galilee and the sight of the Master's face.

Chapter Forty-Eight

A Night Spent Fishing

With the early harvest over, Martha was able to take up her usual rounds again and give Tabitha a well-earned rest, leaving Mary and Tabitha free to progress the weaving. The three of them spent their evenings spinning wool. Lazarus's enquiries for a new shepherd had met with success. An older man had come to ask for the job, bringing his nephew with him. It turned out that the Lord had healed the man in the crowds at the Feast of Dedication, so all was settled quickly. Josh and Jacob had sole responsibility for the sheep, and the new shepherds for the goats. Now it would be much easier to find grazing for the two smaller flocks. Jacob had called in several times, to ask after the kid that Tabitha was rearing. Martha had found them leaning on the stable door, watching it sleeping and discussing its future. She'd had to quickly run inside, so they wouldn't see the big grin on her face.

However, Lazarus was restless, so he had slipped into Jerusalem on the pretext of keeping Elias up to date with progress in the olive groves, but he had spent an equal amount of time with Andrew, Matthew, Thaddaeus and his younger brother James. There had been no news from Peter and the others.

Only Mary was at home when he got back early the next morning. She wondered why Andrew had not accompanied his brother to Galilee, until Lazarus explained that Andrew's ties to the area were no longer as strong as Peter's. Peter still had a wife and family in Bethsaida.

"Didn't Philip come from there too?" Mary asked.

"Yes, I believe so, but Andrew felt he should stay to support Matthew and the others, while Thaddaeus and young James have been helping their mother move to a new house this week." Mary looked intrigued. "Alphaeus and Joses have found work as carpenters, in the temple, so the whole family has moved to Jerusalem."

"That is good news. Praise God," said Mary, brightly. Then she added, through the corner of her mouth, "Will work on the temple ever end?"

"God knows the plans he has for us," said her brother, rising. "I'd better get off then. If anyone wants me, I'll be up in the top groves, and then later back at the threshing floor. I want it ready in plenty of time for the wheat harvest, which is fast approaching. See you later."

Mary continued kneading the dough, lost in thought.

* * *

It was Sunday evening and Martha, Mary, Lazarus and Tabitha sat with the remains of their meal still in front of them while they prayed. Eventually, Tabitha began to clear away. If she hadn't gone into the kitchen at that moment, she probably wouldn't have heard the knock at the gate, despite its loudness. After dark the gate was barred, so Tabitha hurried to open it.

Unafraid, she drew the bar back and to her surprise, saw the shadowy but unmistakable figures of Miriam, Salome and Mary Alphaeus. She threw her arms around Salome then ushered them into the house.

Martha leapt up to greet them, while Mary and Tabitha scurried to the kitchen to fetch wine and more supper for their guests. Quickly they came to the point of their visit.

"Peter and my John and the others are back from Galilee. They arrived just before the start of the Sabbath on Friday," said Salome, with pleasure and a touch of relief.

"And what a time they've had. We couldn't wait to come and tell you," said Miriam. "Besides, it's feeling crowded in Jerusalem again," she joked. "Now the seven are back with us, I hope we don't have to wait much longer for this power from heaven, otherwise we are going to need a larger place to meet." They all laughed.

"So are more people joining you?" asked Mary, her eyes wide with excitement.

"Oh, yes," said Mary Alphaeus, with a smile. "Somehow they find us, or we bump into them."

"But it's tricky, people are afraid to speak openly, especially in the temple courts. It's so wrong," said Salome, shaking her head.

"But at least we are free to talk about the Lord in private. And they cannot stop the people from believing in him," said Miriam, passionately.

"No one will forget the events surrounding his death," said Salome, shuddering.

"The great darkness," said Martha, with a grimace.

"The temple curtain torn in two," added Mary.

"Or the dead rising," said Tabitha, creeping closer to Salome.

"What about the empty tomb?" cried Mary Alphaeus excitedly.

"We will never forget his reappearances and we will never stop talking about him to everyone we meet," declared Lazarus.

"Oh, it makes me feel excited all over again!" declared Mary Alphaeus.

Mary and Tabitha did a little jig of joy where they sat.

"And now for the latest news," said Miriam, her eyes sparkling in the lamp light. She looked across at Salome. "Do you want to tell them? As James and John were there."

"No my dear, you do it best."

"Please!" groaned Lazarus. "Would one of you get on with it?"

Miriam laughed at his impatience as she began.

"It must have been the visit here that some how precipitated Peter into finally going to Galilee, followed by the other six. We've heard nothing in the week and a half they've been away, so you can imagine our delight when they appeared unexpectedly at sunset on Friday. It was a divine appointment, just as the angel at the tomb had said."

"Salome, why didn't you go with them?" asked Tabitha.

"My Zebedee had only just returned home, so I felt it would give James and John some time with their father, without me around," she sighed, "Since the Lord went, I miss Zebedee more than ever," she added. "In my heart I'm beginning to think that the next time I go home, it will be for good. I feel I've done what was asked of me."

"But reserve the right to change your mind," said Tabitha quickly, not liking the idea of never seeing Salome again.

Seeing the frustrated look on Lazarus' face, Miriam continued, "As you can imagine, when they arrived in Capernaum, news of their arrival spread through the town and along the shore quickly. John said the Lord was once more the main topic of conversation, adding further fuel to the stories that had come from Jerusalem after Passover. After the Sabbath John said Peter was restless again, so they borrowed their old boat from Zebedee, and went fishing, taking the others with them."

"Even Philip? Isn't he scared of water?" asked Mary.

"I don't think he minds, as long as the Lord is around. Just in case of storms," said Lazarus, laughing. Miriam and the others knew the story, but Martha and Mary looked puzzled. "They had been caught out on the lake more than once by storms that had shaken even the hardened fishermen among them. Yeshua had commanded the storms to stop and had even walked on the surface of the water. Peter had tried to copy him and nearly drowned, but that's another story. Sorry Miriam, please go on."

"They weren't sure where they should go to meet the Lord, so they stuck together," said Miriam. "It was a long night apparently. Peter, James and John felt like they'd lost their touch, and the others were disappointed too, as there had been no sign of Yeshua or a single fish. It was still early when they approached the shore, and John saw smoke rising from a fire on the beach. At first, he thought someone had come to mend their nets or to work on their boats, but as they drew closer, the man shouted to them. It was hard to decipher what he was saying, but soon they understood that he wanted them to put their nets down on the right side of the boat. John wondered how the stranger could see a shoal of fish from the shore, but Peter didn't hesitate. The nets went straight over the side. John and James raced to help, their hearts beginning to beat with excitement, while the others stood by gaping. Almost immediately, they were heaving a catch on board that most fishermen only dream of. John knew it must be Yeshua. All night long, Peter had kept an eye on the horizon, half hoping to see the Master walking across the water, and now he couldn't contain his excitement, and jumped in, swimming ashore. John and James were left to haul in the catch, with the others struggling to help."

"I'd have been over the side with Peter," laughed Mary.

"Leaving everyone else to do the work as usual," retorted Lazarus, ducking, as Mary took a swipe at him with a ball of wool.

"But you can't even swim," exclaimed Martha.

"I was baptised by John, in the Jordan with you, wasn't I? I'm sure it's not a lot different!" said Mary, grinning.

"Seriously though, why didn't they recognise him until he did the miracle with the fish? Was it lack of sleep or the early morning light? Weren't they close enough to the shore to see who it was?" asked Lazarus, sure he would have recognised the Lord.

Salome nodded. "Oh, they were close enough to see all right. John said it was the catch of fish that did it. It reminded them of the miraculous catch they made right back when they first met him. It was as though their minds had to make the connection before they could actually see him and know who he was. Peter said it felt like the experience in Emmaus, when he and Cleopas didn't recognise the Lord until he broke bread. It seemed to trigger the realisation of who he was."

"We do seem to have trouble recognising him since he was resurrected," added Miriam affectionately. "He really doesn't look any different. It's not as though his eyes have turned blue, or his hair gone white. His beard is as straggly as ever."

"What did they do with all the fish?" asked Tabitha, who had been waiting impatiently to ask her question.

"James sold them to his father," said Salome. "They'll be smoked, or more likely salted and sold. The proceeds will help Peter's family and others. My James is still a good businessman," she added with a touch of pride.

"Please, what happened next?" begged Tabitha, as she slid her arm through Salome's and squeezed tight.

"The Lord had prepared breakfast for them on the beach, so they ate together and afterwards he and Peter walked along the shore, while the others followed," said Miriam. "Then he led them up a hill, where they worshipped him. He'd said all power had been given to him in heaven and on earth, and that we were to go into all the world and preach the gospel, baptising in the name of the Father and the Son and the Holy Spirit. But for me, his best words were when he said he was always with us. When he disappeared this time, they hurried back to Jerusalem as soon as they could."

"What of Peter?" asked Lazarus. "Did he give no indication of what the Lord had said to him while they were walking together along the shore?"

"No," said Salome. "Philip asked him the same question and got nothing. It must have been very personal. But he really seems his old self again, but steadier, if you get my meaning."

"Look out then!" laughed Lazarus.

Martha felt certain that whatever the Lord had said to Peter, it had finally helped him forgive himself and receive the Lord's forgiveness at last.

"What is the Holy Spirit?" asked Tabitha, unable to wait any longer to ask.

"A good question, Tabitha," said Lazarus. "Several of us have been asking that for a while."

"Perhaps I can shed some light," volunteered Miriam. "The night of the Passover supper, the Lord spoke of a helper and comforter that he would send to us once he'd gone. He called it the Holy Spirit or the Spirit of Truth, according to John. Perhaps this is what he means by the power from on high. That first evening he appeared to them, at their lodgings, he breathed on them, and they all had felt different somehow, as if he had breathed new life into them. Their courage certainly returned. But mostly, they are still unclear and unsure." Salome and Mary Alphaeus nodded in agreement. "Dear friends, pray for them, for there is still a battle going on."

"There are evil spirits still trying to confuse them," said Mary Alphaeus. "Nathanael confessed to my James that he still struggles with doubt, even though he's seen the Lord so many times, and even eaten breakfast with him on the beach."

There was silence for a while, each lost in their own thoughts.

Tabitha was curious. "So what did Andrew, Matthew, young James and Thaddaeus do while the others were away? Weren't they disappointed they hadn't gone to Galilee too?"

Miriam looked at Tabitha. "Honestly, not all of us felt we had to go back to find the Lord. Don't forget he had also said to wait in Jerusalem."

"He certainly did," said Mary Alphaeus. "And now God has made it possible for my whole family to be together while we wait. You've heard our news, of course?" They all nodded enthusiastically. "Of course, my boys wished they'd gone to Galilee with Peter and the others. Naturally, they were disappointed they'd missed the Lord, but they did the right thing."

"Indeed, they were a great support to us, talking with all those who came asking about the Lord," said Miriam, and Salome agreed. Mary Alphaeus beamed with pleasure.

"And did you hear what happened to that Iscariot fellow? How terrible was that!" said Salome.

"What an awful end, he must have been in such torment. I can't bear to think about it," shuddered Miriam, her lips pressed together as tears formed in her eyes.

"You think one of the others could have betrayed him too?" blurted out Mary. "It had never occurred to me."

Lazarus returned her gaze steadily before he spoke.

"Many thought the Messiah would come to free them from Roman rule. Even we didn't understand what he was really about. Or maybe," he added with a frown, "we didn't want to understand. We wanted what we thought was best for us, our promised land restored to our nation, fully under our rule."

"When the Lord rode into Jerusalem the week before Passover, everyone's expectations were so high," said Miriam. "The people had all seen the miracles he'd done. They believed him capable of anything,"

"He was capable of anything then, and still is now. That will never change," said Martha emphatically, her voice shaking with emotion. "But what he actually did was far more than we could have ever imagined or hoped for. Kings and battles are how we thought he would do it, but he wasn't just out to save our nation, he'd included everyone else too. All were separated from God by sin, but what Yeshua has done means the barrier between us has been removed."

Salome seemed to light up as she realised this, but still couldn't help adding, "So not moths or wood rot, then." They all laughed.

Chapter Forty-nine

One Last Time and
Then Forever

The wheat began to ripen rapidly in the dry hot days that followed, and once more the harvest dominated life in Bethany. Martha found she had little time to think as the hours flew by, and yet, all the while, a sense of excitement was growing. Finally, on the way to the fields one morning, she shared this feeling with Mary and was reassured to discover her sister felt the same way. Together their prayer found new focus, as they walked to and from the fields each day.

Martha, Mary and Tabitha had made it their mission to ensure that no one in Bethany was left in the dark about the Lord. Many of the sick were encouraged and found a new hope through their testimonies, prayers and practical help. It wasn't hard for their neighbours to believe in the Saviour after the miracle of Lazarus, who walked the streets as a constant reminder. Tucked out of the way in Bethany, they enjoyed a freedom of speech that Jerusalem did not.

Martha watched the sun as it dipped behind the vast shadowed bulk of the Mount of Olives, and sighed. Another Sabbath was over. Nearly six weeks had passed since the Lord had left the tomb alive, but no one had seen him since Peter and the others had been fishing in Galilee. Still, the excitement continued to persist among the women, and this affected the men too, as they continued to meet at their lodgings.

Tabitha was shutting the livestock up for the night, so the house was quiet, but Martha felt restless. She was expecting Mary and Lazarus back from Jerusalem very soon, and couldn't settle. She stood on the roof, her hand shading her eyes from the low rays of sun, her long hair free in the breeze. She heard distant voices, carried down from the greying slopes above. Straining her eyes, she began to pick out small groups of people toiling up the hillside. Tabitha ran into the yard shouting her name.

"What's going on?" Martha called down to her. "Where's everyone going?"

Before Tabitha had a chance to answer there was a hammering on the gate, which flew open to reveal Sam.

"Where's Martha?" he demanded, gasping for breath. Tabitha pointed up to her figure hurrying down the ladder. "Come on you two, the Lord's back!" he cried, and ran through the house and out of the back door, Tabitha hot on his heels.

Martha jumped down the last few rungs of the ladder and sped after them. She caught them as Sam fumbled to open the paddock gate. "Where is he?" she demanded.

"Up there," gasped Sam, pointing to the top of the hill.

"Does everyone know?" asked Martha, hesitating.

"I've yelled out the news to everyone I've seen," choked Sam.

"Now you don't want to miss him, do you?"

Tabitha pulled at Martha's hand, urging her to come, and together they began to run. Tabitha let go of her hand and leapt away like a hind, closely followed by Sam. Martha could see Joseph and Rachel already up the slope ahead of them. Goats and sheep scattered in all directions, bleating in alarm, as all those who could swarmed up the darkening hillside, all eager to see the miracle-maker for themselves.

Martha and Tabitha, sure-footed and fresh from their Sabbath rest, began to leave poor Sam behind. His legs burned with the effort, for he had already run all the way from the lower city in Jerusalem. He brushed tears of frustration from his eyes as he struggled on. Surely this was what they had all been waiting for.

"Please God, don't let me miss it," he groaned.

As Martha struggled up the final slope to the broad almost flat plateau, her breath came in ragged gasps, so she too was forced to pause. More people were arriving with every hammering beat of her heart.

Lit by the last rays of the setting sun, she feverishly sought among the silhouettes for her family and friends. Approaching the central mound, desperation mounting, she finally saw the familiar figure of Mary hurrying towards her. She clutched her sister in a tight hug, but quickly Mary began tugging her forward. Martha's heart still pounded in her rib cage as she gasped, "Has Tabitha found you?"

"Oh, yes," said Mary. "She's with Lazarus and the others, come and see. We've been waiting for you."

"Is he here?" Martha almost sobbed, grabbing Mary's arm, desperate not to loose her in the crowd, but overwhelmed by anticipation and fear. "I haven't missed him, have I?"

"Come and see," said Mary, guiding her towards the others.

She led Martha through the crowd, which parted silently, then closed in behind them. She swam in a sea of familiar faces, but all she could focus on was the overwhelming hope in her heart and her sister, one step ahead. Out of the corner of her eye she caught John bowing to her, as if she was someone important. Somewhere in the recesses of her mind, she wondered at this.

Involuntarily, breath held, tears blurring her sight, she stepped forward into the presence of her Lord and King. Her senses struggled, his figure was blurred, but her heart knew he was there. Wiping her eyes fiercely, at last she saw the crooked smile, the creases around his brown eyes, flecked with the reflected gold of the sun. As he took her hands she gasped, momentarily overwhelmed by his power and glory, but his hands were soft and gentle, and his smell familiar. Finally she crumpled to her knees before him.

His soft voice said, "Stand up, faithful one." She felt the strength in his arms as he raised her to her feet. "After our parting at the Golden Gate, you didn't see me again, but you still believed. When the others had seen me, still they doubted. You are blessed with faith, my dear Martha. I could not return to my father without granting to you the hope of your heart, to see me one more time." Martha looked fully into his eyes and knew that the love of a man could never compare to the all-encompassing love of her Saviour.

Turning away from her, the Lord reached out and touched the extended hands of his friends, who stood closely around them. Then, stepping up onto the summit cairn, he spoke.

"It was written that the Messiah should suffer, and on the third day rise from among the dead, and that in my name, repentance and forgiveness of sins should be preached to all nations, beginning from Jerusalem. You are all witnesses of these things, and now I will send the promise of my father. Remain in the city, until you are equipped and made ready with power from heaven."

Then he raised his voice and spoke to all those who had followed him from Jerusalem, and those that had come up the slopes from Bethany and Bethphage. As one, the people held their breath as the Messiah, the Lord, the man they had called Yeshua, lifted his hands to heaven and blessed them. As he did so, the final rays of the sun blazed like a sword, turning the clouds red and gold around them as he hovered in the shimmering light. Slowly he faded out of their sight. The crowd let out a sigh.

In the breathtaking silence that followed, the people became aware of two tall white figures in the tremulous light who then spoke in musical voices.

"Men of Galilee, why do you stand gazing into the sky?" they asked his disciples. "Yeshua is now in heaven. And some day, just as you saw him go, he will return!" Then they too faded and were gone, leaving the people overawed. Some had fallen to their knees, others simply stood, mouths open, covered by night but filled with light. Like the sound of bees on a summer day, the hum of worship began to rise and drift across the mountain top.

Martha was so lost in wonder that it took her a long while to become aware of her surroundings once more. Her body felt so relaxed as it surrendered to the weight of peace that opening her eyes to see the last red glow in the west beyond Jerusalem felt like coming out of a deep sleep. She recognised Tabitha's form kneeling beside her, and with a great effort lifted her hand and stroked her arm lightly. Like some night creature waking in the dark, the mass of tight brown ringlets turned, and a pale face blinked up at her. Unsteadily, Tabitha leant over, wrapping her arms around Martha, holding her so tight. With familiar sighs and groans, the shadows of their friends began to rise from the ground around them. Slowly one by one, heaven was releasing them.

It was fully dark by the time they had all found one another. Standing close, they clung together, clasping hands, embracing, but unable to speak, so full were their hearts. Sam now knew that the power from God was yet to be delivered, but after what he had just witnessed, he was content to wait a lifetime, if that was what was needed.

Elias, Joachim, Reuben and Sara came slowly towards them, carrying a lamp. The family embraced with passion, but few words could be spoken. Sam pounced on them, overjoyed to know they were there too.

"Where's Mother?" he asked, anxiously.

"It would have been too much for her to come all this way," explained Elias sadly.

Mary saw the tears in Sam's eyes and tried to comfort him.

"Joachim, were you here too?" exclaimed Lazarus in delight.

"I most certainly was," came his uncle's enthusiastic reply, "but only by the skin of my teeth." Lazarus looked from one to the other for an explanation.

"It was just a hunch. An itch I couldn't scratch. So, I sent him a message," said Elias, shrugging.

"I had felt the call too," admitted Joachim. "But I'm not sure I would have come if it hadn't been for Elias' message. I am in debt to you forever, my dear brother."

"I think you were meant to be here, Uncle Joachim. But poor Uncle Josiah, he's going to be very disappointed when he finds out what he's missed," said Reuben.

"Yes. I suppose we had better get back," said Elias reluctantly.

"And let everyone know what's happened," Sam added. "I hope they believe us."

Once more the family embraced, and then they followed Sara and her lamp back down the broad smooth slope to the road and the city. Martha and Miriam stood together watching, reluctant to leave, although the others had begun to drift away. Joanna was the first, with her servants, then Andrew and James as they helped Salome and Susanna across the rough ground, while Matthew and young James hurried to catch up with his parents and brothers, who had gone on ahead. Mary Joseph was escorted by James son of Joseph, her eldest, and John, with Cleopas and his wife. Phillip,

Nathanael, Matthias and Barsabbas called their farewells as they strode off to catch the others.

Eventually, only Peter remained, talking quietly with Lazarus, while John Mark, his young friend, waited patiently with Simon the Zealot and Thomas. Yawning, Mary wandered over to join Martha, Miriam and Tabitha, who shivered a little in the night air. Finally, Peter hugged Lazarus fiercely, then, accompanied by Miriam, John Mark and the two remaining disciples, they disappeared into the night.

Martha shivered as they left the bare deserted mountain top and descended into the darkness, guided by the tiny specks of lamplight still glowing in Bethany. They walked confidently on the rough slopes, carefully skirting the rocky outcrops around the burial ground. Lower down the slope, they heard voices and the sound of loose rolling stones as others slowly picked their way back down in the dark.

Martha stumbled as they passed through the gate into the back paddock, tiredness creeping over her. Mary got the fire going while Martha served bread and wine. In whispers, Lazarus told Martha and Tabitha of the Master's reappearance at the lodgings, and how they had all accompanied him out of the city, gathering a following as they went. It had been marvellous, like his arrival in Jerusalem two months earlier, riding on the donkey. This time, however, he led hundreds of followers out of Jerusalem towards the summit of the Mount of Olives.

"I think he came looking for you Martha, he just wanted to say goodbye to his dear friend," said Mary softly, feeling there was truth behind what she had just said.

"That makes me feel so special," blushed Martha through her tears. "Our friend, the Lord would go a long way for just one of his sheep."

"Yes, even to death on a cross."

"I'm not sure I can identify with being a sheep," said Tabitha, butting in.

Martha smiled. "But you didn't hesitate to follow the Lord when he was with us, did you? Just like our flocks follow Josh and Jacob."

"Well, I see what you mean," said Tabitha. "But when he was here, he could tell us the right thing to do. Now he's gone, how will I know? How will any of us know?"

"Through his teachings, silly," said Mary, stirring the fire.

"But if his disciples, who were with him from the start, can't remember everything he said, how am I supposed to?"

"She's got a point," said Lazarus.

"Well, we've got enough to be going on with," said Martha. "I'm sure he has a plan."

"I'm sure you're right, but I just don't feel it will be that easy," said Tabitha.

"Perhaps," said Martha, following a thought, "something is just around the corner, still out of sight, but very near. We need something like the disciples had, when the Lord sent all those people out with his power in them."

"Miriam said she thought that could be a taste of what's to come," said Mary, a gleam in her eye.

Martha flopped back, thoroughly exhausted, "I'm just so relieved to have seen him before he returned to his father. I hadn't realised how much my heart desired it. When he appeared to Miriam and the others, and then to his men, I wondered if he even still remembered me, but I couldn't stop hoping. Oh, I'm such a silly," she muttered through her tears. "I did matter, didn't I? And seeing him again mattered so much to me!"

Lazarus put his arm around Martha's shoulders and drew her close, "Oh, you matter, more than you will ever know." One day soon, he would tell her that she had been priceless to their father, Reuben. Good men had come forward asking to marry her after

Noah, but Elias had finally confessed that the price his brother had set upon his daughter was way beyond what men thought reasonable.

Chapter Fifty

A Promise Fulfilled

Shavuot

The next ten days flew by as the last of the grain harvest was gathered, though it seemed unimportant and mundane in comparison to what they had witnessed on the Mount of Olives that night. The temple leaders could do nothing to stop the flood of believers this time, and once more the blasphemer who claimed to be the son of God was the topic of conversation, both in the city and in the temple.

The approach of Shavuot increased the excitement as friends and relatives began to pour into Jerusalem once more. Again, the surrounding countryside was filled with visitors, as caravans of travellers began to set up camp on any open ground near the city. It made journeying on the roads slow and tedious, but it was always good for local trade.

Shavuot happened fifty days after Passover, each family bringing an offering made from the first ripening grain of the harvests. It also celebrated Moses being given the law in the wilderness on Mount

Sinai, as the continuation of the nation's story after leaving Egypt.

Martha was looking forward to the festival, especially as their relatives from Gennesaret were coming to stay. They would be eager to hear news of the Messiah first-hand.

In Jerusalem, Peter and the others had been kept very busy as more and more people wanted to hear about the Lord. It was Peter who had announced that they needed to choose someone to replace Judas Iscariot, and this had required a great deal of thought and consideration by the other disciples. There was much speculation by the women as to who would be chosen. In the end, consensus suggested either Matthias or Barsabbas, as they had followed the Master almost from the beginning.

Despite days of prayer and debate among the eleven, they were no nearer to a decision, so they cast lots, in the traditional way, and God chose Matthias.

Lazarus joined their friends in the temple or at their lodgings whenever he could, and often Mary went too. Martha didn't mind, Mary had worked hard during the wheat harvest, and she had much to contribute to the life of the believers in Jerusalem.

Mostly Martha stayed behind, feeling her place was to bring hope to those in Bethany but, on one occasion she had met up with Sara. It had been at an evening prayer meeting and the two had walked part of the way home together, enjoying the freedom. Sara had shared her growing concerns for Elizabeth, whose mobility was more restricted than ever. Elizabeth worried about Reuben and Sam, wishing they were married. There were already too many single members of the family as it was. This had made Martha laugh, as Sara knew it would.

Lazarus and Mary had gone on ahead and waited for Martha by the Golden Gate. They had stood overlooking the Kidron ravine, in warm, moonlight, a trickle of water flowing under the bridge below. Each thought of the windswept night some seven weeks before, when they had stood there with Yeshua, not knowing what lay before them. Even now, despite everything that had happened, they still felt as though they were waiting.

* * *

Martha and Tabitha sat spinning; Mary and Lazarus were just back from Jerusalem and full of news. Mary Joseph and many of her family members were now living permanently with the others. She had met James, Mary Joseph's oldest son, who was beginning to take a more prominent part, meeting with the other disciples regularly to pray.

"I asked James what it was like to grow up with the Lord," said Mary. "He said Yeshua was just like any other older brother to begin with, a bit bossy at times, but he was a really good carpenter, like their father Joseph had been. I got the impression things were fine until his brothers felt he was neglecting his duties at home and getting a bit above himself. Although it sounds as though James is a good carpenter himself."

"I think that's what Mary Joseph meant when she told me his brothers and sisters didn't really know what to make of him around that time," said Martha. "It was like they didn't really know him any more." She was wondering what it would have been like to have had an older brother like Yeshua to take care of her when she was growing up. "Everything that happened around his birth made it very hard for Mary and Joseph to treat him like the others, and that caused his mother a lot of heartache over the years. So, it must be wonderful to have them now understand what she has known all her life."

"It's quite an extraordinary story," mused Lazarus, who had been listening quietly, watching them spin.

"We almost forgot you were there," said Tabitha, coming over and putting her arms round his shoulders.

Martha and Tabitha had their work cut out preparing the house for the imminent arrival of their guests, while Mary took over visiting those they cared for. She was especially excited as there had been an influx of new people to Bethany, resulting in some of the derelict houses lower down the hill being made habitable again.

"I can't believe it's been over a year since we saw everyone," huffed Tabitha as she shook out the bedding. "Do you think the adorable baby Iscah will be walking yet?"

"It's quite possible," replied Martha, smiling at the thought of the baby that had looked so like her mother and Mary. "Ruth is pregnant again, so Ophra will have a new brother or sister soon."

"That'll please Obed," came the reply. Martha looked quizzically at Tabitha. "Ophra will have someone else to boss and fuss over, hopefully," laughed Tabitha. This thought amused Martha as she disappeared downstairs.

In the late afternoon, Uncle Job and Aunt Abigail arrived, with their three grown-up children, Tamar on foot and the four grandchildren, all piled into the small donkey cart with their luggage. Martha was glad to see Ruth was riding on a donkey, which was also laden with the family's paraphernalia. The tired, dusty, fretting children were immediately let loose, and needed no invitation to make themselves at home, racing round exploring every nook and cranny of both the house and courtyard. The exhausted grown-ups were able to relax, enjoying refreshments in the shade of the olive tree.

The family slotted back together as though they had never been apart. Martha was delighted when little Iscah, with her black curly hair and breath-taking smile, took a few steps into her arms from her mother, Tamar. Ophra had not forgotten Mary either, and had raced into the house to find her the moment they had arrived. Mary had come out to greet everyone, with the six-year-old dangling lanky legs from her hips, as she excitedly told Mary all about the new baby that was coming. Perez clung to his father Benjamin, but the tiny flute that Lazarus held out to him quickly restored his more customary boldness as he sat on Lazarus' lap blowing hard into the instrument.

"Quite the flute player," remarked his grandfather, Job, his hands over his ears.

"But very impressive for a four-year-old," said his proud grandmother, Abigail.

"Lazarus, did you make that especially for him?" asked Abigail. "It has a lovely mellow tone."

"Thank you Aunt. I tried to make one that wouldn't sound too shrill," he replied.

Benjamin grinned. "Shortly, Tamar and I will let you know if you've succeeded."

"Thank you, Lazarus. It's beautiful, and thoughtfully made," said Tamar. "Perez, have you thanked Lazarus yet?" Perez threw his arms around Lazarus and planted a big wet kiss on his cheek.

"Will you make me a bigger one next year? We'll come and get it," Perez reassured Lazarus.

Abigail told them that their Aunt Jael and Uncle Joshua would be round as soon as they'd settled in with Cousin Rebecca and her daughter Calah, who lived lower down the hill in Bethany.

"But what good news!" exclaimed Jael. "At last Calah is betrothed. Is he a good man?" Martha and Mary looked at one another and shrugged.

"Elias thinks it's a good match," said Lazarus, helping to unload the cart. "Rebecca will certainly be taken care of."

"Well, that's the main concern, isn't it?" said Mary, with a twinkle in her eye.

"And I hear that you too are to be congratulated, Oren,"

said Lazarus. "Leah, wasn't it?" Oren looked surprised, then embarrassed. He looked down at his hands.

"You did talk about her a lot on our last visit, dear," said his mother.

"An excellent match," said his father, Job, approvingly. "That's all three of my boys taken care of. I don't suppose you'd like some help in that area, Lazarus?" Mary sniggered.

"Do you love her?" whispered Tabitha to Oren, standing beside him with Iscah balanced on her hip. Oren looked down, but a shy grin and an almost imperceptible nod were enough to reveal the depth of his feelings.

The family settled in, while Martha and Mary put the finishing touches to the evening meal.

The sound of running feet as Ruth and Aharon scolded their children playfully came drifting down to the kitchen from the floor above. In the courtyard, Tabitha held Iscah up, while the would-be-toddler insisted upon walking everywhere and her brother Perez was busy building something with the logs from the workshop. Martha came out and was immediately summoned by Perez to inspect his creation. She had forgotten how much fun it was to have a house full of children.

The next two days passed swiftly as they made their preparations to celebrate, and Cousin Rebecca, Calah, Aunt Jael, Uncle Joshua and Micah came visiting. Martha and Mary were delighted to see Rebecca in high spirits following Calah's betrothal. She and Abigail had a lot to talk about with their children's impending marriages.

The whole family sat for dinner, and with so many willing hands, the work was light and easy. After dinner, Martha sat with her aunts, who were keen to hear the story of the Messiah. Martha and Mary in their turn, were surprised at how detailed the reports had been, even in Galilee.

"My dears, when we began to hear news of the events unfolding in

Jerusalem, we were afraid you might have been involved," confessed Aunt Jael, Rebecca's mother. "But I see now the Lord kept you all safe, although events came a little too close for comfort on several occasions, in Bethany and then under Elias' roof. It must have been very difficult for you. We know how very much you all loved the Master, as you called him. To have to sit by helplessly while those terrible atrocities took place must have been unbearable."

"I think it was harder for those who watched him die. We at least were spared that ordeal," said Martha, even now shuddering at the thought.

"But seeing the Messiah taken up into heaven in all his glory, that evening on the Mount of Olives, was the most incredible thing I will ever see in my life as long as I live," said Rebecca passionately.

"You were there dear?" said Jael, her mother. "I had no idea."

"We were just in the crowds with everyone else," admitted Rebecca. "But Martha, Mary, Lazarus and Tabitha were there, close to him, and he spoke with them."

"Nevertheless dear, you were there," said her mother, emphatically. "Just think, my daughter saw the Messiah ascend to the right hand of his father in heaven. The miracle to end all miracles."

"Or just the start of them," laughed Mary. "We've been told to wait for power from on high. And as usual no one is too clear about what that means."

"That's what happens when you put men in charge," laughed Abigail.

Everyone was up bright and early for the start of Shavuot. Tabitha had been counting the days since Passover, and was as excited as the children. She was to stay on in Jerusalem with Elizabeth after the celebration. With a house full, and the growing sense of excitement, Martha had plenty to keep her occupied, so she didn't have time to think too much about Tabitha's impending absence. Which Mary thought was a good thing, as Tabitha was growing up.

Tabitha came wandering into the kitchen, a dreamy look on her face.

"The animals are fed, and I have turned them out into the paddock with extra hay so they should last. Rachel said she would send one of her 'lazy grandchildren' over to check on them this evening, if we aren't back," Tabitha stood, watching Martha taking her precious loaves of bread out of the oven. "They're huge Martha! How did you get the dough to rise so well?"

"Oh, a little honey at the right time, extra kneading, careful proving, and the perfect oven temperature," she said, nonchalantly. "It's just a knack."

Lazarus came in and walked over to admire the bread. "Only the best as an offering to God, I see."

"We have so much to thank him for, it's been one of the best harvests I can remember, and the olives are looking really good too."

"Why do we bother?" moaned Tabitha. "The priests will eat most of the grain, or sell it. It doesn't seem fair for all those poor people who bring things they can't afford,".

"Tabitha, you know that all we have is from God, so we are simply showing him our gratitude and acknowledging he is the source of all good gifts. Many of the temple officials are hardworking people like us. They and their families need to eat too. Don't begrudge them their rights just because of those few who are greedy and spoil it. If we all helped one another there would be more than enough to go round."

Tabitha didn't look satisfied, but she knew better than to argue with Martha, especially on such a happy day.

"Have you put your things together yet?" asked Martha.

Tabitha wrinkled her nose. "I wasn't sure what to pack."

"Take everything," suggested Lazarus.

Martha glared at him. "Be a dear," she said to him sweetly. "Go and see if our guests are ready, we must start soon."

Lazarus departed just as Mary came in carrying the remains of breakfast. "They won't be much longer. Does someone need help packing?"

Martha looked gratefully after Mary as she followed Tabitha up the ladder to the loft. Martha hurriedly cleared away and wrapped her loaves lovingly in linen cloths. She was eager to leave for the early morning prayer meeting at the disciple's lodgings. They would go to the temple later with their offerings. Her guests also intended to visit the temple later in the day and would meet them at Elias and Elizabeth's home to celebrate in the evening. Tabitha had decided to go with the family, a decision Martha had found surprisingly hard to accept. She knew Tabitha was growing up and she had to let go, but she wished it could be just a little at a time.

Chapter Fifty-One

The Promise

Martha was first to leave the house, shouting goodbye to her aunt, uncle and cousins and the children. From behind Joseph and Rachel's gate, on the opposite side of the street, another chorus of goodbyes were called out to her, as she headed up the road, her loaves carefully slung across her shoulders in a leather bag to protect them. She hoped Mary and Lazarus would hurry up, but she couldn't wait any longer.

Already the road was busy, so Martha took the track used by the locals. She had an overwhelming sense of urgency as she crested the southern slope and looked down into the Kidron, the road still a good way below her. She glanced back. Two figures, one short and the other tall, toiled up the slope, a long way behind her. She waved vigorously and strode on purposefully. They had better catch her soon, for once she joined the main road it would be difficult to find one another amongst the crowd.

Before she jumped down onto the rough surface of the road, she glanced back up the slope, but there was still no sign of her brother and sister on the horizon. The main road descended in a curve towards the Golden Gate, but a broad track turned sharply off it to the left and headed south, along the Kidron valley. Martha followed this until it crossed the almost dried-up river bed and headed towards the southern entrance to the city. From the middle of the low bridge she looked back up the hillside, and thought she saw two familiar figures coming swiftly now, along the lower track, towards her.

Reassured, Martha hurried on, making short work of the steep incline up to the city gate. Before she entered, she looked back again to see the unmistakable figures of Lazarus and Mary crossing the bridge. Satisfied, she hurried into the narrow streets, into which the morning sun was only just poking its nose. Many of the buildings were closed up, showing only blank faces, reminding Martha that it was still quite early for most people. Despite this, many of the alleyways were still surprisingly busy. The water carriers were clearly doing a brisk trade, fulfilling last-minute orders. At one point Martha was forced against the wall, clutching her loaves protectively, as two carts tried to squeeze past one another, hurrying in opposite directions. Finally she turned into the street where Miriam and the others lodged.

Martha knocked enthusiastically on the rough, wooden door, waiting impatiently. She began to think they had probably gone already, and then to her surprise, the door opened a crack and a sallow-eyed girl peered out suspiciously. Martha was a little taken aback, but she introduced herself, asking for Miriam and her friends by name. The girl didn't speak at first but looked furtively from side to side, evading Martha's smile.

"Have you lived here long?" tried Martha.

"A few days," mumbled the girl, daring to glance up at Martha's face. "You a friend of Miriam then?"

"Oh yes," assured Martha. "A very good friend." There was a long pause. "I'm just on my way to the prayer meeting. I called in in case anyone was still here. I expect Miriam and the others are there already."

"Yes. They left at dawn. Miriam said I was to join them as soon as I was ready."

"Would you like to come with me?" asked Martha, as gently and encouragingly as she could.

The girl hesitated, frowning with indecision, then nodded. "I'll get my shawl," she said, then added, a little more brightly. "It was a present from Miriam."

"Oh, that was nice," said Martha, wondering at Miriam's choice of gift. The girl didn't look old enough.

As though she had read Martha's thoughts, the girl said, "I'm a lot older than my looks, and Miriam said it would be a good disguise."

"Oh, I see," replied Martha, realising there was a lot more to the story. "What's your name?"

A spark of life appeared in the sunken eyes. "I forgot it, so the women call me Yasha."

Martha smiled. "Do you know what your new name means?" she asked.

"Oh yes. Set free, saved."

Martha smiled as they set off together. "So, Miriam's told you all about our friend, the Lord?"

Yasha nodded her head enthusiastically. "I ran away from my master cos he beat me and did bad things, but Miriam found me and took me in. She says I don't have to go back, ever." Martha's heart twisted with pain.

The market square where the disciple's lodgings were was quiet and still in shadow. A few wooden stalls stood derelict among the rotting piles of refuse. As Martha and Yasha hurried along the street and into the courtyard, they could hear the murmur of prayer from the upper windows. Martha felt her heart begin to race.

As they turned into the back yard, Miriam came out to greet them. "I see you've met my Yasha," she said, softly. "I was just coming to look for her."

"Have I missed much?" asked Martha, disappointed she was so late. "I got here as fast as I could, but we have guests with small children. You know how it is."

"You're here now, that's what counts." Miriam looked beyond Martha to the gate.

"Mary and Lazarus are close behind. I came on ahead. I hope you've got room for us."

At that moment, Mary's figure surged around the corner, followed closely by Lazarus. Both were red in the face and slightly out of breath. Immediately Lazarus disappeared inside, ascending the stairs two at a time. Peter glanced up, giving him a welcoming nod, as space was made for him.

Miriam led the others after him. Martha and Mary were immediately aware of the intense strength of the sunlight streaming through the unshuttered windows, illuminating every dust particle in the air. There was no sound from the street below and prayer filled the room; it would be heard by anyone passing by. The time for hiding was over.

At first, Martha and Mary only listened. Some said traditional prayers, while others vocalised their own personal feelings and understanding. A constant theme was that of the Lord's suffering and sacrifice so that they were free from the penalty of their sin. Martha had never heard prayers like these before. They were full of understanding and boldness. Sometimes they all spoke at once, at other times only one person's voice could be heard, and then there was a heavy silence, as though they waited for inspiration. It became obvious to all that their words were being guided in the direction of the risen and ascended Messiah, the son of the living God.

In the crammed room, a sense of power grew, like the tension before a storm. Martha felt it tingling in her fingers. She adjusted her position, but the sensation got stronger, and then an inexplicable joy began to overwhelm her; she felt light and carefree. Mary, her shining face turned upwards, was weeping. She began to sing, her voice wavering but gaining strength with every pure note. Martha couldn't decipher the words, but others were joining in. Martha listened enraptured, until she found her own voice, her own words. As she sang, she watched herself and marvelled; this was something entirely new. Was this the beginning of what they had all been waiting for? She should have felt afraid, but she didn't. What she felt was pure joy.

The atmosphere became tense, like the moment before a volcano erupts and the power is unleashed. Held by the transient rapture, Martha saw a radiance shine from the faces of all those around her. The sun went in, like a lamp that had flickered for a moment, and then sunlight of great intensity and heat drove every shadow from the room. Almost imperceptibly, a sound followed, like a gentle wind through dry grass on the hills, or the distant fall of water in mountains. Steadily it grew, bringing them to their knees, until it roared with the power of foaming water through a cavernous ravine. From nowhere, a force was felt in the hot air, and it grew until a gale expanded to fill the whole house. When it happened, there wasn't time to be afraid. Great, cool and blinding bright tongues of fire, caressed and settled around each one of them. This was what the Lord had promised, this was what they had waited for: power from on high.

Energy flooded the very deepest parts of their beings. Nothing could be kept hidden. Was this the breath of God breathing new life into them? Life given through the actions of his son?

Time passed, and eventually some found they could hear and feel and open their eyes. Gentle murmurs began to grow into sound, which formed into words, which then poured from tongues that wanted to shout praises, but something was wrong. No one spoke in their native language of Aramaic, nor in Hebrew, which the Torah was read in. They simply could not understand what the others were saying, but despite this, they could not keep silent. Their voices grew in strength and fluency, as they chose to speak the language that God, through his Spirit, was now giving them.

Hearing shouts from the street, Peter staggered to his feet, and leaning out of an upper window, spoke to the people below. Those in the room marvelled at the way he explained what was happening; although they had never heard him speak that language before, somehow they understood. More people came running to see what was going on and joined those already listening in the street below.

Thaddaeus, leaning out of another window, began to talk in yet another language, which he learnt later was Arabic. More passers-by joined them, jostling to see what was going on and to hear what was being said. While Thaddaeus spoke from the window, Peter hurried downstairs and out into the street.

It wasn't long before over a hundred people poured from Magnus' lodging house, and out into the street, intercepting the crowds on their way to the temple.

More passers-by were flowing into the marketplace all the time. Mostly they were God-fearing Jews from far and wide, others were converts to Judaism, but no matter who the people were, they were amazed to hear their native languages being spoken in Jerusalem, and even more amazed to hear what was being said about the Messiah, the one their nation had waited so long for.

Slowly it dawned on the disciples, men and women alike, that what they were saying in other languages they could actually understand. Not always word for word, but it was like they had a sense of what they said. Many of the disciples were amazed at how eloquently they were speaking about the resurrected Messiah, and praising God for the wonderful provision of his son.

The locals, standing around watching, assured the visitors that these were uneducated men and women from Galilee, that they had moved in barely two months ago. In their turn they were astounded by the transformation of Magnus' lodgers, who had hidden away in their rooms after the Rabbi was crucified, but who were now boldly speaking to everyone.

Miriam, and Salome had pushed their way down and were among the men, eager to be involved, the other women quickly following. Some, like Mary Cleopas, joined her husband, while others sought those in the crowds as directed by the Spirit of God within them.

Hesitating, Martha lost sight of Mary, as a young woman, in dusty travelling clothes, caught her eye and gave her a shy half-smile. Martha ventured a few words in Aramaic. The woman's dark, broad face looked puzzled, so Martha tried again, in the language given to her by the Spirit. The woman began to nod enthusiastically. Excited, Martha continued, her fluency improving with every syllable. The girl beckoned to three older women, who hurried over with their children. They were dressed in bright clothes with the same dark complexion and broad features. Although Martha's ears couldn't understand much of what she was saying, she knew in her heart she was praising God, telling these beautiful people about the Saviour Yeshua, and all that he had done and accomplished here on earth. While Martha's spirit rejoiced because the women and children clearly understood her, her mind was astounded at what she was doing.

Miriam found herself talking to one of the local market traders, from whom she bought fresh produce regularly, but the Spirit of God kept suggesting images, phrases and sentences she didn't understand. Realising what was happening, she tried to speak to the stallholder, but this time, using the words she was given. At first the man frowned, but then, to Miriam's relief, the creased, careworn face began to crumple until tears appeared on his leathery cheeks. Miriam continued to speak the words she was given until he wiped his face and looked at her with shining eyes. Then he too began to praise God, and to thank the Lord for his sacrifice and love. Many of the lines in his face melted away as he continued to exalt God and worship her beloved Lord. His fellow stallholders looked on, suspiciously.

A young woman, holding a little girl by the hand, approached the man, staring in disbelief. He gave her a wide toothy grin and opened his arms to the child. In his broad Jerusalem accent, he explained to his daughter that Miriam had just spoken of the terrible atrocities he had suffered as a boy in Libya. Miriam had spoken his whole tragic story in Lebanese.

"Did you understand what you just said to me?" he asked, suddenly turning to Miriam.

"No, not the details," she assured him.

"I'm glad you were spared those," he replied, biting his bottom lip. "I tried to forget the past, telling no one, but today God has revealed himself and his great love, expressed through the sacrifice of his son, and now I am free from my past at last."

"Who would have thought it possible?" cried his daughter. She turned to Miriam, whose eyes glistened with pleasure. "Thank you!" she said. "Look darling, Grandpa is happy," she said to her daughter, bursting into tears as she hugged them both.

All around her, Miriam saw miracles, but the cynics and the sceptical began to loudly provoke the disciples and their friends, suggesting that they had been partying all night and were drunk. Peter responded immediately, but not in anger; he seemed no longer driven by the passion of the moment. Deliberately, he climbed onto a stone block and waited, looking boldly at everyone. The swollen, excited crowd that was jammed into the street and market square, slowly hushed and fell silent.

Peter began to speak, his words full of conviction and authority.

"Fellow Jews and people of Jerusalem, let me explain what you have just witnessed, then you will understand. These people are not drunk; it's barely nine o'clock in the morning. Actually, this is the beginning of what was spoken about through the prophet Joel." Now, Peter had their attention, as he quoted the prophet Joel, unhesitatingly: 'I will pour out my spirit upon all flesh, and your sons and daughters shall prophesy, your old men shall dream dreams and your young men shall see visions'. It was all the more remarkable because as a child, Peter had struggled to memorise scripture, but that morning he astounded them all with his fluency and confidence, especially Andrew.

Peter wasn't the only one who had undergone a transformation that morning, from the moment the spirit of God had been poured out on them in tongues of fire, fear and doubt had been replaced by clarity and purpose.

Peter ended the quote by saying, "Whoever calls upon the name of the Lord shall be saved!" The crowd sighed, understanding at last the full implications of the scripture, but Peter wasn't finished. "People of Israel, listen. You recognised Yeshua of Nazareth by the wonders and signs God performed through him, and as you know, he was crucified by the hands of lawless and wicked men, according to God's plan. However, death no longer had power over him, so God raised him up, liberating him from death.

"King David said, 'I saw the Lord always before me, he is at my right hand so I will not be shaken or cast down. Therefore, my heart rejoiced as my tongue exalted him. My flesh will hope in and anticipate the resurrection. For you will not leave my helpless soul in Hades, nor let your Holy One know decay after death. You have made known to me the ways of life, filling my soul with joy in your presence.'"

"He's gone off into Psalm Sixteen," whispered John to Andrew in admiration.

"Brothers and sisters, with freedom, I'm permitted to tell you about the patriarch David, who died and was buried, but being a prophet, knew God had promised to set one of his descendants on his throne. To this, we his followers are all witnesses, Yeshua is that descendant." Those who had come from the upper room of Magnus' house stood tall among the people listening to Peter.

"But I have more," he continued. "The Messiah was raised up to the right hand of God and has given the promised blessing of the Holy Spirit, which he has just poured out on us, which you…" Peter swept his gaze around the crowd. "Which you have just seen and heard."

As Peter spoke, they understood finally that the Holy Spirit was the spirit of God, and was also the spirit of the son, and it now rested with them, and they would never be separated from them again.

"Our ancestor, King David said, 'The Lord said to my Lord, sit at my right hand and share my throne, until I make your enemies a footstool.'"

"That's Psalm one hundred and ten," whispered James, as though it were a game, causing John to shake his head in mock despair.

"I always wondered why he picked us, especially you dear brother."

James whispered back, "I think that was the whole point. God picked a bunch of bunglers who were incapable of such speeches, so everything that happens from now on points to him and not us."

"Well, that's a relief," said Andrew from behind them.

For a moment Peter was distracted, wondering what was amusing his friends, but there was no stopping him now. He took a deep breath and opened his mouth for God to fill it through the Holy Spirit.

"Let the whole house of Israel recognise beyond all doubt that God made him both Lord and Messiah, this Yeshua whom you crucified."

The crowd stood in stunned silence as Peter's words penetrated their hearts.

"This is terrible," muttered the stallholder Miriam had spoken to.

"What shall we do?" cried a man standing beside him.

"How were we supposed to know? Some of us live far away. What can we do?" cried the women that Martha had met.

"God have mercy on our souls!" they cried in despair.

"Wait!" commanded Peter. "Repent! Change your mind and be baptised in the name of Yeshua, the Messiah, so that you may be released from your sins and forgiven, then you shall receive the gift of the Holy Spirit. For the promise is for you, and your children, and for those who are still far away, to everyone whom the Lord our God invites and calls."

Immediately the people began to praise God loudly, lifting their faces to heaven, asking God for his forgiveness. Then they began to clamour, asking one another who would baptise them. Peter looked down at the disciples and their friends and they knew what they must do.

It was Philip and Matthew who stepped forward first, undaunted by the overwhelming number of people. Quickly, they realised they could use the mikvehs, the hundreds of baths built especially for ritual purification in and around the temple, to baptise the people. Then, directed by the Holy Spirit, they began to call on the one hundred and twenty from the upper room, sending them out in twos and threes with as many as they dared to be baptised. It was only after the first few groups had departed that they realised, they would need them to come back to collect more as soon as they could, while Peter continued to persuade those who were still undecided and to reach out to newcomers with his message.

Lazarus and Mary were called forward and led away excited men, women and children, all eager to be baptised. They walked quite a way, to a less well-used set of mikvehs near the southern entrance to Jerusalem, and here they began their new task. At first Mary hung back, holding belongings while the parents stepped down into the water, their children watching. Lazarus looked up at her questioningly. It was not like Mary to hesitate, and he could not do this without her. As soon as she realised this, her sleeves were rolled up and her long tunic hitched into her belt, so it wouldn't float up as she entered the water. She was clear about what they must do and speak. Lazarus had no idea what to say, but he need not have worried; the words came fluently.

Most people knelt, the water covering their heads, but soon Mary's arms began to ache as she helped them from the pool, or helped her brother raise others from the water. She was relieved to see James and Matthias pushing through the waiting queue. James helped the dripping Mary from the bath and explained that they had brought more people with them.

"Sorry, we'd have been here sooner but it took a while to find you. Philip quickly realised you would need more help. Have a rest and then perhaps you would pray with those waiting." Mary didn't need to be asked twice, but she was glad it was a warm day, as she began to pray for those around her, dripping water.

Matthias had quickly stepped into the bath with Lazarus, and they began to work together, equally matched in strength and height. In different ways, with each person, the Holy Spirit would confirm his presence through tears or tongues, but always with a confession of the Messiah as their Lord, to whom they were now joined. Lazarus grunted as he helped a particularly large man up from the water, and laying hands on him, began to pray. Matthias could see poor Lazarus was flagging, so he encouraged him by describing how

Peter was still talking with amazing results. This brought renewed strength to Lazarus' arms.

Martha and Miriam had stood ready, and when called upon by Matthew, they had led another large crowd away, with John Mark and Barsabbas bringing up the rear. Martha was concerned they might lose some of their group amongst the pilgrims heading up to the temple, but the flow had been somewhat reduced along that road since the Holy Spirit had descended, causing a bottleneck at the marketplace, so, they headed for the temple, hoping some of the mikvehs would still be free.

Martha was bubbling with excitement. She had been amazed at the eagerness of the people, the torrent of questions they had asked her, and how easily she was able to answer them. The first mikveh they tried already had queues, but round the corner, hidden from view, in a shady area under the great wall of the temple, John Mark found one that was more or less free. Here they began their work, standing deep in water that flowed from the intricate cisterns of the city, fed by springs near Bethlehem, the birthplace of the Lord. Barsabbas and John Mark baptised the men and she and Miriam the women and children.

To see the light of her Lord Yeshua shining in their faces as they shed their cares and worries made Martha feel more alive than she could ever remember. This was what true life was all about, sharing the Lord with these hurt and broken people, making them whole through the power of the Holy Spirit, and it brought her inexpressible joy. Many came out of the water praising God, some spoke in heavenly languages, but all were forgiven because they believed in Yeshua.

Salome and Zebedee appeared with more people, so Martha and Miriam continued baptising in the water, while Salome and Zebedee prayed with those who were beginning their new lives. Slowly the queue got shorter, as the newly baptised carried on to the temple, clean once and for all. They went now to thank God for his mercy, grace and loving kindness. The harvest thanksgiving seemed almost incidental.

Martha's arms were beginning to tire when Miriam gave a little gasp of pleasure and pointed to the next person in line. It was Tabitha, and behind her came the whole of Martha's family. Martha surged out of the bath to greet them, overwhelmed by emotion.

"It's a miracle we found you in the crowds," cried Elias, hugging his wet niece. "The whole family has come to receive the Messiah's baptism in the Holy Spirit. We believe in him with our whole hearts and minds." Elizabeth nodded her agreement, and tears rolled down Elias' face. Elizabeth held his arm, overwhelmed by his tears, but her face radiating great happiness. On her other side, she clasped Tabitha's hand over her heart. Martha bit her lip and felt a lump rise in her throat.

Tabitha was just about to step down into the water between Miriam and Martha when Lazarus and Mary came running in, completely out of breath, and still dripping wet.

"Philip told us where you were and sent us to help. But when he said the family had come to be baptised, I never imagined he meant everyone," gasped Mary, blowing kisses to them in her joy.

Miriam stepped out of the water and offered Lazarus her place. Tabitha would be the first. Martha held her hand down into the water. Before either of them could speak, Tabitha announced to everyone that she believed in Yeshua, that he was the son of God, her saviour and king, and that she loved him. With tears running down her cheeks she asked him for forgiveness for all the things she had done and said and thought that were unworthy of his love. Martha and Lazarus held her in the water while it closed over her for a second, and then raised her up to her new life with him, as the Holy Spirit came and filled her. Tabitha began to laugh and then to praise her Messiah and her Father God with words she could not understand. Her mouth dropped open, and she looked round at her family in awe, her eyes sparkling.

"It's good, isn't it Tab?" said Mary. "You're speaking a heavenly language."

"Well, either that, or a language none of us has ever heard before," said her brother.

* * *

It was late in the day when Martha, Lazarus and Mary remembered their own harvest offerings, and accompanied by Reuben, Sam and many of their friends, went to the temple rejoicing. The sun was setting when they finally knocked quietly on Elias' gate and were welcomed in by Sophie. They were surprised when she asked them to wait in the courtyard. Sam, who was famished, grumbled at this, but his brother restrained him from charging off to the kitchen. Elias appeared, leading Elizabeth by the arm, followed by the whole family. He greeted them as if they were honoured guests, and Tabitha, dressed in a new and beautiful robe, ran forward and hugged her beloved Martha. Together they went in and ate with their family.

Martha knew that this was just the beginning; she felt it in Mary's touch, she saw it in Lazarus' smile, and knew it was in Tabitha's wisdom. They were part of something far greater than they could ever have believed or imagined. Now her friend Yeshua, the carpenter, the Rabbi, the Master and the Lord, would be with her always no matter what the future might hold. He was her future.

The Beginning

Appendix

Bible References for Chapters

Prologue

Chapter 1 - Early Morning Guests

John (John) 5:1.

Simon the Leper: Matthew (Matt) 26:6, Mark 14:3.

Salome: Mark (Mark) 15:40, 16:1.

Miriam: Luke (Luke) 8:1-3.

Mary Alphaeus: Matt 27:55-56, Mark 15:40.

Susanna: Luke 8:1-3.

Rabbi Yeshua: John 1:38

Simon and Andrew son's of Jonas (Jona): John 1:40-44.

Phillip and Nathanael (Bartholomew): John 1:43-51, 3:18.

Young James Alphaeus: Matt 10:3.

Matt: 9:1-8, Mark 2:1-12, Luke 5:17-26.

Thaddaeus: Matt 10:3.

Simon the Zealot: Mark 3:18.

Barsabbas and Matthias: Acts 1:20-26.

James and John son's of Zebedee: Mark 3:17.

Thomas: Matt 10:2-4, John 11:16.

Judas Iscariot: Matt 3:19.

Matthew (Levi): Mark 2:14-15.

Joanna: Luke 8:1- 3, 24:10.

Chapter 2 - Purim and Sabbath Rest

Ester

Chapter 3 - Tabitha

Ester, John 2:13-18-22, Matt 4:12, Mark 6:16-29, Luke 3:19-20, Isaiah (Isa) 9:7, John 3:23, 1:29-35-42, Luke 5:1-**11**.

Chapter 4 – Mary and Lazarus Return

John 5:1-16, Deuteronomy (Deut) 2:14.

John 1:35-37

Chapter 5 - Business as Usual

Zechariah (Zech) 6:12-13.

Chapter 6 - Family Ties

Proverbs (Prov) 17:19.

Chapter 7 – Tabernacles and Harvest

John 7:1-9-11, 14, 12-13, 15-29, 31.

Chapter 8 - Eyes Opened

John 8:1- 11, 12-20.

Deut 17:3-7, 19:15-19, 22:22-24.

Chapter 9 – Opposition

John 7:37-45-52, 32, John 8:21-59.

Chapter 10 - An Invitation

Chapter 11 – Dinner

Luke 10:38-42.

Matt 14:15-21, Mark 6:33-44, Luke 9:11-17, John 6:5-14.

Matt 15:32-38, Mark 8:1-9.

Luke 8:2.

Matt 8:14-15, Mark 1:29-31, Luke 4:38-39.

Luke 5:1-11.

Matt 4:13-17 (Isa 9:1-2), Luke 4:31-32.

Matt 4:18-22, Mark 1:16-20.

Chapter 12 - Life Goes On

Chapter 13 - The Dedication of the Temple

John 9:1-41.

John 10:1-11.

1 Samuel 17:34-35.

Apocrypha, Maccabees 1, 2, 3, 4.

John 10:23-39.

Luke 10:1-24.

Chapter 14 - A Sudden Death

John 11:1-16.

Numbers 19:13-22.

Chapter 15 - Martha and the Master

John 11:17-31.

Chapter 16 - The Family Tomb

John 11:32-46.

Chapter 17 - The Tide Rises

John 11:46-54, 55-57.

Isa 53:8, 49:6-7.

Chapter 18 - The Master Returns

Isa 53:11.

Matt 21:1a, Mark 11:1a, Luke 19:28-29a, John 12:1.

Chapter 19 – Going into Jerusalem

Matt 21:1-3, 6-11, Mark 11:8-11, Luke 19:29, 35-36, John 12:12-13.

Luke 24:18, John 19:25.

Chapter 20 - An Anointing
John 12:1-9.

Isa 53:10-11.

Chapter 21 - Friday
Matt 21:4-5, Mark 11:1-10, Luke 19:29-36, John 12:12-19.

Psalms (Ps) 118:26, Zech 9:9

Chapter 22 - Turning Tables
Matt 21:10 -17, Mark 11:15-18, Luke 19:37-48, John 12:17-19.

John 2:14 -17, Ps 69:9.

Chapter 23 - The Sabbath
Matt 1:18-25, 2:1-23, Luke 1:4-80, 2:1-40.

Matt 12:46, 13:55-56, Mark 6:3, John 2:12.

Matt 12:28-45, Luke 11:16-36.

John 11:25-26.

Chapter 24 - A Message
John 12:9-11.

Chapter 25 - The Fig Tree
Matt 21:18-19, 20-22, Mark 11:12-14, 20-26.

Chapter 26 – A Celebration in the Master's Honour
Matt 26:6-7-13, Mark 14:3-9.

Isa 53:7.

Matt 7:14 -16, Mark 14:10-11.

John 2:1-11.

Luke 21:37, 22:39.

Chapter 27 – Leaving
Matt 21:21-22, Mark 11:22- 26.

Luke 13:6-9.

Chapter 28 - The Parting
Luke 21:37, 22:39.

Matt 21:23-27, Mark 11:27-33, Luke 20:1-8.

Parables:Matt 21:28-46, 22:1-14, Mark 12:1-12, Luke 20:9-20.

Matt 22:15-33, Mark 12:13-27, Luke 20:20-40.

Matt 23:1-39, Mark 12:38-40, Luke 20:41-47.

Mark 12:41-44, Luke 21:1-4.

Matt 24:1-3, Mark 13:1-3, Luke 21:5-6/7

Jeremiah (Jer) 3:23

Chapter 29 - Family

Exodus Chapters 1, 11 to 13.

Chapter 30 - A Long Night

Matt 26:17-19, Mark 14:12-16, Luke 22:7-13.

Matt 26:20- 58, Mark 14:17-53, Luke 22:14-54, John 13, 14, 15, 16, 17, 18:1-12.

Matt 20:20-28, Mark 10:35-45.

Chapter 31 - The Brothers Return

Matt 26:57-66, 27:1-2, Mark 14:53-64, 15:1, Luke 22:54,66 -71, 23:1, John 18:12-13, 15-16, 19-24.

Isa 53:7

Ps 110:1, Daniel 7:13-14, Leviticus 24:16.

Chapter 32 - The Day of Preparation

Matt 26:67-68, 27:11-14, Mark 14:65, 15:1-5, Luke 22:63-64, 23:1- 12, John 18:28-38.

Chapter 33 - Pilate and the Lamb

Matt 27:15-31, Mark 15:6-20, Luke 23:13-25, John 18:38-40, 19:1-17.

Chapter 34 - Darkness Descends

Matt 27:45-46, 50-51, 54, Mark 15:25, 33-34, 37-38, Luke 23:44-

46, John 19:30.

Isa 53:8.

Chapter 35 - The Sacrifice

Matt 27:27-33, 38, 44, 55-56, Mark 15:16-22, 27, 40-41, Luke 23:26-27, 32-33, 39-43, 45, 49, John 19:17-18, 25-27.

Chapter 36 - The Temple

Matt 27: 50-51, 57-58, Mark15:37-39, 42-45, Luke 23:44-48, 50-52, John 19:38-39, 3:1-21.

Lev 16, Hebrews 10:1-22, Isa 53:7-8, 4-6, John 14:6.

Chapter 37 - The Passover Meal

Ps 136.

Chapter 38 - The High Day

Matt 27:58-60, 61, 62-66, *55-56, 26:33-35, 69-75, Mark 15:42-47, *40-41, 47, 14:27-31, 66-72, Luke 23:52-53, *49, 54-55, 22:55-62, 39-40, John 19:31-42, *25, 18:15-18, 13:36-38, 18:25-27. *verses listing women at Golgotha.

Duet 21:22-23.

Chapter 39 - Friday Market

Mark 16:1, Luke 23:56.

Isa 7:14, 9:1-7.

Chapter 40 - Change

Chapter 41 - Ghosts

Matt 27:52-54, 5:18.

*John 5:24-28-29 (more relevant to when Jesus returns – but interesting).

Chapter 42 - The First Day of the Week, Sunday

Matt 28:1-10, Mark 16:1-11, Luke 24:1-12, 21-24, John 20:1-18.

John 5:8, Col 1:18, 1 Cor 15:20-24, Rom 8:29-30, Revelation 1:5-6.

Chapter 43 - The Road to Emmaus

Mark 16:12, Luke 24:13.

Matt 28:11-15.

Chapter 44 - Wait!

Mark 16:13-14, Luke 24:13-**34**, 35, 36-49, John 20:19-24-25.

Jer 31:31-33, Ezekiel 11:19-20, 18:30-32, 36:26-27.

Chapter 45 - Going Home

John 11:20-23-27, Isa 53, Isa 25:8, Hosea 13:14, Romans 6:9, Lev 19:9-10, Ruth 2.

Chapter 46 - The Early Harvest

John 20:26-29, 19:31-**34**-37.

Chapter 47 - More Visitors

Matt 26:32, 28:7, 10, Mark 14:28, 16:7.

Chapter 48 - A Night Spent Fishing

Matt 28:16-20, John 21:1-25.

Matt 8:23-27, Mark 4:35-41, Luke 8:22-26; Matt 14:22-34, Mark 6:45-53, John 6:15-21.

John 20:22-23. Matt 27:3-5, 6-8.

Chapter 49 - One Last Time And Then Forever

Luke 24:46-53.

Mark 16:19, Acts 1:6-9-12, 1 Cor 15:3-6, Matt 28:19.

Chapter 50 - Shavuot

Acts 1:12-14, 15-26, 1 Cor 15:7-8.

Chapter 51 - The Promise

Acts 2:1-**15**-41.

Acts 1:15.

Joel 2:28-32, Ps 16:8-11, 110:1, 132:11, 2 Sam 7:12-16, Isa 57:19.

Matt 28:18-20, Mark 16:17, 18, 20.

Printed in Great Britain
by Amazon

12989705R00243